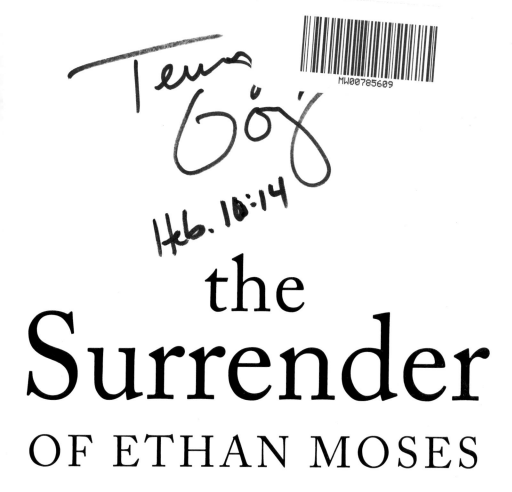

Terra
Góy
Heb. 10:14

the
Surrender
OF ETHAN MOSES

TERRY GOETZ

the Surrender
OF ETHAN MOSES

Tate Publishing & Enterprises

Published by Tate Publishing & Enterprises, LLC
127 E. Trade Center Terrace | Mustang, Oklahoma 73064 USA
1.888.361.9473 | www.tatepublishing.com

Tate Publishing is committed to excellence in the publishing industry. The company reflects the philosophy established by the founders, based on Psalm 68:11,
"The Lord gave the word and great was the company of those who published it."

Book design copyright © 2011 by Tate Publishing, LLC. All rights reserved.
Cover design by Amber Gulilat
Interior design by Nathan Harmony

Published in the United States of America
ISBN: 978-1-61739-730-1
1. Fiction: Christian: Historical
2. Fiction: Christian: General
11.03.03

"How precious is Your
unfailing love, O God!
All humanity finds shelter
in the shadow
of Your wings."

(Psalm 36:7, NLT)

Notes on Scripture Used

All non-paraphrased Bible quotes are NAS, except where noted here.

"A fortune made by a lying tongue is a fleeting vapor and a deadly snare" (Proverbs 21:6, NIV).

"So be content with who you are, and don't put on airs. God's strong hand is on you; he'll promote you at the right time. Live carefree before God; he is most careful with you" (1 Peter 5:6, MSG).

"… the eyes of the blind will be opened and the ears of the deaf unstopped. Then will the lame leap like a deer, and the mute tongue shout for joy. Water will gush forth in the wilderness and streams in the desert" (Isaiah 35:5–6, NIV).

"One day as Jesus was walking along the shore of the Sea of Galilee, he saw two brothers—Simon, also called Peter, and Andrew—throwing a net into the water, for they fished for a living" (Matthew 4:18, NLT).

"Nebuchadnezzar, his face purple with anger, cut off Shadrach, Meshach, and Abednego. He ordered the furnace fired up seven times hotter than usual. He ordered some strong men from the army to tie them up, hands and feet, and throw them into the roaring furnace. Shadrach, Meshach, and Abednego, bound hand and foot, fully dressed from head to toe, were pitched into the roaring fire" (Daniel 3:19–22, MSG).

Dedication

To the angel in my life, Becky, my wife,
who has always believed in me,
even when I didn't believe in myself.

An Angel's Preface

Earth is ridden with the beautiful and the cursed, struggling for the same air. Yet they swirl around each other in some omnipotent harmony that only God could accomplish and use. I'm a chill down the back or goose bumps up the arm for some, a touch of déjà vu for others; my actions are coincidences for many. My name is Levi, and I'm an angel prince sent to Earth as a guardian to protect the fold, ensure God's providences, retaliate against God's foes, and do God's bidding for the redeemed in Christ. This is the story of one of my charges as he successfully endeavors to glorify God and humbly serve man.

Permission to share this manuscript comes with an imperative stipulation that I downplay my contribution. Love not my supernatural powers or my beautiful wings that fly swifter and more surely than the fastest jet. Don't worship me because of my devotion or vigilance to God and mankind. Worship Him who loved you so much He created me and sent me. This writing is only to glorify Him and to allow you to see past the illusion of space and time—into the infinite realm of our God and King.

My only temporal possession is the ring illustrated on the front of this book. It depicts the stone that was rolled away from Christ's borrowed tomb. The full circle contains a ruby, the first stone on the breastplate of the high priest. Red *is* the color of love and the color of Jesus's blood that saved man from eternal damnation—the ultimate love shown.

When Jesus breathed his last breath on the afternoon of Good Friday, it seemed as if Satan had the last word. But the resurrection signifies hope; it embraces power over death and Satan. His resurrection begins your ultimate purpose: To tell the world the good news of God's gracious atonement of all mankind.

Many people get caught up in "who" rolled the stone away. I can tell you, it wasn't for Jesus to get out, but for others to see in. So why does the inscription inside my ring read, "… and she saw two angels in white sitting, one at the head and one at the feet, where the body of Jesus had been lying (John 20:12)"? If I had been one of the angels there, would it give me some undeserved fame and cause you to listen to my words more intently?

The angels on both sides of Jesus's body in the tomb symbolize the angels on top of the ark of the covenant found on both sides of the mercy seat. Jesus became mercy for all mankind. His empty tomb is an open door for you to enter—not unto death, but into life much more abundant that you could ever imagine.

The only Son of God came down from heaven, became a man, and died for you so that you may become sons and daughters of God. What you do in God's name is enveloped in *your* purpose and is not God's work, but your own. Those things define and complete you, giving you great blessings.

Imagine entering massive gates meticulously chiseled out of a single pearl, spanning three and a half miles on each side, their height dwarfing the tallest skyscraper. The gates' intricate design depicts every architectural style devised by man. Roman columns, Gothic arches, Byzantine pendentives, archivolts, and many other styles are blended into one beautiful, harmonious work of art. Tremendous humility envelops your spirit as you realize that all creative energy is spiritual in nature and comes from God. After you enter the gates, you look to your side and notice an ornate border above a shimmering blue wall. As you get closer, you realize that the border is a line of trees with roots underground. Some trees are full of colorful fruit. Some have no fruit at all. Then you realize that it's an ever-changing picture of each Christian's life. What appeared to be a blue wall is a moving stream of crystal water feeding the trees above.

You continue to walk until you enter the great throne room. Suddenly, you notice that you're walking on the most beautiful tapestry you've ever seen, having no end to its detail and color. Then you hear a voice say, "I saw the Lord seated on a throne, high and exalted, and the train of his robe filled the temple." You realize that you've been walking on God's robe. As you closely examine the beautiful vine running throughout the robe, you hear, "I am the true vine, and my Father is the gardener." Approaching the throne, you're greeted with bows from the courtiers; a royal robe and crown are placed upon you and you're given a golden vessel of manna. You look up and say, "Am I going to have to climb all those steps?" Before anyone answers, the King's Son greets you with a kiss on the cheek, places you on His shoulders, and starts climbing the endless height. You notice that He's weary from the strain, but He looks up at you and smiles. It becomes evident that all you had to do was accept His invitation. Then He says, "Take my yoke upon you and learn from me, for I am gentle and humble in heart, and you will find rest for your soul. For my yoke is easy and my burden light." You become hungry and He says, "Break the bread and eat," as he looks at the manna. Profound appreciation overtakes you, as you realize that He's made provision for your journey. He continues to climb the steep steps to the very presence of the King. That's what you receive as a Christian. That's great privilege.

✝

The first time I saw Ethan Moses, he rested in his spiritual gifts. He could read people as if they were stories already told. Where others saw the actions and expressions of the outer person, he always saw their motives, their heart, and their very soul. What lifted Ethan Moses from the realm of the ordinary was his extraordinary capacity to see when others only looked. This journal presents the story he never told. Luke 14:11 says that everyone who promotes himself will be humbled, but he who humbles himself will be promoted. Humility filled Ethan's life and made him pliable to God's direction and intentions, and his life is used even to this very day because of it.

The trumpets blew, the gates opened wide in anticipation of his arrival. He had no crown on earth and no royal throne. He didn't even have a pillow that he could call his own, but in heaven, he was revered—a large crown was placed on his head and the King Himself welcomed him with open arms. Power, love, and self-discipline were your jewels and you carried them with you—my friend.

Go in peace, Reverend William Ethan Moses.

We *will* meet again,

Levi Sarim

... and God Breathed Life into Man

The air was humid and cold as raindrops jiggled on the windows of the bulky car thrusting its way across Clear Creek. You could hardly tell the creek was there, diverted by large concrete culverts and covered with pavement many years earlier. As the gleaming white Cadillac came to an abrupt stop under the portico of the impressive church building, the back passenger door was opened wide with a shout from Dr. Howard, the music minister. "How in the world are you, E?"

Ethan Moses slowly pulled himself to the edge of the plush backseat and proceeded to rise skyward as his old bones unfolded. "Fair to middlin,' Archie. How're you?" he asked, as his thick, gray brows twitched and his left eye rose slightly as he cocked his head toward the dapper little man.

"Good, good. Great to have you with us!" Dr. Howard exclaimed with a gleaming, nervous smile as the two men shook hands. Dr. Howard was like a little boy in the presence of a big-league baseball player, but E was not in the mood for a lapdog. Besides, Dr. Howard was a little too genteel and effeminate for E's taste in men.

It had been an emotionally charged journey through time for E as he reminisced about bygone days and past acquaintances. E had planted that church over sixty years earlier and now it had over seven thousand members.

After a warm introduction, he rose and scuttled with great effort and a sliding gait as beams of sunlight streamed through the stained glass, illuminating his path to the daunting platform. He placed both weathered hands firmly on the pulpit to brace himself and began. "When I was asked to speak at this dedication ceremony for your new sanctuary, they wanted me to tell you what my greatest lesson was in ministry. I've narrowed it down to just one thing that sustained me through all my trials. One thing that I could always rely on when tears, heartbreak, pain, fear, and sorrow paralyzed me. The one thing"—he paused to enjoy the anticipation—"that would comfort me was this." Then he began singing.

> "Jesus loves me this I know,
> For the Bible tells me so.
> Little ones to him belong,
> We are weak but He is strong…
> Yes, Jesus loves me…
> The Bible tells me so."

When he finished, there was a profound silence. Tears were streaming down cheeks of grown men. You could audibly hear E's shoes shuffling back to his seat. "Oh, I've added a few words to that song!" he exclaimed, bristling with new energy and shuffling back to the front.

> "Jesus loves me, this I know,
> Though my hair is white as snow.
> Though my sight is growing dim,
> Still He bids me, trust in Him.

Though my steps are oh, so slow,
With my hand in His I'll go.
On through life, let come what may,
He'll be there to lead the way.
Though I am no longer young,
I have much that He's begun.
Let me serve Christ with a smile,
Go with Him that extra mile.
When the nights are dark and long,
In my heart, He puts a song.
Telling me in words so clear,
'Have no fear, for I am near.'
When my work on earth is done,
And life's victories have been won.
He will take me home above,
Then I'll understand His love."

As he finished, many were hiding their tear-lined faces, but everyone remembered his face. Peace was in his pale blue eyes, glistening with emotion. Contentment was in his melancholy smile. God had given him this day as a gift and it was good.

The day had opened a floodgate of memories for the old man that stirred his heart to the core and transported him back to the earliest days of his ministry. The years melted away as he recalled standing on the banks of Steeple Creek in southeastern Texas where he was preparing to be baptized in the cold creek water of fall. Steeple Creek fed into the Sabine River about seven miles downstream. It was a perfect day filled with cerulean blue skies and gentle breezes. You could hear leaves rustle, as they gave way to the tug of gravity, adding color and texture to the soft ground below. The chatter of wrens was in the air, creating background music for the setting. The year was 1915, and E was only twelve.

God began to softly speak to him, "Lay down your nets—leave the things in your life that have no purpose. Stop following your path and adopt mine. It's the best and most rewarding." He was frozen in shock that God's voice could be so clear and resolute. As he looked up at the big cherry tree losing its leaves in the trickling water below, his eyes widened again as God continued, "Lose the dead and put on the new." As E looked deep into the moving water below, God instructed, "Running water purifies everything it touches, brings peace to all who hear it, and refreshes all who taste it. But most of all, it feeds, nourishes, and satisfies everything that it comes in contact with. Your purpose is to be my water, E."

The moment God finished speaking, the minister looked up and motioned for E to come into the water. He walked slowly with great effort against the moving water to where the minister stood.

E's posture tensed as he gazed across the water's glistening surface. It seemed to take on the characteristic of a dividing line, separating good from evil. He realized that God was delivering him from a worthless life and placing him into His precious, wonderful light. With both hands, E grabbed the minister's arm. Brother Gerald sensed the hand of God on E, stirring his soul, so he interjected, "There's somethin' you can always rely on, Ethan, God's love." With those words, he plunged E deep into the icy cold water. "You can let go now." Brother Gerald uttered as E broke through the water's surface and took a large gasp of air.

Life was carefree for E and filled with great possibilities, with each day bringing its own peculiar joys. He took full advantage of any opportunity to fulfill his goals, which included working for Miss Margaret Clark, an old lady in the community who had never married. She never cared much for the opposite sex and really not much for her own. Maybe it was because of her state in life, but most found her to be morose and bitter. Miss Clark was never friendly; no one ever conceived of her as cheerful or particularly sociable. However, she found herself drawn to the disheveled little E. She would pay him to do odd jobs for her in the afternoons, after school, and after his chores at home were done. Once, while he was working for her, she noticed that he was mumbling to himself. She quickly and correctively retorted, "E, you're much too young to be doin' that prattlin' to yourself!"

He immediately replied, "Ma'am, I love recitin' scripture. Not because it comes easy, but I find that God lives in His Word. It brings me closer to Him and makes His voice clearer."

She was embarrassed for jumping to the conclusion that he was mumbling to himself and asked, "Are you tellin' me, son, that you've memorized that much of the Bible?" She released a self-effacing chuckle as he bobbed his head up and down, answering her question.

After that day, she spent hours thinking of questions to ask him, just to see what unique wisdom would flow out of his youthful mouth. One late afternoon, when he was helping her in the garden, she looked him square in the eyes and asked, "Why did God give us the Ten Commandments if he loves us so much, E? I mean, it's hard enough to live on this God-forsaken ball without tryin' to adhere to rules that can't possibly be followed!"

He stared at her for a few moments, smiled, and said, "They should draw you to Jesus when you realize that you need Him to be your substitute for what God demands. It isn't a list of dos and don'ts for us to lose sleep over. They're to show us God's nature, His heart, His character. When you try your best to follow His Law, it should be out of love for God and what he's done for you. The Law should always be our compass."

When he finished, she wiped her eyes with her apron. She couldn't remember the last time she had shed a single tear. E had touched her heart, and in turn, he had gained her eternal gratitude.

It was not by chance that I guided Winston Churchill to a certain door in South Africa after his escape from a military prison. In that same vein, I guided E to Miss Clark's door. She had prayed many years earlier that God would allow her to be useful to Him before her heart grew cold and bitter. God's providence had brought E to her door, many years after she had given up hope and had long forgotten about her prayer.

The School of Life

School was easy for E and he found great pleasure in teaching the other children when he got the chance. He would make mental notes of weaknesses that he could help them with later. Ellie was six years younger than him. He had observed her and studied her from afar, almost like a science experiment, not that he thought of her in that way; it was just the particular way it turned out. Ellie was a doormat for all the other children at Red Star School. E tried his best to stop the abuse, but he had very little success. She was always a mess, her hair was never combed, and her dresses looked like they had been worn one too many times. Often she didn't have adequate clothing for the weather. Miss Miriam Thacker, the schoolteacher, would take her to the backroom, and Ellie would reappear with a coat or sweater that she hadn't come to school with.

On the opposite side of the room was Naomi Porter, daddy's little princess. She had curls that went on forever in her perfectly bowed, black, shiny hair and always wore the daintiest dresses with frill and fanciful lace. Her shoes shined like mirrors and her socks always complemented her attire. Vanity, arrogance, and manners she had, with curtsies and crossed legs, making the snobby and prudish proud. E studied her almost as much as Ellie. Both seemed to be damaged to him, neither being the norm.

Soon, E was in his twelfth year at Red Star School and was considered to be Miss Thacker's aide and confidant. She relied on him heavily and trusted him implicitly.

"E, we've got to do somethin' about Ellie!" she exclaimed as she exhaled in a long, heartbroken sigh. Her body went limp as she settled into her chair.

"What is it, ma'am?" he asked, frozen in shock at Miss Thacker's pale appearance.

"Well, E, this is to go no further, but her mother committed suicide last night and her good-for-nothin' father's a drunk. He was admitted to the hospital for alcohol sickness and all the school board will say is they'll look into it. If I had any gumption at all, I would give them an ear full," she whispered indignantly with wide eyes as she moved close to E's ear.

E asked through trembling lips, "Where will she stay, ma'am?"

Miss Thacker's mouth tightened into a thin smile, knowing E was worried about the little girl and said, "Well, right now, she's staying at the hospital with her father, but make no mistake, I'm goin' to get her."

Miriam Thacker was a comely, single woman, full of grace. She had many gentlemen callers and even a proposal; however, she tried to keep her head and wait for that "right man." She used E to block for her on more than one occasion and he was honored to do it.

"Miss Thacker, why did she—?" E asked, not finishing his question as he moaned with sadness and a single tear found the crevice of his right cheek.

"Well, E, I'm not sure. She had Ellie before she was out of the tenth grade, and the father finally married her after he was paid to do so. I'm just sad that I didn't go see her. If I'd known she was having such a hard time, I would've dropped everything," Miss Thacker said gravely as she looked at the floor, shaking her head. She had an enormous heart and really cared for her students and their parents. However, she couldn't wait to give Ellie's father a piece of her mind.

"Mr. Bosch, my name's Miss Thacker and I'm Ellie's teacher at the school," she stated while folding her arms across her chest and standing over his hospital bed. "I'm greatly concerned about this whole matter, Mr. Bosch, but mostly I'm concerned about Ellie. I would like to keep her until you get better, if that's all right," she asked with a high-pitched voice of authority and resolve, shifting her weight forward and raising her brows high.

Jakob Bosch had received the news about his wife, Jenny, just hours earlier, but he was too delirious to really let it sink in. He lowered his eyes in contrition at Miss Thacker and nodded yes.

Now that Miss Thacker had little Ellie in her care, she wasn't going to let her suffer any more indignities. She went straight to her uncle, the honorable Judge Thomas Thacker, to petition his help. "Well, Miriam, I can get you temporary custody, but understand it's only temporary. It's an uphill battle to get children away from their parents. You better have some real hard evidence against him," he prompted with great skepticism, as he peered over his glasses.

"I'll get the proof, Uncle, and thank you," Miriam said with resolution as she gave her uncle a kiss on the cheek. As she was leaving, she proclaimed, "I have to protect Ellie from her 'monster' father."

As soon as Jakob got enough strength to stand, he checked out of the hospital and went straight home to rest. The next day was Saturday, so he got dressed and went to Miss Thacker's orderly and immaculate residence close to downtown. Miriam had tried to get information from Ellie, but she was unable to break the child. Ellie kept insisting that he was a good father and a good husband to her mother. She also insisted that he never drank or abused either of them. Miriam was discerning enough to realize that something didn't add up.

"Miss Thacker, I've come for my little Ellie. I do appreciate you takin' care of her, ma'am," Jakob Bosch stated with great humility as he bowed his head low.

"Well, Mr. Bosch, it's unfortunate that I have to tell you this, but I have temporary custody of Ellie," Miriam said as respectfully as she could under the circumstances.

"Excuse me, ma'am? You have what?" asked Jakob naively, as color drained from his face.

"Please, come in, Mr. Bosch. I'd like to speak with you frankly, if I may," Miriam said, softening her stance slightly.

"Sure, ma'am," Jakob answered, as he took off his hat and cautiously walked into the parlor. Miriam was confounded by his manners and his persona; this was not the monster she expected to entertain, and she wondered if it all was a performance to impress her and win her over.

"Mr. Bosch, please have a seat," she insisted, as she continued to stand.

"Miss Thacker, I can assure you that I'm a good father. I treat Ellie as if she were my own child," Jakob groaned, sounding like the breath had been knocked out of him.

"Are you telling me that you're not Ellie's father?" a perplexed Miriam fired back in a higher pitch.

"Ellie was an infant when I married her mother. I don't know who her real father is," Jakob answered softly and with great sincerity, as he looked down.

"Well, it's all around town that you *are* her father, Mr. Bosch, and that you were paid to marry Jenny," Miriam stated as her eyes flashed, thinking she would corner the big liar.

"Oh, no ma'am, she's not my biological child, but if 'saving my life' is payment, then I guess you're right in that assumption," he answered, as Ellie ran down the stairs into his arms. She hugged him tightly as she cried and told him how much she had missed him. Miriam was truly touched by what she was witnessing, but she was still resolved to finding the whole truth.

"Mr. Bosch, could we talk without Ellie for a few more minutes?" she asked, trying to stay focused.

Jakob whispered something in Ellie's ear and she ran back upstairs. "Sure, Miss Thacker," Jakob answered with a kind gleam in his eyes and a purposeful smile.

"Well, would you mind terribly if I asked you to start at the beginning?" Miriam asked.

"Not at all, ma'am," he answered.

Jakob's Ladder

Jakob Bosch was a fine-looking man who had a muscular build, with sandy brown hair and blue eyes. He joined the United States Army on April 27, 1917, and ended up at Camp Mills near New York. Then he sailed out to war on Cunard's Mauritania. His father and mother were proud as peacocks that Jakob would eagerly fight for their newly claimed country. His family had immigrated to the United States in 1912 from Austria and eventually settled in Hershey, Pennsylvania.

After a brief stay in England, Jakob went on to France. He carefully noted all the towns he passed through on the back of his mess kit. Even though Jakob was not from Germany, he had a German-sounding accent and name, causing many of the soldiers to take out their frustrations on him. The fact that the French called the German soldiers "Bosche" (blockhead), didn't help matters either since his last name was Bosch. His nickname became Bosche. The men would pull pranks on him, like putting salt in his shaving water. It would burn like fire, but he could take it. His father had taught him to place truth, honor, and integrity above even his own happiness.

Lieutenant Colonel David Lynn was a true Southern gentleman. He didn't stand for shenanigans and had defended Jakob on several occasions, thinking that he was not getting the respect he deserved. That fact rang true on the morning of December 15, 1918, when Jakob put his life on the line, retrieving several men who had been "downed" by a sniper. After going back the third time, he took a bullet in his right leg, straight through the bone.

"Hey, Colonel, ole Bosche went after Willie, and they didn't make it back," John Franklin, one of the men that Jakob had saved, bellowed loudly.

Suddenly, one of the largest blizzards ever to hit that area came through with a vengeance. You could hardly see your hand before your face. "Colonel, we gotta do something!" exclaimed a frantic Edward Eliot, the second man Jakob had pulled from gunfire.

"Y'all stay put, I'm on it," stated the colonel, making his way through the thick blanket of snow and wind.

It was a long three miles and even though Willie was dead, Jakob was very much alive and in excruciating pain. Colonel Lynn ordered, "Just try to help me get you up with your good leg, Wag." Jakob's rank was a Wagoner in charge of supplies. "Now, if I can get you on my back, we'll be back to camp in no time," the Colonel said while stooping very low to retrieve Jakob and retracing his steps the best he could in the blizzard. Once back to camp, Jakob and the others were taken to the first-aid station where they quickly made an assessment of Jakob's leg. They planned to send him to the surgical hospital near Langres for amputation.

The colonel had taken the trip with the men, and when he got the news, he flew into a rage and burst into the operating room. "What do ya mean, takin' the boy's leg off? You peons are always lookin' for the easy way out! This boy's a hero and he's to be treated as such. You save that leg, and that's an order!" Colonel Lynn was not the type to lose his head, but when he did, people took notice. Dr. Powell did his best, but he was pessimistic of the outcome and told the nurses to watch him closely because they would probably be cutting it off anyway.

Two months later, Jakob Bosch was on his way home with both legs intact. Colonel Lynn had made several trips over to see him before he was shipped out, and Jakob had expressed his gratitude to his newfound hero who had saved his life and leg. Jakob hadn't heard a word from his parents for months and was looking forward to getting home.

When he finally found his way back home, he noticed several quarantine signs on front doors throughout his community. He stopped by Mr. Prepelite's bakery to inquire about the signs, and the old man gave Jakob a warm hug that was filled with emotion. "I'ma so, so sorry, my son. They were sucha good people, your poppa and momma." Jakob looked at him, dumbfounded. Mr. Prepelite finally realized what he didn't know and proclaimed, "I am such a *boccalone*. I'ma so sorry, Jakob. So, so sorry. I thought you knew. Thata influenza swept through here like a soma plague. They were so tired and weak, worried sick about you all the time, they just didn't hava a chanca, you know? You stay with us, Jakob. Okaya son? We'll taka good care of you. You don'ta worry." As Jakob stiffened with disbelief and ran out the door, Mr. Prepelite said to himself, "*Chiudere il becco*, you *cicciobomba*!" He popped himself on the forehead with his palm and rolled his eyes back in his head as he went back to work.

There was no sign of life as Jakob limped up the steps of his boyhood home. He knocked on the door, but no one answered. He cried out, "Poppa, Momma, it's Jakob! Your son's home at last!" But no one came. He knelt on the edge of the porch with tears running down his cheeks as if a floodgate had been breeched.

Felix Strasburg, who lived next door, heard Jakob's cries and came over to console him. "We took good care of them, son. Your poppa, he told me to give you this," Felix said, as he handed Jakob an envelope containing a letter and key. After a few moments, Felix continued, as he glanced to the sky, "You know, son, your father's last words to me were, 'I'm goin' home, but I'll be watchin.' For sure, I'll be watchin.'"

Jakob was now all alone in his new country. His parents were gone and his dreams of a new life were gone with them. He couldn't force himself to read the letter; it was just too painful. So he let himself in the back door with the key, made a fire in the fireplace, and cried until first light of morning. Then he got up, shaved, took a bath, and went down to see what needed to be done to sell the place. He had come to grips with everything at some point in the night and had resolved to move close to Colonel Lynn, his wartime hero, for a fresh start.

He brushed off his well-worn brogans with the back of his legs and walked inside Mr. Mahoney's elaborate office on Main Street. Mahoney was a ruthless and selfish businessman whose motto was, "Business is business and personal is personal." He claimed to keep the two separate only to ease his conscience.

"Well, Jakob, good to see you, son. How's your leg?" Mahoney asked with forced cordiality and an insincere twinkle.

"It only hurts on days like this, Mr. Mahoney. It seems to know when I'm going to get hornswoggled," Jakob retorted, as he leaned forward and raised his brows.

Mr. Mahoney nervously chuckled and resumed, "Now, Jakob, I'm not one to profit on hard times, but you know real estate's not what it used to be. One dollar will only buy you four bits' worth these days."

Jakob, not giving him a chance to soften him, gathered his courage and commanded, "Just tell me what you're willin' to pay, and I'll be on my way."

Mahoney's vest buttons tightened as he inhaled to answer, "I have a number in my head that I'll give ya for the old place, Jakob. Why don't ya tell me what you would take?"

Jakob was young, but the war had hardened him and made him weary of men's petty games. "Mr. Mahoney, tell me what you had in mind, and then I can tell you whether you can jump in the lake or not. How 'bout that?" Jakob asked, raising a skeptical, wrinkled brow.

Mr. Mahoney quickly realized that Jakob had become a man since he had last seen him. "Oh, now, Jakob, I'm sure we can work this out," Mr. Mahoney smoothly replied, pulling a piece of paper out of his coat pocket and handing it to Jakob. He had written "$1,000.00" with all the zeros to make it look as large as possible.

"Are you out of your mind? I happen to know that my parents paid over $2,700 for that house and land. Are you saying that things have depreciated that much?" Jakob demanded loudly as his eyes narrowed with rage.

"Well, that's what I'm tellin' ya son. Exactly, yes. And besides, your parents kinda let the place go down …" he answered politely as his voice trailed off.

"I'll let you know, Mr. Mahoney," Jakob almost screamed as he stormed out of the office, slamming the ornate, wrought iron door behind him. As he leaned on the old oak tree by the street, the letter his parents had left him jutted out of his jacket pocket, demanding to be read.

> *Dear Son,*
>
> *It's with a very heavy heart we write you this letter. We didn't want to take anything away from your recovery, son, so we decided to leave this letter with a friend. If you are now reading it, that means that we will not be sharing your days in our new country. But we're both assured that you will make us proud as we look upon you from above. We've asked God to protect you and we both have felt that God has ordained a path for you to follow. We have prayed fervently that you will follow that path. You've been a wonderful son, and we've enjoyed being your parents. We know that you'll want to start fresh, and we understand. Don't make the mistake of going to Bob Mahoney to sell the haus. Joe Morrison has already agreed to buy it for $2,000 if you want to sell. I also put our life savings of $5,000 in a milch jar hidden underneath Frau Mullen's rug, under the third floorboard—you know where. It's buried about a foot down in the dirt. It was the least we could do for you, son. We both love you so much.*
>
> *Make us very proud,*
> *Poppa*

The letter was a firm reminder of why he'd lived the way he did. He had to make his parents proud. He sold the old house and furniture and packed his bags for Artesia, Texas, with $8,000 in his wool military money belt. He was excited about the possibilities, and his imagination conjured up a life full of graceful living and warm friends.

The bus trip to Artesia was long, with numerous connections. He was finally at a friendly place, or so he thought, until the townspeople heard his accent and judged him harshly. After a period of earning empathy from a few businessmen, he opened Bosch Hardware in an old, abandoned grocery store. He had a lot of work to do to get it "spic and span," but he completed it in record time. After he settled in and got his store open, he looked up the family of his hero, Colonel Lynn, and knocked on their door.

"Who is it?" asked a soft whisper from inside the door.

"Jakob Bosch, ma'am," he answered. Soon the door creaked open slowly. "Ma'am, I don't know if your husband…" he started, as the little lady interrupted him with a hand gesture.

"Why, you're the boy that saved all those soldiers, aren't you?" she asked.

"Oh, no, ma'am. I don't deserve any praise for that, ma'am. It's your husband who's the hero," he insisted as his eyes fell in embarrassment.

"Well, come in, and we'll make some coffee," she said, opening the door wide. Soon they were on a first-name basis as he told Mrs. Carol Lynn about his escapades through France with her husband.

As he was sitting in the parlor, David Lynn's younger brother, Samuel, came through and shook Jakob's hand. Samuel had moved in with his brother's family when both of his parents had died suddenly within a few months of each other. Jakob had a wonderful time, and they insisted that he stay for supper. Afterwards, he told more stories as they enjoyed the cool evening breeze on the veranda.

As he was leaving, Samuel grabbed his arm and proclaimed, "I'll see him out, Carol. Don't worry, he'll be back to see us. I promise." As the two men walked out, Samuel's posture slacked as he said, "Jakob, I want to apologize. It's usually a lot happier around here, but we can hardly show our faces around town because of all the rigmarole."

Jakob said, "I don't understand." Samuel's face turned beet red and he started to stutter. Jakob stopped him and added, "Look, I'd be the last person on earth to say something bad about the Lynn family."

Samuel just looked down at the ground and mumbled, "Jenny, my brother's oldest girl, started slipping out of the house after everyone had gone to sleep, and the next thing we knew, everything has gone awry and she's expectin.' So to make a long story short, now she's had this bastard child, and everyone's a gawking at us like we have ten heads."

Mrs. Lynn had told Jakob that Samuel was so lazy, he wouldn't work in a pie factory as a taster. Jakob was also put off by Samuel's proclamation that he had "beat the draft by three months," but when Jakob heard those words, he saw so much of the colonel in him. His mannerisms and his voice inflections were comforting to Jakob, as he thought of his hero, Colonel Lynn.

"So what about the father? Doesn't he have responsibility in this?" Jakob asked indignantly, getting passionate about the double standard.

"Well, of course not," Samuel answered curtly with a quick release of air. They said their good-byes, but not before Jakob got an invitation for lunch the next Sunday.

As he climbed the steps again a week later, he felt many eyes on him through the curtains. "Come on in, Jakob!" Mrs. Lynn said brightly, as she swung the front door open wide. "Go sit in the parlor. We'll be eatin' soon," she said as she made her way back to the kitchen. Samuel was napping when Jakob walked in. They talked for a few minutes, and then it was time to wash up. "Jakob, you must sit here by me," Mrs. Lynn insisted as she pointed to the chair closest to her.

"Yes ma'am," he answered. Soon, there was some clattering down the hallway and two girls appeared. "Jakob, this is my oldest daughter, Jennifer, and my youngest, Katherine." The two girls curtsied and took their seats at the table.

After lunch, Jakob was back in the parlor with Samuel. "What'll happen to Jenny and the baby?" Jakob asked in a whisper.

"Well, they'll give the baby up, of course. But Jenny's so unstable, they just keep puttin' it off. It's ruined our family name and it's gotten so bad that we have to slip into the back of the church after the singin' starts and slip out during the final hymn. The owners of Mosley's store told Mrs. Carol that she had to go elsewhere to shop," Samuel stated.

Jakob was shocked that people could be so cruel. At that moment, his inspired idea even surprised himself. "Samuel, I owe my life to your family. What if I were willing to marry Jenny and give the baby a good home and a good name? I would love her as my own," Jakob pleaded as he stood.

Samuel, stunned that Jakob would make such a sacrificial resolution, stood up and stared into the distance for several seconds before he urgently asked, "Jakob, you'd be willin' to do that?"

Jakob quickly and boldly answered, "Yes, I would."

Samuel chuckled heartily at his lucky fate and ordered, "Well, don't be sayin' nothin.' You just let me handle this." A few weeks later, Jakob and Jenny were married in her mother's backyard, officiated by David Lynn's first cousin who was a pastor near Houston.

Jenny seemed to be happy for a while, but her depression soon returned and became worse than ever. Jakob tried to make her happy. He would work all day, come home and make supper, clean the house, and take care of Ellie. He was wearing himself to a frazzle, trying to make things as pleasant as possible. For twelve years, he fought an uphill battle, but Jenny was not getting better—only worse. Little Ellie was now in the sixth grade. Jakob had to dress and feed her and make sure she got to school on time. If that wasn't bad enough, people at the church began to boycott his business and spread several rumors about him. They were very successful in almost shutting his business down. He was having a very hard time providing for his family.

Jenny's friends told her about all the rumors, and it was almost too much for her. After the news came that her father, the Colonel, had been killed in France, Jenny took an overdose of bromide sleeping pills and alcohol. That same night, a customer found Jakob passed out on the floor of his hardware store. The doctor assumed it was alcohol poisoning, but Jakob was literally worn out—dehydrated and malnourished. Jakob had been living on adrenaline and finally his body shut down.

The rumor mill was ruthless as it curled around the little town like a constricting python, smothering out the life of those in its path. The rumors now had Jakob physically abusing Jenny and the little girl, while spending all of their money on booze. Of course, none of that was true.

By the time Jakob had finished telling his story, Miriam was staring at him through tear-filled eyes. She couldn't believe that people could be so cruel, assuming that they know a man's heart—especially Christian people. She also thought of her own callous thoughts as she felt her face warm. Miriam was truly touched by his life story and found that she was strangely attracted to him. He had been through so much, yet he had an inner strength that was so admirable.

"Well, Mr. Bosch," she said in a sniffle as tears ran down her cheeks.

"Please, call me Jakob, ma'am," he interrupted, while giving her his handkerchief.

"Okay, Jakob, I hate to tell you this after being convinced of the truth, but you have a hearing in front of a judge in two weeks. He's going to be looking for evidence that you're unfit to be Ellie's father," she mumbled reluctantly, dabbing the corner of her eyes with his handkerchief. Capturing his eyes with her own again, she then asked, "Jakob, would you mind telling your story one more time?"

Jakob humbly answered, "No ma'am, Miss Thacker."

She insisted, "Call me, Miriam, please." She took Jakob by the arm and escorted him over to see her uncle. He told the whole story once again, convincing the judge also of his innocence.

"Jakob, I would like to find out some more details about all this, if you don't mind," Miriam said, letting her curiosity get the best of her.

"What like, ma'am?" Jakob asked with hesitation as he wrinkled his brow.

"Well, I'd like to find out who Ellie's real father is and also why all these rumors are floating around, if I could," she pleaded, with a friendly smile.

He just nodded yes and said courteously, "Thank you again, Miriam, for believin' in me and for helpin' us. You know, when I've prayed about this, I didn't ask God to take away my problems or to make things better for us. I just asked Him to be glorified in whatever happened."

Miriam brightly smiled, opened the front door, and patted Ellie on the back as they left.

Three nights later, Miriam stepped out into the bright moonlight, throwing a blue cloak over her shoulders. She wondered how the old lady would take the news as she knocked delicately on the weathered, white door of Mrs. Lynn's house. She paced with nervous anticipation on the porch as she knocked a second time. Finally, the door creaked open only a few inches.

"Mrs. Lynn, my name is Miriam Thacker and I—" she started.

Mrs. Lynn quickly interrupted her, raucously saying, "Yeah, I know who you are. It seems that you've been puttin' your nose into some places it don't belong, Miss Thacker."

Miriam was taken aback by her comments, but she understood that she was only hearing one side. She looked at the belligerent woman with great humility and said, "Mrs. Lynn, I assure you my intentions are honorable. I have some news for you that will be disturbing, but it's important that you know."

At those words, Mrs. Lynn started to slowly close the door. Miriam shoved her right foot into the crack and begged, "Please, Mrs. Lynn, it has to do with Ellie!"

After a long pause, Mrs. Lynn opened the door a few inches again. With widening, piercing eyes and a loud voice, Mrs. Lynn announced, "You leave Ellie out of this. She's innocent in all this mess!"

Miriam had hit a nerve, but she had Mrs. Lynn's attention. She smiled slightly and proclaimed, "I wholeheartedly agree. My snooping was out of my great concern for her. You see, I wanted to get to the bottom of all the gossip and the accusations. I love Ellie with all my heart."

Mrs. Lynn opened the door further and moved to one side, gesturing that Miriam come in. Once inside the parlor, Miriam continued, "Mrs. Lynn, this whole thing is distressing to me too, and what I have to tell you isn't going to be easy."

Mrs. Lynn was a hardened war widow that was not shaken easily, so she said nonchalantly, "Let's have it, whatever it is."

Miriam looked about the room to make sure they were alone and quietly said, "Samuel is Ellie's father and he is also the one spreading the rumors, or at least starting a lot of them."

Mrs. Lynn took a deep breath as her eyes fell to the floor. "Even though I don't want to believe you, my intuition says otherwise. I guess I entertained the thought a few times, but I fought it off. Thank you for your courage and your perseverance. Now the hard part…I have to evict him," she said as she hugged Miriam with some apprehension.

Miriam hugged her back without apprehension and stated, "Let me know if I can do anything to help."

Mrs. Lynn nodded with a smile as she opened the front door for Miriam.

The Walk

"He has told you, O man, what is good. And what does the
LORD require of you but to do justice, to love kindness, and to
walk humbly with your God."

Micah 6:8

It was 1921, and "the Babe" was well on his way to taking the Yankees
to the World Series. E had finished high school and was turning
eighteen soon. World War I had been declared "over" two years
before, and everyone was finally getting back to work. A new car
called the "Able" was being driven around the old town square.
Cotton was the crop of choice for farmers in southeast Texas with
plenty of land but little money for fertilizers or irrigation.

E's father had stayed on past the end of the war to help with the
repatriation of the very last of the German POWs. As soon as he
returned home, he found the old farm in great disrepair. The family
had tried their best to keep it up, but it proved to be too much for
them. It would take a very long time to get it back in shape; in the
meantime, Oswald had to find work.

He took a job at the Liberty Gin in Artesia on the second floor, where the cotton was separated from the seeds. It was good money by their standards, but it was dangerous work with long hours. Oswald Moses was not scared of hard, dangerous work and after all, he had seven mouths to feed at home. It was harvest time and cotton was one of those crops that wouldn't wait. Working late one night, a weary, worn-out Oswald got his right sleeve caught in the gin. Before he knew it, his right arm was detached all the way up to his shoulder.

E had been waiting up for his father that night to tell him about his call to the ministry. By 8:00 p.m. there was no sign of Oswald and E's mother was frantically pacing the floor. Finally, at a quarter to nine, a messenger boy from the telegraph station had been sent to deliver the bad news. It would take a long time for Oswald to heal and return home. E felt he needed to wait to tell his news.

Life was anything but easy for the Moses family. E's father was a great believer in buying things when you had the money to pay for them, so they had no debt. In those days, job security and disability didn't exist, so Oswald found himself out of a job. George Housman, the gin owner, was an ornery old man with ill regard for anyone, especially Oswald.

"No, no, no," he told his foreman, as his jaw tightened and his eyes hardened to small angry dots. "We're not runnin' some charity here, especially for greenhorns, so stop your gripe. Shoddy work from a one-armed man—just what I need! Pack his plunder and get him out. I blame him for almost a half-day's ruin. And get those hayseed grangers of yours back to work. We gotta make up time."

As George murmured on, the foreman looked over his shoulder at the surprised men with open mouths and commanded, "Boys, let's get back at it."

Crabby old Housman was little thought of around Artesia but he owned most of the town, so people tolerated him. He had long outlived his wife, Katherine Banks-Housman, daughter of Howard Banks, Sr., founder of the Banks Oil Company of Houston. Katherine had given George money to start his business enterprises but knew little of his crooked dealings and underhanded shenanigans.

Many called Housman "Nabal" because of how he treated Oswald, but Oswald never said one unkind word about how he was treated. He was not one to carry grudges or let people get him down. In his mind, God had let all this happen for a reason, and who was he to question God's intentions? Oswald learned to use his left hand almost as well as his right in no time. No one could outdo him on a shovel, so the county road crew hired him. After a long time, he was able to work his way up to supervisor.

In the meantime, E was the oldest in the family, so it became his lot in life to help provide for them. E could have questioned God about his fate, but he didn't. Oswald had taught his children to make the best of every circumstance. "When life hands you lemons, make lemonade" was their family motto; however, they added one more line: "then give that lemonade to someone who really needs it." Believing in God's provision wasn't something they just prayed for at the Moses home. It was something they lived.

Saint Nick

Poppa Nick, E's maternal grandfather, had moved in with them after his wife died from influenza during the pandemic of 1919. Poppa Nick was a renaissance man who had been a barber, cook, dairyman, and butcher, and had even owned a team of mules in his lifetime. They liked to joke that he'd not been a candlestick maker yet, but give him time. He wasn't much help around the old house, but he could play a mean game of checkers, and no one could tell yarns about the good old days like the old man. Oswald thought Poppa Nick was a little too garrulous and called him "Nick Knack" at times, but in reality, he wished he had some of the qualities of the old man.

Poppa Nick's wispy, white hair hardly ever saw a comb. His tobacco-stained mustache curled up on end, and he had a little tuft of a goatee on his chin. Every time he would come near, he smelled like Velvet pipe tobacco, which he smoked on occasion. His eyebrows would move like flowers pulling at their roots in a big wind, and his rosy cheeks glowed like hot embers as he lost himself in his embellished storytelling.

"Have I told you boys about the time my grandparents met Jesse James and his gang?" Nick prompted, his mustache twitching as if electrified. "My family homesteaded on a farm outside of Russellville, Kentucky, in the days when things were still wild and lawless. Three horsemen lookin' rougher than a wagonload of cobs rode in early one mornin' while my grandpa and father were out doin' chores. As the dust cleared, the lead man said, 'Say, old man, you got some chow? We're banded.' Grandpa nodded politely and hitched their horses to the ole' post in front of the house. Two went in to eat, leaving the third outside attending the horses. He would take off one saddle at a time, curry that horse, and then move to the next one, looking over his shoulder the whole time. When the other two went in, they rearranged the plates at the table so that they could see out all the windows. As they sat down to eat my grandma's fried cakes, the lead man reached across his chest and pulled out a barkin' iron that was backwards in its holster and placed it carefully on the table in front of him. It was a Navy Colt with several notches in it. He was so familiar with that pistol my grandpa reckoned that he used it as a pillow. As soon as the other man got through eatin,' he went out to relieve the man outside currying the horses. Then that man came in. The lead man that stayed inside glanced over at my grandma and said, 'Ace-high, ma'am. Thank ya.' Then he flicked one coin up in the air. It hit the table with a ringing noise, spun and wobbled, then fell flat. My grandma said it was an 1856 gold Liberty coin worth twenty dollars back then. He tipped his black hat and they all left without another word! It was one of those stories I heard a million times growin' up. My grandpa said they called the lead man with the gun 'Jesse,' and later they discovered that the James Gang had robbed a bank in Russellville the day before those men showed up, but there were only two at the bank robbery. They always suspected the third man was waitin' nearby with fresh horses," Poppa Nick said, while fumbling inside his white grosgrain vest pocket. Soon he brought out that old gold coin, and to the boys, it made everything come to life as they put the coin in their hands and studied it with big eyes.

When Hannah told the girls to get their baths, the rest stayed to listen to Poppa Nick tell more stories. As his eyes darted about the room with an unnatural energy, he asked, "Did I ever tell you boys 'bout the time I had a fryer sale in my butcher shop? I got a great deal on a wagonload of hens, but I didn't have the space for em, so I decided to have an 'all day' sale. Some of the finest, plumpest birds you ever did see … that is, except for this one crate full of birds that looked more like parakeets. They were so little you could use the drumstick as a toothpick! So I decided to take the small hens and put them inside some medium-sized ones so everyone would get their money's worth. The next day old Miss Eunice, who wasn't known for her great intellect, came by to thank me for her hen. She said with great repose, 'Mr. Nick, I gotta thank ya, sir, for that great hen you sold me. But ya know, I feel like I cheated you!' What she didn't have in brains, she made up for in heart. Then she said with great excitement, "That hen was gonna have a baby!" Everyone rolled with laughter as Poppa Nick took another draw off his old pipe while gray swirls of smoke danced about his head, joining in the levity.

At that moment, E got a providential idea. If he could get his grandpa to teach him how to be a butcher, maybe he could cut meat, pack it, and sell it out of the back of the wagon. "Poppa, you think we could do it?" E asked earnestly.

Eliciting a serious look from Nick, he answered, "Well, sure, son, if that's what you'd like to do." So E told Poppa his plan while Hannah and Oswald got ready for bed. "I like it, E, but we'll need some good knives and equipment," Nick declared with a proud twinkle.

"Yes, sir!" E said with excitement.

Soon the venture was a phenomenal success and E became known for his honesty, integrity, and sincerity. If you ordered a pound of shank, he would give you a pound and a quarter. He even named his business and painted it on the side of the wagon: "E-licious Meats." E's meat sales kept the family afloat during a very dark time. It soon became "E-licious Foods" as he expanded the business to include eggs, cream, milk, and butter.

Running a business, doing his chores, and working for Miss Clark was tough on E, but it served to temper his resolve to eventually go on to college and then seminary. He knew that God would supply, but he dared not mention anything about his dreams yet. He didn't want his family to feel bad about the way things were then and the direction that life had taken them all.

A Pocket Full of Poseys

Red Posey was a huge black man with a voice like a freight train and a heart made of gold. Red's wife, Zate, had worked for the Moses family as a nanny when Oswald was at war and Hannah worked in the ammunition factory. Zate had taught E how to fish and had a lot of influence on his calling into the ministry. Red and Zate were God-fearing, hardworking people ensconced in the black working class of the South. Red would always come to the Moses home for his eggs and cream. "Ya' sees, I don't want you to go to tha' trouble, E. You lets me come to you. It bees best for everybody concerned," he told E when E tried to deliver to his house. E loved the Posey family with all his heart and thought that a lot of the trouble between the whites and blacks could be alleviated if they would only get to know one another. E had always thought that the black image in the white mind was altogether different than reality. On one occasion, that point could not have been "driven home" any better to him.

Red was on his way home, walking in the well-rutted shortcut that took him through a thicket to his humble house. It was exactly a mile to the sawmill, and he made the trip twice daily; however, this day he was very late leaving. Darkness was already beginning to cover the community, and he was trying desperately to see with very little light. Red was a big, muscular "man's man," so no one would ever guess that he was deathly afraid of the dark. As a small child, he had been locked in a closet as part of some punishment bestowed on him. As the glow of the sunset faded from the sky and was replaced by an indigo blue, he began to panic and started running full gape into the pitch-blackness. That stately pine had been standing there for years and was not about to yield to Red. He was out cold.

It was Red's birthday, and several had already gathered at his home for the "big surprise." Twyla, his youngest daughter, stood by the window and blew on the glass, making hearts with her finger while her father's birthday gift bumped against her leg. She had been teaching her daddy how to read, so her mother, aunts, and uncles had saved all the money they could to buy the gift. He had always wanted to read the Bible but couldn't, and now he was going to finally have the opportunity to realize his dream.

There was a circle of intense community that they all shared. Maybe because of the pressures of the world against them, or maybe it was because of their increased enlightenment of what was important in life. That shiny, new Bible was a symbol of hope for that family—hope in God's revelation and in His provision.

"Where is he, Momma?" Twyla asked in a concerned, high-pitched voice.

"He'll be here. Just you don't fret, child," Zate answered, hiding her own fears. Soon the minutes turned into an hour and they all started to worry and pace.

In the foggy darkness, Red woke up dazed and sat by the tree, affixed in terror at the night sounds that were surrounding him. Before long, a lantern glowed in the distance and grew to full light.

"What do ya think, Nubby? Is he drunk?" asked Sam Chatman.

"Shoot yeah, Sam. He's drunk as a kooter!" Nubby chimed, as he shook his head from side to side.

Before Red could say a word, the men were gone. "Ain't that ole Red from the mill?" Sam asked as they hastily walked away, not even checking on Red's wellbeing.

"Yep. Worked with him some last summer. Never knew he was the sort to get snookered, though," Nubby answered, without much thought as he mumbled on.

Soon Zate was frantically concerned and gave a lantern to Red's uncle. He struck out in the night toward the mill, but he didn't know about the shortcut and missed Red completely. He came back and told Zate there was no one at the mill and everything was dark. Zate took the lantern and went straight to the Moses house for help. It was a good three miles there, but she made it in record time. After she explained what had happened, E got a lantern and his horse.

"You stay here, Miss Zate. I'll be back soon," E said calmly. He finally found Red sitting by the big tree. "Are you okay, Mr. Red?" E asked nervously.

"I thinks so. I's took a big hit on my ole gourd, though," he said humbly with a forced laugh.

E loaded him on his horse and walked him back to the Moses home. After Zate and Red embraced for a moment, E went out to hitch the mules to the wagon to take them home. As he rode up, Twyla ran out to greet her daddy. He picked her up with one arm and hugged her tight.

"E, would you stay for some birthday cake, please?" Zate pleaded with a smile.

E answered, "Well, all right, ma'am, I can stay only a few minutes." As they sat by the fire, E found himself studying the Posey family in the pulsing glow that filled the whole house and lapped at the humble furnishings. He was impressed with Red's innocent wisdom shining brightly in the darkness of the Steeple Creek community. Red Posey, like his name, was in full bloom.

Suddenly, there was a great upheaval outside. They looked out and saw two hooded men on horses with torches. Red staggered to the front door, asking loudly, "What do you mens want?'

One of the guys on horseback answered, "We want to have a word with you, Red. We understand that…"

While the man was still speaking, E walked over to the door, recognizing the voice. "What are you doing here, Mr. Edwards?" E asked with great surprise.

There was a moment of silence while both hooded men regained their composure. "We know that Red's drunk and we're here to make sure that don't happen again," commanded the second man.

"What are you talkin' about? He ran into a tree in the darkness and it knocked him out! This is his birthday, and he got a Bible as a present," E said with resolve. Before he could finish, the men quickly rode off into the darkness. E gained a world of experience that night. It would prove to serve him well in the years to come. He would adhere to higher values and not be condescending toward anyone for any reason. He would humbly desire to understand people where they lived, never assuming anything and not judging anyone.

Artesian Well

The next day, more news hit the streets of Artesia; the pastor was leaving for good on December 12 to celebrate Christmas with his family. Old Brother Gerald was retiring and moving to Dallas where his kids had settled, so Steeple Creek Church was actively searching for a new preacher. Brother Gerald had been a circuit preacher before the church called him to serve full time seven years earlier. Back then, the deacons were the ones who picked a new preacher. Being a deacon was a very prestigious honor and a status symbol. Harland Boyd, chairman of the deacons, owned and operated the sawmill near the outskirts of town and employed several men who were members of the church. Although E's father was a Sunday school teacher and a very active member of the church, he had continued to resist having his name added to the list when it came time to vote on new deacons. He felt like he could serve God in better ways and wasn't interested in status. Oswald was very modest, but Hannah always thought it was his shyness that kept his name off the list.

E was well known for his benevolence. At Christmas time he always tried extra hard to help the widows who had lost their husbands in the war. He had heard about Mrs. Chamber in the community who needed her shingles fixed on her old, run-down house. He spent his entire Saturday fixing her roof, raking her yard, and fixing a loose banister. When he told her he had finished, she said, "Joe Earl, you're always helpin' your granny and I appreciate it so much, sweetheart. Let me bake you a pie or somethin' to take home?"

"No, ma'am," E answered, never telling her who he really was.

Later that evening, E's mother got a call from Doris Watson. Mrs. Watson was much better than the newspaper at keeping everybody up with community happenings. Of course, she was not a gossip; she considered it sharing in Christian love. After Hannah got off the phone, she called E down from his room.

"E, Mrs. Watson tells me that you weren't over at Mrs. Chamber's house today. Is that true?" she asked as her voice rang with surprise.

"No ma'am," E decisively answered.

By that time, Oswald had taken an interest in the conversation. "Well, you wanna explain?" Hannah asked, knowing there was an explanation.

"Yes ma'am. I finished doing what needed to be done and I went inside to tell her, but she kept calling me Joe Earl."

Hannah looked over at Oswald with a grin. "So you didn't correct her, did you?" she asked.

"No ma'am," E answered. Immediately she changed the subject because she knew that E was selfless in doing for others and she expected that from him.

"E, I've baked some teacakes and they're coolin' on the stove. Go get you a couple," she ordered. He got his teacake and some milk and joined the family listening to the radio in the living room.

That same night, after suppertime, the deacons at Steeple Creek had decided to meet at the church to vote on a man most of them wanted for their new pastor. They locked the door behind them as they went in the church office, then went inside the pastor's study and locked that door too. As they sat around the old desk discussing the matter, Brother Boyd brought up a problem he had with calling the man. It seemed that some had some dealings with him a few years back and were very concerned. It wasn't something you could really put your finger on. He just seemed to be very complacent and careful about not offending anyone. Saying little most of the time is a good character trait to have, except in his case. Brother Flanders was a little too perfidious, conniving, and accommodating. Brother Boyd thought he was too much into feathering his own nest. Harland tried to convince the group to proceed with caution, but to no avail. Harland said to himself, "They just want someone to pet and pamper 'em." Harland was called on to pray before the vote, so he asked God to block it somehow if he was not the right man. His prayer got several *amen's*.

Meanwhile, E was getting ready to eat his favorite dessert, pecan pie. But for some reason he was quickly losing his appetite. He felt in his spirit that something bad was happening. He had a sinking feeling in his stomach, and pecan pie was the last thing on his mind. He went into his bedroom, hit his knees, and started praying, "God, I don't know what's happenin,' but I ask that Your will be done. I'm available, God." At that very moment, he heard God's voice say, *Go to the church.* He didn't know why, but he knew he had to go.

As he passed by the kitchen, he said, "Momma, I gotta go. I'll be back soon." Any other time, she would've asked questions, but this time she didn't. Somehow she knew that he was doing something very important. He mounted Goosebumps, his horse, and rode steady on the old wagon trail illuminated by a setting sun throwing long blue shadows across the old wagon ruts. The road ran alongside Steeple Creek, and he could see the water sparkling from the sun cutting through the trees. His trot turned into a full gallop as he wondered what could be happening.

After Harland prayed, they got paper together for the vote but couldn't find anything to write with. They looked in every drawer and on every shelf. One of the deacons decided to go into the church office, so he unlocked the door and scrounged around the church office through all the drawers and cabinets but found nothing, not even one pencil in the entire church office.

As E dismounted by a clump of bushes behind the church, he followed the light that brought him inside, waiting for God's direction. All he could hear in his mind was, *He is not the right man.* But what did it mean? As he stood in the hall by the locked office door thinking how foolish he felt, the door opened.

It was Mr. Boyd and he asked, "E, what're you doin' here?" But he didn't wait for a reply. He just kept frantically looking for something to write with.

E caught his attention again, however, when he said, "He's not the right one."

He looked at E with big eyes and asked, "How did you know that we were considering anyone, E?"

"I didn't, sir," E answered.

At that very moment, Harland remembered his prayer and his face turned pale. "E, would you mind telling the group what you just told me?" Harland continued.

"No, sir," E replied humbly.

As E walked through the office and into the study, all eyes were on him. "He's not the one," E proclaimed to the group.

Mr. Edwards, one of the deacons, demanded with squinted eyes, "Would you mind elaborating on that, son?"

E looked over at Mr. Boyd and shook his head no. When Mr. Boyd realized that E had nothing else to add, he quickly shuffled him out and told him thanks and that he would do what he could.

E found himself staring at a locked door again. At that moment, God gave him tremendous peace. He had done what he was called to do. As he mounted Goosebumps, God continued to talk to him. *Some men say they want me to guide them. They say they want my will and even pray that I block things if they're not right. But in the end, they just want my will to be theirs.* Then Luke 9:23 came to E's mind. "If anyone desires to come after me, let him deny himself." Suddenly E had a rumbling in his stomach for some of his mother's pecan pie. He was hoping that it was still on the table when he got home. It was getting dark, but the full moon was coming up over the trees, illuminating his way. The deacons voted yes for Brother Flanders. It went to the church floor for a token vote the next Sunday morning and passed with no opposition.

The new pastor was everything the church wanted. His watered-down preaching on sin eliminated black and white absolutes—everything was gray. His sermons were boring and lifeless, having no real-life application to Christian living. He petted and pampered the sick and old and befriended the influential in the church to solidify his job security. He soothed the lukewarm Christians with words of approval and stomped out any sparks of true Godly living with his empty words.

The Remnant

Every Sunday, E would be up before daybreak, putting the feed sacks on the mules and hitching them to the wagon. He would get an old quilt that his grandmother had made and put it down on the hard seat for his mother to sit on. Oswald would get the family up and ready. His mother, Hannah, would have breakfast cooking over the wood burning stove that E had filled and lit before he went out that morning. It was a long trip to the church down by Steeple Creek, so they packed to stay the entire day with dinner on the grounds. It was a place where E felt like he belonged. He would soak up the atmosphere of the old church that Oswald's father had helped to build many years earlier. E didn't like where the new pastor was taking the old church, but he trusted that God knew what He was doing.

God had chosen E as a remnant of the Great Awakening at the turn of the century. By the early '20s, God and His will were the last things on most people's minds. God had heard their prayers during the war, but they had quickly forgotten those things—forgotten God and put Him away for a time that they might need Him again. It was much like Moses and the wilderness. The Israelites prayed and prayed to God for deliverance, and when He delivered them, they were not appreciative and even complained of their plight.

E learned at an early age to totally rely on God. So many of life's lessons had already taken hold in his life. He was talking to his father one day about prayer and said, "Pap, I believe that one of our greatest sins is that we don't ask for enough when we pray. We don't take what God's willing to give, because of our unbelief. Not once in the Bible does it say He didn't have enough to go around, and I don't remember Him ever saying, 'Don't ask too much!' In fact, I do remember Him saying, 'Ask and it shall be given.' However, I don't believe He was talking about asking for things that we don't need and that might even be bad for us. Our prayers should be accounted with our giving. I think what the preacher said about that ten percent tithe thing is phony and elementary, too. I don't think we can settle how much we ought to give so easily and compactly. The only safe rule is to give more than we can spare, not only of money but time, talent, and as I said, prayer. And what the preacher said about why most people don't give their ten percent in tithes is hard to swallow, too. I believe that most people don't give or give very little out of a fear of insecurity, not greed. Those people should read Luke 6:38, 'Give, and it shall be given to you: good measure, pressed down, shaken together, running over, they will pour into your lap. For whatever measure you deal out, it will be dealt to you in return.' Do we not believe that anymore as Christians?"

As E finished, Pap gave him a quick nod. He was not one for many words. E knew the nod was as good as gold, because his father was always very frank and lacked any pretense. He was so honest and aboveboard that he often came off as lacking tact. E's mother would scold Oswald for being too honest at times. She thought it was too cutting and lacking in feeling. Of course, she knew that he really wasn't like that. He masked his big heart quite well.

He would walk through the house in the morning saying, "Idleness is the parent of all vice—get up before the sun warps your teeth!" Oswald was one of those people you could set your clock by. He was in bed by 8:00. He and Hannah would talk about the day, world events, and other things while lying in bed, usually no longer than thirty minutes, and then he was asleep by 8:30. Much of his day was the same way. Procrastination wasn't a word in his vocabulary. If he said he was going to do something, you could expect him to do it promptly. On the other hand, he expected everyone else to be the same way. Sometimes that would get him in trouble.

A lot of the neighbor kids would get to stay home during harvest to help out with chores, but Oswald would never let any of his kids miss school. However, when they came home, they had plenty to do. E's younger brother, James, was in charge of feeding all the animals and making sure the chickens were on their roost and closed up tight at night. E's oldest sister, Jane Eliza, was in charge of milking Betsy, the family's Jersey cow. Betsy was very particular about who touched her, so her job was set in stone twice a day. Janie was full of life and forcefully convincing on any subject. She had her father's quick wit but definitely her mother's heart.

Mary Mae was the youngest sister and everyone's pet. She was supposed to gather eggs and skim the milk after the cream separated and came to the top, but on many occasions E would be caught doing her chores for her. She was not the physical type, anyway, and she loved to read books. Mae Mae, as they called her, was definitely the finest of all the kids, getting her good looks from Hannah's side of the family. She was also the most creative, loving music and art. Grandpa Nick really took a liking to her, of course.

Mr. Withers had stopped Oswald one evening on his way in from work and handed him a puppy that had been roaming around the community for weeks. "Oz, can't you find someone who wants this puppy?" asked Old Man Withers, who lived about a half mile up the road.

"Well, I guess—" said Oswald.

Before Oswald could finish his statement, Mr. Withers interrupted, "We just can't keep feedin' him, and mother's bedridden. I would appreciate it, Oz."

Oswald was stuck. John Withers was a great hand at helping Oswald—whenever he could. "Where'd he come from, John?" Oswald asked.

"Somebody must've dumped him here," answered Mr. Withers.

It didn't surprise Oswald. Several years back, they had found an X in the middle of a circle on one of John's oak trees by the road. Nick said it was a hobo sign, meaning, "This house is good for a handout." The Withers family was very hospitable, and some people will take advantage of that. As Oswald took the dog in to look him over, E met him at the door.

"Pap! I always wanted a little puppy! Thank you so much, Pap," announced E as he hugged tight on the little dog.

The excitement on E's face was too much for Oswald to say no, but he did tell E that he was to look out for the dog and not let any of his chores lack. "You fix him a place to stay outside and you'll be responsible for him," Oswald sternly told E.

"Yes, sir, pap!" E answered with excitement.

"What'ya gonna call him?" questioned Oswald.

"Micah, and he's going to be my best buddy in the whole world," E said.

As Oswald examined Micah, he realized that the dog was full of birdshot. After some detective work, he found out that Mr. Miller, who lived at what they called the "Upperline," had one of his prize golden retrievers get loose and mate with his wife's fancy chow chow. He waited for the pups to wean and then he shot them, stuffed all of them in a gunnysack, and tossed them into the creek downstream. E knew that Micah had survived for a reason, and that reason was to be his dog. As the years went by, Micah became the patriarch of the farm and he took his job very seriously as friend, defender, and even counselor, at times. Micah was E's hero, not because he did some heroic act, but because if a heroic act were ever needed, he would not hesitate. His unconditional love, unending vigilance for duty, and quite friendly nature was inspiring to the entire family.

Micah would sit by E while he read his Bible and fished. The Bible was so easy for E to understand and learn. He would go around the house quoting scriptures and advising people much older than him. He knew it was a spiritual gift from God. Everyone did.

The Furtive Miss Clark

"You know, E," Miss Clark said, "I never liked men. I thought all of them were selfish and manipulative and women… well, they're just plain mean. But you've given me hope in mankind. You've made me realize that God is still working in this cold, heartless, evil world we live in and maybe it's not a goner yet."

She smiled at him and paused for a moment, waiting for his reply, but all E did was smile. "E," she continued, "I need to tell ya somethin.' I know you think of me as an ornery old maid in this community and that's probably true."

After E shook his head no, she continued, "And most people say I eat little children and I have a big, black cauldron in my basement. You know that's just talk, but I do have a deep, dark secret."

E was deathly silent as she told her story, intently watching her lips. She continued, "I'm the illegitimate daughter of George Housman."

E was not easily shaken, but he really squirmed at this news. He was sure that his mouth was on the floor as his chin gave way to gravity. God had gifted him with great wisdom for his age, but this was real deep water to tread. All he could see was the face of that miserable, wretched old Housman. If there was one man in the world E could hate, it would be him. Soon a scripture was almost screaming in his head, "Give, and it will be given to you. They will pour into your lap a good measure—pressed down, shaken together, and running over. For by your standard of measure it will be measured to you in return." But why was he getting a scripture about giving? Finally, he couldn't hold it any longer and just blurted it out. Miss Clark started crying incessantly. What had he said? For the first time in his life, he felt totally inadequate as his face turned white. But his face only served to convince her even more that what she was about to do was the right thing.

Old George Housman got his just reward on December 13, seven days before Miss Clark's conversation with E. He never figured on dying, at least not yet, so he never went to the trouble of making out a will. In line for all the fortune was old Miss Clark and only Miss Clark. Years earlier, her mother had made sure the right paperwork was in place for that to happen, or should I say God did. George had lied to Margaret Clark's mother many years ago, telling her that he would marry her. She was so in love with him, she believed everything he said. But after he heard about the pregnancy, he married the Hughes girl for her money. To add insult to injury, he made a confidential arrangement with an attorney in town to pay Margaret's mother off monthly, and if she didn't keep quiet, he would "take drastic measures."

The money stopped coming soon after Margaret was born, so her mother went back to the attorney, but he couldn't get George to pay any more than he had already paid. He sent word through the attorney that if she tried to get any more money from him, he would have the child picked up by the authorities and declare her unfit. That attorney's name was Hilton Speed; he was the grandson of Nora Clark Speed. Nora was Miss Clark's first cousin, so she made sure that her son filed the right paperwork to take care of Miss Clark in the future. Miss Clark was now a very rich woman. She had asked God for a confirmation of her plans. The scripture that E had quoted was all she needed.

She finally settled down enough to make coherent sentences again. "E, I'm a very wealthy woman and I want to send you to college. Would you let me?" This was yet another curveball coming E's way. He was still thinking about old Housman and how she resembled him. She continued, "Just pray about it, okay? And, if you're willin,' I'll come over and talk to your father about this later." All E could do was nod up and down as his lips trembled and his legs became wobbly and offered little stability as he tried to stand.

That night, E didn't sleep. Tossing and turning, his mind would race back and forth over the conversation with Miss Clark. It was his "dream come true." Finally, he could see a glimpse of the providence of God, just in time for Christmas.

When Things Go Bad, Don't Go With Them

"There are a thousand
hacking at the branches of evil
to one who is striking at the root."
—Henry David Thoreau

Within the walls of Baylor College, E found solace from the shallow thinking of the outside world and the boundless hopelessness it espoused. He was preparing for midterms when he got a call. It was his mother. "E, the doctor says that Poppa Nick is not going to make it much longer. I asked him if he had made his peace with God, and he replied, 'Peace is a gift given to us to die gracefully and gratefully as Christians, so peace I have.'"

E tried to study, but he found it hard to concentrate on his books. He finally grew very tired and fell asleep on his bed. Something kept him from resting soundly, and soon he felt my presence in the room. His eyes sprang open wide in a paralyzing fear, and he was surprised to see me standing by his bed. My manifestation was pitch black, cloaking my brightness that was illuminating the wall behind me. As E tried his best to gather all his strength, he quickly sprang to his feet and screamed at the top of his lungs in terror, "Help!"

Instantly, I commanded, "Peace, be still!" So E had no recourse but to calmly settle back into his pillow. Then he heard me say, "E, you're going to go through a lot soon. Just be faithful and you'll be fine." Then I melded into the darkness of the room and was gone. I made sure no one heard E's screams for help, and he returned to a deep sleep, getting more rest than he had gotten in a long time. When the next night came, it was harder for him to get to sleep, as he was wondering if something would happen again. But nothing did.

As with each man, Satan has his day. And the day had come for E to be tested. Satan and my nemesis, Azazel, asked God if they could sift E into dust. God, of course, said no. But God was very pleased with E's faithfulness, so He agreed to their testing within His limits.

E was really enjoying college life. Professor Chambers was a dapper little man with more hair on his forearm than on top of his head. What little white hairs he did have up there looked like they couldn't decide which way to go. He taught E physics, an elective class that he enjoyed tremendously. "E, you have an incredible gift. Have you ever considered changing your major?" Dr. Chambers asked with great exuberance.

"Well, no, sir, I haven't. But, I'll consider it. Thank you, sir," E answered with humility.

"Well, make sure you do, I want to take you around to the other professors as soon as possible," Dr. Chambers said, confident that he would make the change.

There was a chill wind that seemed to saunter across campus, taking the school captive. It came without pageantry to the busy students running to and fro. It ran its ugly hand right through the cracks between buttons on E's jacket and whispered words in his ear like, "You owe it to yourself," and "It's now or never."

"No, no, no! That's not what I've been called to do. It's not my purpose, and you know it," he seemed to say to someone other than himself.

The chill wind continued to erode away his good reasoning as he heard it again. "God didn't mean for you to give up on your dreams. God really didn't mean for you to be a minister. He meant that you're to minister in whatever you do."

As Azazel slithered into E's head, a scripture came to him. "Did God really say, you must not eat from any tree in the garden?" As he pondered the scripture, warmth came over his skin, giving him goose bumps. At that moment, he resolved not to go against God's will. He promptly visited Professor Chambers and told him he was not interested in changing his major. E wondered if that was what I came in the night to warn him of.

Professor Chambers continued to insist on the change. E found himself avoiding him, but Azazel would not accept defeat that easily.

Her name was Lydia Murphy and she glowed like a star in the drab, dreary universe of Baylor. Not many girls were on campus in those days. Lydia was working in the infirmary after she would finish classes in Denton a few miles away. Her mother was the head nurse at Baylor, and Lydia wanted to follow in her footsteps.

During exams, E was struggling with an illness that seemed to zap his energy. He tried his mother's homemade concoction, but it didn't seem to help. It was all he could do to maintain his studies.

Byron Wilson, E's boyhood friend, was next door in room 313. "E, are you all right?" By asked, as he knocked on E's door.

By heard a small, barely recognizable voice say, "If I had just a little more energy, I could tell you how little energy I have." By quickly opened the door to find E lying in his bed, wrapped in blankets.

"E, you're burnin' up! We've gotta get you to the nurse," By said while putting his hand on E's forehead.

Fighting delirium, E opened his eyes to the beautiful Lydia. "How are you feeling?" she said in an angelic voice, compressing a wet cloth to his forehead.

"Hey, you sure are pretty…you mind if I touch you to make sure you're real?" he asked, putting his hand on her cheek. She just giggled as her face blushed. E got better as the days got shorter. Fall was such a beautiful time of the year in northeastern Texas and Lydia embellished it with her good looks. E suddenly realized that he was falling in love with a girl he hardly knew.

"Lydia, would you consider going on a picnic with me?" he asked, thinking that it would be a safe outing for getting to know her better.

"A picnic? Why a picnic? I was thinking about Cavetti's, that nice restaurant that just opened," she retorted, with a mischievous twinkle in her eyes.

"Well, I was thinkin' that a picnic would allow us to get to know each other better," E offered, thinking that she would understand. But to Lydia, he only sounded cheap.

"You take me to Cavetti's, and then I'll go on that picnic with you. All right?" she insisted, seeming to have her mind made up.

"You got it," E conceded, squinting his eyes.

Lydia had found out that E had money and she was out to hook him. She put her best dress on and spent hours getting ready for their date. Then her phone rang. "Lydia, I just found out that my grandfather is very ill and I need to go home. I hate to do this, but I need to postpone our date," E told Lydia reluctantly.

Seizing the opportunity, she replied, "Oh, E, that's okay. I could pack a bag and go with you." She really wanted to meet his family and see where the money came from.

"Well…" he answered in a state of confusion. "Let me check and make sure that's all right."

"Okay, bye," Lydia answered, confident that she would be accepted as a guest.

"Lydia, you look lovely!" E professed as he got her bags and placed them in the trunk.

"Oh, you're too sweet," she said, pretending to be shocked by his compliment.

E was on his way home. It was a pleasant journey with Lydia, but the more he thought about my ominous visit, he realized that at least part of it had to be about Poppa Nick.

"Mother, how is he?" E quizzed with concern as his mother opened the door.

"He's fine and resting in bed," Hannah said as she mused at them.

"Mother, I want you to meet Lydia," E said with a proud smile.

"Well, it's a pleasure, Lydia. Come in, E can get your stuff out of the car later," she said as she hugged them.

Miss Clark was paying for E's tuition, meals, boarding, and even a car, but at home there were still a lot of chores to do. E checked on Poppa Nick and walked out on the porch to swing with Lydia. "I'm so glad you came home with me this weekend, Lydia. It really gives us some time to talk and get to know each other. I have a lot to do around here, but I've saved some time for us," E announced as he reclined and readied himself to talk further.

"Oh, I enjoyed meeting everyone, E, but I'm afraid I can't stay. I just talked to my mother and she really needs me at home," she said curtly.

"Is anything wrong?" he asked, raising his brow in frustration.

"Oh, no, it's just that she really needs me," she responded sharply.

A bewildered E paused for a moment, then he responded, "Well, do you need to go now?"

"E, I really hate to ask, but I really do," she answered, as she busied herself with her things. She was almost insistent on coming with him and now she was already prepared to go. He suddenly realized that he would never understand women.

"Mother, something came up at Lydia's house and she needs me to take her home," E said as they walked inside.

"Well, where does she live?" Hannah asked, sounding suspicious.

E sensed her concern and answered, "It's only thirty miles or so. I'll be back before bedtime." They got in E's car and drove off down the road without a "good-bye" or "thank you" from Lydia.

"Oz, I really wasn't trying to eavesdrop, but when she said 'squalor,' I stopped in my tracks," Hannah told Oswald in bed.

"What?" he asked, forcing a laugh.

"Yeah, she said it. She told her mother she was in a shanty with *squalor* and that she thought E had money, but he didn't," Hannah answered as her eyes widened in shock with every word.

"She said that?" Oswald asked as he sat up in the bed.

"She did," replied Hannah with boldness.

"Well, it's best that she leave then. What in the world is E doin' with her?" he asked in frustration as he shook his head.

"I think she just turned his head and he really didn't know what she was like," she stated as Oswald grunted. Hannah continued, "I think she saw that nice car and thought she had herself a meal-ticket."

Oswald asked as his eyes danced, "So you think she's a gold-digger?"

Hannah answered, "I do."

They said their goodnights and went to sleep. Thirty miles turned into almost fifty, so E didn't get back until late. Hardly anything was said the whole trip. He tried, but she was not in the mood. He reasoned with himself that something was wrong at home and she didn't want to talk about it.

The next morning came early as E sat with his parents at the kitchen table eating breakfast. Nothing was said about Lydia. They had already decided that if E wanted to talk about her, he would have to bring her up. Oswald soon headed off to work, and E made his way around the old farm, inspecting fences and cleaning up around the feed stalls for the cow and horses. He went over to the edge of the garden where the turnip greens were and picked an arm-ful for supper. The tomatoes had long since played out, but there was at least a mess of peas left, so he picked them. After doing all he could around the weathered barn, he turned his attention toward the old house. Some cracks around windows had to be sealed before winter and the pipes had to be wrapped tight. He walked down to the spring where they had placed a pump to check on things there. He wanted to get as much done as possible before Oswald got home from work. He slopped the pigs, fed the chickens, hoed out the fall potato patch, and made sure Micah had plenty water and food.

"Hey, Micah, you wanna take a walk with me to the pond?" he asked the old dog, who seemed to answer with a jump. Nick had stocked the pond with catfish, so E grabbed a bucket of fish food. Micah watched and barked as the fish churned the water where they ate. It was a hard weekend, and as E sat there with Micah's head in his lap, he pondered all that had happened. Micah just listened patiently as E poured out his thoughts and feelings on the old dog. It was a great show of love for Micah to listen, and E realized it. Time flew by and before he knew it, he was packing his bags for school.

School Dazed

"Monday morning got here too quickly, didn't it, Mrs. Wilkins?" he said as he headed to class. Mrs. Wilkins was a nice black lady who worked around campus, mostly cleaning and mopping. E met her in the lobby of the dorm and would make casual conversation with her. One day he found out that she had a son who had been crippled since birth and that the father had abandoned them years earlier. He wanted to do something special for them since it was almost Christmas, so he decided to buy some toys, package them up, and leave them on their porch in a bag. He also decided to get Mrs. Wilkins a little something, too. Since she was on her feet all day, he got her some slippers to wear when she was at home. On Thursday night, before he got out for Christmas, he drove up to the humble shotgun house south of town and left two bags on the porch with a card that read, "Merry Christmas and may God bless you!" No one knew about the gifts but him, and that was the way he wanted it.

Lydia was not talking to him, and even though he didn't understand, he thought, *Something's going on with her, and I just need to give her space.* He sent her a Christmas card that read "I Wish You a Merry Christmas" on the front. His mother had taught him that there was no excuse to be cold to anyone for any purpose, no matter how they treated you. Hannah would say, "We're called on to love and forgive," and E lived those words.

Baylor's president had agreed to let the Lone Star Colored Baseball League use the baseball field for practice off-season as long as there were no other activities scheduled. The group had formed in Texas at the end of the 1800s, but they lacked good organization or financial backing, so they did their best to tap into every charitable opportunity to better themselves. The administration was shocked at the entourage of players, managers, and followers as they made themselves at home on campus.

One fall morning, a group of trashy, white ne'er-do-wells had formed what looked like a lynch mob in the parking lot in front of campus, and reporters were swarming everywhere. There was a large truck next to the hedges that bordered E's dorm, and a line of reporters ran from the telephone pole to the truck. E and others in the dorm stood at the front door watching the crowd heckling and shouting obscenities to the blacks on campus. Suddenly, they surged toward this one black woman trying to make her way through their lunacy. E recognized her immediately as Mrs. Wilkins. She was simply trying to get to work. He instantly made his way through the crowd to bring her to safety.

Just as he got to her, a policeman appeared and warned, "Son, if you put one hand on that woman, you're goin' to jail!" He'd obviously mistaken E for one of the troublemakers. The policeman, along with some of his men, escorted Mrs. Wilkins into the building.

A few weeks went by, and the weather became nippy as E gathered up his things for the trip home for the holidays. It was always a happy time for the Moses family around Christmas. They set the mood for the entire community, putting up lights, singing carols, roasting marshmallows, and popping popcorn in the fireplace. E was looking forward to a nice rest; it had been a long semester and he had crowned his achievements with five As and one B. It would have been six As, but Chambers said his "class participation was less than satisfactory." E knew the real reason for the B, but he was just glad to have it behind him.

He was on the top of the world when the dorm resident knocked at his door and announced, "Your father's on the phone."

E ran downstairs thinking someone was either hurt, dying, or dead. "Hello!" he said as he grabbed the receiver.

"E?" Oswald asked with a great exhale.

"Yes sir?" asked E.

"Son, we got a letter from your school, and I think it's gonna to be very disappointing to ya," his father said reluctantly.

"Sir, what is it?" E asked, frozen in place.

"Well, it says that you've been suspended."

"What? What did you say, sir? I'm what, sir?" E asked in hysterics.

"Now, E, keep your head. I wanted to give you a call so you could take care of this matter before you left," Oswald commanded, having faith in his son and knowing that it was just a big misunderstanding.

"Yes, sir, I will," E said as his eyes glazed over.

"Well, just take care of it and we'll be waiting for you, all right?" Oswald asked.

"Yes, sir. But what does the letter say?" E asked, as his mind reeled.

"You have a copy in your mail folder at school. Bye, son," Oswald said as he hung up the phone.

"Suspended!" E said loudly as it echoed down the hallway of the dorm. He ran to the campus post office and quickly opened the letter addressed to him:

Dear Mr. William Ethan Moses,

It has come to our attention in the Dean's office at Baylor that you were involved in the scuffle that ensued on campus on November 28 of this school year. An employee turned your name in to this office because she feared for her safety. This type of inappropriate behavior will not be tolerated at Baylor in any measure. In accordance with Baylor's Suspension Policy, you are officially suspended from your degree program. This suspension is effective as of the beginning of next quarter and your suspension period will last at least four quarters. During your suspension period, you may not take courses from any accredited college or university. You will be dropped from any courses in which you are currently enrolled, and the tuition for these courses will be refunded to you. At the end of your suspension period, you may apply through the admissions office for readmission.

While this action is disappointing, you should view it as an "attitude adjustment period." Reexamine your motivations for coming to Baylor and goals you wanted to accomplish while here. Use your suspension period productively and accumulate evidence to justify your readmission to Baylor, should you choose to reapply. If you have any questions regarding this action, contact this office. We have placed a duplicate copy of this letter in your student mail folder in case you did not receive the copy mailed to your home.

Sincerely,
Jacob Bardwell
Dean of Students, Baylor College

The news spread like wildfire in dry sage through the halls and across the dells of Baylor. By told E, "Obviously you're not livin' right. God's punishing you, and you need to search your soul and your heart to find out what you're doin' wrong." By continued, "First your sickness and now this!"

Then E remembered what one of Job's friends said about him in the Bible. "Consider now: Who, being innocent, has ever perished? Where were the upright ever destroyed? As I have observed, those who plow evil and those who sow trouble reap it. At the breath of God they are destroyed; at the blast of his anger they perish."

After giving By his ear, E felt hollow inside as he made his way over to the Dean's office.

"My name is Ethan Moses, and I'd like to see Dean Bardwell, please," E said with great humility.

"I doubt if he'll be seein' *you*, but I'll check," the secretary huffed in an emphatic manner. E noticed something very sinister about the woman, and for good reason. Azazel had embodied a woman secretary and was trying his best to keep E away from the dean. "Dean Bardwell is extremely busy and will not have time to see you. I will check his book to see when you might talk with him," she said with contempt, looking at the schedule after the holidays.

"Ma'am, I realize that he's busy, but my reputation and character are in question. Don't you think I deserve some explanation and a rebuttal?" E asked the belligerent woman.

Still not wanting to be agreeable, she stated with a supernatural force and a fake smile, "Well, maybe you should write him, Mr. Moses."

E cocked his head to one side and responded, "Ma'am, how's a letter going to give me answers?"

She didn't even look up as he walked away and went to the water fountain located in the hallway to get a drink. I made sure that Dean Bardwell happened to be walking through to get a drink as well. "Dean Bardwell," E asked, "would you consider giving me just a second of your busy day, sir? It's very important."

Dean Bardwell, not knowing who E was, answered, "Absolutely, son, come in. We'll go through my back door. Now, what's your name?"

When E told him, he turned red, but he had already committed himself to the conversation. "Now, what can I say other than what the letter stated?" he asked E.

"Well, sir, I've never been prejudiced toward anyone in my life. In fact, I like Mrs. Wilkins and often talk with her on campus. I was trying to get to her to help her, not harm her," E stated desperately.

"Well, that sounds contrite, Mr. Moses, but that's not what she, or the policeman who tried to stop you, said. I think you just got your hand caught in the cookie jar, Mr. Moses. Facts are facts, and you'll just have to accept that. Now, if you'll excuse me, I have people to see that I *can* help. Good day, sir!" the dean said with hostility as he quickly opened the door to the hallway and literally pushed E out.

E couldn't help but question God's motivation for allowing this to happen, but if the scripture from Job was any indicator, he was in for a bruising. As he went back to his dorm room, he felt a thousand eyes peering at him. It was as if everyone on campus was looking in judgment. Back in his room, he found some paper and started writing Mrs. Wilkins a letter. He explained what happened and hoped she would understand, but he fought the urge to tell her anything about the Christmas presents. No matter what happened, that was still between him and God. He also wrote a formal letter back to the dean, highlighting what they had talked about and restating his insistence of innocence. He made three copies: one for himself, one for the president of the school, and one for the dean.

When he got to the campus post office, he noticed a card in his folder from Lydia. She had sent his Christmas card back and had written on front, *Don't call me, don't write me, and definitely don't talk to me. I'm embarrassed that I ever knew you. I hope you realize now that you don't belong here. Go back to your pigs.*

She was waiting for a good "out" with him and now she had a great one. She was now dating his friend, Byron. They both considered themselves so much better that E. Byron had family money and was going to school to be an engineer. He planned to make lots of money and knew God would bless all of his endeavors because he deserved it. Lydia hitched her wagon to his because he was her kind of man—an arrogant, self-important man with means.

In life, blessings are often disguised. E was experiencing what he thought was the most horrific day of his life, but what God saw was a faithful man, even in the face of adversity. Azazel was not happy with the outcome, as E made his way back to the dorm to quickly finish packing. E couldn't wait to put that school behind him and get home.

He was so spent, he could hardly see straight as he pulled up to the side of the barn. As he got all of his bags out and stepped foot on the porch, his mother came running out to greet him with a hug.

"Are you okay, son?" she asked with great concern and wide eyes.

"I will be, ma'am," he said, thinking that some rest would help him. After a bath and a changing of clothes, he felt much better, but he still was in shock.

Oswald counseled him, saying, "E, I could've questioned God when I lost my arm, but I decided to let God work through it. What good is it to fret about things you can't change? Worry in one's life is caused by self-centeredness, always self-centeredness."

"Oh, E, Miss Clark phoned and said she wanted to see you as soon as possible," his mother said as she grabbed his dirty clothes bag.

"I guess she's heard the wonderful news," E stated as his eyes rolled around, then lowered to the floor. He continued, "I better get over there, but first I have to go do something." He went upstairs to his room and shut the door.

"What do you think he's doing?" Nick asked as his brows rose with concern.

"Well, he's probably prayin'," answered Hannah with a smile.

E prayed, "You have unending love and amazing grace. You're forever mine and I will forever follow you, even now." He got up, washed his face, and went out the door to confront Miss Clark.

Mrs. Wilkins had gotten E's letter in her mail folder at school. She read it with incredulous eyes and threw it down on the end table by the sofa, walking off to the kitchen to work on supper. At the very

moment E prayed, I made sure Mrs. Wilkins's son looked on the coffee table at the letter E had mailed and noticed that the writing was
the same on the card with the gifts, especially "Merry Christmas."
He called his mother into the living room to show her his discovery.

E and Micah ambled down the familiar dirt road to Miss Clark's.
"Now, Buddy, don't you go chasin' those cows of Mr. Finley's, okay?"
E said with sarcasm. Micah seemed to understand, but he made no
promises as he wagged his tail and barked.

"Come in!" Miss Clark bellowed as E knocked on the fancy maple
door. He went inside, but she didn't meet him like she usually did.

"Hello?" he quizzed, as he cautiously entered the foyer.

"Come on back, by gum!" she commanded loudly.

As he entered her bedroom, he noticed the nurse at her bedside.
"Are you all right?" he asked as his voice quivered.

She looked up at him and brightened. "Gooder 'n grits! Joy,
please excuse us for a spell, would ya?" she asked the nurse with a
smile. "Come sit by me. Your eyes are buggin' out like a stomped
on toad frog. Is it because you're concerned about me or is it those
ment'lly deranged uppities at that school o' yours?" she asked, trying
to get a glimpse at his eyes.

"Well, both, I guess," E answered as he looked down in defeat.

Miss Clark lifted her chin and said, "As far as that rigmarole at
school goes, it's their loss. If that door's been closed, I have faith to
know that God has another door for you to go through. And, if'n
you're worried 'bout me, you should be hearing the scripture, 'Who
of you by worrying can add a single hour to his life?'"

E released an emotionally charged laugh; he had definitely
rubbed off on the old woman.

As they sat there and talked, E found rest for his spirit. She had
assured him that God was working His plan and had not forgotten
him. She continued, "E, don't fret. You just go enjoy your family and

rest. You have my prayers as always, my friend." With those words, she motioned for the nurse to come back in. As he was leaving, she added, "Come see me before you go back to school." And then she gave him a wink.

E wondered to himself if she was being facetious, senile, or just optimistic?

On the way home, Micah wanted to go to the pond, so E grabbed his fishing pole underneath the boat propped on the willow. E sat there on the levee with his hook in the water, looking out over the surface and thinking about God's words about the water many years earlier. "Micah, maybe God's saying, 'Don't go to school, just preach,'" he said to the old dog, who was comforted by E's voice as he put his head in E's lap and watched the sun go down.

Poppa Nick, recovering from his illness, hobbled over on his cane to open the door for E and said, "I know this is bad timing, son, but you'll realize it soon enough."

"What now, Poppa? I don't think I can take anymore bad news," E stated as he shook his head and pushed his palm out at the old man.

"Well, the family meat and eggs business is kaput, and your brother's left home all bowed up." You could tell that Poppa Nick really didn't want to say it, but he thought E could help find James. "Your parents are fit to be tied, but they didn't want to add more on you right now. I hear tell your brother didn't take care of his customers. In fact, several claimed that he had shorted 'em. He was never on time and messed up so many things. His heart was never in it, anyway. He had his eyes on the big city lights and couldn't wait for the day he could fly the coop," Nick continued, as he exhaled with a long, nervous sigh.

"E, there's a call for you on the phone!" Hannah said excitedly.

"Momma, I just can't talk to anyone right now," E said with frustration, as everything came crashing down on top of him.

"E, I think you'll want to take this call," she commanded with great insistence. He nodded in meek compliance as she shoved the phone in his hand. "Just answer it, son," she demanded with a gleaming smile on her face.

The boy's mother was too upset to talk, but Mrs. Wilkins's son explained that he had made the handwriting discovery. "My mother has gone to the school president to tell him the truth! We didn't want you to go through Christmas worrying," he said as E's eyes started to well up, hiding his face against the wall.

Trying to keep his composure, E thanked the boy with a shaky voice and got off the phone.

Hannah was there hugging all over him when Oswald came in from outside.

"So I'm thinkin' that things are all right now and we can have a good Christmas?" Oswald asked, cocking his head to one side. He got a few nods and was satisfied as he pulled down his reading glasses from his forehead and went into the parlor to study his newspaper.

Prodigally Speaking

James was the younger son in the Moses family and very much the prodigal. You might blame his friendships for his pursuit of the fleeting pleasures of this world. You might even blame his older brother, who seemed to be the "chosen" in James's eyes. James struggled spiritually and emotionally throughout his childhood, thinking he had let everyone down, including himself. He chose to remove himself from the warmth of his father's home and lose himself in the lights and glamour of the world. James had "the gift of gab" and thought, *I need to find a job selling something.* He started looking for that one sales job that would make him a name and plenty of money. He could just see himself driving up to his father's house one day in a fancy new car.

James finally made it to Joe Calhoun, an infamous used car salesman in Texarkana. "Well, son, I might take ya on, ifin you're willin' to learn," said Joe, flipping his cowboy hat up past his hairline.

"Yes sir, Mr. Calhoun, anything you say!" James answered.

"You work with the mechanics for a while, fechin' for um and thangs there, and learn all you can from them grease monkeys, and I'll put you up in the back of the shop. We'll talk about your sales abilities later, son," Joe said, as he rubbed his bulging middle and sucked on a broom straw.

Concerned about eating, James humbly and quietly asked, "Sir, what about pay?"

Joe lowered his eyes at the youngster and offered, "Tell ya what, I'll get you some groceries and thangs there, and you can pay me back when you sell your first car. Don't that sound just great?" James nodded yes, but his heart said no. Joe sent his floozy secretary out to get a few groceries for James to put in his new living quarters, which consisted of a rickety old army cot, a nightstand that had seen much better days, and a chair that was missing one arm. There was also an old potbelly stove that had seen better days. When James was ready to settle in, he found his bag of groceries on his cot. The secretary also brought him an old black skillet and a handful of mismatched plates, glasses, and silverware.

"Now, Jimbo, I expect you to make that food and thangs there last," Mr. Calhoun commanded as he brushed off his fancy cowboy boots with his bright red and black handkerchief, cocked his hat back on his head again, and went out the door to sell to another customer fell prey to his underhanded business savvy.

James could've been a mechanic in a short period of time, but he hated getting dirty, and besides, he wanted to make real money. The year 1923 was a good year and Mr. Calhoun was capitalizing on people's bigger pocketbooks after the war. Hook or crook, he was out to relieve them of as much of their money as he could.

Meanwhile, E was trying his best to find James. The only one who might have some idea where he'd gone wasn't talking.

"Ben, I can't tell you how important it is that I find James. He could be in real trouble. Would you like that on your hands?" E asked as his eyes widened and his brows raised.

"Okay, okay. I'll tell you the town, but you're gonna have to find'em yourself. Texarkana," Ben surrendered with reluctance as he looked down.

Businesses in Texarkana grew quickly after the war and it flourished because of its close proximity to agriculture and the railway. Honest Joe's Car Sales was right on State Line Avenue, straddling the state line of Arkansas and Texas.

"Momma, I'm goin' to talk some sense into that brother of mine," E stated, as his eyes flared with anger.

Hannah quickly followed him to the door and added, "E, be careful and tell him that we love him and to please come home."

E's eyes met his mothers as he turned and released a reserved smile, saying, "Yes ma'am, I will." His mother handed him a bag of groceries and toiletries to give James as E cranked his car for the long trip.

The man in charge of the "bread line" had seen James the night before, so all E had to do was wait. The line soon started forming and it went out the door and up the street. E aggressively walked up and down the bastion of despair trying to get a glimpse of his brother, but he had no luck. He would ask people in line if they had seen James, pulling out an old photo from his wallet.

"He was here last night. He said he worked for some automotive place," an old man interjected as he saw the photo.

"Did he say what place?" E asked. But the old man had nothing else to add.

After visiting every car dealership in town, E drove up to Honest Joe's. It was not by accident he found him. A small beam of light was leaking out into the alley behind the mechanics shop and it drew him closer and closer like a star. A holey pipe from the wood heater had filled the room with smoke and allowed for a dramatic entrance as he walked through it. James was attempting to read a mechanic's manual by a dim light bulb hanging from a ceiling joist.

"Brother, you really should fix this door. Any bum off the street could come in and do you harm," E said, startling James right off his cot and into a standing position.

"What are you doin' here?"

"Well, Merry Christmas to you too, brother! Tell me, James, what're you tryin' to prove here?" E asked as his eyes scanned the humble surroundings.

"Well maybe I'm tryin' to find my own way, chart my own course. You know, just maybe I'm tryin' real hard not to be you!" James almost screamed.

"Look, James, I didn't come here to pick a fight. I came to try and talk some sense into ya."

"Well, brother, maybe it's sense that I have."

Realizing James's resolution, E retorted, "Well, you do what you want, James. I know you will anyway, but your parents are worried sick and would appreciate it very much if you would at least come home for the holidays."

"You know what I'd like, E? I would like for everyone to stay out of my business. That's what I'd like."

E knew he was getting nowhere fast, so he said his good-byes, kept the invitation open, and laid the bag of goodies from Momma by the door. As E started home, he couldn't help but be concerned about his little brother in that pigsty. Back home, E told Oswald and Nick where he found him, but he didn't want to startle his mother with the absolute muck James was living in.

"I tried to talk sense into him, Pap, but he's so bull-headed! Everyone else is wrong and he's right," E said as he sat with the men in the parlor.

Even with James gone, Christmas was good that year and E got a letter from the college president reinstating him. The president also stated that the dean was "on report" for his inappropriate behavior. Nick told his famous *'Twas the Night Before Christmas* story, with a twist, of course, and Oswald carved the big bird. Mae Mae said the prayer, and everyone ate until they couldn't fit another crumb.

Soon James was finally making money, but not at Honest Joe's. He went to work for his competition across town. Honest Joe had really taken James for a ride, not giving him commissions on cars he sold and taking leads that James had developed and selling to the customer behind his back.

The Buick dealership was excited to give him a shot at new cars on straight commission. He really loved it and was making good money, but his eyes saw a bigger game that made much more money. He was connected with several loan sharks who could guarantee loans at a very high rate of interest for those people who couldn't get credit from banks. He decided that being a loan shark was the business to be in, so he started making his own deals with people who couldn't afford cars any other way. Soon he had a booming business on the side, but the owner of the Buick dealership found out and fired him without hesitation.

Like Lambs among Wolves

E finally finished at Baylor with honors and set his sights on the seminary. It was much more intense than college, but he was finally in his element. The following is an excerpt from E's journal:

> *Thursday, 10:30 p.m.*
> *It's getting late and my eyes are feeling the effects of little sleep while studying for almost a week. However, I have some thoughts I must put to paper. It makes them stick in my memory.*
> *Last week I was leering across the commons in some sort of half-focused gaze, only to see my professor, Doctor Safire. Like the gem of the same name, but different spelling, he was radiant as he walked. I realize that the sunset was illuminating his frame from*

the other side of campus, but there was something supernatural about the glow. It reminded me of a painting by Michelangelo with the flames of fire above the apostles' heads. While I was watching him meander down the bending sidewalk, a quote from T. S. Eliot came to mind: "And the light shone in the darkness, and against the Word the unstilled world still whirled about the centre of the silent Word!"

Why, God, do you continue to put such wonderful, grace-giving men down here on this troubled, undeserving planet? Then God gave me the scripture in Luke 10:3 where He says that He is sending us out like little lambs among the wolves. The key word there would be "like," but God and His angels are watching out for us.

I've been sitting in Safire's class for more than a month now. My desk is about three-quarters back in a packed classroom. In the very back are a few older men who are just sitting in without taking the tests. In the very front are the legalists and rebels. Their only goal in life, it seems, is to catch the good doctor in some travesty or heresy and if they succeed in trapping him, they gain favor with their group of peers. I looked with amazement, thinking that Jesus had to endure the same.

I have to say that he has become my favorite teacher. His style is warm and energetic, but mostly his humility punctuates his delivery. He makes the Bible very relational to the modern day. And although he wrote the textbook we're using, he always listens to other views, no matter how farfetched. And when he has a view, he always says, "In my opinion" before it.

Shawn Hazlitt is a quick-witted student of the Bible. If there was ever a time when I thought I was "Bible smart," I lost that prideful occasion around Shawn. He's the perfect student with a 4.0 average and he knows his Bible perfectly (or close to it). Although Shawn is not the worst of the legalists in class, he's a borderline "law whore" as the grace crowd calls them. Nevertheless, I really like Shawn and I've found myself spending time with him on campus.

Taking notes in Safire's class is a great challenge. His diction is not the clearest, and he spins through words like they're his very own playground. I told Shawn that we should compare notes and comprise one good copy to study by. It was a great idea, and we *continued to do it until recently, when I found that Shawn had not taken any notes at all since our last test. A few days before the test, I tried to call him, but there was no answer. I finally decided to go by his dorm room. As I knocked on the door, I heard some unrecognizable words and then the door slowly opened. Shawn was standing there in his robe, but the thing that really hit me was how "white" he looked. I know I must have looked shocked, because he immediately started with some gibberish about fasting. I put my arm around him, took him back to the bed, and insisted that he sit down. This is where it got bizarre. I'm going to try to put this down as best I remember it.*

I asked him what was going on, and he proceeded to tell me about his life growing up. His father was off at war and his mother was working. He had an uncle and a cousin who abused him sexually. His uncle even tied him down and said if he told, he would swear that he was lying and he would get into real trouble. The abuse continued until he was twelve, when he told them "no more." After that, his goal was to do so well academically that he could go to some foreign land where they couldn't find him—where no one could. In college, God got hold of him and changed his heart and gave him different goals. But the demons of the past were still there (literally).

It got so bad at one time while he was in college, he went to talk to his pastor and he told him that he just needed to pray and obey God and everything would be fine. But it wasn't. He continued to struggle. When I asked him what he was struggling with, he said he thought he had an addiction. Well, of course I am thinking alcohol, but then he said it was sexual. And no one could tell him what to do about it.

Finally, he went to see Safire in his office. Safire told him, "You have demons, son. Do you want them out?"

Of course, Shawn said yes, so Safire told his secretary that they were not to be disturbed.

Shawn said that he poured his heart out to Safire. He said that somehow, Safire knew the names of the men who had abused him. Safire then led him in a very long prayer of forgiveness for those men and for himself. Then Safire told him that he couldn't expel the demons out of him because these demons had to go a different way—by fasting and prayer.

I asked him if he was a Christian, and he looked at me like I was crazy.

Then, he said, "I really thought that Christians couldn't have demons too. Satan's been lying to the church and to me for years. God showed me in scripture where they were having orgies in the outer courts of the temple while God was in the holy of holies. And we are that temple, my friend."

So I asked him to proceed with his story. He said he went back to his dorm room after leaving Safire and started to pray. He prayed all night until he couldn't pray anymore and then he fell asleep. I stopped him there and told him to put on his clothes; I was taking him to lunch. I was thinking that he might have some opposition to the idea since he'd been fasting, but he didn't.

At the diner, we met up with my friend, William Spark. I trusted Will and I wanted him to help me with Shawn, or at least get his views. We all greeted each other and sat down at a table in the corner. Shawn wanted to start where he left off, so I caught Will up on the story.

Shawn said that he had a dream after he fell asleep and it was as real as you could imagine. I looked over at Shawn and asked him, "Did it have anything to do with dogs?" He looked at me, whiter than before. He asked me what I had dreamed, and I told him that I was running with him and we were trying to escape these wild, ferocious, black dogs with red eyes. They looked ravenous, with very large teeth. He wanted to continue with his version, so I let him. He said that we would go through a door and close it, but the dogs would come through it like it was paper. They finally caught up with us and one of the dogs tore both arms off Shawn. One dog grabbed my arm, but I shook him off. Then I picked Shawn's arms up and put them back on him. I agreed with his dream, raised my left arm up to show a red mark on it, and asked, "This arm, Shawn?" and he nodded. All Will could do was stare at us with his mouth open.

I asked Shawn what happened next and he said that for the next three days, he fasted and prayed. Then the night before I came *to his dorm room, he went to take a shower. While in the shower, he started yelling at God, "What do you want with me, Jesus? Swear that you won't torture me!" Then, in the midst of his yelling, Shawn heard a small, loving voice say, "Mark five." Then he asked, "Mark five what?" But, the voice just kept saying "Mark five." He got out of the shower, dried off, and went inside his dorm room to look up Mark 5.*

He said when he saw what the demons were saying to Jesus, he started crying, because it was the same words he was yelling in the shower. He reached his hands up toward God and he blacked out. The next thing he remembered was me knocking on his door. By this time, Will was just a shadow of his previous self. He was perplexed with the whole story and not able to eat a bite, turning whiter than Shawn ever was. I asked Shawn how he felt now, and he said, "Happy and sad." I asked him what he meant and he said that he was so happy to finally be free from bondage, but he was sad at the time he had lost, but God had already made it very clear that He was going to use his experiences to His good and to Shawn's.

I knew what I had to do. God had already been leading me to do it. As soon as we got back to the dorm, I told him that I had to restore him (put his arms back on). God was ready to do a new thing in his life, but we had to get the past out of the way. So I led him in a prayer and he cried some more, then I left.

Today, I went to see Safire in his office. He looked at me, smiled, and asked, "So how's Shawn?"

I must have looked like I'd seen a ghost. All I could say was, "Sir?"

Then he asked, "Well, did you restore him?"

I just nodded. He got up from his desk and said, "We're all gifted by God, Mr. Moses, for some higher purpose, and for whatever the cost, that purpose must be attained. You've been used, my friend, by God, for someone else's purpose to be attained. But being useful to God is not work; it's the biggest blessing you could ever hope for. Learn from this, Mr. Moses, and God will continue to purpose your life. I see Him working in you."

Just yesterday I heard someone talking about Safire. They told me that three years ago, his daughter was murdered in a burglary attempt at their home. His daughter was by herself and she had surprised the man who broke in, and he shot her dead. Dr. Safire went over to the jail to see the man that killed his daughter. They were hesitant at first, but they decided to let him go in with two guards. He went in, prayed for the man, and forgave him for what he had done. The man ended up crying on his cot, and Dr. Safire left a Bible there beside him.

So as I end this journal entry, I get another verse from God, "I have raised you up for this very purpose, that I might show you My power and that My name might be proclaimed in all the earth" Exodus 9:16.

Seven days later, here is more from E's journal:

3:00 p.m. on a Thursday
This is my second journal entry concerning Shawn. I saw him today and he looked great! He definitely had a glow about him; however, the rumors had hit the campus. People were talking about the "pervert" he was and judging him on his past—a past that was as far as the east was from the west. The lion was trying to devour Shawn and stop him. I can't help but wonder what God is going to do in his life. For Satan to try so hard, it must be great. I felt compelled to call several of my friends together and pray that "the lion's mouth be shut." Afterward, the seven of us felt approval from God for our efforts. We will see what happens next, but I have faith that God has fixed the problem.

From the height of the highest peak and to the deepest depths of the seas—you are an amazing God!

When it Rains, it Pours

E finally finished two years at seminary and was looking forward to starting on his doctorate program in the fall, after spending his summer at home. There were some fences that needed mending down by the pond, so he got a crowbar, gloves, some nails, a hammer, and a bag of feed for the catfish and made his way down the old familiar dirt road that had watched him grow up. "Come on, boy!" he shouted, and soon Micah rounded the corner and moved past him, scouting out the trail ahead. "You sure get around for your age, Micah!" E said as the dog moved out of hearing range.

While Hannah was making lunch, the girls were washing clothes and cleaning the house. Suddenly, running down the road, crying, and yelling for E was Mae Mae. "E, please, it's terrible. Please come!" she yelled as she ran.

"What is it?" E asked with a look of terror. He just knew that Poppa Nick was dead.

"It's Mother! Come quick!" she answered while fighting for breath.

"What?" E asked, as he shot back to the house like a bullet, leaving Mae Mae behind in the dust. He flew through the back screen door of the house, finding Janie holding mother's head in her lap.

"What happened?" asked E, but his sister was too distraught to respond. He picked her up off the floor like he was Superman and carried her to his car. "I'm goin' to the hospital. Tell Pap to meet me there," he ordered. Then he flew down the road like the wind, leaving a trail of dust behind him.

Soon, Oswald and the family arrived at the hospital, only to get bad news. "She's gone, Oz," said the doctor as Oswald tried to enter the room.

"What? I gotta see her!" Oswald said as he pushed the doctor's hand away.

E was sitting in a chair with his head in his hands. A sheet had already been placed over Hannah's head. Oswald walked over to her like he was walking up to a queen. With all the love and reverence he could muster, he removed the sheet from her head and started crying uncontrollably. E looked up and started crying too.

"Pap, I'm so sorry. I tried to save her," he told his father through his tears.

Oswald looked over at E, smiled, and nodded. "I know, son."

At that moment, Oswald took Hannah's hand, held it tight, and prayed, "God, I will praise you in this difficult moment. I know that she's with you now and even though it hurts like I've never hurt, I'm satisfied with the outcome. Take care of her, because she's so loved and appreciated by us. Thank you for lending her to us. She has filled our lives with joy, and our hearts are full to overflowing because of her love for you and for us. She chose to be a blessing in her brief life, and that is her heritage. Amen."

Then, looking at her, he continued, saying, "Honey, I love you more than life itself. We will miss you, and our lives will never be the same in your passing. Thank you for allowing me to be your husband. My love for you is deathless." With that said, he put her hand back under the sheets, gave her a small kiss, and pulled the sheet back over her head.

Many people had already stopped by the Moses house with food and cards. Several of the family came in and made themselves at home, eating and talking. Oswald joined right in with the talking and reminiscing, but found it very hard to look at any food.

E went to the outside porch to get some fresh air.

"Mae Mae, where's Micah?" he asked his sister.

"I don't know. When I was going to get you at the pond, he shot out like a racing horse across the yard. Sis said that Micah was the one that got her attention about mother."

E thought a while and decided to go out and look for him. It was a chance to get away from the crowd and gather his thoughts. As he walked down the road, he wondered if he had tried to get old Mr. Withers's attention. E went up the drive and didn't see Mr. Withers's truck in the barn. As he approached the side door of the old house, he noticed that a lot of things looked different around the old place.

He knocked, and a strange man came to the door. "Oh, I'm sorry, sir. I was looking for Mr. Withers," he explained.

The old man aimed some spittle at the ground and said, "Old Withers sold me the place first of the week, and I just moved everythin' in yestaday. After his wife died, it got to be too much for 'im, I guess."

E didn't know what to say; Mr. Withers had been a permanent fixture around there for so long. "Well, sir, my mother died this afternoon, and I was hoping to find my dog—he ran off in all the commotion."

"Well, your dog wouldn't be yeller, would he?" the man asked, as he took off his hat and scratched his head.

"Yes sir!" E answered excitedly.

"Well, I thought ur dog was tryin' to get at my hens, he was makin' such a fuss and all. I hate to say it, son, but I shot'em," the man said without a flinch.

"Well, is he okay, sir?"

"Oh, I doubt it. He's out by the fence gate there if'n you want to take a gander," the old man said with no feeling.

E immediately shot across the yard to Micah. If he had been alive, he wasn't anymore. He took him in his arms with all the care that one would hold a newborn baby and walked slowly back to his house, crying all the way.

The man said as he passed the door, "I kin' get'ya another dog, son."

E just shook his head no. The man just went back inside and closed his door.

"Another dog?" E spoke to himself as he cried. "He's more that just some old dog. Another dog? Good luck in finding another dog like this one, mister. No dog could ever replace you, Micah. Never!"

E was sure that Micah was trying to get Mr. Withers's attention. Just as he was thinking that, I got out of my car that was parked by the street. I started walking alongside E, who was headed toward the Moses house, and I said, "What a small sacrifice he made, compared to Calvary. Don't you think? If you had to go, wouldn't you like to go being a hero to those you love?"

E laid Micah down inside the gate and looked around to see who I was, but I had already disappeared. So he went to the storeroom in the barn and got a shovel and started looking for the perfect spot for Micah to be buried.

He started to dig the hole through his tears, blubbering, "I think you will like it here, Micah. You have a view of the house. There's the pond where you liked to swim in the summer, and you can see my room from here … so you can make sure I'm okay."

The day had just broken his heart into a million little pieces and put quite a dent in his spirit as well. "I'm goin' to make you a fine tombstone, Micah. You just wait and see."

After meditating by Micah's grave for almost an hour, E skirted the large crowd and went straight to his room. Even though there were a lot of people in the house, it felt empty without his mother there. She was the glue that held everything together. She was always the peacekeeper, the one who first initiated forgiveness, and always the last to do anything for herself. Her love permeated the walls of that old house. As he looked around his room, her presence was still there in the folded clothes at the end of his bed. Her sweet smell was still in the air from when she came in to prepare for E to come home. He was pondering the last words that he said to her, when Mae Mae knocked at his door.

"Come in," E said with reluctance.

Mae Mae rushed to E's arms, crying and weary. "Were gonna be fine, Mae Mae, just fine," he said, trying to calm her down.

"Did you find Micah?" she asked while crying, hoping that all was not lost.

"Momma didn't wanna go to heaven alone, so she took Micah with her." He sighed as he stroked her hair. Mae Mae just cried on his shoulder for what seemed like an hour. She finally went to sleep, and he laid her on his bed and covered her with the quilt that his mother had laid there for those nights when he would get cold. Things were going to be different around the old homestead, and he grew anxious about the possibilities.

†

Several years passed since his mother's death and while E never finished his doctorate, the wisdom of the Lord filled him and opened many doors to begin his ministry. His reputation as an evangelist spread quickly, and he traveled and preached where the Lord led him.

Die So That You Might Live

"More things are wrought with prayer
Than this world dreams of."
—Alfred, Lord Tennyson

The town seemed to recede as he drove down the long, winding procession of blackness drawing him into some doom. E should've been on top of the world, but something wasn't right. He had prayed so hard before this revival. He had made great preparation, but his heart ached inside his body and he found it hard to swallow. He slowly parked his car and stared for several minutes at the big tent that was lit up like the circus was in town.

Pastor Jasper Flynn was the man in charge. His church had decided their sanctuary was too small to hold the revival they wanted to have. "Well, Brother Ethan, what d'ya think? Pretty impressive, huh? Now this is how I see things comin' together. We have all our deacons at the back by the doors to make sure the right people get in and then—"

Right at that moment, E knew why the Spirit was weeping. He interrupted him and said, "Right people? Brother Jasper, we're all but filthy rags before the Lord. Don't you agree? My Bible states that God looks at the heart of a man, not some skin color or economic status."

Jasper was sweating profusely as he challenged. "Well, Brother Ethan, I know that we are all equal in His sight, but I like the idea of separate but equal." Jasper was the type of preacher that E couldn't stand. E's gripe with Jasper was that he wouldn't stand for anything unless there was some personal gain in it.

He tightened his right fist, cocked it a few inches from Jasper's chin, and demanded, "Brother Jasper, I want all those deacons of yours to meet me down front. Then I'll pray with them and excuse them to go back to the church, where I want them to hit their knees and pray for these services every night. If that's not what happens, you can find yourself another man. Is that clear?"

Jasper was stammering and stuttering, as his shoulders sagged and his eyes fell to the floor. "Now, now, Bro...Brother Ethan—" was all Jasper got out.

E cut him off with, "Am I clear?"

Jasper didn't dare breathe as he shook his head up and down, his face reddening with remorse and shame.

E ran his fingers through the indentions in his hat, tapped the rim, promptly placed it on his head, and, in military style, turned on his heels and quickly walked out. He knew what he had to do next; he was going to give Chapel Hill Church more than they'd bargained for.

He steamed and snarled as he peeled out in his black Chrysler roadster, sending multi-colored leaves swirling across the pavement in his wake. After he calmed down, the Spirit finally spoke to him with scripture, "Judge not or you will—"

"Well, that's right, Lord. He's judging on skin color or on economic status, and that's wrong, wrong, wrong!" he blurted out to the traffic, cutting off the Spirit.

Several minutes went by while the Spirit let him ponder his response. As he leered at himself in the rearview mirror, he crinkled up his lips in an ambivalent scowl and apprehensively proclaimed, "You didn't mean him, did you, God? You were talkin' about me. I was pretty hard on him, wasn't I? Well, I guess there's only one thing to do."

When he got back to the big top, everything was dark except for a small beam of light escaping from the changing room behind the stage. E reluctantly entered the room and saw the silhouette of a man with his posture wilted in defeat, head in hands.

E softly said, "Jasper, brother, I'm sorry. I had no right to judge you so hastily. In fact, I have no right to judge you at all."

As Jasper pulled his head up out of his hands, E continued, "Look, I was on my way to get a black friend of mine to come sing at tomorrow night's service, but God stopped me dead in my tracks."

The transformation was surreal. Jasper went from down and depressed to excited, instantly emitting a nervous chuckle and asking, "You were really goin' to do that?"

"Yes, I was," answered E decisively.

Jasper wagged his index finger at E and stated, "Well, I've gotta say, you have guts. I really need to explain why I'm not so gutsy. When you have one of the grand poobahs of the Klu Kluxers as a deacon, all your absolutes seem to get fuzzy. I don't mind tellin' you, brother, he scares me to death. And he's so indignant, he doesn't just stop at the blacks or migrants. Just last week his gang beat a white woman to within an inch of her life. You wanna know why? She's a single mother and they just thought she had to be doin' somethin' wrong! Say…" Jasper surged forward toward E with bulging eyes.

"What'ya thinkin'?" E asked, wrinkling his brow.

With an impish grin, Jasper asked, "I'm sure it will be my ruin, but do you think you could still get that friend of yours for tomorrow night?"

E smiled and nodded yes.

Andrew Jackson Wilcher was a big black man that stood six feet and eight inches tall.

"AJ, would you do me a favor and come down to the tent meeting tonight to sing?" E asked, as he shook the big man's hand.

"Brother Ethan," AJ answered, "there's nothin' I'd likes better, sir, but is all those white folk gon go fur dat?"

"You just let me and Brother Jasper worry 'bout that," E answered, with a big smile as he looked at Jasper.

"Yessir, Brother Ethan," AJ answered with apprehension.

E had befriended a black preacher named Armstrong Ludlow, writing him first and telling him how impressed he was with his book, *Our Fight for Families*. After several letters of correspondence, Reverend Armstrong invited E to speak at his church. It was a gutsy thing for him to do, because there was a lot of animosity toward "Whitey" among the black deacons. However, he was well received and afterward was smothered by black women in big hats.

One in particular approached, him saying, "Brother, you might bes white on the outside, but you bes black on the inside!" E smiled and was flattered by her comments.

AJ had sung at that meeting and E felt like he had entered into heaven. He had never heard anyone more anointed in his life, and his tenor voice rattled the church rafters. If anything prepared E to speak that night, it was AJ's song.

"We have to get AJ fitted for a nice suit, Jasper," E said tenaciously.

"Where on earth you gonna find a suit that big?" Jasper asked with a giggle as he shook his head.

"I've got an idea," E said, while squinting his eyes toward the door. "There's a tailor that owes me a favor or two. I'm not sure he'll do it, but I'll try."

Old Herman Insull had been through the fire, and E had been there with him. E had helped him, consoled him, and prayed with him as his wife lay dying. He was about the only one who would come see her. Not knowing if she was contagious or not, many stayed away and wondered why she deserved such a fate. As E pulled up to the old man's shop, Herman met him at the door with a large hug.

"Brother E, it's so great to see you!"

"How's business, Brother Herman?" E earnestly asked.

"Fair to middlin,' Brother E. We've got to work on that suit of yours. Do you use it as a strainer?" Before E could say anything, Herman had his coat off, examining it.

"Brother Herman, I have something to ask of you," E said reluctantly.

"Anything! What is it?" Herman asked excitedly, still fidgeting with E's coat.

E motioned for Jasper to bring AJ inside. As the large black man walked into the store, Herman asked in a giggle, "And what's this, E?" Then he walked over and started measuring the large man. "Well, let me see if I have enough fabric to make him a black suit with a nice white shirt," he said as he excused himself to the back of the store.

E and Jasper looked at each other in amazement and a scripture came to E. "They went and found a colt outside in the street, tied at a doorway. As they untied it, some people standing there asked, 'What are you doing, untying that colt?' They answered as Jesus had told them to, and the people let them go." Because of their obedience, God had provided providentially and without question.

Herman came out of the back with several reams of fabric and said, "Men, why don't y'all go do what needs doin' and leave him here with me for a while?"

E looked at Jasper with his eyebrows slightly lifted and said, "Brother Herman, he's all yours." As the men got in E's car, they couldn't help but wonder what would happen when a big black man came bounding onto the stage in a nice new suit and sung his heart out.

After the Great War, many Americans sought new ways of doing things. Old-fashioned values and traditional things were openly mocked and disregarded by an "enlightened" modern era. A culture-war brewed between the forces of fundamentalism and modernism. E and Jasper found themselves in the middle of the struggle for America's soul. The modernist thought invaded the schools through Darwinism. The Bible was no longer the rule of truth, and the ACLU became the defender of evolution. The '20s became an era of clashing belief systems in America. Sensuous dancing, flapping shoes, promiscuous sex, cigarettes, lipstick, and wild parties were all rolling against E and Jasper at break-neck speed.

"Jasper, there's a link between persecution and revival, like in the book of Acts, isn't there? The Holy Spirit had anticipated where persecution would come and prepared His people for that day. That's true here too, isn't it?" questioned E. Jasper nodded yes and E continued, "The blessings of revival seem to always precede an onslaught of evil."

"Let's get some lunch at the diner and we'll go back to check on Zoot Suit Jackson!" E joked as both men laughed.

As they made their way back to the big tent, Jasper handed a bag of food to AJ. "Nawsir, I jus can't eats before I sing," AJ said, as he handed it back to Jasper.

"Well, keep it in the dressing room for later," Jasper said, as he shoved it back to AJ.

The first night soon came and Jasper became jumpy as he paced and watched who was coming in the doors of the big tent. The deacons had gotten there early and were already discouraging several from entering. Jasper felt like he had a sling against a huge giant. He felt sick inside as he went to find E.

"They're already doin' it. They're turnin' um away," an overwhelmed Jasper stated.

"Well, let's see what they do if we go back there with AJ?" E asked with an impish grin.

"Probably call their friends in law enforcement!" Jasper answered, with a sigh of frustration.

"Oh, Jasper, I think we're better connected than they are," E said calmly.

The large tent soon proved to be too small to contain the crowds flocking to hear the good news. In fact, they soon overtook the small bastion of deacons. All twelve deacons found themselves pushed all the way up to the platform in a matter of seconds. It was at that moment and not a second sooner that Reverend Ethan Moses parted the curtains on stage and said, "Ah, I'm glad you deacons are down here. I need to pray with you, and then I want you to go back to the church, get on your knees, and pray for this service. Pray with all your heart that God will move here in a mighty way this week."

After his long prayer with the deacons, he scooted them out the side door where Jasper had their transportation ready. When the banners came in through the side doors, the Spirit of God fell like a bomb inside the big tent. E heard the Spirit say, "You have given a banner to those who fear you, that it may be displayed because of truth." Jasper grew a spine that night and decided to live boldly for God, no matter what. As E was praying in the back, he felt God's hand on him so strongly that if he didn't get this message out now, he was going to explode. He ended his personal prayers the same way each time: "God, I'm a living sacrifice to reach the world for you. I'm just a gatherer in your fields. I love you, God. Let me live your Word, and let others see You in me. Amen."

E was a very animated showman and he loved playing to a big crowd. Excitement was in the air as he went to the microphone and said, "I love the Lord with all my heart, soul, mind, and strength. Do you know why? Stick around, and I will tell you after our special music."

Brother Daniel, the music minister, was kept in the dark about the plans, mainly because his father-in-law was Charles Nye, a Klansman. Jasper had already given Brother Daniel's wife, the pianist, a copy of the music that AJ was singing. Brother Daniel was stunned as the gigantic black man came bounding through the curtains and made his way to the microphone. Without looking up, Daniel's wife began to play. The entire tent was completely silent, giving that moment a defined reverence as AJ sung his heart out.

E was not a faith healer and had never had an occasion to lay hands on the sick in a service, but he felt the Holy Spirit telling him to pray for a blind lady in the crowd that night. AJ was singing "Amazing Grace" and when he got to the part, "was blind, but now I see," E called out for a blind lady to stand up, and one lady stood in response. E looked at her, rebuked the blindness in the name of Jesus, and commanded that her blind eyes be opened.

Suddenly there was a cry of, "I can see, I can see!" After the song, the woman made her way to the platform. She was handed a Bible by Jasper, and with trembling hands, she read where Jesus healed the blind man. The congregation erupted in shouts of praise and thanksgiving to God, and eighty-three people came to the front during the altar call that night.

So many times, right after a great spiritual victory comes great struggle. This struggle's name was John "Stout" Jones, and he was the Grand Wizard of the Klu Klux Klan, prominent member of Chapel Hill Church, deacon, and Sunday school teacher. He was also the albatross around Jasper's neck. After the first night's services, Jasper was "called on the carpet." First Stout tried to get at Jasper without the other deacons present, knowing he didn't have their support, but E told them that Stout was in the dressing room, and they hurried into the room. Stout had Jasper pinned to the wall with one hand on his neck.

"Stout!" exclaimed the chairman of the deacons. "What in tarnation do you think you're doin'?"

"Well, now, boys, me and the preach were just comin' to some understandin,' that's all," Stout snorted with disdain, doing his best to conceal his shortness of breath. "You all know that I have the best of intentions for our fair church. But I'm afeared that our preacher has left his calling to become a n_____ lover."

At those words, the chairman, Brother Bridges, pushed Stout into the same corner, pointed his finger in his face with contempt, and said, "Look, Stout, you have little regard for anybody or anything other than yourself. And you know, as well as the rest of us, they have souls, too."

"Well, now, I'm not so sure 'bout that," Stout said, as he slithered out the door and disappeared into the night.

Jasper had truly been shaken. "Reverend," said Brother Bridges, as he dusted Jasper off and straightened his jacket, "I think the best thing you could do is resign and start fresh somewhere else. You'll never live this down, even though we're not opposin' to ya. That…"—there was a pause as he was trying to think of a "churchy" word for Stout—"well, he won't rest until he's got everybody up in a lather and you on a rail."

All the men made their way out as Jasper got his hat and started putting the lamps out for the night. "Well, I thought you handled that well," E said, with a facetious grin from the shadows.

"How long you been standin' there?" asked Jasper in a miffed tone.

"Oh, the whole time," E answered.

"So you weren't gonna help me? Jasper asked.

"If you needed any," E said, as he surged forward into the light.

"Well, what do you think I need to do now?" Jasper asked, still reeling from the confrontation.

E looked doggedly at Jasper and started, "John Wesley once said, 'Give me a hundred men who fear nothing but sin, and desire nothing but God, and I will shake the world.'"

Jasper replied, "So you think I'm a coward?"

E answered, "No, Jasper. I think you need to rethink your priorities. My daddy said when he was training for war, they told him to accept death and it would give him an edge. Accept it as a possibility at the beginning of each mission. I believe that is what Christ meant when he said, 'Take up your cross and follow me.' I believe it has a much deeper meaning than just a physical death, too. I think He means death to self."

Klandestined

The next day came with a knock on Jasper's door. About ten o'clock the night before, Stout had gotten together with several of his Klan buddies and decided to pay Jasper a visit, but on the way, I made sure they had a flat. While Stout was fixing it, he fell over with a heart attack, so the men quickly put the spare on and rushed him to the hospital.

"Who is it?" asked Jasper warily.

"It's Joe Bridges. Got some bad news, Rev.," Joe said somberly. When Joe Bridges told him what had happened, he started to feel sorry for old Stout. "I came to get ya, preacher. He's been askin' for ya," Joe said, like he was on some special mission from God.

Jasper's eyebrows went up to almost his hairline in shock. "Okay, Brother Bridges, just let me get some britches on."

The commotion woke E and he ambled out of his room to hear the last part of the conversation. "I'm goin' with y'all," he told them, grabbing his coat.

The hospital smelled like alcohol and floor wax as they made their way down the dimly lit empty hallway to Stout's room.

"Boy, I'm hatin' this," Jasper said, as he approached the room.

"What are you talkin' about, Jas?" E questioned, cocking his head to one side. "There ya go getting all negative! He could very well recant all the bad things he's done to ya and turn his life around!"

Jasper looked at E like he had just grown donkey ears and a tail. As they entered the room, everything looked so sterile and cold. For Jasper, it was hard to look at the man who had been so diametrically opposed to him and his values. As he ran his eyes over

Stout, not fixing on him for any length of time, he couldn't help but notice how helpless he looked without his cigar and hat that was two sizes too small. The doctor motioned for the men to come out of the room. At that moment, Stout motioned for Jasper to come over to him. Jasper had visions of him grabbing his throat and choking him to death right there in the hospital, but he fought his urge to run. "Jasper," he started with great effort and kind eyes, "I … I want you … " was all he got out. They rushed Jasper out of the room as the nurses and doctor took over.

"What's happenin,' doctor?" Jasper asked as he walked out into the hall.

"He's just been overdoin' it, Reverend. You'll have to wait until he's had some time to recover," the doctor commanded.

Jasper nodded and both men sat in the waiting room in silence, just staring at the floor. After a while, E resumed, "Jas, what was he gonna say?"

"Let's see," Jasper answered facetiously. "He would start by sayin' how he's been so burdened by all this and it finally caught up with him, and the very least that I could do is give a dying man his last request!"

"You don't really think that, Jas!" retorted E. "I just bet he was goin' to apologize."

"Boy, are you gullible. He's the most conniving, manipulative man you could ever imagine. He told his own daughter and grand-daughter that he didn't want to see them ever again, after they had an argument with him over his bigotry! E, you have no idea how rotten to the core this man is. Rotten … just awful rotten!" Jasper exclaimed, as every muscle in his body stiffened.

At that moment, E caught a glimpse of me as a girl in her early teens as I passed by the nurse's station. I had a single rose in my hand as I went into Stout's room.

"Jas, what does his granddaughter look like?" E asked.

"Stout's granddaughter, why?" asked Jasper.

"Well, I think she just went into his room."

Jasper picked his face up out of his hands and looked down the hallway. "Was she a thin teen with almost white hair?" asked Jasper.

"That's her," E answered, shaking his head.

Stout just looked at me in disbelief. I had become the granddaughter he had treated so shoddily, and I was telling him how much she loved him. All the rage that had filled his soul for so many years suddenly left him. Unexpectedly, he grieved for his pitiful life and how he had wasted it and made others miserable because he was so miserable. He looked up at my angelic face and saw tears streaming down my cheeks. To his astonishment, he began to weep as well.

As the nurse escorted me out, I turned to him and said, "God loves you too, Grandpa."

He smiled and raised his index finger of his left hand to his lips and blew me a kiss as I left. "A pencil," Stout whispered to his nurse with great effort. At first, she resisted and told him to get some rest, but she soon realized that he was adamant with his request.

About 6:00 a.m. the next morning, the nurse in charge heard Stout talking to someone in his room. As she turned the corner, she scolded, "I told that preacher to let him get some rest!" Then she realized that Jasper and E were both asleep in the waiting room. As she opened the door, he had a big smile on his face, but he wasn't moving.

"Y'all might as well go home and get some rest. Mr. Jones has passed," the nurse said.

Jasper and E immediately jumped up from their sound sleep to make sure they heard her right. "Ma'am, he's gone?" Jasper asked. The nurse nodded her head.

The day was empty and without comfort for Jasper as he went around to the family and paid his condolences. "I prayed so much for that man, E. I don't know why, but it was like I had some attachment to him!" Jasper exclaimed as his eyes welled over, sending tears streaming down his cheeks. "I wanted God to do a real number on him, change his heart, and all that. And I really felt like God was going to do it, too. I really had peace about it. Now his poor, pitiful family and that poor little girl … how can I face her?" he asked as he shrugged his shoulders and knocked on their door.

Annie was the only child of Stout Jones's daughter, Gertrude Barrow. Gertrude's husband died in a hunting accident shortly after Annie was born. Stout had cut them off from any help, even though Stout's wife would sneak things over to them. Jasper really was not looking forward to this encounter. He really liked Gertrude, even though she was much older than him.

"This is how she'll remember me—the guy that told her that her father was dead," he said as he knocked on the door again and removed his hat. "Miss Barrow, how are you, ma'am?" Jasper asked.

She looked at both men like they were ghosts and asked, "So it's true?"

That was all she got out of her mouth before the little girl exclaimed, "I told you, Momma. I told you!"

Jasper, thinking that someone had already told them the news, added, "So you've heard, ma'am? I'm sorry."

She answered with a shocked look, "No, Annie told me you would be here."

Jasper, shaken from his pastoral stance, continued, saying, "Someone told your daughter, ma'am?"

Shifting her eyes toward the little girl, she answered, "Oh, you could say that. Come in and let me take your hats and coats. Annie woke me up early this morning and said her Poppa had been to see her. I told her that was impossible; he was in the hospital. She not only insisted that he came to visit, but he told her he had to go away for a long time, but he would see her again one day."

You could tell that she was beginning to lose her composure, so Jasper grabbed her hand to console her. "You don't have to continue, Miss Gert," he remarked with exaggerated concern.

"No, I need to tell you this, Jasper. Annie said my father left a note and a key for you at the hospital and that he loved us more than we would ever know." By then she was a mess, crying on Jasper's shoulder. He just looked over at E with a puzzled look, exhaling in a long, forlorn sigh.

Jasper whispered, "Miss Gert, I'm so sorry. If there's anything I can do, please let me know. When I saw Annie at the hospital last night, I worried about how she would—"

"Annie never went to the hospital last night," Gert interrupted in shock.

All Jasper could do was look over at E with incredulous eyes. At that moment, the hospital called for Jasper. They had been looking for him since early that morning. "Hello," Jasper said on the phone, with crinkled brow. "Well, okay…I guess right now. Yes, ma'am. Thank you. Bye." As soon as he got off, he whispered to E that the hospital had something for him from Mr. Jones. Jasper composed himself and asked meekly, "Miss Gert, I hesitate to tell you this, but the hospital has something that your father left for me. Would you like to go?"

As Gertrude, E, Annie, and Jasper walked down the same hallway in the hospital, Jasper got a chill up his spine as he wondered what this could be about.

"Well, here it is, Reverend," said the hospital director as he gave the key to Jasper.

"Was this all?" Jasper asked with a grimace.

The administrator, trying his best to cover himself, answered curtly, "Well, the nurse in charge said Mr. Jones had written a letter and put the key inside it, but she was busy with her duties, so she laid the letter on the bedside stand. When she went back to check on him early this morning, the only thing left was the key."

With a nebulous face, Jasper asked, "I'm very confused. Why are you giving me this key?"

"The nurse was sure you were to get the key and she did say Mr. Jones wanted the revival to go on as planned. That's all I know," finished the mealy-mouthed administrator.

E and Jasper dropped the others off and started toward Stout's home, where they had left his wife earlier that day.

"We just wanted to check on ya, Mrs. Jones," Jasper said, as he tilted his hat and walked in the door. It was a musty and cold old house, cluttered with bric-a-brac. They could smell pine kindling burning in the living room fireplace as she ushered them through the dark foyer.

"I'm so happy you both came back, won't you eat a bite with me? People have been bringing food by here all morning," she proclaimed brightly.

Before they could say anything, she was getting dishes down and pouring tea in glasses. They both realized that she needed to wait on them. It made her feel better about the whole situation she was in, so they didn't say a word. They sat by her for what seemed like hours while others came to pay their respects. Old Mrs. Nye came by and went on about why this had happened. Others came by with advice, but E and Jasper just sat there by her, listening when she needed to say something and answering politely when she would ask a question.

They both got up at the same time to leave. E told her, "Mrs. Jones, we have to get ready for tonight's services, but if you—"

She interrupted him with, "Men, I just wanna say this has meant more to me than you know. You just sat here by me and said very little when all these people were trying to give me advice and console me with words. I was hoping they would leave, but I hate to see you go."

Jasper sincerely stated, "I'll be back to check on you, ma'am." She nodded with a smile as they put their hats on and went on their way to the parsonage.

Hoping that he could change the subject, Jasper said to E, "I've got somebody special that I want you to meet. She's going to be at the service tonight."

"Who is it?" E curiously asked.

"No, no … it's gonna be a big surprise," Jasper answered with a high-pitched voice.

E just nodded, knowing that Jasper just needed a diversion from the emotional rollercoaster they had been on.

"What do you think the key fits?" asked E, changing the subject back because of his curiosity.

"I have no idea. Take a look at it and see if anything looks strange to you," Jasper said as he handed the key to E.

"It's to a safe deposit box. It's got a number on the tag," E answered.

"Yep, and what number would that be?" asked Jasper with raised brow.

"91206. So?" asked E.

"So 9–12–06 is my birthday!" answered Jasper.

"You're kiddin' me," E stated with surprise as he shook his head.

Stout had told the nurse that he wanted the revival to go on and his funeral was not to get in the way, and the family was in agreement. So Tuesday night's service was dedicated to Stout.

God led E to continue a sermon named, "Hanging out with Sinners." He started with four things Jesus did for Zacchaeus. It was a simple message, but the Spirit was stirring strongly in that tent. AJ sang once again with the help of the choir, and the altar call was incredible, with over one hundred decisions. E moved in front of the pulpit as the people were crowding their way forward. And there she was—the most beautiful girl he had ever seen was right in his line of view. He couldn't help but be mesmerized by her. He tried to focus elsewhere, but it was if some very large magnet was drawing him and he couldn't pull away.

Her hair was like harp strings of gold, strumming the tune "Like a Lily among Thorns." Her eyes looked like rays of sunlight shooting through the bluest of ocean waves. She glowed as she looked intently into E's eyes—into his very soul. He wondered if he would ever feel the same about anything.

At that very moment, Jasper came over to her and gave her a kiss on the cheek. E thought back to when Jasper said he had someone special coming tonight. A sick feeling overcame him. He wondered how he could've lost himself so quickly to Jasper's girlfriend or possibly even his fiancée. As they approached, Jasper was called away by one of the deacons.

Jasper looked at E and said, "I'll be right back. E, meet Elise."

"Hi, E," the sweet little songbird of a voice said, melting his heart. "Jay's told me so much about you."

She smelled like a thousand gardenias. He really wanted to say something—anything would do—but he was wordless and mesmerized by her overwhelming presence. Trying hard to save face, he blurted out, "Yes, well, yeah. It, it was a pleasure. I gotta run. People to greet and all…ah…aah…my pleasure, yes." He backed away, running a poor little lady down that was standing behind him. He stumbled away like a gangly, inexperienced prom date, mumbling to himself as he escaped through the crowd.

First, she thought he was just nervous, but the more she thought about it, the more she decided that he was just being an arrogant snob. As soon as the deacons finished with Jasper, he made his way through the crowd until he found Elise, still stunned and staring into space. "Where's E?" Jasper asked very innocently.

"Well, I wouldn't know, cousin. Your arrogant little twit of a friend said he had better things to do," she stated very indignantly. "I'm ready to go. Let's get outta here, Jay," she continued.

Jasper stopped her and said, "Whoa, hold on to your horses now. Let me find out what's going on here."

But she wouldn't have any of it and broke free from his hold. "I'll be in the car, and don't bring that 'friend' of yours over either, and, by the way, don't you dare tell him who I am!"

"Okay, okay, just let me tell him I'm takin' you back to school," Jasper answered with resolve.

"E, what in tarnation did you say to my cousin?" Jasper asked, as he found E shaking hands near the street lamp outside. E turned a thousand colors of red and for a brief moment was relieved about her being his cousin. But when he realized what a buffoon he had made of himself, he became mortified. He looked at Jasper with the most pitiful eyes. "I'm so sorry—your cousin?" he said, shaking his head and closing his eyes in disbelief as his face reddened.

"What are you talkin' about, E?" Jasper commanded with a wince.

While taking his handkerchief out of his back pocket and rubbing his forehead, E answered, "Jas, I thought she was your girl. She's the most beautiful girl I've ever seen, but when you came over and gave her a kiss, well..."

Jasper started, "E, my cousin was so tired of me talking about you on the phone for the past couple days, she wanted to see you for herself. Now she doesn't wanna hear anything about you *ever*. In fact, she's sittin' in my car, waitin' for me to take her back to school...tonight."

E held his head low. "I'm so sorry, Jas. I really am sorry. Please tell her how sorry I am, please?"

Jasper trudged to his car while E continued to stare out into space, wondering how he could've botched things so badly.

"Elise, he feels awful," Jasper said in defeat as he opened the door to the car.

"Well, isn't that nice," she said facetiously.

"No, really...you don't understand!" Jasper continued. When he explained what had really happened, she acted as though she was still upset, looking out the side window. But when he told her that E thought she was the most beautiful girl he had ever seen, she grinned with a faraway look in her eyes.

"You didn't tell'm who I was, did you?" Elise asked, snapping back from her dream.

"No, but one day you'll have to," Jasper commanded. She just smiled as she looked out the window at the blurred landscape.

By the last day of the revival, 230 people had made professions of faith. E was excited about how it all had gone; he couldn't wait for the last night. By the time Jasper got back from taking Elise to school, E was fast asleep. At six the next morning, there was a knock at the door. It was Charles Nye, second in command of the Klan. He had been with Stout the night they were going to see Jasper.

"Come in," Jasper said as he opened the door and walked to the kitchen. "And how are you, Mr. Nye. Would you like some coffee?" Jasper asked, trying to hide his disdain.

Charles answered, "No thanks, Reverend."

"So what can I do for ya, sir?" Jasper asked.

"Well, Reverend, we all want you to stop this revival. It's been a failure from the start and it's only gettin' worse. It seems like the only people comin' to this thang is ne'er-do-wells and blackies. Less and less of the good church people are even showin' up!" he said, with a curious tilt to his head that revealed his arrogant ignorance. Charles was a self-righteous, cantankerous man who thought he didn't sin anymore and that people who did were going to hell. He and Jasper had had some very heated discussions on the subject. He was quite the prude, too. He felt that if a woman and a man even hugged, it was lusting. So none of that was tolerated around him, even at home … not even among relatives.

"So let me get this straight, Mr. Nye. You consider over 230 decisions as being a failure?" Jasper asked, as if he were thrusting a punch right into his gut. By this time, E was standing at the doorway of the bedroom listening in stunned silence.

"Well, we think—" Charles started.

E interrupted him with, "'We' is exactly who, Mr. Nye?"

Charles, leering over his shoulder at E, said with a gesture of his hand, "Now, Brother Ethan, this don't concern you." Charles had been a deacon in years past, but several people in the church got tired of his legalism and voted him out. But he still had many friends who thought like he did. "Brother Jasper, if you don't call this circus off, we will." Charles threatened, as he hastily got up like someone had heated up his seat. "You just make sure you call it off and quick," he continued, as he shot out the door with a wide gait and a bright red face.

Jasper looked over at E and said, "Ah... and a good morning to you, too!" poking fun at the uptight Mr. Nye.

E heard the Lord's voice as he sat down for breakfast with Jasper. *I will bring peace in the storm.* E confidently stated, "Jas, I don't think we're gonna have to worry 'bout tonight."

Before Jasper had a chance to respond, there was another knock at the door. It was Stout's daughter, Gert. "Well, Miss Gert, won't you come in?" Jasper asked with exuberance.

"Well, just for a minute," she answered, looking over her shoulder like someone was following her.

"So what or who brings you out this early, Miss Gert?" E asked her, noticing Jasper's flirtatious manner.

"Well, I wanted to warn both of you that Mr. Nye has been getting people worked up against the revival, even though my father put his blessings on it. His problem with it is the quality of people you're attracting," she said, not trying to offend. "I wanted you to know that my family told him that if he continues to make waves, we'd make trouble for him like he'd never seen. You see, he worked for my daddy and now that my mother's running the company, he works for her."

E looked at Jasper and said, "What a strange irony."

Meanwhile, Mr. Nye was paying a visit to Mrs. Jones. "Now, Mrs. Jones, I respect your husband's wishes, and you know that he was like a father to me, but I really think you need to read this," Charles said, while pulling some paper out of his coat pocket.

"Read what, Charles?" she asked, not really wanting to listen. He handed her the three handwritten pages of the last words of Stout Jones.

"How'd you get this?" she asked belligerently.

Charles started, "I went to see Stout the mornin' he died. When he saw me, he was elated. He wanted me to throw that note away and tell you to stop the revival and fire Brother Jasper immediately. He said that they had tried to blackmail him."

"Blackmail! About what?" she asked.

"Well, read the letter," Charles added.

> *Dearest Family,*
>
> *How I argued with our Lord over letting me tell you this in person. You know how hardheaded I am. I'm no longer hardhearted though. I guess by now, my little Annie has told you that we made our peace. I'm a man of few words; over the years, those words were not good. I've hurt you and so many others, but God had forgiven me as I hope you will too. My flesh, my pride, and my big mouth have been shut on this earth, but I guarantee that it will be wide open in heaven, praising Him. Thank you for loving me Gert, Annie, Rob, and my beautiful wife, Mildred, when I was so unlovable. And yes, I knew, Millie, that you were sneaking things to Gert and Annie. Remember what we talked about, Annie. I will be watchin' to make sure you do it.*
>
> *I know that my Redeemer lives, Brother Jasper, my son. I'm so sorry to tell you this in a letter, but you have to know. Your mother was going through a rough time with your father, so I consoled her. We were both young and vulnerable and we made a very big mistake. When I found out she was pregnant with you, I panicked and tried to put distance between us. When her husband was killed in the accident, it was the perfect opportunity to cover up everything, but it was still very hard for me to look at you. I am sorry, son. I am so very sorry.*
>
> *When I was changing that tire, a man came up to me and said he knew you and that I was to respect your calling. I do, now, and*

I'm asking my friends and family to respect your calling too. The key is to a safe deposit box at the First Commonwealth Bank of Dallas.
 The contents of the box are all yours, Jasper, and your name is on file at the bank. I have one more thing to add. Take it from a dying man—die to self, so that you may truly live.
 Don't live selfishly as I did.
 Love to all of you,
 Stout

Charles continued, "I guess you can see what they were trying to pull, the two of 'em. They'd found out Jasper was his son and they were going to tell you. He also said to get the key back and give it to me, because he always considered me to be his son."

At those words, Mrs. Jones's mind was made up. She got her coat on and went out the door to her car. Charles opened the door for her and helped her in.

"Charles," she said, as she cranked up the car, "thank you for setting all this straight. I won't forget it." As she sped away, leaving a blue-gray haze of exhaust smoke, Charles couldn't help but chuckle out loud. He even did a little jig in the driveway then caught himself, stopped, and looked around to make sure no one saw him.

Meanwhile, at the parsonage, Gert was getting up to go. She went toward the door and Jasper sprinted over to get it for her.

As he opened the door, Gert's mother walked in. "Mother?" Gert blurted out, startled.

"I'll see you at home later," Mildred said, as she made herself comfortable.

"Mrs. Jones, I'm sure you came over to say the same—" Jasper started, but was interrupted.

"Reverend Ethan, would you mind if I talked to Brother Jasper alone?" Mrs. Jones asked courteously.

"Not at all, ma'am," answered E as he made his way out to enjoy some fresh morning air.

As she told Jasper what transpired, he turned white. "I can't believe that anyone would make up such stuff," Jasper said in a terror-stricken voice.

Mrs. Jones continued, "Well, when he said that Stout thought of him as a son, I knew that that feckless blowhard was lyin.'"

Jasper asked, "So you don't believe him?"

"Don't believe him?" she exclaimed loudly. "I wouldn't put anything past that snake. Stout didn't like Charles. In fact, he hated his guts and thought he was a proud, pretentious, self-centered windbag!"

Jasper asked, "So what are you gonna do?"

"Well, the first thing I'm gonna do is give you this letter that belongs to you," she stated, while pulling it out of her purse.

He couldn't believe his eyes as he read the letter.

"Well, Brother Jasper, I'm sorry that you had to find this out now, but it's best to get it all out in the open and deal with it the best we can. Wouldn't you agree?" she asked.

Jasper just nodded.

She continued with firm resolution. "The revival goes on as planned and as Stout wanted it. I'm leaving now; I'm sure you have a lot to think about."

"Thank you, Mrs. Jones, for everything," Jasper said while she walked out the door. Jasper motioned E inside and let him read the letter from Stout. They both chuckled nervously, thinking of the implications.

"Tell me something, E?" quizzed Jasper. "If that wasn't Annie that we saw in the hospital, why did he say he made his peace with her in the letter? I know that he visited her after his death, but that was also after the letter was written?"

E, thinking out loud, said, "So what you're sayin' is, the girl *was* Annie, but she didn't know it?"

"I don't know if that makes sense," said Jasper. "I'm gonna have to think this out some more."

E mused, "You know, a scripture came to me when you were talking to old Charles. Jesus rebuked the religious leaders of His day, often when they had too high of an opinion of themselves. When He was at the house of Simon the Pharisee, a woman who was known to be a sinner came in and began to wash His feet with her tears, wiping them dry with her hair and anointing them with oil. When the Pharisee saw this, he thought, 'This man, if He were a prophet, would know who and what manner of woman this is who is touching Him, for she's a sinner.' Jesus knew his thoughts and told a story of a creditor who had two debtors who were both unable to pay their debts. The point of the story was to show the Pharisee that though this woman was indeed a sinner, so was the Pharisee; neither had the ability to pay for their sins and they were essentially in the same leaky boat. The Pharisee's problem, however, was that he thought himself more righteous than the woman. He was so self-righteous, he couldn't see his own sin—a lot like old Mr. Nye there. In fact, I think I just saw my topic for the night's services played out in front of me."

Jasper just smiled, but his thoughts were about that bank safe deposit box and his real father.

The final service went off without a hitch. Mrs. Jones was successful in shutting down any opposition Charles Nye had organized. The tent was packed to standing room only, and over one hundred decisions were made. There was even a little boy who couldn't hear that came up to the front. E was so touched by him, he went over, hugged the little boy, and prayed with him personally while Jasper counseled others. When E finished praying with the boy, he put his hands on both of his ears and gave him a kiss on the forehead. When he did, the boy fell out cold in his arms. He put the boy on one of the front chairs while his mother attended to him and went on to others who were coming up the aisle. Suddenly, the boy's mother started crying and praising God. E went over to see what was going on. "Joshua can hear!" she cried loudly. E hugged her, went over to the boy, and held him in his arms for the rest of the night.

After the services were over and everyone finally had gone home, E and Jasper washed up and went to the Jones's house. "E," Jasper started, "I thought you'd planted her."

"What?" E questioned.

Jasper continued, "The old woman that couldn't see…They taught me in seminary that God didn't work that way anymore, so I really thought you put her there for effect."

E just smiled, shook his head, and said, "Why would you think I planted a woman that couldn't see?"

"Oh, maybe to get things rollin,'" Jasper answered.

E wasn't offended by Jasper's honesty; he really liked that about him. Gert was there waiting for Jasper at the door and hugged him so tightly, he could hardly breathe.

"Jay, I knew I was drawn to you for some reason, I just never imagined that you were my half-brother!" she stated with pride and emotion. They all hugged and thanked Brother Ethan for a great week of revival.

Jasper and E drove back to the parsonage to collapse with fatigue. They were both spent and could hardly make sentences. "E, please consider going to Dallas with me. I'd really appreciate it," Jasper said.

E just looked at him, frowned with duress, and asked, "What in the world for, Jas?"

Jasper incredulously answered, "The safe deposit box!"

"Ah, I forgot all about the key!" E exclaimed, as his face seemed to heal quickly. "The good Lord willin' and the creek don't rise…just get me back here by 7:00 p.m. tomorrow, I have a train to catch."

"No problem," Jasper answered with a smile, as both men just stared into space the rest of the drive.

Contents of a Friend

It was cool and dry as they made their way to Dallas on Monday morning. The sun was just making its way above the horizon as they

pulled out onto the heavily patched two-lane highway that meandered its way toward the big city.

"Well, here we are!" Jasper exclaimed as they pulled up to the
large bank.

"What if it's a whole bunch of confederate money?" E asked
humorously before getting out of the car.

Jasper just looked at him with disgust as one side of his lip went
up. The anticipation was killing Jasper as he hurriedly got out of the
car and almost sprinted up the steps to the front doors of the bank.

E looked at his watch and chuckled a little. "I think we should wait
a bit, Jas!" he exclaimed to Jasper, as he quickly moved away from him.

"And why would we do that?" Jasper questioned loudly, while
closing in on the front door.

"Well, the bank won't open for another thirty minutes or so!" E
answered with laughter.

Jasper looked back at him and noticed that he was smiling bigger
than a Cheshire cat. Then he looked at his watch but couldn't help himself—he still had to try the doors. Of course, they were locked, and
Jasper slowly descended the big, white steps back down to street level.

He didn't even look E's way when he got back in the car. "Okay,
okay. I don't want to hear it," Jasper said, cutting off any comeback.

"What if it's a deed to a goldmine?" E continued with his eyes
widening.

"What if it's just an empty old box?" Jasper added.

"No, I don't think he would pay for a bank box that had nothin'
in it," E said, shaking his head and squinting.

Finally, they saw a bank worker open the front doors. Jasper was
out like a shot and up the stairs again before E even had a chance to
open his door. By the time E got into the bank, Jasper had the bank
president opening the vault.

Jasper looked over at E and pleaded, "Would you look first?"

E answered, "Oh, come on, Jas. You need to do this."

Here is what he found:

- *A deed to thirty acres of land*
- *An old dusty leather journal*
- *Seven $500 Marshall Field & Co. Gold Bonds*
- *A deed to seventy-seven acres of family land northwest of Shreveport*
- *An old brass compass*
- *Several old coins*
- *A will*

Old Stout had left everything to Jasper except for the family business and house. He left those to Gert and Annie. What Jasper couldn't understand was why. Why would he do that and why would he act the way he did toward Jasper if he felt this way? It was just a giant puzzle in his mind. As he drove E to the train station, they talked about the *whys* and *what fors*, but they came up with no answers.

"Jas, what if he always had the intention of telling you, but he couldn't get past his history?" E asked.

"What do you mean 'history'?" Jasper asked.

"Well, you know he had this reputation to live up to. Suppose there was a good side to him that wanted to get out, but didn't know how?" E answered as Jasper just stared into space.

"You might have something there," Jasper pensively replied.

They said their good-byes for then, but not farewell. They had bonded as friends, and the years to come would only solidify that friendship.

No One Is Good But God

"…Why do you call me good? No one is good except God alone."

Mark 10:18

The year was 1929. The Grand Teton National Park was established. Herbert Hoover was inaugurated as the thirty-first President, and then there was October 29, which was later called "Black Tuesday"—the beginning of the Great Depression. The very next day was a solar eclipse, and there were several who came out to say God was judging America. E thought God was chastising America and possibly trying to get its attention, but definitely not judging—at least, not yet.

E stayed busy with revival after revival throughout the South. When he would get settled for the night, he would often write Jasper. Here is one of those letters:

Dear Jas,
Hope this letter finds you well. I'm sitting in a hotel room in Norman, Oklahoma, bored beyond words, so I've decided to ask

you some very pointed questions. I'm asking myself the same questions. Here they are:

Why do we put a mammoth priority on the salvation aspect of Jesus's Ministry (which I totally agree with, by the way), but we almost exclude the healing and deliverance part of His ministry? There are examples of Jesus healing and casting out evil spirits over and over again in the gospels, and He gave his disciples the authority to do the same. As believers, we have that same authority through the Holy Spirit. Are we missing an important aspect of the power of God by not focusing on healing and deliverance as well as salvation and, by the way, discipleship? Would our hard-hearted Christian culture respond to seeing the real power of God work or have we put blinders on? Or better yet, has God put the blinders on us because we don't have the faith of a mustard seed?

I wonder if our watered-down approach is disallowing many Christians to live transformed, victorious lives, free from bondage. It's truly a burden of mine. I realize that there have been abuses and fakers when it comes to spiritual things, but have we literally thrown the baby out with the bath water? By taking a stand against deception, haven't we become the greatest deceivers of all? And what about intercessory prayer? All I hear in our churches is "God help us." I'm so sick of the self-centeredness in the church as a whole. And our prayers seem to always be about the physical realm. Is that what we've watered ourselves down to?

Seminary taught nothing about deliverance or the gifts of the Spirit. In fact, these things were ignored even when students brought up questions. I had one teacher who taught that they no longer existed and another teacher who was a Spirit-filled man that knew the power of God, but he kept those things under his hat and was very careful who he talked to about them.

People need a deeper relationship with Christ—one that includes all facets of His ministry and His whole armor. It's not some smorgasbord that you choose from. All of it's vital; we need His power, His wonder-working power, more than ever.

You ever studied the verse where Jesus called out to Lazarus? I had one of my teachers say that he was showing His personal relationship to Lazarus when he called him by name. His tears showed that personal relationship! I think he said, "Lazarus, come forth," because if he would've left his name out, all the dead would rise, and it wasn't time for that to happen yet! Why can't we realize God's tremendous power?

I was thinking about how we pray in church. "If it be your will, God, let it be done." There are two types of people who pray that prayer. One prays it because of his unbelief. It's almost a disclaimer on everything he asked for before that statement. In saying it, he's already admitted that God will not come through. The second person who prays that prayer wants God's total rule in their life. They've had enough experience with God to know that He knows best, even when they think they might know what to ask for. One has total faith in God and the other, no faith at all. But they pray the very same prayer! What a paradox!

Now, my next "hot button"—racial and economic integration...I know I stand very much alone on this (you remember what we went through), but if we're to look at the stories in the Bible and learn from them, such as the Good Samaritan, then I have to say, as ministers, we're doing a pitiful job. I mean, for Jesus to even consider using Gentiles to carry his message was unbelievable in His day. Do you realize that when a Jew went through an area with Gentiles, he dusted his sandals off when he left? Gentiles were not only another race; they were the undesirables, the unclean. So that takes me to the Samaritans. They were not only half-breeds, but also they were a great embarrassment to the Jews, yet Jesus used them positively in several of his examples. For us to get high and mighty and think that we have some superior aspect to our race or our economic status or our capacity to learn or even our denominational beliefs, it makes us no better. Unity is what God wants in his church. Unity is what He blesses and unity is how His message of love is spread. The only good in me is Jesus. The only purely good thing coming from me is His love. The only master is Him. And the only race is the race of his hand coming to carry us, to sustain us, to love us—all.

And now the reason for bringing all this up: Last week, I was in a church outside of Houston. We were in our final night of the revival when a man on the third pew from me stood up and start-

ed saying quite loudly, "I am free, I am free, I am free," over and over again, flailing his hands in the air. A deacon went over and physically took the man out. Then the pastor got up and apologized for the outburst. The Spirit was stifled so badly, I almost couldn't continue preaching. Afterwards I inquired about the man who got up in service, and the deacon who took him out said to me proudly, "I told him never to come back, we didn't stand for that kind of stuff in our church." I tried without success to find the man.

I would love to hear your comments on these topics. It's getting late, and I have some ground to cover tomorrow, so I better get some shut-eye. Hope to see you soon.

E

Elise on Life

E didn't see Jasper again until that next Christmas. The Great Depression slowly ground on. Things were meager all around, but the Moses family decided to have a modest Christmas party. E invited Jasper's family to come, secretly hoping to reconcile with Elise. He also wanted to see if that feeling was still there from the night they met. The party was to be held on December 20 and it came quickly.

E was rushing around wrapping gifts for everyone and preparing food. That night, right before the party, it started to snow. Jasper had just arrived and they all watched in amazement at the anomaly from the front porch.

"Mother, this is E," Jasper said.

E was happy to meet her, but he was really looking for Elise. As his eyes gave way to a compelling impulse to scan the vehicle, his mind won out over his heart, and he walked back inside to help in the kitchen. *It was just wishful thinking*, he thought, reflecting on the bitter truth that she was gone for good. He'd only missed her by a second as she got her gifts out of the trunk of the car. As they all gathered in by the fire, E spotted her. His heart began to thump, and he felt his whole body give way to the percussion. His face was burning, and he knew it wasn't because of the fire in the fireplace.

She was much more beautiful than he had remembered. He tried not to stare, but his eyes wouldn't listen. She seated herself right by Oswald, and he seemed to know her as he put his arm around her shoulders. In fact, it seemed that everyone knew her, but E reasoned that it was just that everyone was imbued with the Christmas spirit.

She radiated, creating an air of energy that enveloped the whole house. When she smiled, the whole room laughed. She would listen, and the house seemed to have a reverence toward her ear. Her very presence seemed to drown all hopelessness in the world. He had wondered for a long time if he would feel the same around her as before. He wondered no more. She had his heart—every bit of it.

As she brushed her beautiful golden hair back from her face with two fingers, she looked intently into E's eyes. No doubt she noticed his trance. He couldn't move and was very sure that the whole world had stopped rotating as well.

"E, come over here. Have you met Elise?" Oswald asked with a shifty smile and a burgeoning laugh, bringing E back to some state of consciousness.

As he glared at them sitting there, he suddenly realized that he was "on," so he stood to make his way over to where she was sitting. "Yes, I'm afraid we got off to a bad start. Hi Elise, I want to tell you how sorry I am for our first meeting," E said as his voice cracked with great humility.

She seemed to be charmed by his heartfelt words as she gave him her hand like a queen would do before her subjects. "I might be remiss, but I do believe that we've met long before the occasion you recollect," she said, looking deep into his eyes with a pensive stare.

"No, Elise, I believe I would remember meeting you," E defiantly stated with a nervous chuckle.

"Do you, by chance, remember a girl named Ellie from Red Star School?" she asked, as she rolled her head around removing hair from her face.

E felt his face erupt into a full-blown bonfire. He felt the whole room spinning out of control as he tried to keep his composure, steadying himself on the back of the couch.

"Little Ellie! You're not telling me … " is all he got out before the whole room exploded with laughter. It seemed like "the big joke" was on him. He was the clown that had not figured out the obvious. He looked at Elise and realized that he was being made fun of.

He excused himself quickly and walked outside to get some fresh air as an apprehensive silence descended on the old house. Elise, feeling sorry for the way everything came down, quickly followed him. "E, it was never my intention to make you feel dishonorable or stupid. I kept my true identity from you because I was mad at you at first. Then I kept it from you because I was afraid of how you would feel about me if you found out. I was afraid of losing what mystique I had acquired by you not knowing," she pleaded honestly.

"Elise, I think I understand, but could we just start over? Maybe from the beginning?" E asked. She found his eyes with hers and smiled, took his arm, and walked over to the swing.

"You know, I always looked up to you. I would watch you in class, and you seemed to always know what you wanted out of life. You were the only boy that was nice to me in school. I do remember that. After you left to go to college, Miss Miriam married my dad. She really helped me to find myself," she said meekly while patting his arm.

E just sat there with his mouth open, still shocked at the whole affair. "Elise, I'm sure you will forgive me for sincerely remarking that you are the most beautiful girl I've ever met. And I'm not just speaking about your looks. I have to admit, I've never felt this way about anyone before. You speak to my soul and it jumps for joy at your presence. I know I'm blubbering on about things that people talk about when they've known someone for a very long time, but I feel as though I've known you forever," he stated with honesty and a sincere smile.

Elise, not expecting the very direct resolutions, swallowed hard and seemed to pull herself away from E gradually. He had scared her with his honest thoughts and feelings, and she needed time to think about what he was saying.

"You're all I think about. I can't imagine being with anyone else," E continued.

Then, as she pondered his words, she began to think he was trying to make a conquest. She was the goal, and he was trying to gain victory. Her sweet, melancholy demeanor became a defiant rejection. Soon she excused herself to the powder room as he sat there making plans for a life of blissful love. He had found the one he wanted to spend the rest of his days with, but she would not be that easy to convince.

"E, Elise has suddenly become ill, so I'm going to take her home. I really do appreciate everything. Thanks again for inviting us. Let's get back together soon," Jasper said as they left.

E had poured his heart and soul out to Elise and she was gone. Was this his second strike? Would he ever see her again? He was bursting with joy one minute and in absolute shreds the next. His heart ached at the anticipation of living one day without her...even one second.

He tried very hard to get her out of his head, but she was there for good. Nevertheless, he tried not to think about her and affixed a quote that Leo Tolstoy told his son on the dash of his car. It said this:

The goal of our life should not be to find joy in marriage, but to bring more love and truth into the world. We marry to assist each other in this task. The most selfish and hateful life of all is that of two beings who unite in order to enjoy life. The highest calling is that of a man who has dedicated his life to serving God and doing good, and who unites with a woman in order to further that purpose.

He didn't totally agree with Tolstoy, but it helped him to cope with his despair. He tried three times to call Elise, but she refused his calls, using one excuse after another. He had to move on and make the best of life without her.

Meanwhile, Elise was wondering when he might call her again. Azazel embodied a girl named Judith and befriended Elise only to destroy any further plans of Elise and E getting together. If he could destroy that, he could destroy E's ministry. Judith told her to make him sweat and to play "hard to get." Elise wasn't too fond of the idea of not answering that third time he called, but Judith insisted. Judith answered the phone and was very cold and curt to E. "She's out on a date. You'll have to try back some other time," she bellowed while hanging up. Azazel knew that was all it would take to foil the relationship. It had been over a week without any calls and Elise was beginning to think that she had gone too far. Her heart ached at the anticipation of never hearing from him again. She tried to look at other men and get back into the groove of dating, with Judith's help, but she just didn't have the heart for it. E had her heart—every bit of it.

Pride and Prejudice

After the holidays, E had become very successful on the road as an evangelist and he began to get a little too proud of his accomplishments. While he was crossing through northeastern Texas toward Oklahoma and at the moment was thinking how good he was, he ran out of gas on one of the most God-forsaken roads in the country. There was nothing for at least thirty miles, maybe more, both ways. He thumped the gauge and it went right down to below the *E*. "Just what I thought," he said to himself. "The stupid gauge was stuck." He looked intently at the *E* and realized what had happened. It was him, the *E* was E, and God was telling him to empty himself out so he could be totally useful. Pride is of no use to God. The second he became receptive to the words from the Spirit, two lights showed up in his rearview mirror. As the lights moved farther apart, he became excited until he realized that it was the worst jalopy he'd ever seen.

"Oh, no. Please go on past, just go on … go on … no, no, no!" he shouted, as the car rolled to a stop right behind him. Soon I got out of the car with a fellow angel and walked toward him. I was wearing old dirty overalls with one side snapped and a grungy old cap with a big red *O* on the front. The fellow angel had the appearance of a woman who was as big as a mule as she waddled with no shoes.

We were a dowdy and unkempt couple. I walked over to E and asked, "Ken we hep you, boss?"

E looked in my eyes and recognized something about me. Just as he got out of his car it started to rain.

"Well, I think I ran out of gas," E told me as we all hurried back to the jalopy.

"That ain't no problem, boss. Mabel, move over and let the man sit by the winder," I said as I got into the driver's seat.

"No, no, I'll just sit back here," E insisted as he tried to open the back door.

"Oh, naw boss. You won't wanna be sittin' back there. That old seat has sprangs comin' right out of it. Besides, that door don't work," I stated, as the other angel opened the front passenger door and moved over to the middle on the bench seat.

E fastidiously settled on the passenger seat, closing the door just in time for a big backfire from the exhaust pipe. He hugged the passenger door, but the angel who looked like a woman seemed to be moving closer and closer to him. The springs were in terrible shape in the front seat as well, and E felt like he was sitting on the side of a big hill. The right windshield wiper didn't work and the left one only smeared things around on it, making it almost impossible to see out.

E tried to make small talk by asking, "Well, I guess it's about thirty miles back to the nearest station, huh?"

I emphatically answered, "I b'lieve it's thirty-three miles to Old Man Marvin's fillin' station." E just nodded his head and grunted. I continued with a set of questions. "So what kinna business are ya in, boss, if'n I keen ask?"

E answered, "Oh, sure—I'm an evangelist."

I replied with bright eyes, "Ah ha! That sure is interesting. I guess you take your orders d'rectly from God, huh, boss?" Without room for a reply, I continued, "I guess you could say that you truly are a servant to the Lord if you're an evangelist? Like Galatians 2:20 in the good book, ya know?"

E's mind went blank. Why couldn't he remember what verse that was? Before too much time lapsed, he replied, "Yes, I guess you could say I'm a servant." He thought, *Good save*, but I was less than impressed as I released air from my nostrils and nodded.

I had an old, rusty gas can on the backseat that I filled up. The ride back was mostly chitchat except for one statement that I made that stuck with E for the rest of his life. "You're a preacher man. You know the scripture I like?" I asked, without giving time for E to respond. "Luke 10:20. Ya know? Where Jesus says somethin' like, 'Don't rejoice in your successful service, but rejoice because of your right relationship with me,' or somethin' like that. I think we serve God best when we just throw ourselves into the world like it was parched land or somp'in and we were the water. Don't you, boss?" E just looked at me and grunted, but his heart pounded out of his chest. He wondered if I had a crystal ball and knew his thoughts, desires, and even his weaknesses. E thought, *How could that be coming out of a man that looks like he does?*

We finally got back to E's car with the gas can, and E was just about to pour the gas in when he realized that he'd not paid me for the gas or the ride. He reached for his wallet and turned around, but there was no trace of us in either direction, not even a taillight in the distance. E got a chill up his spine. Goose bumps ran down his arms as his heart pounded, and his legs gave way. He looked down in his wallet and found seven new gas ration stamps next to his money.

"That man was right behind me!" he nervously said to himself. He finished pouring the gas into the car and got in to go. He looked down at the needle on the gas gauge, expecting it to register a quarter tank at best. It was full, even past the *F* on the gauge. *What a strange night*, he thought, as he cranked the car and pulled back onto the desolate, crackled and worn pavement.

His Bible almost leaped at him when he sat down in the seat, so he looked up Galatians 2:20 and read aloud, "I have been crucified with Christ, and it is no longer I who live, but Christ who lives in me…" He thought, *Of course, I know that scripture. Why in the world couldn't I… God, I'm so hardheaded. I was taking a bow, when all I did was make myself available to you. I need to be totally available, and then there are no restraints on you, right God? And those people looked like they did because I was getting a little too proud for my britches. Isn't that right? And no man is too low for me to serve. I have to put myself under the lowest of the low in order to serve all man. And when he mentioned Luke 10:20, that hit too close to home. I know it's about relationship first and usefulness second.* He went along his way, reflectively smiling at the night's festivities and wondering about those people who had picked him up. Then he thought about the gauge and the tank of gas that was empty, then full. What a night indeed!

Hopeful

As the lights of Hopeful came into view, E thought of his friend, Jasper. He said to himself, "Salt Creek is not far from here; I think I'll give him a call when I get in my room for the night."

"Do you think he'll call?" Jasper frantically asked his new fiancée.

"You know he will," she answered with a confident smile.

"Well, he better. I'm tired and I have a long drive tonight. We should've told him that we were dating, but it's your big brother's fault. He introduced us," Jasper replied with a defiant brow.

"Well, you just have more to tell him now, don't you, honey?" Janie said, as she giggled with excitement.

"I just hope he takes the news as well as my cousin Elise did!" Jasper continued. "And speaking of my cousin, I hope he takes *that* news well, too."

Janie just groaned and shook her head.

"Elise and By together! You know, E's pretty sore at his old friend from school anyway; I think our news will pale in comparison to how he responds to that blow! Elise is the second girl By has stolen from him," Jasper stated with great emotion as he sighed.

"E, I haven't heard from you since you bought your new car. How are you?" Jasper asked E on the phone.

"I'm good, just wanted to call since I'm this close," answered E in a tired and low voice.

"Well, I hope you didn't get a room. I want you to stay here," Jasper insisted.

"I did, but I'll see if I can get my money back … if it's no trouble," E answered with renewed vigor.

"Absolutely not. We have a lot of catching up to do," Jasper answered forcefully.

E went to the desk clerk and he gave all but a small bit of E's money back, for housekeeping to re-make the room. It was a short drive over to Salt Creek and he seemed to regenerate energy as he thought of his old friend. He couldn't wait to tell him all the things that had happened to him on the road.

"How in the world are ya, Jas? Haven't seen you in a coon's age," E said as Jasper opened the door wide.

"I got so much to tell ya!" E continued.

"We do too," Jasper replied as Janie came out from behind the door. "Come on in and have a seat. I'll get your bags." Jasper said as E looked at both of them, stunned with silence. "Well, at least he didn't hit me, Janie," Jasper continued. "It's your fault, you know? You introduced us at the family Christmas party," Jasper said as E looked like a deer in headlights, trying to get his composure back. "Well, stop catching flies with your mouth and say somethin'!" Jasper continued with a nervous laugh.

Without further hesitation, E said, "Couldn't have happened to any worse people. You deserve each other!" he said, giving them a pert half smile. "Did'ja really think this was a big surprise? Jas is an ole' skunk-ape, and you, Jane Eliza, are a screamin' banshee … so you match perfectly! You know, Janie, Jas is tighter than Dick's hatband? He'll have you wearin' ole' flour sacks for dresses!" E continued as he surveyed the surroundings.

They both laughed hardily, and Janie gave E a big kiss on the cheek. She knew that all the banter was his way of approving of their union.

"E, we have some more news," Jasper said reluctantly.

"Good news?" E asked brightly.

"Well, not exactly. My cousin, Elise, is engaged and is getting married in June," Jasper replied.

Silence was not golden at that moment. E just stared at Jasper for several seconds as he came to grips with the news, then he said, "Well, I hope they'll be very happy. She deserves someone wonderful." Then there was an uncomfortable pause before E asked, "So tell me what's been go'in on, other than you two pulling the wool over my eyes?"

"E, it's By," Janie said, turning to get Jas's hand.

"By? Elise is marrying Byron?" E asked as his eyes widened in shock. Jasper just nodded his head up and down.

E sighed, releasing years of pent-up emotion and said, "You know, there's an old sayin' that goes, 'In choosing a friend, go up a step.' So I guess that goes for husbands, too. By's a wonderful guy and a much better catch than I," he said with a self-deprecating chuckle. He continued, "If you see them, send them my very best wishes. Now … I'm famished. Do you have any vittles in this old hovel? Or do y'all live on love?" He had improved upon an old Russian proverb and made it his own:

"Fear the goat from the front, the horse from the rear,
and women from all sides."

"Elise, I will make you the happiest girl in the world. I promise," By said, as he went down on one knee with great earnestness. "Please say you'll marry me?" he pleaded.

Elise just looked into space, regretting her doom. She had only dated By to make E jealous, but nothing brought him back to her. He was gone, and she just had to make the best of life without him. Her whole being told her to abstain from By's advances, but something else told her she better grab someone before it was too late. She was already being called an "old maid."

She looked intently into By's eyes. He was so respectable; besides, an engagement was not necessarily permanent. *Maybe that would be the thing to shake E up?* she thought.

"Yes, By. I'll marry you," she said, melting By's heart.

"Oh, Elise, thank you, thank you. You'll not be sorry, I promise. I'll make you so very happy!"

As she looked at his sincerity, she had a sick feeling in her soul. Somehow, she'd missed it before. She had realized for the first time how By really felt about her. She just smiled at him, wondering how in the world she was going to get out of this gracefully.

Suffocating in Sin

"Pleasure is the bait of sin."

—Plato

James took the money he made from loan sharking and moved to St. Louis. After "Black Tuesday," he was having trouble making ends meet, so he played small bit parts in a "wire-store" for some con artists and a part or two in a bait-and-switch scam outside the city, but there were only a few con artists he even liked. He considered most of them to be marauders, not caring who they hurt. He tried to keep a good conscience by telling himself that he was only hurting those who made their money on the backs of the poor and helpless. He would even give money to the charity balls he attended, believing he was doing what was right.

His hat was set on a wealthy railway tycoon, so he moved in for the kill. Phelan Kidd had made millions on the backs of underpaid migrant workers slaving for him in his rail yard and gashouse. James found out that his pigeon was going to be attending the opening of a new school for the deaf. He knew that those types of social gatherings attracted the very wealthy and even the very crooked. He also surmised it was about guilt or maybe they were trying to "save face." Obviously he was right, because the crooks truly came out of the woodwork. James had spent a lot of money on a newly tailored suit and wanted to make a good impression on the man. He paid off the maitre d' with a Benjamin for an introduction and got the waiter to bring a glass of Madeira and a bowl of macadamias to the rich tycoon. James had done his homework and knew what Phelan liked.

"Mr. Kidd, this is Mr. James Moses. He has given a substantial amount to the school," his paid advisor told the old man. James knew he would get nowhere without a formal introduction.

"Mr. Kidd, what do you say to some fresh air?" James asked while the maitre d' rolled his eyes and turned from them to serve others.

"Sure," responded Phelan, as they both walked out onto the veranda. He was proud of his education and was culturally savvy. Phelan was in no way a self-made millionaire but considered himself to be almost as good—doubling the family fortune in a matter of a few years in the worst of economic times.

"I do say, Mr. Kidd, the financial climate in our nation is tremulous at best, wouldn't you agree?" James questioned, trying to steer the conversation.

"Yes, quite so. I'm just glad they finally have that FDIC in place. Can you believe that Mr. Mellon, the Secretary of the Treasury, saying that the government's business is in sound condition? What a melon head!" Mr. Kidd exclaimed, sipping his drink and wadding a large handful of macadamias into his more than ample mouth as his jowls flapped.

"Agreed. They have no idea what's goin' on up there," James replied, getting ready to bait his hook.

"So what exactly do you do, Mr. Moses?" Phelan asked, trying to see if there was an angle to the conversation.

"I'm with a division of New England Mutual," James answered.

"Life insurance!" exclaimed Phelan sharply, spitting small pieces of macadamia nuts into the air, thinking he had just wasted his time with an insurance salesman.

"Oh, no, sir, Mr. Kidd. Have you ever heard of mutual funds?" James asked with a calm timbre, trying to affect the mood of the conversation.

"Sure," retorted Phelan, not wanting to look dumbfounded as he stuffed another handful of nuts into his mouth.

"Well, my division has a two-hundred percent return. As you know, the Dow is doing incredibly well these days. It's a very good time to get in," James said smoothly and with poise.

James was selling himself as a mutual fund manager. He had already roped three high rollers and was quickly working on his fourth. James was aware that Phelan knew little about stocks and bonds. He had purposely stayed away from the market since the crash in '29, but Phelan also knew enough to realize that it was rebounding.

"Tell you what…You get all your paperwork to my secretary Monday morning, and I'll get back with you," Mr. Kidd said, not really planning to call James back. But James knew he was in the door, and once in the door, there was no way to stop him.

He was successful at getting Mr. Kidd to bite and found himself in charge of three million dollars in funds from four high rollers. He rode the wave for two years, paying himself a handsome salary. He was able to afford a well-appointed apartment, a new car, and several nice, tailored suits. He also was able to keep a checking account with an average balance of over two thousand dollars. When he saw the market taking a dive, he bailed, handing over all accounts to an apprentice he had been training. He bilked the fund once again for himself before he packed up to move to Chicago. It was almost Christmas, so he took a minute to write his family:

Merry Christmas!
    I won't be able to be there for Christmas, but please know that I am well. I have spoken to E, and he told me of Poppa Nick's passing, and it saddens me. Hopefully the money I've enclosed will help to perk everyone up.
    Love to all,
    James

Along with the letter, he sent a hundred-dollar bill. Oswald promptly took the money and placed it in the offering plate that next Sunday at church. Oswald's heart was breaking. He stayed on his knees a lot, praying that God would protect James while he was in his "depraved" state and bring him to his senses soon. A scripture came to E after hearing about the letter and the money. "A fortune made by a lying tongue is a fleeting vapor and a deadly snare" (Proverbs 21:6, NIV).

Chicago Underground

Chicago was a cold place in the winter, and the wind coming off the big lake was sharp. James couldn't help but wonder what the weather was like in northeastern Texas. He was truly homesick, but he would not succumb to such a notion and fought off the feelings of a warm fireplace and family gatherings. Besides, he was successful. Chicago was known for its lawlessness in the '30s and also for the confidence men and mafia that roamed its streets. James was not interested in getting into that network of liars, cheats, and swindlers. He was looking for his own meal ticket. He had kept a good job, a decent checking account, and great clothes and had secured a Diner's Club Card. He knew all those things would help him in his quest to obtain what he was looking for.

    The Chicago Tunnel Company was building a new section of underground tunnel for freight underneath the city and needed a supervisor. It was the perfect opportunity for James. He was great with people and even greater at getting people to do things. Now he had to make it look legit, so he called his printer friend in St. Louis.

"Clark, can you make it look impressive? It has to look authentic," James insisted.

"No problem, James. I happen to have a picture of the real thing to go by," Clark said, while wrapped in an ink-smeared printer's apron.

"Great, let's do it. And don't forget my resume, some cards, and those letters of reference," he reminded Clark.

Meanwhile, he secured an interview with Mr. Stevens. James had already found out that Joe Stevens had been roped into doing all the hiring for the tunnel company. Joe was a vice president for Chicago Telephone and Telegraph. Chicago Tunnel was a subsidiary that was not making the money they had hoped, so Joe had to turn things around quickly.

James had discovered Joe's favorite cigars, his likes and dislikes, and what he was looking for in a supervisor. He also knew he loved to deer hunt, was a Democrat, and hated statistics with a passion. He thought you could get numbers to say what you wanted them to say on paper. And if there was one gift James had, it was with anything financial. He was great with numbers, so he had already mapped out a business plan for the project from what information he could obtain.

With his best suit on and a handful of Emilia Garcia cigars in his vest pocket, he strutted into Mr. Joe Stevens' stuffy office, which smelled of leather.

"Hello, Mr. Stevens. My name's James Moses and no, I don't part waters, but I can part the earth," James said with confidence and a big smile. Seeing the deer head on the wall behind Mr. Stevens, James continued, "Did you hear the joke about the statisticians that went deer hunting? Three statisticians went hunting and came across a large deer. The first statistician fired, but missed by a foot to the left. The second statistician fired, but also missed by a foot to the right. The third statistician didn't fire, but he shouted in triumph, 'On the average, we got it!'"

That clinched the deal. James pulled out his resume with a handful of cigars. "Here, do you like Cuban cigars, Mr. Stevens?" he asked, knowing the answer.

"Call me Joe. So I see here that you got your engineering degree from MIT?" he prodded.

"Yes, sir, and it was a great experience. Boston has a lot of pretty girls!" James answered jokingly, hoping to change the subject.

"Well, I have to talk to the others on the board, but I feel confident enough to say you have the job if you want it," Mr. Stevens said, as he chuckled and heartily shook James's hand.

"Well, sir, thank you!" James said exuberantly.

Every Monday morning James would have all his contractors in for a big roundtable discussion that lasted two to three hours. He would take all the problems, ask the group what they would do, and made a decision based on that consensus. For six months, everything was great, until he got into a real problem that had to have an immediate solution. When he was not able to respond quickly, they started checking out his references, and he was fired promptly.

The next weekend was July Fourth, and he had been invited to a barbeque with a friend he had made at work.

"You know, James, I knew you never went to MIT," said Robert.

"So why didn't you say something?" James retorted.

"Well, I guess I was having too much fun watching you and admiring your talents," Robert continued.

"What're you talkin' about, Rob?" James asked, tinged with self-loathing.

Robert smiled and said, "You never went to college, yet you know things that college men could never learn in books. Horse sense … an intuition unlike anything I've ever seen. You're an amazing man and you could really do something great with your life if you had a mind to," Robert stated, trying to pick James up after being fired. "Tell me that you'll come; that's all I want to know, and I'll leave you alone,"

Robert relentlessly continued. "I'd count it as a personal favor. I'll have no one to talk to otherwise."

Out of all of Robert's classmates in college, not one had scruples. They didn't care who they hurt or stepped on while working their way to the top. But here was a man who lived a lie, was not a college graduate, and yet was very careful about whom he hurt. James finally said yes to his invitation.

Her name was Sarah Michelle Lindt; she was his best friend's sister. At first, it felt unusual for him to be attracted to her, but she was unusually attractive.

"Sarah, this is my friend, James," Robert said.

The weather was warm and the sky was blue, but James saw none of it. He didn't even see the fireworks display over Lake Michigan later that night. He couldn't keep his eyes off Sarah. She was really enjoying the attention that James was giving her, but he found out quickly that she wouldn't be one of his conquests by tongue, as he was accustomed to. He could talk all he liked, but Sarah was interested in deeper things like character and honor.

"Why won't you go to dinner with me? Just dinner, and then I'll take you home?" he asked, as if his life depended on it.

"Well, James, I really do like you and I know that I would love our dinner together, but I don't want to lead you on. I'm not interested in anything long term," she said, breaking his heart in two.

"If you like me, let's just take it from there—real slow," James pleaded.

"I don't think you understand, James. I really think we want different things from life and I don't want to lead you on," she said with resolution.

James, not conceding yet, pleaded, "Sarah, I can learn to like anything you like."

Seeing that James was not getting the hint, she asked, "So what you're saying is, you could learn to have good morals and an honest job?"

It was as if she had stabbed his heart with a dagger and turned the blade. Suddenly, and with amplification, he felt the blow of all his sins. Even if he had rationalized his way of life before, none of it made sense anymore. Wrong was wrong and right was right: no *ifs*, *ands*, or *buts*. He felt his legs tremble as they gave way, and his face and ears became hot as fire. For once in his life, he was speechless, with no pithy comebacks as his eyes fell to the floor in shame. He quickly excused himself without another word.

"Sis, where's James?" Robert asked Sarah.

She just looked at him in horror as her eyes welled up.

"Sis, what's goin' on?" he insisted.

She finally gathered a couple words together, "He's gone."

Robert flew outside, but James was nowhere to be found. His posture tightened as he came back inside only to find his bewildered sister standing by the door in disbelief.

He whispered, "What happened?"

Reluctantly, Sarah told him what she had said.

"Oh no!" Robert exclaimed, while shaking his head in long gestures.

"What?" Sarah asked, dumbfounded.

"I didn't tell you he had just lost his job and I was really trying to pick him up with this barbeque. He's really a wonderful guy, sis."

Sarah shook her head with insolence and asked, "Why didn't you tell me this? You told me all these stories, making him look like some unconscionable shyster. Now you're telling me he's not?"

He just shook his head no. After a few moments he continued, "He knew more about honor than anyone I've ever met. Maybe he went about things the wrong way or made some wrong choices, but he has more heart than he has brains. And he has a lot of brains. For someone who's a con artist, he's the most caring, encouraging person I know. And he only conned those who had made their millions swindling innocent, hard-working people."

Through her tears, Sarah replied sarcastically, "Well, brother, thanks for telling me this now!"

Weeks crept by without a word from James. Robert had spoken to E and the family on several occasions, trying to find him, with no luck. Sarah was still very upset over the whole affair and was not speaking to her brother. James seemed to slip into oblivion and was furtively subsisting in some other universe.

Life Application

"James, I can't take this money!" insisted Phelan Kidd. "You earned it. I realize that you lied to get my money in the beginning, but I made a fortune on your speculations in the market, James. Even now, it's not doing as badly as it could be. I'll not accept your money. Take it and get into college or trade school or somethin.' You really have some talents you need to hone. Get some book smarts to go along with those street smarts of yours and you will be unstoppable. You just make sure you come see me when you do," Phelan said, slipping the stack of bills back into James's coat pocket and shaking his hand. "But, thanks for apologizing, James. That means a lot to me, and I won't forget it," Phelan continued with a gregarious grin.

James was on a quest to right all his wrongs. He knew it was futile, but he was going to do his best. He thought, *How do I take back the wasted time? How do I take back the things missed because I was looking in the wrong places for satisfaction? I was so blind with the lusts of this world, God. How can I start all over at my age?*

For the first time in his life, he heard God's voice as clear as a bell. "I don't want you to start over, James. I might have chopped down the tree, but the stump and the roots are still intact. I want you to take what you've learned and apply it differently. I want you to rearrange your life, not repeat it."

As E prayed about James, God began to speak to him through His Word. Jesus's parable of the prodigal son begins with the statement, "A certain man had two sons." When the prodigal son returned home at long last, the father and his household rejoiced. The elder brother, hard at work for the father in the field, heard this merry-making and came to investigate the cause. When he saw the reason for the rejoicing, Jesus said, "He became angry with a passionate rage."

E responded to God by saying, "I understand, God. I'm now facing the other prodigal son's problem, and it's important how I respond to James's return. God, please don't let me be swallowed up by rage or jealousy. Please give me the strength that I need to be a supportive and encouraging brother."

For Whom the Wedding Bells Toll

At Jasper's wedding reception, E finally saw Elise again.

"Elise, I wanted to tell you how happy I am for you and By. You couldn't have picked a better man. I really do wish you both the best," E said with all the sincerity he could muster as his heart broke in two.

She looked at him in horror, then erupted in tears and ran outside with her face in her hands. As if the breath had been knocked out of him, E exclaimed, "What did I say, Jas? For the life of me, I'll never figure out women!"

Jasper answered with great reserve, "Elise broke off her engagement with By three weeks ago. She told him that she didn't love him and couldn't continue to lead him on."

E asked, "Why didn't you tell me this, Jas? Boy, I really stuck my foot in my mouth again! I can't seem to get anything right when I'm around her. Am I just snake-bit when it comes to Elise?"

Jasper calmly smiled, pointed to the door, and said, "Why don't you go find her, E?"

E went outside to look for Elise, but she was nowhere to be found. She was gone and that was strike three. He walked over to the lake that bordered the church property and sat down beside the water. Watching the white swans glide gracefully, he remembered the time he saw Elise in the tent revival. As he looked into the blue-green water, he couldn't help but wonder what God had in mind. Was this yet another test of his resolve? He looked down at the reflection of his face in the water, distorted by the small wake the swans were creating. *That's me, being pulled in every direction*, he thought. Suddenly the water was like glass and another face appeared over his shoulder in the reflection. It was Elise. As both heads came together in the water, there was some providential symmetry to it all. They seemed to meld into one another. Even with her face smeared from wiping away tears, she was radiant. With the risk of soiling her dress, she started to sit beside him. He quickly jumped up, took his coat off, and laid it down, offering his hand for support. For several minutes, they just sat there, looking over the water at the swans preening their feathers. E noticed that the two swans were forming a heart in the reflection and wondered if Elise saw it.

"Elise, I…" was all he got out before she put her index finger over his lips to stop him from talking. Her touch gave him goose bumps as her beautiful eyes found his; then in a wistful tone that intensified the moment, she said, "E, I only agreed to the engagement with By to make you jealous, but I only ended up hurting myself and him, too. You scared me when you said all those things on the porch that day, but I wasn't 'put off' by them, I just needed time to think. It was my girlfriend Judith's idea to make you sweat and not answer your calls—I really wanted to. I know, now, that I feel the same way you did."

"Elise, I hope you won't think this too presumptuous of me, but if I don't do this now, I think I'll absolutely explode," E resolved. He stood up, got down on one knee, took Elise's hand tighter than he would hold it usually, and said, "If I have enough time on this earth,

I want to take every second of it to show you how much I love you. You make me feel like I've never felt…like I could soar to the highest height and with rushing speed, go anywhere and do anything. I want to be with you always. I lay my heart in your hands. Elise Bosch, would you marry me?"

Tears welled up in her bright eyes and streamed down her face as she smiled with a blissful stare into his admiring blue eyes. "Yes," she said softly, with a nod. They hugged. He wiped away her tears with his handkerchief and gave her a soft kiss on the cheek. Then they went arm-in-arm back toward the church.

"Jas, I have an announcement to make," E said abruptly and nervously as he paced.

Jasper went over to the punchbowl, hit it with the big spoon, and announced, "Attention, everyone. First we want to thank you for being here on our special day. We love you and appreciate all of you very much. And now I want to yield the floor to my good friend and Janie's older brother, E."

E started, "A toast to my good friend, Jasper, and my sister, Jane Eliza. May your love endure beyond the last sunset. May both of your lives be long and happy, your cares and sorrows be few, and the many friends around you prove faithful and true." He lifted his cup and then took a small sip. "Now for my news," E continued as he motioned for Elise to stand by him. "I'm happy to announce on this auspicious day that Elise Bosch has made me a very happy man. She has agreed to marry me."

Jasper and Janie came running over to hug both Elise and E, and the whole reception party erupted in applause and cheers. "E, when I told you to go find her, I had no idea this would happen! Congratulations," Jasper said, as he held his cup up.

Janie came running over to E, gave him a big kiss on the cheek, and said, "Brother, I hope you're both blissfully happy. Y'all deserve it." Annie, Stout's granddaughter who was now going by "Ann," came up to E and gave him a small box. "Grandpa made me promise

I would give you this at Jasper's wedding." E just looked at her bewildered, wondering how Stout knew he would be at Jasper's wedding.

"What is it, E?" Jasper asked as he cocked his head.

"It's a ring," E replied, losing his composure. He nervously reached over for Elise's left hand, and as he slid it on her finger, it fit perfectly.

Elise looked shocked and bewildered, but forcefully proclaimed, "A beautiful red ruby! I love it!"

Jasper looked over at E with wide eyes and whispered in his ear, "Remember the Stout note? It said for Annie to remember to do something." E just looked at Jasper, thinking that he was off his rocker. Elise was thrilled at the beautiful red ruby, so what was a man to do but enjoy the moment and not look a gift horse in the mouth? As he looked down into the empty box, he noticed a small piece of paper with a verse handwritten on it:

> So be content with who you are and don't put on airs. God's strong hand is on you; He'll promote you at the right time. Live carefree before God; He is most careful with you.
>
> 1 Peter 5:6 (MSG)

That verse became E's motto through life and he quoted it on many occasions.

Oswald walked up to the same table, took the spoon, and rapped on the punch bowl once more. Everyone stopped talking and looked intently at the old man in wonder.

"I have an announcement to make also. I've been waiting for the right moment and it seems like I better get on this train before it leaves the station!" he exclaimed with a shy laugh. He motioned for Miss Clark to stand by him, and E looked over at Jasper with great surprise. "I've asked Miss Margaret Clark to be my bride, and she has succumbed to my incessant badgering and said yes," Oswald finished with a grin.

Everyone started cheering and clapping again. E ran over to both of them and hugged them tightly, his eyes welling up with tears. Jasper, Janie, and Elise all came running too.

Mae Mae, who was now going by "Mary," picked up the spoon and tapped on the bowl once more. You could have heard a pin drop. "I just want to announce that I have no plans to marry anytime soon," she said with a playful giggle. Everyone just laughed and went on enjoying themselves. It was a wedding reception like no other.

E and Elise, with Oswald and Margaret, were married in a double ceremony in the old Steeple Creek Church on a beautiful summer afternoon, Saturday, June 3, 1933. Miss Clark insisted on paying for everything, including separate honeymoons.

E's father and new stepmother wanted to see the newly opened Mount Rushmore, but Elise had always wanted to go to Venice, Italy. They stayed at the Hotel Royal Danieli. The old hotel was the setting for much rest, relaxation, and intimacy, getting E and Elise ready for life in the fast lane once they returned home.

Venetian Blend

People seeking refuge from barbarian invasions settled Venice. It was once home to Marco Polo, the great merchant and explorer. Polo, befriended the great emperor of China, Kublai Khan. E was amazed by Khan's protection and provision for Polo and his company as they traversed China and the Orient. They traveled through the bandit-ridden interior and were given horses and anything else they needed for a safe journey. He felt it was a great analogy of what God does for us.

E had been reading the *London Times* and sipping his wonderful Venetian coffee on the terrace when Elise sauntered through, getting ready for a day out and about. They walked arm-in-arm while E fed the pigeons outside St. Mark's Cathedral. A gondola boat ride took them on a tour of the city. The water was beautiful, reflecting the intense blue skies from above and the beautiful architecture.

Then E heard God. *Blue is the color of my glory. You are to reflect my glory as this water reflects the sky.* As he heard the Spirit, he realized that it was no mistake that Elise picked Venice as their honeymoon site. It was, after all, the water city.

An old man kept shouting "*Pericolo!*" over and over as he ran from a body that lay face down at the edge of the Basilica. E wasn't sure what the little man was saying, but Elise thought it meant "danger" or "beware." As the sunset illuminated the ornate architecture of the square, creating long blue shadows, E tried to get the man help.

A priest came over, looked intently into E's eyes, and said, "*Uomo di Dio, sì?*"

E, thinking that someone at the hotel had told the priest that he was a man of God said, "*Sì.*" The priest spoke to two men in Italian, and they dragged the man off who was face down. Elise thought he said something about him being drunk. Then the priest motioned for E and Elise to follow him inside Saint Mark's Cathedral. E was shaken by the beauty and sense of awe the beautiful church evoked.

"*Buon giorno, mi chiamo Padre Francisco Caravello. Parla Italiano?*" the priest asked.

Elise shook her head and said, "*Non capisco.*"

E whispered to her, "I think his name is Father Francisco Caravello."

The priest asked excitedly, "*Ou speak Inglese?*"

E told the man, "*Sì.*"

The bright-eyed priest exclaimed, "A *uomo* came yeesterdey at Trenta!" He held up three fingers, meaning three o'clock, and continued, "He speak *Inglese*. I no capisce, but I pray. God say He send *uomo*"—he pointed at E—"over *corpo!*" He motioned for them to walk down a massive hallway to a small room.

"Did I hear him say that God had sent you to a man who spoke English?" Elise asked.

"I think so," E answered in confusion.

Jack Donaldson had been out on the Mediterranean for more than three months, still a greenhorn on the high seas. God had called him into the ministry later in life after he had finished college and medical school. Jack was more than ready to accept whatever God had for him, until he lost his three-year-old son to polio. His wife, not being able to handle the loss, was put into an asylum. It was too much for him to bear, so he found the first freighter in Bass Straight leaving Tasmania and got a job aboard, working in the galley. He kept having visions and dreams on board and told several of his shipmates about them. Disaster after disaster followed the boat and its crew since he came aboard. They all decided that he had done something against God and they were all being cursed for it.

First the ship hit a quay wall and a sailor fell to his death from the mast. The list kept getting larger, including a fire, an explosion that killed three people, and dysentery. While the ship was somewhere off the coast of Trieste, heading back southwest, they decided to send Jack off in a life raft in the middle of a large storm, and he ended up in Venice, close to death.

"I kept havin' this vision that I was on a schooner going over the sea in a different time. I looked down and I had a beard and a robe on. The kind of clothes people would wear thousands of years ago. This kept happening throughout the voyage!" he said as he looked up at E. "When they put me in that raft, I was relieved for them as well as me. I just said to them, 'No hard feelin's, mates.'"

E suddenly realized that he was seeing Jonah from the Bible played out before his eyes. He looked at the man intently and asked him, "Why have you relinquished your calling?"

Then the man broke into tears, telling his sordid tale.

"Well, there's only one thing I can do. I have to restore you and send you to where you're supposed to be serving. What you were seeing in your visions was Jonah on a ship trying to escape God's hand thousands of years ago."

Elise looked into the man's eyes and said, "You're a doctor, aren't you?" E looked at Elise with a smile. He saw God's hand on her and he suddenly realized how much God's providence had brought them together. She was going to be much more than a wife and a friend to him.

The man nodded yes to Elise, and she smiled at E and said, "He's suppose to be a medical missionary to the aborigines." Jack was shocked and knew she spoke the truth. He had felt it in his bones for years. If he didn't take up his cross and go, nothing would ever be right in his life again. He hugged both of them and thanked them.

"I still feel bad for that poor ship I was on and all the destruction that I caused her mates," he said with a sad face.

"What was the ship's name?" E asked, scratching his head.

"The Royalist ... a softwood clipper that had tea, gold, some wool, and a lot of Australian wheat on board," Jack answered dispassionately.

E looked at him with relief and smiled. "Jack, you weren't the curse on that ship. She mysteriously went down yesterday, somewhere in the strait with no survivors. The desk clerk was talking about it at our hotel and said that the ship was really a German freighter in disguise."

Jack was speechless as he stared at E. "Your blood should be bottled, mate," he said, giving E a piece of paper with his family's home address written on it. "It's been my honest assessment that nothing happens by circumstance when you walk with God, and I don't think our chance meeting is to be all of it, chap. Please stay in touch and I'll do the same, Tiny," he said as he left to gather his things for home.

"What did he say about blood? And did he call you 'Tiny'?" Elise asked. E just shrugged his shoulders and shook his head.

The next day, E and Elise found a wonderful bakery and spent the rest of their francs on breakfast as they sat and watched the beautiful sunrise over Aldebaran Canal. Elise walked over to the edge of the water and dropped a white rose in, saying, "*Arrivederla Venice*." It was time to leave the serene city of water.

After a long walk back to the rail station, they got on their train and went through the numerous connections to get back to Milan. In Milan, they caught their flight to Paris... then to London. The right prop went out on the old eighteen-passenger Curtiss Condor and they had a rocky landing, but E was not worried. He knew that their purpose in life was yet to come and God would be faithful to protect them until they had finished it. After a Clipper flight to Greenland, they were finally headed back across the "big pond" to the States in a brand new Boeing 247. It was no first class ride, but at least it was air-conditioned.

E looked out the window at the large blue ocean and realized something he had never completely realized before. Water made up most of the planet. If he was to be the "water" for God, his reach had to be huge. At that very moment, he pulled the little piece of paper out of his coat pocket. It read, *So be content with who you are, and don't put on airs. God's strong hand is on you; He'll promote you at the right time. Live carefree before God; He is most careful with you.* He realized that it was not he that had to do the reaching.

Moses and the Mountain

As a new pastor, E found out that time for himself and his new wife didn't exist. Even so, E decided that being on the road all the time as an evangelist was no life for newlyweds either. God had provided a nice church not far from home, so E could keep a close eye on his father and his failing health.

Miss Bernice, the church matriarch, was a great woman, but she would get "wigged out" about the smallest things. When she called E, he would usually say, "I'll be right over." But this night he had already received a call from Mary concerning his father. They were taking him to the hospital, so he glued himself to the phone. He had already called all the people on the party line to make sure the line stayed clear. "How is Pap?" he asked Mary, his voice trembling.

"He's resting, E. Don't worry. I'm staying here, and if anything changes, I'll call you," she said with great affection.

When E told Miss Bernice about his father, Miss Bernice was on her way. E tried to discourage her, but she was hardheaded and big-hearted. She was a war widow and consoled herself by trying to comfort others. Miss Bernice could be pushy at times, but E knew that she meant well. As she got into her big Desoto and hurriedly made her way to the parsonage, the truck seemed to appear from nowhere. They took her to the hospital, but she was in a coma and had several broken bones. The doctors didn't expect a woman of her age to pull through such a terrible ordeal.

E's father was finally stable, but there was no news on Miss Bernice. E felt horrible and hadn't been out in days from fasting and praying. Elise was staying at the hospital, first with Pap and now with Miss Bernice. E was in great need of some fresh air. He started walking down to the bridge that spanned the small creek about a half-mile from the church. Heavy spring rains had made the creek look like a giant river as it thrust itself under the vulnerable bridge with immense force. As he stared into the rushing water, he was reminded of God's words about him being the water. Then he realized that water was strongest after a storm. As he was thinking that, he looked down at his soiled black patent leather shoes and noticed that his reflection resembled Christ on the cross as he stretched out his hands on the wooden girders of the bridge.

Then suddenly he realized there were two more shoes by his in the reflection and he heard my voice say, "She's fine." He quickly jerked his head up to get a look, but I was already gone. E stared at the spot where my shoes were standing for a moment, then he ran back to the parsonage as fast as his legs would take him. He got in his car and rushed to the hospital just in time to meet the doctor coming out of her room.

Still not sure of the situation, he asked, "How is she, Dr. Bridges?"

The doctor, with a surprised look, said, "Well, she's fine, Reverend."

E couldn't help but repeat the words back to the doctor. "She's fine?"

Dr. Bridges, looking more positive, announced, "Yes, fine."

Elise, who was sitting by Miss Bernice, got up and gave E a big hug. E insisted, "Honey, why don't you go home and I'll stay here tonight?"

Relieved and exhausteded, E slumped into the chair by Miss Bernice and fell sound asleep. At three in the morning, he was startled by Miss Bernice's hand patting him. She had a big smile. She was still too weak to speak, but her face said a thousand words. She was touched that he had stayed there beside her, and a small tear trickled down her cheek and was caught in the wrinkle of her smile. Robert Browning once wrote, "Ah, but a man's reach should exceed his grasp, or what's a heaven for?" Ethan Moses had touched many lives already in his young life. But he had just begun.

As soon as fall came around, Oswald took a turn for the worse, so the doctor told the family to gather in. Miss Clark sat there, thinking that she didn't have enough time with him. They had enjoyed each other's company so much and she couldn't help but think how lonely she would be without him.

As she sat there, E came over, hugged her, and said, "Miss Margaret, I know what you're thinkin,' and don't. You have a family now, and no matter what, we'll always be a family." She smiled at his spiritual intuition and realized that he had grown very deep in his faith and walked with great power.

As she held Oswald's hand, she looked over at E and said, "He's gone."

Everyone gathered around the bed and E decided the most appropriate thing to do was pray. "God, your love comforts us. When all hope is gone, you carry us. You are the giver of every breath we breathe, but we are alive because we are alive in you. My father might be dead to this life, but he is very much alive in your presence. He will always have a great place in our hearts and we can hardly wait to see him again. Thank you, Pap, for giving us a living example of how to live our lives. Thank you for your unpretentious, simple way of seeing through the vain clutter of life. We love you, Pap, and the grave will not change that. Rest in peace until we meet again. Amen."

E turned to Margaret Clark and thanked her for making his father's last days happy ones. He also told her that she was moving in with them.

"No, E, I can't accept, but I will expect you to visit often and every holiday," she said with a smile. Then she continued, "I love your father and I'm going to miss him immensely, but I'll be fine. Remember, I've lived alone before."

E and Elise stayed at that church for three more years and had their first child while there. Faith was a beautiful baby—seven pounds exactly. At three months old, she was sleeping all night. She had big, beautiful, blue eyes and blond hair like her mother. She was the apple of her daddy's eye.

Growth Pains

The third year, E decided to invite an old friend to lead the revival at Sweet Briar. The church was getting ready to build a new sanctuary because they had well outgrown the old one.

"Shawn, it's so good to see you after so many years! So how've you been?" E asked.

Dr. Shawn Hazlitt answered, "Doin' great, E. It's good to see you, too!" Shawn had gone on to finish his doctorate, took a large pastorate in the west, and had written several books. He had also been teaching in a Bible college for the past few years.

"Shawn, I opened up a large can of worms three nights ago. We were having cottage prayer meetings to get ready for this revival. A woman came to the meeting with her eight-year-old daughter. She was very nervous and asked if she could talk with me in private. As I listened, she told me through tears about her little girl's brain tumor. The doctors gave her no hope, saying that it was inoperable and the little girl had six months, at best, to live. I could just see my little girl sitting there. What could I do? Well, I wasn't going to play around. I never felt the power of God so strongly, so I anointed her on the forehead with some olive oil and had everyone lay hands on her and we prayed for complete healing. By the time the story got around to the church, it took on a life of its own and probably picked up things that didn't really happen. Anyway, the chairman of the deacons called me last night and they want to talk with me this afternoon. I just wanted you to know what you're stepping in here," E stated.

Shawn just looked at E and said, "Thank you, Lord, for bringing me here. Now I know why. There's hope for the hopeless, grace, forgiveness, mercy, and healing to the brokenhearted and the down and out. Now I know why God gave me the sermon topic, 'How far do we have to fall?'"

E just looked at him, smiled, and said, "I'll let you know how far I fall," as he raised his eyebrows.

Three hours later, E stepped into the cramped office where six deacons were waiting like vultures on a branch. Mr. Leonard would have made it seven, but he chose to stay away since he had been at the cottage meeting and had no problem with what had happened.

"Brother E," said Ray Winnow, chairman of the deacons. "I wanna get right into this and get it over with. We all agree here that we don't want to lose you as our preacher. You've been instrumental in getting this church back on track. However, if you'll take a seat, I'll read what the deacons in attendance want you to do for us. First no more 'laying on of hands' and no talk from the pulpit about healing, deliverance, or them spiritual gifts. Second, no talk about how we need to love our neighbors no matter what color, creed, values, or position they have. And thirdly and most importantly, the deacons will make all arrangements for any speaker, singer, or evangelist that wants to stand behind our pulpit. Now if you're in agreement to these things, just nod and we'll be on our way."

E smiled at the curtness in Ray's voice—the same Ray that cried in E's arms when he lost his father. E paced back and forth in the small room, looking intently in each man's face. Several minutes went by without a sound from E. Then he stopped dead in his tracks, looked Ray right in the eyes, and said, "Nothing in this world stunts our spiritual growth like fear, and nothing edifies our spirit and starts the healing process like love. What I did for that little girl was out of love. You men are talking out of fear. Sometimes fear causes us to use a destructive power and equate it with success." Then he paused for a second and stated, "No, I will not give you a nod of 'okey dokey.' The reason why is clear—it's not my call to make. So if that's all fellas, I have a revival to get ready for."

Ray was getting red as a beet, but he was determined to have resolution before anyone left. "No. Now pastor, we haven't called this meeting adjourned. It's either the list or else," Ray demanded, trying to corner E.

"Well then, Ray, I guess it's the 'or else.'" E stated with resolve as he turned and walked out.

As soon as E was out the door, Joe Thomas crawled Ray for making such an unyielding statement of intent and said, "Now, you've gone and done it. It'll get around the church that we ran him off. Do you want his blood on your hands, Ray? Do you really want to split the church?"

Ray had just realized what he had said, but he was not the type to say he was wrong or apologize. "If he's a mind to leave, then let him go!" he proclaimed as the others just shook their heads.

"Well, Shawn, they wanted me to denounce what we did the other night along with a laundry list of other gripes and grievances. I told them it wasn't my call."

Shawn just shook his head, smiled, and said, "E, people wear masks to try to navigate our world or fit in, but not you."

E replied, "Masks are to keep our true identities secret because we fear being judged or fear losing love and respect. It says in Psalms that God discerns my going out and my lying down; He's familiar with all my ways. There's no need to forget that. We might be going into unfamiliar territory, but it's not unfamiliar to God. And forgetting who we are in Christ is serious. Very serious."

Shawn interjected, "A little infant has arms and hands, but it's quite a while before they figure out they have them, and then more time goes by before they realize what wonderful tools they are. These men are like infants, not realizing what wonderful tools God has gifted them with and what power He has given them to make those tools work."

E just smiled in agreement as they walked around the edge of the yard toward the front porch. A few minutes went by while Shawn and E sat down on the porch, then E said, "Shawn, I think God wants us to have a 'walk-on-water' faith. What intrigues me about the story of Peter walking on water is his faith. First, you think he's resistant to any belief, but then he shows a bold expression of faith, asking Christ to let him walk to him. The others didn't do that. So he's cheered on by Christ with a prompt answer, 'Come!' What faith it must've taken to descend from the vessel, set foot on stormy water, and walk over to Christ. We also see where his faith evaporated. 'When he saw that the wind was boisterous, he became afraid.' Fear overtook his faith! That's where most of us live, Shawn—alternating between a calm trust in Christ and a cowardly fear of circumstance."

Shawn smiled and shook his head up and down promptly. Soon it was revival time and the house was packed. As soon as E and Shawn entered, the dull roar of the crowd quickly quieted to a few cackling voices, including old Mrs. Hensley. She was giving her views on some important issue that couldn't yield to reverence.

E got up behind the pulpit and said, "It's good to have all y'all out tonight for the starting of our revival. Dr. Shawn Hazlitt and I went to seminary together. He's a good friend that's been preaching out west and doing some teaching as well. It's so good to have you, and thank you for coming. As soon as the special music's over, I will invite Dr. Hazlitt to come up and address us."

The first night was over without a hitch and Shawn, E, Elise, and little Faith all walked back to the parsonage together. The next morning uneventfully started at the dining table. Elise had cooked breakfast and brought everything to the table.

She looked at them with their deep thoughts and serious faces and said, "We get so caught up in things, we forget to have fun. Laughing and playing aren't frivolous things just for kids, guys! Our joy in Christ is the most undeniable evidence of our faith in God. It's His gift to you when you renew your faith in God's unshakable and protective love. Enjoy it!" Then she shuffled off to the kitchen.

E just looked over at Shawn, started laughing, and said, "She does that to me all the time. When I get too serious or too full of myself or even when I get depressed, she's always there to thump me on the head! The Holy Spirit might be saying it to me, but Elise is my confirmation and she's a loud one." Both men laughed and decided that they had to do something that was fun. E grabbed his fishing tackle and said, "I know just the place for us to release some tension and maybe catch some supper."

The second night of revival went well with five people coming forward for baptism. Afterward E decided that they would all go to see the little girl who had caused so much commotion.

"Susan, this is the revival preacher I told you about," E stated with a kind smile. The beautiful little girl smiled and melted Shawn's heart. E said, "Susan, I know you're probably sad, but I just wanna say this illness is not you. It doesn't define you as a person. You're a child of God and that means you have His qualities."

He looked around the room and tears were falling from everyone. Elise went over and hugged Susan tight, and then Susan said, "I don't know why everyone's so sad. I know God healed me."

Susan's father looked at E and Elise with red eyes and said, "We wanted you to be the first to know that these tears are not tears of despair; they're tears of joy. The doctor's are completely stumped. They x-rayed her twice today and found nothing, not even a scar.

They're out there scratching their heads now, wondering if it could be their film or some other anomaly."

E just broke down, crying. Elise came over to give him a hug and she started to cry as well. They both looked at Susan at the same time and noticed a peace on her face that was not physical. She believed, and that was that. E and Elise learned a lot that day looking at her simple, childlike faith, and they realized that God was giving them a revelation, something they could apply to their own lives for years to come. Shawn was shaken too and went out to see for himself the X-rays and to talk to the doctors.

You would think the news would be good at Sweet Briar, but it was the contrary. After the revival was finished and Shawn was gone, the deacons started another jacquerie. This time they decided they would get their way. Ray had gone over to talk to one of the little girl's doctors and believed the first X-ray was faulty. He came back to report to the group his findings. God gives you lessons in your life. If you don't listen the first time, He brings them around again. And the lessons become harder and have more consequences each time. Sweet Briar had not learned a very important lesson. God is not bound by traditions or very narrow views of His truth. E was God's anointed man and those deacons were treading on shaky ground. E had been the salvation of that church. In fact, attendance was up three hundred percent. He and Elise had served them selflessly. Yet they were ready to judge the best pastor they'd ever had.

Arrogance had caught up with them and it ranted and raved, "Do it our way, or else." The word had been handed down almost like a death sentence—not for E, like they would think, but for the church. It was written up, typed, and handed to E with a place for him to sign. By not signing, he immediately forfeited his position and was to take the letter as his notice of termination.

First, his stomach twisted into a dozen knots and then he realized that the prize was in the moment…in that seemingly bad moment. He suddenly realized that God was getting him ready for the next step in his ministry. He began to get nervous, but then a scripture came to him. "Saul said to the servant who was with him, 'Come, let's go back, or my father will stop thinking about the donkeys and start worrying about us.' But the servant replied, 'Look, in this town there is a man of God; he is highly respected, and everything he says comes true. Let's go there now. Perhaps he will tell us what way to take.'" *What could that mean?* E wondered. Then he knew through a revelation of the Spirit: Saul was out looking for donkeys, but God had something else in mind.

E decided to go to the deacons individually in an effort to resolve the problems. When he went to Ray, he could sense the rage as he stood before him. He got chills as he looked at his face and noticed pitch-blackness. He was seeing in the Spirit, and there was evil afoot as Azazel had his way with Ray.

E asked with humility, "Well, I guess you've made up your mind, haven't you?"

Ray stiffened with defiance as he leered at E in disgust and stated, "No, if you sign the paper, things can go back like they were."

E chided, "Don't you see that's not possible? You act like everything is based on circumstance, and it's not. That's God's call and He's in control of my actions."

Ray challenged, "Well then, if He's in total control of you, maybe He's telling you to leave."

E looked at him with a penetrating stare and conceded, "Maybe He is." E left, thinking Ray was right for once.

"Elise, the deacons are trying to force me to sign that dimwitted paper again. This time there's no out. They're saying that my termination is imminent if I don't sign," E said to her, sighing with frustration.

"E, hasn't God always been faithful to us? I'm not worried. But what do ya think it means?" Elise asked with a solemn face.

E looked at her with a half smile and said decisively, "I think He's getting us ready for something new. He gave me a scripture today about Saul out looking for donkeys. Saul just ran right into his destiny."

Elise said, "Oh, it wasn't by chance, E. And I will agree, He's getting you ready for something new, my ole' donkey hunter!" she exclaimed with the quick laugh that she had made her own.

"Ha, ha. Well, you might not laugh if I can't put food on the table," E replied, raising a skeptical brow.

"Well, I guess we could go live with Miss Margaret," Elise said, as she shuffled off to check on Faith.

"Miss Clark, that's it! I need to go talk with her!" he brightly exclaimed as he jumped up.

A Word to the Wise

It had been several weeks since Miss Clark had talked to him on the phone, so she was glad to see him. "Sit down and tell me what's goin' on," she said.

As they sat in the parlor, he poured out his heart to her, telling her about the little girl and the letter that the deacons wanted him to sign. But she seemed distant, almost uncaring. He tried not to think such thoughts, but he couldn't help himself. She was not concentrating on his words and the only thing that would come to his mind was that she was losing hers. He stopped talking for a moment to see what she would do.

She slowly turned to look him straight in his face and said, "I was wondering when you might tell me in all of your yammerin' if there's some purpose to this? I know that you realize there is"—she paused—"purpose." After she said it, she smiled at him.

"So what're ya sayin,' Miss Clark?" E asked.

"E, you know as well as I do that you were never meant to be at that church for very long. Now, I realize that being on the road all the time is a big strain on a new marriage, but don't be deceived. God has bigger plans for you. And I'm not completely convinced it's being an evangelist," Miss Clark said enthusiastically as she flashed her eyes at him, making him wonder what insight she was privy to.

E laughed heartily and said, "Boy, you scared me for a minute. I thought you had really lost your mind!"

They both laughed while she asked one of her housemaids to get them some lemonade. "Look, E, all you have to do now is put your future in God's hands. He'll never let you down. You tell those deacons they don't have the brains that God gave a billy goat. You, Elise, and little Faith are coming to stay with me until God's timing is complete. And don't you say no. I won't hear of it. Besides, it'll give an old woman some great company and make me very happy," she commanded with great resolve.

E smiled at her and conceded as Miss Clark shoved a glass of cold lemonade in his hand. He knew it was pointless to fight the tenacious and highly spirited old woman; besides, he knew it was the right move. "Whoo! It's hotter 'n the hinges of Hades in here," she said as she took a big sip of lemonade. "Martha, get those fans revved up!"

"You ever read John twenty-one, where Jesus appeared to the disciples by the water after His resurrection?" E asked.

She lifted and pushed together her eyebrows, pursed her lips, and answered, "Don't think I have."

E continued, "Well, I was thinkin' about that story today. They're out there doing what they'd done in the past—fishing. After all, Jesus wasn't there to follow anymore, so they didn't know what to do with themselves. We often go back to what's familiar when God has something bigger in mind."

Miss Clark asked, "So what are you thinking? That this is one of those times?"

E replied, "Maybe." As they sipped their lemonade, E stated, "And ya' know, there's something else about that story that's strange. There Jesus was with a fire and coals and everything and even some fish, but he told them to bring some of their own fish. What do you think that means? This is Jesus we're talking about. He didn't need their fish."

Miss Clark laughed and said, "I can tell you this for sure, you're a deep thinker!" They both laughed and she said, "I know that Jesus didn't need their help, but what if He's saying, 'I desire for you to be a part of this, not because I want you to work, but because I want you to be blessed'?"

E smiled and shook his head affirmatively, realizing that she had come to the same conclusion he did. After seeing Miss Clark, it was time for him to face the music. While he was gone, the whole church community was stirred up. Soon the lines had been drawn and E saw an inevitable split in the church.

E hugged Elise as they sat on the porch swing. Several minutes went by before either one said anything. Then E broke the silence with, "A weary mountain climber, high up in the mountains, was trying to reach the very top peak. While he was climbing one of several narrow, rocky paths in his quest, he met a wise man. In frustration, he asked the wise man which of the many paths would take him to the summit. The wise man pondered the question for several minutes and then replied, 'It's simple, just make sure that every step you take goes up, and you'll reach your goal.' Elise, I can't let this split the church. We've got to make sure that doesn't happen." E was going to make sure he kept his walk on the "high road." Every step he took was going to be a step up. He and Elise talked about it some more and prayed fervently.

The next day was Sunday and you would have thought it was Easter. People came out of the woodwork to see the big showdown. E totally avoided everyone before services and quickly entered his study and put his *Counseling Session—Please Do Not Disturb* sign on the door. At a quarter to eleven, he quietly cracked the door to make sure no one was lurking and quickly shot inside the sanctuary and positioned himself in his chair. As the pianist played, he made sure not to make eye contact with anyone.

Soon the music stopped and he walked slowly up to the pulpit and recited part of his favorite hymn. "Thy bountiful care, what tongue can recite? It breathes in the air, it shines in the light, it streams from the hills, it descends to the plain and sweetly distills in the dew and the rain." He looked down for a few seconds and then said, "I know that many of you have heard that I'm thinkin' about leaving. Well, I want to say it has nothing to do with you. I took this pastorate because I thought it was what God wanted me to do, and to tell you the truth, I welcomed it because I believed that being on the road all the time would not be good for a new family. However, God has made it very clear to me that He gives me what I need and He makes everything good. So the rumor's true—I'm leaving to complete that which God has called me to do. I hereby give the church three weeks notice, as agreed to in our bylaws. This church will always be special to us, and we both thank you from the bottom of our hearts for allowing us to be a part of you for over three years. Now enough of that … let's get down to some worship." E motioned for the special music to begin.

After the service, Mr. Clayton, vice chairman of the deacons, came almost in a gallop to where E was. "E, I want to shake your hand," he said. "I've been around for a long time, but you have to be one of the most Spirit-filled men I've ever known. You took something that could've been a disaster and made it into something beautiful. That's very God-like, you know? My heart was hurting for this church, Pastor, but now I know we'll make it through."

Mr. Leonard came up to him after everyone had left and hugged him. "Brother, I'm gonna miss ya. These people don't realize what went on, but I do. And I wanna apologize. You're a God-fearing man who I will never forget. They don't know what they …" he said as he wiped his eyes with this shirtsleeve. He wanted to say more, but the emotion of the moment got to him, so he smiled, slowly turned, and went out the door.

Elise was watching E from the corner of the sanctuary. She had been reading Shakespeare's *All's Well That Ends Well* and she was thinking about what the king said. " … see that you come, not to woo honor, but to wed it." Although it's not exactly what Shakespeare meant, she had wed honor and she couldn't be happier.

Patience is a Virtue

Weeks had gone by without one call. Did he zig when he should have zagged? Nevertheless, E had a fire that was building in him with no place to burn. God was doing something new in his spirit, but patience had to be a hard-learned virtue for both of them as they waited day by day.

Three months later, on a Saturday afternoon, a black Nash drove up to Miss Clark's house. E was writing in the study like there was no tomorrow, Elise was rocking little Faith to sleep, and Miss Clark was ordering her cook around the kitchen. Elise, hearing a knock, put Faith in her crib and looked out the side window then flew down the hallway and quickly swung open the door.

"Daddy!" she said, as she hugged Jakob tightly. Miriam got out next and they all hugged and greeted one another.

"So how are things, E?" Jakob asked.

Everyone stopped talking to listen to E's reply. He looked at everyone and said, "I knew that you were coming today and it has something to do with our future. I sensed it when I was praying this morning."

Jakob was amazed at E's spiritual perception and said, "E, you'd be right about our trip—it does concern y'all, but I wasn't totally convinced until now that it was the right thing to do. You know that we live just northwest of Shreveport in Graceville … It's a spiritually dead area with very few churches until you get into Shreveport. Miriam had this idea that maybe you could plant a church there and we would be some of your first members. It would take a large step of faith, but I think you could do it after hearing you speak."

E didn't know what to say. He was touched by their sentiment, but where in the world would he get the land or the money to build such a church? It was a monumental task, but he decided not to discount it yet. He smiled graciously at them all and nodded.

Just at that moment, Margaret Clark entered the room. "Oh, I'm so glad to see everyone! What a wonderful surprise! Elise, did you know your parents were coming?" she asked with wide eyes.

"No ma'am." Elise answered.

"Well, no matter. Let me go and make preparations for supper. I'll have to put the big pot in the little one!" she said excitedly as she rushed off to the kitchen with her cane.

"Don't go to any trouble for us, Miss Clark. We didn't come to eat," Jakob announced.

"Now don't be silly. It would give me great pleasure to have y'all stay and eat!" she stated as she moved away, not looking back.

E looked over at Elise and smiled. She was already reading his mind. "Say, I have a wonderful idea. Couldn't we all just have a little prayer meeting right here before supper?" she asked, looking at her father.

"You know, that's a great idea, Elise," said Miriam, and Jakob agreed with a grin.

So they all gathered around the table in the dining hall and held hands. E started the prayer and it went around the table until it got to Elise. She prayed, "God, we're not putting you to a test. If anything, we're asking you for perseverance and patience while we wait. We want your timing and we want your will and your hand to be on this." The second she finished, the phone rang.

"E, pick up the phone!" Miss Clark shouted from the other room.

"Hello," E answered apprehensively. "Well, hey, Jas. How are you? Yes, yes,"—he gave a long pause—"Are you sure that's what you wanna do? Well yes, we do. Okay...well, good to hear your voice too. Bye," E said as he hung up the phone.

Elise was about to pop with anticipation. E looked at the group with a sad face and then all of the sudden he smiled and said, "We got it! We got the land! And it's close to Graceville!" Solemn faces were not what he expected. "Oh, come on, I was just messing with ya!" he exclaimed.

Elise looked at him with a scowl and asked, "You're just kidding about the land, right?"

E said, "No, no. That's all true. You know the family land that Stout left Jasper? Well, Jasper wants us to have it for whatever God's planning!" Again, he looked around and everyone was looking away with solitary stares. He said, "What's wrong with y'all? This is great news!"

Miriam looked up at E with a pleasant smile, but tears were running down her cheeks. She said, "E, I'm just so touched by this. I'm just embarrassed."

E looked at her and asked, "Embarrassed?"

She shook her head and continued, "I have to tell you, I never expected God to act so promptly." Jakob was touched too and he agreed with a nod.

"Now, come on, Mom and Pop, you can't douse this great news with apprehensions or fears; this is a time for joy!" Elise said with great enthusiasm.

"You're right!" Miriam said as she got up to hug everyone.

Jakob got up and shook E's hand and said, "Now, what do we need to do to make room for everyone at the house?"

At that very moment, E heard God's voice say, *Moses answered them, "Wait until I find out what the Lord commands concerning you."* E remembered that verse in Numbers and said to Jakob, "We'll wait until we hear from God."

Yet more waiting for E and Elise, but God didn't keep them waiting long. The phone rang in the parlor of the large house three days later. "Hello," E answered. It was the planner of a men's retreat in North Carolina. They needed him to be one of the speakers for the week if he was available. The man that they had scheduled had to go in for surgery. It had to be what they were waiting for.

"Well, I'll have to talk to my wife and of course pray about it," E stated with enthusiasm. As he got off the phone, he jumped so high that he almost touched the ten-foot ceiling.

Mountaineering

The mountain air was crisp and dry, and the sky was a deep ultra-marine blue as they pulled up to what seemed to be a dream. It was a beautiful setting—a placid lake at the foot of three mountain peaks. Cabins embedded into the sides of the slopes. A trellised bridge spanned the lake on the far end that led to a path that meandered up the mountainside to a bright green knoll. The whole picture from where they parked was so meticulously manicured, E found it hard to see how heaven could be an improvement. It was fall, and the colors of the leaves up the sides of the mountains were breathtaking. A trickling brook not far away made fitting sounds as the water found its way over the worn rocks and down to the lake below.

"Are those horses?" E asked, as they retrieved their luggage for a brisk walk to the cabins.

"Yes, horseback riding is included," Jason Slate said as he checked them in and gave them their meal vouchers. He continued, "Now, don't be late for supper. Our visiting chef is from the Waldorf Astoria in New York and he's incredible!"

"Come on, Jas, let's set up our bunks. I want the bottom!" E exclaimed hastily, like a little boy at summer camp.

"I still can't believe I let you talk me into this. Now I've left that large church in Florida waiting on my answer for a whole week while I'm up here with you. I was so sure that God wanted Janie and me to be missionaries. We both felt it in our bones, but when our application was thrown out by the denomination because we had two adopted kids and two of our own … well, that was God closing that door very hard and very loud," Jasper said as he got his luggage and met E on the walk down to the cabins.

"Just smell that clean, crisp air!" E said as they walked. "What a great place to renew the spirit, huh, Jas?" he asked, still trying to get Jasper to loosen up and forget his troubles. "Hey, take a look at that slide that goes right into the lake, Jas. That looks like a lot of fun!" E stated with gestures and exaggerated enthusiasm. Jasper just grunted with ambivalence and walked on without examining anything except the ground in front of him.

Soon it was time to eat. E and Jasper went down to the dining hall to see if the hype was anything close to reality, and it far surpassed their expectations. After the night speaker, they sat out under the stars by a large bonfire.

"E, I want to thank you for insisting that I come," Jasper said, breaking the almost holy silence under the stars.

E looked over at Jasper, smiled for a few seconds and said, "Ya know what? I think we're both gonna come away from this mountain closer to God and closer to each other. This really is a special place, isn't it?" Jasper smiled and nodded. E said, "Jesus took Peter, James, and John up to a high mountain, and there before them, He was transfigured. He became dazzling white … 'raiment white as snow,' the Bible says. And they saw Him with Moses and Elijah. And you know, Moses went up a mountain and also had an encounter with God when God gave him the Ten Commandments."

Jasper looked at E for a moment, snickered, and said, "E, you're thinkin' too hard. Relax and enjoy this beautiful night."

E, looking up at the stars, continued, "Oh, I know. But think about it—mountaintop revelations are so common in the Bible. It just makes me wonder what God's up to, that's all." Jasper didn't say anything, but he wondered too as he stared into space.

The next day was filled with a well-planned agenda: breakfast, intensive Bible study, and then small prayer groups. E and Jasper walked up the small trail to a plateau that overlooked the camp. It was the perfect place for prayer. It evoked a reverence for God like no place they knew, and then they understood why God used mountains so much in the Bible.

"E, I will lead and then you can end," Jasper said as he got on his knees and bowed. He prayed for a good thirty minutes and then there was silence. It wasn't a silence to allow E to begin. It was a silence of listening, a silence of reverence in His presence. Jasper was speechless. Nothing would come out. He felt a tightness in his throat as he tried to raise his head but it wouldn't move. E got three words out and found himself in the same predicament. He tried to get up, but all he could do was slightly open his eyes. It was so bright—much brighter than he remembered before he closed his eyes. Soon the grass blades that were a bright green became white. E noticed a shadow that seemed to go to his right and left. And then he realized that the shadow also striped the grass from the top of his head out. He was in the shadow of the cross.

Several seconds went by before E could finally get something out, and he asked, "God, what do you want of me?" Several seconds later God's voice came and it was like a soft rain. *I only want to show you my love, E.* E waited for a few more seconds, but nothing else came, so E asked, "But God, why did you bring me here?" The same response came from God: *To show you my love.*

E waited a few more seconds and then he asked, "What do I do, Lord? Where do I go? I want to follow you, but I need to know what to do." This time there was no pause before God commanded, *If you're following, then be content in knowing I'm in charge. I brought you out of bondage and slavery. Behold, I am going to send an angel before you to bring you to the place I have prepared.*

And then it was all over. The bright light was gone; the shadow of the cross was gone. E got up and sat there on the grass. Jasper, still visibly shaken from the celestial adventure, took longer getting his bearings. For several minutes, they just sat there looking into the lake below as the clouds and sky reflected in the water. Finally, E looked over at Jasper and said nervously, "That was interesting."

Jasper just shook his head affirmatively without eye contact. They finally made their way back down from the mountain and soon sat at a table to eat lunch. Both men were very silent while they ate.

✝

It was time for E to prepare for his turn on stage. The theme of the week was "A Drink Offering," so he decided to speak on 2 Samuel 23:16, which says, "He would not drink it, but poured it out to the Lord."

"Jasper, I figured it out. God is telling me to give all of the blessings back that He has given me. And if I don't, it could corrupt me; it could ruin me and destroy my ministry." Jasper looked at him and said something unrecognizable. "Jasper, did you see the shadow of the cross?" E asked.

"What, what are you talkin' about? All I saw was that man with his hands on your head."

E looked over at Jasper with wide eyes, like he was crazy, and said, "What? You mean you didn't hear God's voice?"

Jasper, with big tears welling up in his eyes, said, "Oh, I heard Him. I still don't know if I can talk about it though."

E had just realized they had different experiences on that mountain. He scooted closer to Jasper and asked, "What did you hear, Jas? What did He say to ya'?"

Jasper, swallowing hard and trying to keep his composure, said, "That me and Janie have been called to be missionaries and I have to stay true to that calling no matter what things look like. Looks can be very deceiving. Oh … and that He doesn't answer to some missionary board."

E asked with great curiosity, "Was that it? I mean, was that all?"

Jasper had been looking away from E's eyes while he was speaking, but he slowly turned, met E's eyes, and said, "No, he said that when you give your blessings back to God, He will give them to me."

E was entranced. He thought this week was for him somehow, but it seemed like it was really for Jasper. The next day was a "free day" so they both decided they were going to hike up the mountain. Would they see another epiphany? They couldn't help but wonder.

"Hey, are y'all goin' hikin' up the mountain?" I said as I seemed to come from nowhere. "My name's Aamir. What's yours?" I asked, as I stuck out my olive-skinned hand. Soon I was a part of the trek up the mountain.

"Hey, Aamir, have you ever had an experience with God that was so unbelievable that you didn't have words to describe it?" E asked.

I looked over at both men and said, "Our words are containers that are inadequate to hold our experiences with God, men. When John was trying to describe his vision of heaven, he probably had that same problem."

Jasper looked over at Aamir and asked, "Aamir, why aren't you sweating and breathing hard like us? You must be in some great shape!" I just laughed.

A few minutes went by in silence and then E asked, "Why do you think God likes to give us great experiences on mountaintops?"

I replied, "Maybe it's the closest to God's perspective that men can have. You get a small glimpse of the big picture." Both men looked over at me and smiled.

After a short pause, I asked, "I don't wanna meddle, but what's this great experience you both had?" Both E and Jasper told me of their experiences and waited for my response. I smiled and said, "Sounds like you both had a real mountaintop experience! However, you've got to follow Jesus back down into that valley. That's where most ministry takes place, you know?"

For the first time, E looked directly into my eyes and thought he recognized something about me, but it wasn't something he could really pinpoint. I quickly looked away from E and continued, "It also sounds like both of you have contained God into what's predictable and boring, and God's anything but boring and never predictable. You know, Peter tried to contain and confine Jesus when he said, 'Master, let's build three booths here . . .' We have to open our minds to God's abilities and then we'll see supernaturally. God is definitely getting both of you ready for a deeper walk with Him."

E, mystified by my great pearls of wisdom, tried to look into my eyes and asked, "Well, Aamir, what do you think God meant when He said I was to give my blessings to Jas?"

I smiled, looked off into the distance, and answered, "Whatever God's leading you to do will feed what God is leading Jasper to do. I'm sure of it."

Soon, we had reached the peak. The view was breathtaking as we gazed over the landscape, seeing as far as human eyes could reach into the distant, soft blue mountain range. It mesmerized the men to the point of silence as they pondered God's beautiful world from a different viewpoint.

"So *this* is what God sees?" Jasper asked.

E chuckled and I asked, "Whata ya thinkin,' E?"

E answered, "Oh, all of the sudden, I got this picture in my head."

Jasper, who was looking over the edge at the camp below, worked his way over to E and asked, "Okay, E, let's hear it. Share with us this funny picture that's in that funny head of yours."

E answered, "Well, I was just imagining ole' Nimrod on top of his puny tinker-toy tower to the heavens, and there he was, probably screaming to the top of his lungs, 'I am god! I am in control of my destiny!' And to God, he probably sounded like some high-pitched rodent on top of Popsicle sticks. How funny and pathetic he probably looked to God!" We all laughed and nodded our heads in affirmation. We finally made our way back down the mountain just in time for lunch.

"Boy, I'm famished. Let's change and get over to eat," Jasper said.

So they all went into the cabin to get ready. "Hey, where's Aamir?" E asked Jasper.

"Wasn't he with you?" Jasper asked. They both looked at each other then ran over to the door to take a look, but there was no Aamir.

"Nope, no Aamir. In fact, there's only two middle-eastern men registered," answered Jason. "We do have a Jewish Christian speaker for the lunch hour tomorrow though!"

"Well, that has to be him then," Jasper stated with resolve.

"No, his name is Joseph," Jason announced, with brows raised.

The two men just looked at each other for several minutes and then E said, "I thought I recognized him. I looked into his eyes and something looked familiar. Jas, you don't think he could have been that angel that God mentioned, do you?" Jasper didn't say a word, he just kept eating. But his expression said everything as his face grew pale and his posture slumped.

"Well?" E continued, trying to get a response.

"I don't wanna think about it," Jasper quickly said. After a few more seconds, Jasper asked, "You said you recognized him?"

E looked over at Jasper with a sinister grin and said, "I thought you didn't wanna talk about it." Jasper pursed his lips, shook his head, and continued eating.

A few more minutes later, Jasper said, "Okay, my imagination is gettin' the best of me. Tell me what you know."

E started, "You remember me telling you about the man that picked me up when I was out of gas?" Jasper just nodded. "I think the man's the same . . . well, not the same in appearance, but I think he was—"

Jasper interrupted. "No, no, wait a minute. How can he be the same and not the same? Don't pull my leg, E! I thought you said that man was white?"

E, laughing, said, "Well anyway, I think he was the same guy and I think he was an angel."

Jasper, still somewhat white from the whole experience asked, "Do you think we'll see him again? Because I don't think I can face him. This whole thing is gettin' a little too weird and crazy."

E, trying to calm Jasper, said, "No, I doubt he'll show again. I think we're to take what he told us and apply it, though."

Jasper asked, "Can you remember all he said?"

"I think so," E answered.

John Fredrich waited for quiet before he addressed the crowd at lunch. "As you all know, this retreat is non-denominational, non-racial, non-status, and non-confrontational. We're not here to talk about the five percent that we disagree on; we're here to talk about the ninety-five percent we do agree on and to show God we can 'play well together.' Psalm 133:1–3 says how good and pleasant it is for brothers to dwell in unity. It's like precious oil upon the head. It's like the dew coming down upon the mountains of Zion. Worship him this week and see how He blesses unity. There's a reason you're here, men. I've been coming since the beginning and it always amazes me how God transforms lives, starts new ministries, builds bridges, and shows His great love here on this mountain. Now I want to call on Joe Bennett to pray for our meal and anything else he feels inclined to add. Brother Bennett…"

Soon Joe Bennett climbed the steps to the podium and started, "We come as broken men in search of God's purpose to this mountain. In this very building, there are two men who have heard from God today. They're wondering what to do now, so here's a poem that God gave me just a few minutes ago for them. I call it, "The Pearl Rose."

In the heart of the earth, a seed was anointed with oil.
God buried it deep inside; pitch black as night
A tiny plant lay fast asleep in the confining soil.
"Wake," said God, "And reach to my light.
Dance with delight in my rain and my toil."
Perplexed was the whole world.
A tender shoot could break free the confines
Of hardened hearts and minds.
"Breathe, my chosen seed unfurled.
Breathe and bloom, my lovely flower of pearl.
Grow in the Son and in His warm embrace.
You will be my fragrant rose, full of grace."

He continued, "God is so good. Let's all endeavor to live for Him. Let's pray." Bowing, he said, "Father, in our secret place, in the depths of our very souls, help us to know you, to touch you, to see your face. You're everything we hope for, everything we live for, and everything we need. Thank you for the road that brought us here. Bless this food and bless this day that you have made. Amen."

As Joe walked down from the platform, you could have heard a pin drop. God's strong presence was everywhere. E's eyes were full of tears as he tried to compose himself. Jasper sat there with his head bowed low. Somehow, the wonderful food that was before them paled in comparison to the wonderful washing of grace that they all just shared. God held them all close, feeding them spiritual bread.

Walking toward the conference center to hear the afternoon speaker, Jasper finally composed himself and asked, "And you thought this week was just for me? That poem was directed at you, my friend. Wasn't it?"

E, trying not to get emotional, answered, "The breeze did seem to blow my way."

"All right, what are you not telling me?" Jasper asked as his eyes winced.

"God was speaking to me the whole time that man was talking. How does He do that?" E asked, looking far off into the distance.

"What do you mean?" Jasper asked.

E continued, "If two people were talking to you at the same time, could you understand them both? I did! That man would say something and then God would say something on top of it. How do you explain that?"

Jasper just smiled and asked, "So what did He, or they, say?"

E looked over at Jasper and said, "Well, my friend, the weight of the world has been on our shoulders, but God told me that he was taking that heavy load off. In fact, he never wanted us to take on such a load anyway. We're to do one thing and one thing only."

Jasper asked, "Well, what is it?"

E answered, "Be available to God."

Jasper looked at E with a tilted head and raised brow and said, "That's it?"

E motioned for Jasper to take a walk with him outside before the speaker started and said, "No, there's more. The church is to be called "Pearl Rose" and it's already been planted on that land you gave me. I'm to pastor the church for thirty-three years and no longer."

Jasper's eyes were getting bigger and bigger, and then he asked, "So where do I come in?"

E looked in Jasper's eyes, smiled, and said, "Well, you're the ole' junkyard dog, of course, and I'm to give you scraps every day!"

Jasper just shook his head and said, "Come on, E, tell me."

E, looking more serious, said, "You and Janie *are* to be missionaries and my church will be the first of twelve to fund your efforts. In fact, God said that you would eventually have a Bible school for young pastors and an orphanage, too." Jasper was now looking into the distance himself and smiling.

After several seconds, Jasper asked, "So that's what He was talkin' about on the mountain?" E just nodded up and down, and they both just sat there pondering it all until the bell rang to be seated.

The rest of the week was a relaxing calm in contrast to the fear of the unfamiliar early on. It was as if God was massaging His message in with subtle experiences, reminding them of His love, His promise, and His unending provision.

Streams in the Desert

"…the eyes of the blind will be opened and the ears of the
deaf unstopped. Then will the lame leap like a deer, and the
mute tongue shout for joy. Water will gush forth in the wilderness and streams in the desert"

Isaiah 35:5–6. (NIV)

The year was 1940 and the South was trying its best to move past
the Great Depression. After all, it had been over ten years since
Black Tuesday and ten is symbolic for completeness. The average
salary was $1,299 in America. Antarctica had been discovered as a
continent, and everyone was looking forward to a brighter future.
However, looming ominously in the air were rumors and fears that
the war in Europe would inevitably become their own.

It had been three busy years since the men's retreat. E and Jasper
were ready to see progress on the new church. E continued to be
an evangelist, saving his money to put toward the building project.
Jasper had decided to take the church in Florida, only as a means
to an end. He realized that he needed to be on the mission field

as soon as God opened that door. E met Jasper in March and they started praying together while they walked around the property by Cross Lake.

"We have to continue to remind ourselves that God says this is His work and we only have to make ourselves available," E said, as he sat on a stump near the building site.

After Jasper took a big drink of water from his canteen, he responded, "I really have no idea how He's going to pull this off, E."

"Well, buddy, if we saw the whole picture, I'm sure we would try to get ahead of God. No doubt in my mind. Jas, I've saved enough to get the framing done on the sanctuary, but that's it," E stated, as he pulled out lunch from Elise's picnic basket. "Jakob's contributed so much to this project already and he's givin' us our lumber out of his sawmill at a third the going rate. We should be able to get all the framing up and then we're going to have to raise more money."

Maybe the great winds of the Dust Bowl had receded from the prairie lands, but the great winds of evil had not. They would have to face some difficult times ahead and they knew it. Graceville was the closest town to the church land and it had a large train depot. As the men finalized plans and did some more prospecting, they both made their way to the depot.

"Jasper, I appreciate ya, brother. I do. Have a good trip back to Florida and give Janie a kiss for me," E said, as he watched the train release steam beneath its wheels and slowly pull away from the station.

Jasper was on his way back to Florida, and E had a couple of hours to wait for his train. The smell of coal smoke was in the air as he watched Jasper's train disappear down the tracks. He sat there thinking about the future, trying his best to imagine what it would be like.

E saw a water fountain close by, so he walked toward it for a drink. As he looked down, he noticed a sign that said, "Coloreds"; then he heard a voice running toward him, "Stop! You can't drink from that fountain. It's for coloreds, mista!"

E just looked at the small, stringy black woman and said, "The water I drink is for everyone. We're all children of God, you know." She looked at him like he was crazy, but he continued, "In the book of John, it says everyone who drinks this water will be thirsty again, but whoever drinks the water that Jesus gives will never thirst again. And that water becomes a spring welling up to eternal life."

The woman was visibly shaken by God's Word as she looked at the ground. There was a colored section on trains and on buses. Coloreds could sit in those places, but whites could sit anywhere. She saw yet another injustice when E took a drink from her fountain. At that moment, E was given a word from God about her. She was an alcoholic with three kids at home. Her husband had left her, and when she caught up with him, he was in prison. The whole world seemed to look down on blacks, and even most blacks looked down on women in her position. The only consolations she had in life were the borders and barriers that gave her some small drop of freedom and privilege.

As he looked into her blood-shot eyes, his heart broke in two. He could see the pain and unrest in her spirit. Then he said, "He's the only one who can give peace and rest. In fact, He's the only one who gives freedom and privilege. Be still and know that He is God. Rest in His holiness and in His comfort."

She quickly got her composure back and exclaimed, "How's somebody likes you knows what I goes through? Yous've no idea, mista!"

E looked into her eyes and solemnly said, "I know about your kids. I know that your husband's in prison. I know that God is concerned about you and He loves you." She had tried to cover her broken heart with rage, but E had broken through her facade. She just stood there with tears streaming down her stoic face.

After several seconds she asked, "So how'd you knows 'bout me? Yous a part of tha Klan or sumpin'? You gonna run mes out a heow?" Somehow she couldn't get it in her mind that E really cared for her. She knew that there had to be some agenda or sinister purpose behind his concern. After all, she was not used to anyone caring, especially a white man. Before he could answer, she said, "Well, you won't haves to worry 'bouts me much longer, mista!" At that moment, E got another word from God. She was going to end her life. She had been planning it for weeks.

E looked at her again and said, "You know in your spirit that I have no ill will toward you. You also know that I was not sent to deal with you by man. The one that sent me loves you and doesn't want you to do what you've planned. It's hard to be free if you don't reach and accept true freedom when it's offered. It's hard to believe if you don't trust, and it's hard to see when the rain's pouring down so strongly on top of you. But the Son can shine through that hard rain. And true freedom is not given by man or country. That freedom's from God and it will make you free indeed. Nothing compares to the greatness of knowing His love and His freedom. Don't live for the day. Live knowing that days exist for you. Don't look at the world as some prison. Break free from that bondage that Satan has put you in. You're free to live in great privilege. Through Him, there's no longer a land of darkness—only light." As he continued to witness to her, pointing out John 3:16 and other verses in the Bible, she began to glow. It started slowly in her eyes and moved down to her lips as they expanded into a pleasant grin. Then her whole being was enveloped in joy and peace.

"Are you ready to pray to receive what Jesus has for you?" E asked. She just shook her head yes, crying incessantly as E led her into the very presence of the King. She was a new creation and he knew it as they got off their knees. "Now, I want you to continue to pray that God reveal things to you and when I get the church built, I want you to feel free to come," E stated with kindness.

"You don't needs ta be talking to me, preacher. You see those peoples lookin' at us over there? Yo' color decides who yous are in dis town, but talkings to me makes you a doofus. I do 'preciate tha invite to yo' chuch, though, but that would bes a onion act to dos that. And there *is* a land of darkness, and you needs to stay out of it. Do ya wanna be called a n———lover? I's get into a good colored chuch. I promise."

E asked, "Could I ask your name?"

She looked at him, smiled, and said, "Mary."

"Mary, I'm available to talk to you any time you need me and you're always welcome at my church and into my home," he said, as he reached into his pocket, pulled out a five-dollar bill, and gave it to her.

She took the money with big eyes and said, "A nickel note! Is you crazy, preacha? Yous can't gimme dis!"

E laughed at her expressiveness and said, "I just did. Now go in peace and know God's grace is sufficient for you." E had found the five-dollar bill on the ground by the train tracks. He knew that God had placed it there to be used; he was just waiting for the right opportunity. In E's mind, there was no such thing as luck and everything had purpose when you walk with God. Mary's chin was raised and her eyes glowed with a new anticipation of a long-sought-after new beginning.

As he sat back on his bench, waiting for his train, he saw a porter coming toward him down the platform. "Sir, are you by chance waitin' for the three-thirty-three to Fort Worth?" he asked, courteously waiting for E's reply.

"Yes, sir, I am," E answered as he nodded.

"Well, sir, you needs not sit out here in this heat and wait. It'll be a good while yet. Come inside to the waitin' area and I'll get you some coffee and a paper," the porter insisted, as he motioned for E to follow him.

Inside the large fans were spinning at maximum speed on the high ceiling. The porter neatly folded the paper with his gloved hands and handed it to E. "Thank you," E said with a nod.

"Now, could I get you some coffee, sir?" the porter asked.

"No, I don't believe, thank you," E answered, wondering why he was getting first-class service.

Soon a stout black man with a porkpie hat came over to him and asked if he would like a shoeshine. "It bees paid for already, mista," he told E as he waited for an answer. E looked around the room to see if he could spot the benevolent donor, but everyone was looking elsewhere.

"Paid for by whom?" E asked.

"Oh, sir, that would bes none a ma business," the man answered as he looked down. E raised his eyebrows and followed the man to his stand in the corner. E was still searching the room for any eye contact but found nothing. Soon the black man had worked up a shine on E's shoes that you could use as a mirror. E reached into his pocket to give him a tip, but he wouldn't accept it.

As E got down, the man said, "Ya know, sir, Mary works here at the depot." E was starting to get the picture, but he was still unclear about why he was being treated royally. Soon his eye caught the eye of a black man seated on the opposite side of the room, tapping his foot to the music that was playing behind the glass window of the stationmaster's quarters. Two white men were seated by him in the section that was called "no man's land." It was not the white section, and it was not the colored section—well away from the potbelly stove and coffee pot.

Soon the old black man approached E slowly. Everyone in the room was watching intently. For a black to confront a white man in the white section was unheard of. "Sir, I wonder if I might talk with you for a moment," the old black man asked with humility. E looked over at the stationmaster behind the window, and he motioned for them to go outside to conduct their business. They walked onto the platform and continued down the long covered area beside the tracks.

"I want ta thank ya, sir, for what you did for that girl," the man said in sincerity.

E looked at him in the eyes, thinking that he might be some angel, and said, "You don't have to thank me. It was my privilege."

The man just smiled with an amusing cackle and said, "Well, I would like to shake your hand anyway, if you don't mind, sir." E looked back toward the depot and noticed that the two men had followed them out and stayed by the doors leading inside.

E put his hand out and asked, "Could I ask your name, sir?"

The man smiled and looked back at the smiling men who were with him. "My name's George. Could I ask for yours, sir?"

E looked at the man and said, "Oh, sure. All my friends call me E."

The man smiled, shook his head up and down, and said, "It's a pleasure to meet you."

Then, one of the men who was standing by the door came over and said, "Dr. Carver, the train's rounding the bend."

George looked over at E and said, "Sir, what's your profession, if I may ask?"

"I'm an evangelist, and I'm planning to build a church at Cross Lake," E answered.

Dr. Carver just nodded and said, "Well, you have a good day, sir, and God bless your efforts."

E smiled and said, "Thank you." The three men went over to the boarding area. E watched them leave as their train followed the curve of the tracks around the bend and slowly out of sight.

Soon E's locomotive thundered into view, pulling a long line of coaches behind it. "All aboard the three-thirty-three to Fort Worth and points in between," the conductor yelled, as the long whistle blew, waking E from a half-sleep. He groggily got aboard as the train came to life with a series of short puffs, sending a plume of black smoke skyward. He was finally headed back toward Texas. He couldn't wait to tell Elise all about his adventures on the rail.

A Birthday Wish

As soon as he walked in the door, she met him with a kiss and exclaimed, "E, honey, you got a letter from your brother!" She was hoping it was good news for E's birthday, which was coming up in less than three weeks.

Many happy returns of the day,

E, I know it's been too long, but I have some wonderful news and it's only God's providence that allows me to share it with you so close to your birthday! First, I want to apologize to you for all my wayfaring. I know that I helped to put our parents in an early grave and I will never forgive myself for that. I'm not sure why you've continued to believe in me when I didn't even believe in myself, but I do appreciate it more than you will ever know, brother. I died several deaths before I was awakened to new life, but I finally made it. As to why my head was so hard or my heart so cold, I have no excuse. However, I can tell you that I'm a new man and proud to be your brother.

I have so much to tell you, so I'm going to give you the most of it in this letter. But you will have to wait to see me to get the rest! I was at the end of my rope when God reached me. What unending love and amazing grace He has! My hope has been secured, and as long as my life endures, I am His.

E, I fell in love with the most beautiful girl when I was a despicable person. Her name is Sarah. I thought I had lost her because of my sinful lifestyle, but she saw something in me that gave her hope. I left her abruptly and tried to make all my wrongs right, but she soon caught up to me, and we have been engaged for three months.

More news—While I was trying to get my bearings, I joined the marine corps. I know you think I'm crazy, but I wanted to be an engineer, and they are sending me to school free of charge. However, now I have a special duty assignment in Europe, so we have to bump up our wedding date. I want to ask you in person if you would marry us on April 30. So keep that in mind.

Love to all,
James

E got a call from James and rejoiced with him over the news of his marriage, but mostly because of his turn back to God. "Of course I'll marry you and Sarah. I wouldn't miss it for the world!" E exclaimed with a giddy laugh.

The weather was perfect on that April day, and old Steeple Creek Church never looked lovelier. "Elise, I would love to give them a nice wedding present, but I don't have any ideas," E said apologetically.

She smiled with bright eyes and asked, "E, don't you still have that old gold coin that your grandpa gave you on his deathbed?" E just went over and kissed her on the cheek as he went to get the old coin out of the bureau.

E was glad to finally meet Sarah and see her brother Robert again. "James, she's absolutely the second most beautiful girl in the world!" E said to James, looking over at Sarah with a wink. Elise looked over at E, giggled, and hit him on the arm.

At the reception, E made a little speech about having his brother back and toasted their marriage. Once again, Mary stepped up to the punch bowl and tapped it with a spoon. Everyone was looking at her as she said, "Brother, I couldn't be happier for you and Sarah. She's the sweetest person I've ever met, except for one that's just a little sweeter. I know that many of you thought you would never see the day that James would get married and many more of you thought you would never see me get married—the old maid."

At that moment, Robert walked up to Mary, put his arm around her, and said, "I've asked Mary to be my wife."

E and Elise ran over and congratulated them both. "How did you even meet Robert?" E asked naively.

Mary answered with a laugh, "At your famous Christmas party, of course, brother!"

Soon James and Sarah were off on their honeymoon to Santa Fe. E took the opportunity to visit the old creek where he had been baptized. As he looked into the water, he heard God's voice. *Don't let the rocks change your direction, E. Remember to stay true to your purpose, even when things look murky.*

He was on the top of the world and everything was going the right direction in his life. He had his brother back, he was only months from starting the new church, and his youngest sister was getting married. He asked himself, "How could God be giving me this kind of message?" He couldn't help but wonder what was ahead.

As he looked over the surface of the water running near his feet, God continued. *Sometimes the land rejects water and makes it hard for it to flow. Just remember, water that follows my direction always finds a way.*

God's Spirit was so strong and so loud that E felt disrespectful sitting at the edge of the water. He slipped his shoes off and lay there with his face down on the ground. Several minutes went by as he gave reverence to God with his silence, waiting for His guidance and words. Then God asked, *E, My servant?*

E softly said with a shaky, humble voice, "Yes, Lord?"

God said, *You have served me well, but remember—water is to take the shape of what surrounds it. It never possesses a shape on its own. Let me surround you and make you into my image.* Then it was over. He slowly got up and sat there for several minutes, thinking about God's words.

Soon James was back from his honeymoon and had just a few days before he was shipped off. It was Monday, and E was in Louisiana, prospecting on the new land, so James wanted to surprise his brother. He got a rail ticket and was waiting down by Clear Creek Bridge for E when he started back toward Graceville at the end of the day.

When E saw James, he quickly ran over and said, "James, is everything okay?"

James laughed and said, "E, this is your new, improved brother— not the old one. Everything's fine, but I would like to talk to you. I have so much to ask you about. And by the way, the property's perfect; I can see a church sitting out there!"

As they walked, James started, "E, I'm almost over the grief I've had for my earlier life and I look forward to a renewed life. I can't wait to get to know you and the family better. Ole' Beelzebub has stolen so much from me, but God tells me there's no shame because He has taken all that away."

Then he looked intently over at E with a leering stare, raising his eyebrows like Poppa Nick used to do, and asked, "I have questions, though. Like, how did I get so far off course? Why was I so hell-bent on sowing wrong seeds?"

Just at that moment, E got a scripture—"And he arose and came to his father." E grinned and said, "Well, you were blinded by your sinful lifestyle. The Spirit beckoned you to come to your senses, but until you walked down the road toward home, the truth was not revealed to you. When you decided to surrender all is the moment when you really began to *live* and really see things the way they truly are. Look at the prodigal son in the Bible. He had already 'come to himself.' He looked at his past and saw how foolish he was and what would happen if he remained in his sin. Then he decided to do something about it. There's a time when thoughts must turn to *action*."

James smiled at his brother's wisdom and asked, "I'll go with all that, brother, but what do I do with all my regrets?"

E started walking back toward the bridge and said, "No doubt you have regrets. I have regrets. The prodigal son was deeply grieved that the son of such a father was living with pigs. But what's the use of regret if we continue in sin? Regret that doesn't continue to repentance is just regretful death. It's good to regret and mourn over sin, but so many people live in regret. The consequence is that your future becomes a reflection of your past. When you harbor regrets, you're simply reinforcing those aspects of your life that you don't like. Just let your regret continue into obedience to God. God's love is stronger than gravity. His grasp is deeper than the deepest seas. His wisdom and understanding is endless. Totally surrender to God, and He will transform even the things in your life you thought could never be used. I'm proud to have a brother that sees through spiritual eyes. I'm not ashamed of you, and God's not ashamed of you, either. He's proud to call you His son."

By the time E finished, they were back at the bridge. James was visibly shaken by E's God-inspired words. E sat by the bridge and pulled his wedding gift out of his satchel. He had put it in the hand-carved box depicting Christ's tomb with the stone rolled away on the front that had held Elise's wedding ring. "Here, I meant to give you this before you left on your honeymoon."

James reached out his hand that was already shaking, took the box, and asked, "What's this?"

E smiled and said, "I wanted to give you a wedding gift and Elise had this idea … well, just open it!"

James asked with a wrinkled brow, "What's this on the box?"

"I thought the empty tomb was an appropriate theme for you … *a resurrected life*," E stated with a chuckle.

James opened the box and found it hard to hold back the tears as he put his hand over his mouth. He knew that he couldn't say anything, so he just pulled the old coin out and stared at it with big eyes. E smiled and said, "I thought you should have it."

James just hugged E and wiped his eyes with his right shirtsleeve. "Thank you, brother. Thank you for never givin' up on me. But you didn't answer my other question."

E smiled and said, "We better get back to Graceville if we're gonna catch the train."

James, with his eyebrows raised, waited for E's response to his question.

Finally, E asked, "Why do you think you went down the wrong road?" James rubbed his hand across his brow and answered, "I can't blame anyone but myself. I can't blame my circumstances, my family or even you."

E smiled at him and said, "Right answer! The prodigal son's ideas of self-justification were gone when he said, 'I have sinned.' Which is worse, to sin or to deny the sin? To deny sin shows an unhealthy heart. He laid bare before God his sores and ulcers of deep, dark depravity. The way to God's mercy is to cry out, 'O Lord, have mercy on me for I am a sinful man.'"

The two men continued to walk back to Graceville and waited for the train to take them back to Texas. James and Sarah left the next day to spend some time with her family before James left for Europe.

"Elise, I hope I have some more time with him to talk. We just scratched the surface," E said, as they watched them drive off.

Pearl Rose

Jakob headed out to meet E at the depot in Graceville on Tuesday, May 7. Most of the materials needed had been delivered to the site on Monday, and excitement was in the air as E waited for Jakob's Model A truck to arrive. It was unusually hot for May, but a spring rain the night before made it tolerable. The framing crew had started work at daybreak to take advantage of the cool of the day.

Russell Cayton, the rotund project foreman, said, "Ya know, Brother E, this is gonna cost five, maybe even six 'Gs' by the time we knock this out."

E looked over at Jakob and he shook his head like he knew that already. "Russ, we already know the cost. You just worry 'bout that crew of yours. We wanna make some good progress today. Half the day's already gone and we have lots to get done."

Russell pulled his hat back on his head slightly, wiped the sweat off his brow, and said with confidence, "Jus you don't worry none 'bout my boys. They're not afraid of hard work in the sun. If we need to stay longer, we'll do it. We might even come back after it cools a bit if they're not fagged."

Jakob smiled and said, "Now, Russ, keep ya hair on. I think we can get plenty done by three if we stay at it."

E looked at both men vying for the title of boss and said, "This project is in God's hands, fellas, and things will get done on His schedule." Both Russell and Jakob chuckled at E as they shook each other's hands.

"You got it, preacher. I gotta stop chewing the fat and get back to my boys," Russell said as he hastily walked away.

"You know, he's right. It's gonna be close to six thousand with the steeple and everything, even with my discount," Jakob stated hesitantly.

"Mr. Jakob, no matter the cost, it's the right thing to do and the right time to do it," E said with confidence.

Jakob was testing E's resolve and he was satisfied with his findings. "Okay, E. You have my full support," he said, as he picked up the bocky, or dried gourd, and dipped out of the barrel of water on the back of the truck. Both men decided to prospect the grounds, so they started walking as they looked at the walls going up from all the different perspectives the land provided.

"What do you think about the war in Europe, E?" Jakob asked.

"I think we'll end up in it, but the war's not what troubles me most," E stated with authority.

"What da ya mean?" Jakob asked.

"America's doomed if we don't get a handle on family values. What common creed do we follow in this country? Something the government doles out? The first words in our Constitution are 'We the people,' not 'We the government.' I think that in the '20s we had a false sense of security—a security based on who we were. When the depression hit, we took the security we had in ourselves and in our abilities and put it into government. Neither is correct. God is the only answer to our security and prosperity," E said as he finished his mini sermon.

Jakob smiled and asked, "So what's the closest church to here, E?"

E looked over at Jakob and smiled, knowing that he was reeling him back in. "Well, me and Jas found a little Jehovah's Witness church down there," E answered, pointing northwest.

Jakob's eyes widened and he said, "Witnesses … they might give you trouble. There's one of those churches by us and they stay mad as hornets!"

E looked surprised and asked, "What're they mad about?"

Jakob said, "Oh, the whole war thing and patriotism in general. They burned our flagpole down in front of our church. We had the Christian flag and the American flag flying, and they burned both of them down and put up a sign that read, 'Idolaters' in big letters!"

E, not hindered by Jakob's belligerence, raised a brow and said, "We were sent here to learn how to live together in harmony, no matter what foes we face."

Soon the sun was straight up and the loud tinning of a dinner bell rang on the back of the teardrop trailer parked under the big oak. Men hurried like ants to get in line to eat.

"Okay, men, thirty minutes and we've got to get back at it!" Russell yelled, as everyone tried to glimpse at the day's fare. Soon, men were laid out under any shade they could find for a short nap before the bell rang again to go back to work.

E walked over to get in line, but Jakob pulled him back and said, "Miriam made us somethin' special." Both men walked over to the truck and Jakob grabbed the basket that was covered with a red-checkered tablecloth. "So, how's my Elise doing?" Jakob said, feeling like he could talk more personally while they were alone.

"Oh, she's fine. Just ready to finally get settled somewhere," E answered. Jakob smiled and nodded in agreement, as he grabbed a fried chicken leg and took a bite.

Hastily the clock sped around to three and another bell rang for the men to stop for the day. E and Jakob surveyed the progress with Russell, and everyone was satisfied. Soon E and Jakob were back at the Bosch home to visit a while and eat supper with Miriam and Elise before going to bed. The next day would start early.

After three days, the building was beginning to take shape. The framing of the steeple was completed and a place for the bell was left. The sub-flooring was down, all the doors and windows were roughed in, and the roof was to be the next order of business. E was going to stay one more day, then he had to go back to work in Texas.

That night, right before midnight, a lone boy sneaked onto the new church grounds. With a can of kerosene, he doused the fresh-cut lumber until the fuel was running through the floorboards onto the ground below. There was a single strike of a match thrown into the air as he ran away from the impending doom. Soon the incredible blaze could be seen for miles, billowing its ugly, black smoke into the indigo sky.

"Preacher! Preacher!" screamed Russ, as he approached the Bosch home. By the time the men got to the site, they couldn't even get over Clear Creek. The fire had already made its way to the bridge and burned it to a crisp, leaving only halves of black smoldering sticks in its wake.

E watched the fire burn out of control from across the creek. He could see the reflection of the blaze in the water as it consumed his dream and made it a nightmare. He looked back across the edge of the creek at the line of men's expressions illuminated from the light and saw their pain and their heartbrokenness. He had been at this place of faith before and he would not make the mistake of questioning God again. He had too much experience with God to question anything.

The flesh wanted to scream, accuse, and ask why, but at that very moment, he received a scripture from Psalms: "Don't sin by letting anger control you. Think about it overnight and remain silent." So that's what he did. He remained deathly silent even when others were offering their opinions on what happened and who started it.

Russ chimed up and said, "I know who did this—those crazy Jehovah's Witnesses! They did this to ya,' preacher! That's who did this!"

E had a dream that same night about a field of beautiful red roses. He was pruning and watering the roses when a fire came through like a thief and consumed them right in front of his eyes. Nothing was left but ashes. Then an ivory-colored rose came up through the ashes and it had twelve blooms on it. It was much more beautiful than all the other roses before it and it seemed to reflect the blue of the sky as it swayed in the breeze. E found himself wide-awake, sitting up in bed and thinking about the dream.

Elise stirred from her sleep, touched E on his arm, and asked, "Are you okay, honey?" E looked over at her and told her about his dream. Trying to wake enough to make sense of things, she said, "Well, that's similar to my dream."

E insisted, "Tell me what you dreamed!"

She sat up in the bed and started, "I saw you with a sling in your hand like David against the giant. You were spinning it faster and faster over your head and finally you let it go. In the sling was a single white rose, and as it went through the air, the petals came off and filled the sky. As they fell to the ground, they turned into snow. The ground, the trees, and everything were covered with a thick blanket of white snow. Then I heard a voice say, 'Though their sins be as scarlet, they shall be as white as snow; though they be red like crimson, they shall be as wool.'" E just smiled and glanced over at the Big Ben illuminated by the moon on the bedside stand. Both hands were on the three.

"You know that the Great Chicago Fire that laid ruin to downtown Chicago started an economic boom and spurred the development of one of the most populous cities in America? What I think God is saying is, 'This is the way I'm going to build my church!'" E told Jasper on the phone the next day, trying to convince him of God's tremendous providence in the matter.

"Well, E, maybe God does have some miracle in mind, but for now, we have no recourse but to start from scratch," Jasper said, feeling overwhelmed.

After breakfast, E loaded up in Jakob's truck as they made their way around to another bridge, finally taking them to the church site. The big oak that was the centerpiece of the property was severely burned, and the only thing left of the church was the large foundation stones. Even the building materials that were stacked on the ground were gone. Then E noticed a small, burned sign nailed to the big oak tree. He went closer, trying to make out the writing. It said, "This church worships money, not God."

Jakob walked over and said, "Told ya it was those Witnesses." E just looked at him in disbelief. He couldn't fathom anyone doing something so dastardly, even if they disagreed with his beliefs. Jakob said, "Well, one thing about it…there's not much clean-up to do. The fire pretty much burned everything."

The next day, E, Elise, and little Faith were on their way back to Texas. They sat there on the train, silently pondering all the things they'd experienced. E broke the silence with a single statement, "We have to choose love and forgiveness as our weapons in this war!" Elise looked over at him and smiled. She had been thinking the same thing.

Grace Bestowed

On December 7, 1940, E and his family were once again headed to Graceville. Jakob had cleaned up the property and was anxiously waiting for them at the depot. E looked over at Elise and asked, "What do ya think your father's up to?" She shrugged her shoulders, wondering herself what this suspicious meeting could be about. As the long whistle blew and the train slowed, a hard clanging was heard and felt as each car took up slack in its couplings. Soon the train stopped, letting steam escape underneath its belly toward the depot. After the white smoke cleared, E and Elise saw an anxious Jakob pacing close to the tracks. As they exited, Jakob quickly grabbed their luggage and walked toward the truck.

"So how was the trip?" he asked, as they briskly walked together.

Elise, knowing her father's peculiarities, said, "Daddy, what's goin' on? You're actin' strange."

He moved toward Elise, smiled, and said, "Sweetheart, no day could be finer." E just smiled and looked at both of them curiously. Jakob looked over at E and started, "E, I had a dream about two wheels. I was one of the wheels and the other wheel was called 'Circumstance.' Most of my life, I've felt tied to *that* wheel, but in my dream, I noticed another wheel, a wheel that was much larger and greater. I noticed that the larger wheel went at a consistently faster speed, while the smaller wheel I was attached to was very inconsistent and slow. Then I noticed that my wheel was attached to the smaller wheel with a belt, but I really wanted to be attached to the larger one. I tried and tried to work my way toward that larger wheel, only to fail over and over again. Then I heard a voice say, 'All you have to do is ask, and it will be given.' So I did, and soon I was attached to that larger wheel. Then I saw on the large wheel two words—'Christ Jesus.' I realized right then that our wealth isn't tied to the largesse of others, luck, economy, or even our hard work. Then I realized that wealth as I had defined it was not correct either. Wealth to God is not the same wealth that man declares. God's wealth is not measured by status, but by humility. God's wealth is not holding lots of money, but holding higher thoughts. Value is not in the dollar, but in our character and in the way we live our lives."

E looked at Jakob in amazement and said, "Sir, you really did have a revelation!"

Jakob smiled and said, "E, you have no idea!"

Soon they were parking against the curb in front of Graceville Bank. Jakob looked over at Elise and said, "Sweetheart, why don't you take the truck and drive to the house. Mother's waiting for you and Faith. We'll get a ride home."

Elise looked solemnly at her father, and without waiting for a question, Jakob smiled and said, "Don't worry, Mother will fill you in!" She smiled and gave both men a big hug and kiss. As they both walked through the double doors, a man escorted them to the conference room in the back. Eleven businessmen were seated at a very large table.

"E, take a seat, please," Jakob said, as he took his position in the twelfth chair.

"It's with great irony we sit here today," the man in the lead chair said. "You see, Brother E, we realize that you wanted to set the world afire with your church. However, what happened is that we set your church afire. I don't mean *us* literally, but someone in our community did, and that makes us all responsible." The chairman of the board at Graceville Bank had spoken and then he looked over at Jakob to finish.

Jakob said, "God has given each of us so much. We didn't resist the gifts and talents that God has so freely given us, so we don't think we should reject His calling to be of service to one of His servants. It's the unanimous decision of these businessmen you see seated here to rebuild Pearl Rose and to also build a parsonage for you and your family."

E was speechless as he sat there almost in tears. He knew that God was up to something, but he really didn't expect this. He got his handkerchief out of his back pocket and wiped his face of the mixed sweat and tears. As he stood to make some sort of impromptu speech, all the men rose and started shaking his hand. They seemed proud of their contribution and couldn't wait to see what would come of it. E couldn't wait to call Jasper and fill him in.

Soon the new church building was going up again, but this time it was triple in size and there was a parsonage, too—with a real bathroom!

"Brother E, there's a telegraph boy here for ya!" Russ said, as he yelled over to where E was standing. He walked over to sign for it, putting his hand in his front pocket for a tip. The telegraph said:

From: *Tuskegee College*
To: *Rev. Ethan Moses*
Date: 12 *December,* 1940

It's with a heavy heart I respond to your regrettable tragedy. However, through some of my friends in your area, I've made arrangements to supply you with plants and flowers for the new church grounds, including a new rose that I've developed here at

Tuskegee. Also, we are sending several five-gallon cans of paint for your project as you rebuild. Please feel free to respond to the return address if you need anything further, and God bless your endeavor.

G.W.C.

As E stood there in shock, looking at the telegram, I had embodied a truck driver, and I drove a big truck into the construction area with a large, covered load in the back.

"Are you Brother Moses?" I asked.

"Yes sir. How can I help ya?" E asked.

I looked at E and said, "Well, Reverend, you can supply me with some strong men. I have a bell in the back of this truck and it's some kind of heavy!"

With a puzzled look, E asked, "A bell?" He just shook his head as I got out. Soon, Russ was by the truck, calling some of his crew over to get the bell on the ground.

"Okay, preacher, just sign this," I insisted, as I shoved a pad and pencil into E's hands.

"Wait just a second. Who's this bell from and who's paying for it?" E asked, puzzled. I felt in my front shirt pocket and pulled out a small, folded envelope and handed it to E. The handwritten note inside read:

Please take care of our centuries-old chapel bell. The Nazis are stealing all of our church bells to melt them into bombs and bullets. With many lives jeopardized, we crated it and smuggled it across the channel out of Holland in hopes of keeping its beautiful music alive. We all grew up hearing the sounds of this beautiful bell at weddings, funerals, and many happy festivals. They're trying to steal our souls by stealing the music from our hearts, but by keeping the bell ringing, you are restoring our hope that one day we will be at peace again. Please stand with us in our solidarity and pray for our country. Maybe one day we will visit our lovely bell again.

—The Village of Katwijk

E just stared into the distance as Jakob came over to see the note. "Did you have somethin' to do with this?" E asked curiously, looking at Jakob with a raised brow.

"Nope. I'm from Austria, not Holland!" Jakob exclaimed with a shake of his head.

"So how and why our church?" E asked as he squinted his eyes, still not buying into Jakob's innocence.

"I have no idea. Really, E, it's a mystery to me, too," Jakob answered, slowly shaking his head. But E wasn't entirely convinced that Jakob didn't have something to do with it.

"Seek God's kingdom first! Start from within and stay conscious of His presence. Love Him with all your heart, mind, and strength. If you want an abundant life, have a consuming appetite for God," E said to the young boy who had started the church fire. The boy had boasted to his friends about being the arsonist, and soon it got back to E. The boy's father had made several snide comments about the church. It was also his father's idea to burn the church down and give the credit to the Jehovah's Witness church down the road. He might've been just mouthing off to his family, but his little boy took it to heart and acted on his father's words.

E forgave the boy, but as part of his payback to the church, he was to do seven hours of work a week at the church for three years. E had an opportunity to witness to the boy and he had made a profession of faith in Jesus Christ. Now it was E's duty to teach him and let God mold him into an upstanding young man.

"David Wolfe, in Matthew, Jesus said, 'Stay here and watch with me.' What'd he mean?"

The boy just looked at E with a blank face. E answered, "He's saying that we aren't supposed to have some private point of view or agenda. He invites us to take part in His bigger, more rewarding point of view. Most Christians can't get past their own agendas.

Their prayers tell the story. It's all about them. Open your eyes and see the larger picture, a picture from God's perspective, and your life will take on an uncommon abundance, an unending peace, and tremendous grace. God is not in need of anything we can give Him. However, he allows us to be a part of something bigger that gives us great blessings. Experience God like all those men in the Bible did."

The church had been finished for three months, but now the parsonage was complete and it was a great monument to God's provision. Soon Miriam and a pregnant Elise were organizing things in their new home. The twelve men who met in that room at the bank were made the elders of Pearl Rose Church. Those twelve men and their families would move the church forward, reaching out to the community and beyond. E had explained God's plan for a missionary effort, and all the deacons loved the idea of supporting Jasper and his family as soon as possible. E stayed busy studying the Word and ministering to his parishioners and the community as a whole, and the church flourished like that beautiful white rose that adorned the front flowerbed.

Big Fish

"E, you have a letter from your brother!" Elise said, running up to E, who was standing in front of the church. He couldn't believe it. It had been years since he had heard anything from his brother. Sarah kept him informed usually, but E hadn't heard from her in a very long time either. He kept looking at the letter with hesitation.

"Well, go ahead and open it!" Elise commanded, letting her curiosity get the best of her.

"What if it's bad news?" E asked.

"Would you open the letter?" Elise exclaimed with giggles as she paced nervously.

E began to read:

Dear Brother,

After commando training abroad, I find myself in a special ops division in England with the Allies. I'm working through a secret department where most of the characters are numbers and not names. I would ask that you please keep this to yourself. The military censors would have a field day with this letter; however, I'm in a place where they can't touch me. If you haven't figured it out already, America is about to be dragged into this crazy war. Most of my job consists of reconnaissance, and I can tell you Hitler is up to some nasty stuff and his quest for world domination doesn't stop at the ocean.

I hope you've received the bell by now. The Vicar was hoping to hide it, but the Germans are ruthless at finding much smaller things, so I had this great idea!

I dedicated it to our mother's memory before I shipped it out with the help of my friends in the underground and, of course, God, to whom I've entrusted its safe journey. Send my love to Elise and Faith. I hope to see you all soon.

Love to all,
James

E looked over at Elise with tears welling up in his eyes. Elise grinned with caring eyes as she hugged him. "Your brother was lost, but now he's found. I think it's wonderful," she said, as she put her head on E's shoulder.

"My brother. Who woulda guessed it?" he asked, as he looked up at the bell. At that very moment, the sun shot a beam of light through the trees, hitting the bell's skirt and causing E to squint at the bright, metallic sparkle. He knew there must be a deeper meaning to that old bell and maybe one day he would know the full story.

Elise, sensing he was wondering about the bell, said, "You know, I read somewhere that a bell is symbolic of the Trinity. It forms three points like an 'M.' The two points upward are the Father and the Son and the point downward that makes the beautiful music is the Holy Spirit."

E looked over at her with amazement and said with a grin, "You never cease to amaze me, Elise Moses."

Elise soon gave birth to their second little girl, named Joy, and she filled their lives with many days of joy as they settled into the community they would call their home. It was May at Pearl Rose, and soon the whole environment around the church changed like a vibrant butterfly escaping the bonds of its cocoon and soaring freely through the spring air. Cross Lake bordered the church land and it became E's favorite fishing grounds. The lake gave him an outlet to enjoy himself in a peaceful setting, while escaping briefly without interruption. He might've escaped his pastoral duties, but he was available to God twenty-four-seven and that's how he wanted it. In fact, the water seemed to make conversations with God easier and less encumbered.

Ben Wolfe was sitting on the banks of the lake, leering out at E with belligerence and contempt. His son, David, the same who had burned the first church to the ground, had been working on Ben's heart for some time, hoping he could turn his father toward God. The boy was relentless in his quest, but the old man was not taking the bait. Stout had promised he would sell that church land to him. He had saved his money; waiting for the opportunity to expand his farm and his prosperity. When E showed up, he felt he had been robbed. He had coveted that land for such a long time.

The water was clear and the sky had a purity that seemed to bathe E, making him feel renewed as he slowly reeled in his crank bait toward the boat. As he brought the bait up to the pole, he shot it out again toward some brush not far from Ben. As he started reeling it back in, a seven-pounder nailed it, then the reel handle came off in E's hands.

When Ben saw what had happened, he started howling with laughter. It was almost like a release valve was going off. E didn't think it was that funny, but he immediately saw an opportunity to make some in-roads with Ben. With exaggeration, E grabbed at the line and started pulling it in with his hands. He started laughing, too, at the great spectacle as he finally got the fish into the boat.

Ben was still laughing as E rowed over to the shore where he was sitting. "Well, Ben, I'm glad I gave you some amusing entertainment today!" E laughingly said, as he pushed his boat up on land with his oar.

Finally, Ben settled down enough and scoffed. "Brother E, that was the funniest cast I've ever seen. You sit right there and I'll be right back with some real fishing gear," Ben said, like there was never any animosity between them. Fishing was Ben's weakness, and E had finally broken the ice.

E looked up with a smile and said, "Thank you, God, for my wonderful catch."

Within a few minutes, Ben returned with fishing gear, sandwiches, and a water jug. "Now, let me show you how this is done, Brother E. This is my homemade bait I call the Big Bad Wolfe. I'll show you a few secret patterns I use to catch the big ones," he said, as he climbed in the boat and shoved off with his foot. Soon the whole Wolfe family were active members of Pearl Rose. E had baptized them all and was determined to disciple them into a closer and closer walk with God.

"Brother E, I feel totally to blame for burning the church. Isn't there somethin' I can do to make amends to you and the church?" Ben asked, with great emotion in his voice.

E looked at the man and felt that he knew his heart. "There's one thing that would make the church complete. But you have to understand this is not necessary for you to be accepted. If you do this, it won't be considered as payback for the past. As far as God and me are concerned, that's been forgiven and forgotten. Do you understand?" E asked.

"Okay, preacher, I understand," Ben answered.

E looked over at Ben, smiled, and whispered, "A covered bridge. I just think that would finish things out. After the fire burned the original bridge, the county built a less than adequate bridge to replace it and it always floods."

Ben looked at E with a smile and said, "That's funny."

E asked, "Why?"

Ben answered, "Well, my father was a bridge-builder, and I happen to know quite a bit about building bridges."

E wasn't surprised. He knew the Holy Spirit was guiding his words and when that happens, you live beyond the natural with common conclusions. Ben was happy because he could show his love for God, and E was happy because that bridge became the centerpiece of the church.

E's old boat became an altar to God where he sacrificed time and effort in convincing many to turn to God. As the summer's heat began to subside, the war was beginning to heat up. E had gotten more letters from James as he gave them insight on what was happening. He and Elise felt like they had that information for one reason—to pray for America and the world in general.

In the Trenches

"God whispers to us in our pleasures, speaks to us in our conscience, but shouts in our pains: It is His megaphone to rouse a deaf world."

—C.S. Lewis

On Sunday, December 7, 1941, at 7:58 a.m., the squelch of an alarm went off. "Air raid, Pearl Harbor. This is not a drill! Repeat, this is not a drill!" Japan's single, carefully planned and expertly executed attack took out most of America's battleship fleet. Within a very short period of time, five out of eight battleships were sinking and the rest were heavily damaged. The shocked and enraged American public, who were previously divided on involvement in the war, became purposefully unified.

It was the end of a peaceful era in America and the beginning of a tumultuous future. Soon the industrialized boom that was building the States into a major world power slowed to a halt. The same factories that were building cars and products for the public were now building military vehicles, guns, bullets, and bombs.

In 1942, the United States, Russia, and Britain took some very big hits in the war, but as the calendar turned on a new year, the tide began to turn. British forces captured Tripoli from the Nazis and fifty bombers mounted the first all-American air raid against Germany. E thought it was very ironic that he got a letter from James while he was helping a non-violent German resistance group called the "White Rose." They became known for an anonymous leaflet campaign, lasting almost a year. E just knew that James had something to do with those leaflets and the name. Those same leaflets were smuggled out of Germany and copies of them were dropped all over Germany by Allied planes.

James was now a corporal and was reassigned to a Field Artillery Observation Battalion. He soon found himself right in the middle of what would later be called the Battle of the Bulge. Though his unit was doing reconnaissance and didn't carry any heavy armament, they were directly in the path of the German spearhead. For a period of six weeks, Allied troops faced superior enemy numbers, rugged terrain in the heavily forested Ardennes region, and bitter winter weather as the German forces launched a desperate attempt to halt the steady advance of the Allied Forces. James would write E with stories of blowing tracks off Panther tanks with bazookas, setting mines, and doing reconnaissance missions behind enemy lines. Then E got a letter dated December 16, 1944:

Well, big brother, I finally feel like I've done something with my life that's worthwhile. The indications are very strong that we will move in a day or two—perhaps tomorrow on my birthday. We will be on our way to Luxembourg and should see plenty of fighting. Hitler is like a cat that's been cornered.

In case I'm not able to write you again, I feel provoked to write lines that may fall under your eyes when I am no longer. Not my will, but God's be done. If it's necessary that I should fall on the battlefield for our wonderful country, I will without hesitation.

Just know that I love you all very much, and don't worry, God and me are finally on good terms.

I've written Sarah, but in case she doesn't get my letter, tell her that I love her very much and look forward to spending the rest of my life with her at my return. There's so much in my life that I'm ashamed of, but God has forgiven me and given me peace about everything. I have strongly felt His presence lately and I'm so proud of you for "staying in the fight." You might not realize it, but you are in a war that's much more brutal that this one. When I return home, I will tell you about a dream I had. I was walking on God's robe! It will astound you, brother!

Love to all,
James

On December 24, Christmas Eve day, E, two beautiful little girls, and a pregnant Elise made their way back home to see Miss Margaret. E knew that this would probably be the last Christmas they would spend with her because her health continued to decline. He had invited Jasper and Janie to join them and they were supposed to pick up Sarah and little James Jr. on their way, but E had not heard a word from anyone.

As they sat by the fire and reminisced about bygone Christmases, there was an ominous knock at the door. E opened it to see Sarah standing there hooded and at the point of hysteria.

"Sarah, you didn't travel here alone, did you?" E asked, thinking about her wellbeing. When he got no reply, he realized that something was dreadfully wrong.

Soon, Elise came barreling through, hugging Sarah and bringing her inside. As she sat by the fire warming, she finally started talking as her eyes welled over, sending tears streaming down her face.

Two sharply-dressed officers came to Sarah's parents' house to find her, bringing the official bad news. James had gone missing, presumed dead, during the Belgium Initiative that later was called the Battle of the Bulge. Much later, they found out that James had been murdered by SS troops on December 17, 1944, near the Belgian town of Malmedy. The Germans had captured almost a hundred men. While they stood in a field with their hands over their heads, the SS gunned them down. James had managed to strike a single match on his boot and throw it into several jerry cans of gasoline before they shot him. The firestorm ignited three German vehicles, creating a huge fireball. One of the Panzer flamethrowers had blown up, starting a domino effect and laying ruin to tanks and half-tracks.

Soon Jasper, Janie, and their kids arrived and were briefed by E on the porch about what had happened. Christmas was sad and colorless, as the family just survived from day to day. If it hadn't been for the kids, it would have been an intolerable Christmas for everyone. At that moment, E would have given everything he had in the world to have just five minutes with James. Sooner or later, everyone discovers that the important moments in life are not all the lights or fancy wrapped presents or even the food. It's much simpler than all of that. It's the simple moments, simple conversations, and laughing with people you love. Worth will inevitably be measured by the unnoticed, unglamorous, unselfish time spent with each other.

Weeks after Christmas and the official news of James's death, E was still ridden with guilt for letting James go off to war. He got up one morning and told Elise that he had to go. He just had to do it. She was very upset that he was taking it so badly, but she understood and told him to do what he thought was necessary. Soon he found himself in line to join the armed services, but during his physical, the doctor said that he had a heart murmur and turned his application down. He knew it was God who had stopped him—his heart had no murmur—but he at least had to try. He felt like he owed that much to his brother. For so long he had anticipated James's return. The letters E got from him only fueled his desire to rediscover his long lost brother and now he would never have that opportunity. It seemed as though as soon as he was able to communicate with James on a level that was his own, he was gone.

Then God gave him the scripture, "Remember how fleeting is my life. For what futility you have created all men! What man can live and not see death, or save himself from the power of the grave?" E had finally heard God through his grief and began to realize that James's destiny was on a different plane from his.

Liberty Rings

By the spring of '45, E was setting the world on fire with his preaching and calmly ministering to all the people who had personal losses during the war. The healing rain was falling down around Pearl Rose, as God's Spirit began to console and heal the land. In April, the Russian Army had met the American Army near Toragau, Germany, and only a few days after that Hitler took his own life. Even though Japan was still fighting to the bitter end, the American people began to see the light at the end of a long, dark tunnel. The "war to end all wars" was finally coming to a close. By the end of '45, the overall personal income level in America rose from $72 billion in '39 to $172 billion, and there was a big shift from lower incomes to middle incomes.

E drove over to the west end of the lake one Saturday to go fishing and he saw the sheriff's deputy, Lawson Hanks, badgering a man who was sitting by his truck beside the road. From E's perspective, the man looked like a Mexican. He slowly stopped and got out, ambling his way over to the commotion that Lawson was making. The man never looked up and never responded as the deputy continued to get louder in a feisty tone. "You dad-blame mangy ole' spic. Why don't you look at me when I'm talkin' to ya? Huh?"

E had been in run-ins with Lawson before and realized that his bark was plenty loud, but his bite was nothing to worry about. "Hey, Lawson, what's goin' on?" E challenged as he startled Lawson from his proud stance.

"Oh, nothin' that concerns you, preacher. Just move on," he said, knowing that he would never get rid of E that easily. E looked intently at the man sitting by his truck. He had already figured out that he wasn't Mexican by his boots and said, "Baa shini."

The man immediately looked up at E and asked, "You feel bad about what?"

E smiled as he looked at the deputy who was dumbfounded, then back at the man, and answered, "Oh, about what's happened to you."

By this time, E had the man's full attention and he slowly stood, brushing himself off. Lawson got in the stance of a gun-fighter, getting ready to draw. E looked over at the deputy and demanded, "Deputy Lawson, has this man done anything unlawful?"

Lawson stiffened with defiance but soon shook his head and admitted, "Well, no, but he don't need to be loitering around the lake unless he's in designated areas for the public."

With a penetrating stare, E stated, "Well, deputy, you don't worry 'bout that. I'll take care of things from here. He'll be movin' on shortly."

Lawson, realizing that he was beaten, flared at the situation, saying, "Okay, preacher, but I'm holdin' you accountable." Shaking his index finger at E, he walked back to his patrol car.

"So how much Navajo do you know?" the man asked, as he skeptically studied E.

"Not much. My great grandmother taught me a few phrases before she died, but I was too young to remember most of 'em. She was half Navajo. My name's Ethan Moses, and yours?" E asked, as he stuck out his hand.

"Harrison. Harrison Todychini," he said, shaking E's hand hard.

"So, how'd ya know somethin' happened to me and how'd you figure I was Navajo?" Harrison asked, as both men sat down by the lake.

"Well, Harrison, it wouldn't take a brain surgeon to figure that somethin' was wrong!" E said with a laugh, "But as far as how I knew something had happened to you ... well, I listen to a higher power for those sorts of things," E said, trying to break the ice and get Harrison to talk about spiritual matters.

Harrison skeptically looked over at E and said, "Yeah. I heard the lawman call you preacher, but don't give me any of that mumbo jumbo. How'd ya know I was Navajo, though? Did some higher power tell ya that, too?"

E smiled as he saw his opportunity and answered, "I'm sure that my God showed it to me, but that's the Navajo Yeii Spirit on your boots—a spirit considered by the Navajo to be a mediator between man and his Creator."

Harrison looked at E with increased respect and said, "Where I am right now, no Yeii Spirit could help me—not even your God."

E looked over at Harrison and said, "Early one morning, Jesus, the great mediator between God and man, got hungry. He saw a fig tree by the road, so he went over to it, but it had nothing but leaves on it—no fruit."

Harrison, still not taking the bait, said, "So did Jesus miraculously make figs appear?"

E had hooked a big fish. Now he had to reel him in, so he began again. "Oh, no. He looked at the tree and commanded, 'May you never bear fruit again!' and instantly, the tree withered and died. When Jesus's disciples saw this power, they were amazed and asked, 'How did the tree die so quickly?' Jesus answered, 'I tell you the truth, if you have faith and don't doubt, not only could you do what I just did, but you could tell that mountain to throw itself into the sea and it would be done.'"

Harrison was still skeptical. "You have no idea what—," was all he was able to say before a largemouth bass shot up through the water right next to Harrison. The splash startled both men as they looked at the size of the fish as he danced out of the water into unfamiliar air. E giggled at the experience as Harrison quickly got to his feet in amazement.

"Some fish!" Harrison said.

E looked over at Harrison, smiled, and said, "Some God!" Soon, E had Harrison where he wanted him—in his boat. As they fished, the two men talked about everything, and E was able to lead him to a saving faith in the Lord Jesus Christ. E explained the deeper meaning behind the fig tree, and Harrison realized that God was looking at the fruits he bore as well.

E found out that Harrison Todychini was not only a Navajo Indian, but also a true American hero. He grew up on the reservation in the Glen Canyon area of Arizona, but soon he decided he wanted to be an engineer. After school, he was working in Taos for a construction company when a friend of his came up with the idea of using the Navajo language for war communications. Soon he was part of a group of highly specialized marines called the "Navajo Code Talkers." When Harrison came back home after the war, he found out his wife had been unfaithful to him. Overcome with grief, he got in his truck and drove east until he ran out of pocket money. That's where Lawson found him.

E fed him, put him up for the night, and then gave Harrison some money to get back to Taos to forgive his wife and put his life in order. He later moved to Cross Lake with that same wife, who also became a believer and was baptized in Clear Creek. They became very active members of the church, and Harrison was always looking for things to do to help E out when he was off work.

Harrison asked, "Preacher, that bell's somethin' special, isn't it?"

E just nodded.

"You know, I looked at that bell up close and it's got some writin' on there that looks like code. It has to be code."

E looked at him like he had been fighting the war for way too long and said, "Well, Harrison, that probably would be Dutch."

"Oh, no, I would recognize Dutch. That's definitely some type of code," Harrison insisted.

E was mesmerized and seemed to lose himself in the thought. Then E got a scripture in his head from Exodus. "The sound of the bells will be heard when he enters the Holy Place before the LORD."

"I think I can break it," Harrison said confidently, before E could say anything.

"You really think it's a code?" E asked, not believing his ears.

"I do," answered Harrison.

"I knew there was somethin' special about that ole bell. I just knew it!" E exclaimed.

The next weekend, Harrison had three days off from work because of Good Friday, so he started working on the inscriptions found in three columns on the haunch of the bell. Two days had passed and on the third day, Harrison climbed up to the belfry once more after Easter services. E, exhausted from preaching two sermons and teaching Sunday school, went home to take a nap. At a quarter to three, he went back over to the church to take Harrison something to eat.

As he entered the small hole in the belfry, Harrison exclaimed, "Preacher, I think I've got it!

> When I ring, God's praises sing;
> When I toll, pray heart and soul;
> Be meek, and live in rest;
> Give thanks for God's best
> I, sweetly tolling, men do call
> To taste on meat that feeds the soul."

As Harrison finished, E looked at him and said, "It's beautiful … but that's it? Why would they put that in code?"

Harrison laughed heartily and said, "Oh, no, that's just the large type. To hear the rest, you better sit down."

As E got comfortable, Harrison continued, "In the year of grace, 1643, a humble merchant from London, zealously interested in the Reformation and freedom from the Monarchy, instigated my fabrication in Holland for use of his fellow citizens and placed me in the cathedral overlooking their humble abodes. My function was announced by the impress on my bosom: *ME AUDITO, VENIAS, DOCTRINAM SANCTAM UT DISCAS.*"

Harrison stopped for a second and explained, "That means, 'Come, that you may learn Holy doctrine.'"Then he continued, "And I was taught to proclaim the hours of God's clock ticking down the circle of time. One hundred and thirty-three years had I proclaimed His imminent coming when I was broken by the hands of an inconsiderate and greedy king in want of my treasure for war. Rescued, I was cast into a fiery furnace and when my metal glowed red as blood, many sacrificed their golden trinkets to me, praying for my return. I was re-founded in Holland and set to my sacred vocation once again. May my sound of true liberty ring forever! Reader, you will also know a resurrection—may it be to eternal life with God!"

E had a large lump in his throat as he looked with great affection toward the inspiring golden bell. He stood there mesmerized, eyes affixed upon the delicate curves of this Easter bell—not just any old bell, but one that had escaped two wars where freedom was at stake and had been reborn to new life again. Without warning, a hymn started ringing in E's ears:

"Alleluia! Alleluia! Hearts to heaven and voices raise.
Sing to God a hymn of gladness; sing to God a hymn of praise.
He who on the cross as Savior, for the world's salvation bled,
Jesus Christ, the King of Glory, now is risen from the dead."

He swallowed hard and in his spirit, the resurrection of Christ took on a more firm reality because of the bell. Then, counting in his head from 1643, he excitedly exclaimed, "This bell was re-founded in 1776!"

Harrison looked over at E and nodded affirmatively.

Then E continued in a whisper, "Harrison, we can't breathe this to a soul, do you understand? God meant for this bell to be heard, not gawked at in some stodgy museum. It beckons people to God and that, my friend, has to be its lifelong calling."

Harrison smiled at E and said, "I'm the last person who wants to see that bell bound from singing, preacher. My grandfather had a saying: 'If a man is to do something more than human, he must have more than human hands.' Who really dares to say he owns this bell that has proven itself of bigger hands? It wasn't cast and hasn't survived by men's hands, and we must leave it to God."

E looked at the old Indian and smiled, realizing that he understood.

"I want you to see somethin,' Harrison," E said, as he pulled the letter that came with the bell out of his pocket. When Harrison finished reading, he shook his head and exhaled loudly. "What is it?" E asked.

"That village it talks about … the Germans completely demolished that place to make way for their Atlantic Wall," Harrison said with a deep groan. E just shook his head in disbelief as his eyes lowered.

The sound of that bell was much sweeter and mellower the next time both men heard it, and they realized even more how precious grace is and how great it is to have the chains removed and set free from bondage, to let eternal freedom ring.

The Fiery Furnace

"Nebuchadnezzar, his face purple with anger, cut off Shadrach, Meshach, and Abednego. He ordered the furnace fired up seven times hotter than usual. He ordered some strong men from the army to tie them up, hands and feet, and throw them into the roaring furnace. Shadrach, Meshach, and Abednego, bound hand and foot, fully dressed from head to toe, were pitched into the roaring fire."

Daniel 3: 19–22 (MSG)

The year was 1948, and E had just gotten back from North Carolina, where he had escaped for a few days with Elise. Only once did he leave her to do God's bidding. One night, while sitting by the fireplace, he suddenly sprang to his feet and exclaimed that he had to go. When he arrived at the small cabin overlooking a breathtaking line of hazy blue mountains, three men were praying inside. He made his way over to the oldest man in the room. A nice, handsomely built man—he had to be the one he was supposed to talk to.

Then God said to E, *No, he's not the one.* Then he changed direction, going toward a man who was a little younger and not quite as handsome. Then God said, *Not him*. After pausing, E looked up and down the tall, scrawny young man. He seemed to be the shyest and most unsure of all the men.

Then E said to the one they called Billy, "I've come to anoint you as an evangelist to the world. A packed crusade in Los Angeles will be your confirmation." He laid his hands on his head and prayed. The men were visibly shaken that God would answer their prayer so quickly and boldly.

Before they had a chance to ask who E was, he had slipped out the door. They tried to follow, but it suddenly started raining hard while a large clap of thunder rumbled over their heads. A strong wind pushed them back inside as they watched E slip away into the darkness of the mountainside, illuminated only by occasional flashes of lightning.

As soon as they returned home, E took his ordained position behind the pulpit to deliver yet another discourse to the hearts of his congregation. God's Spirit enveloped E to the point of almost making him laugh because of the joy he felt. It had been years since he had felt God move so abruptly upon him while he was preparing to speak. He already knew what the Spirit wanted him to say; he just needed that extra nudge of confirmation to give him confidence in his delivery.

The atmosphere was tense as he stared into their souls. Almost immediately, Jim Winter's face was supernaturally illuminated in the crowd. Some considered him the "seed of Satan" at Pearl Rose. E knew he was calloused and confused, but he never completely gave up on him.

The war to end all wars was over, and the soldiers, including Jim, were back home, back to their jobs, and back with their families. The war had changed Jim and made him untrusting and unfeeling. He was hell-bent on cleaning up society with tight rules and cracking whips. As he looked at E, he saw a weakling, a measly wimp of a man who had never faced utter terror or unmitigated debauchery. Jim knew how despicable people really were and what they were capable of. In his mind, all they needed was a stiff kick in the rear to set them straight.

E stared for a few seconds more into the congregation as the Spirit came down on top of the people. On cue he began, "Back in 1913, there was a children's novel written called *Pollyanna*. It depicted this spiritually strong young girl who had to face incredible adversity, including the loss of her parents. Yet her faith in the goodness and grace of God remained undiminished. After her loss, she was sent to live with her Aunt Polly, a very crotchety and unhappy rich lady. Aunt Polly used her wealth to run the entire town, even the church. The pastor preached what she told him to preach and the sermons were always harsh and legalistic, designed to inflict as much fear, pain, and guilt on the congregation as possible. Pollyanna, full of faith, grace, and wonderful optimism in people and in God, refused to be daunted by the legalistic guilt her aunt imposed on the people. By the end of the book, the town, the church, and even Aunt Polly had been transformed by God's grace that had shown through little Pollyanna. It's a wonderful picture of the triumph of authentic Christian freedom over soul-destroying legalism.

"In your bulletin and on the sign out front, I've given you a hint of my topic today—legalism. So right after the special music, that's exactly what I'm going to talk to you about."

As E sat down, Jim Winter quickly skirted the crowd and went out the side door, followed by Jack Burns and John Cooper. Elise had joked about them being the "Three Stooges" only to lighten E's mood and get him laughing. She had even called Jim "Sanballat" a few times. Nevertheless, the three had been quite divisive in the church.

My old nemesis, Azazel, had tried to cause problems for E by calling attention to his belief in spiritual gifts and using them to heal and deliver, but too many people were scared to touch that subject. Soon Azazel realized that he could play an old card that had worked so easily in the past and had caused endless havoc and division in the church, even in its earliest days. The old "ace in the hole" was legalism. C.S. Lewis once said, "One of the marks of a certain type of bad man is that he cannot give up a thing himself without wanting every one else to give it up. That is not the Christian way. An individual Christian may see fit to give up all sorts of things for special reasons—marriage, or meat, or beer, or the cinema; but the moment he starts saying the things are bad in themselves, or looking down his nose at other people who do use them, he has taken the wrong turning." Legalism was the key to Pandora's Box, and Azazel had his henchmen lined up inside Pearl Rose to start opening it up. He knew that if he could give legalism a toe-hold, the Christians would spend all their time trying to "win" God's approval and judging others. He also knew that it would create strife and discord in the body of Christ by riddling them with guilt and shame.

E walked back up to the podium after the music and began. "We can't go 'round accusing someone of being legalistic unless we truly know their heart, and only God knows a person's heart. Instead, what I would encourage each of us to do is to daily examine our own hearts. I think Pollyanna would agree that we can't beat them with the same stick they're using on us. Pollyanna was able to accomplish success by living what she believed. My friends, that's all God asks of us." As E continued, you could see the relief on people's faces as they began to settle down and listen intently.

E continued, "Brothers and sisters, one of the signs of falling from the truth of God's Word is bickering and disunity. Jesus said in John 13:35 that the world would know His disciples by the love they have for one another. In Colossians 3:14, the Bible says that love is the perfect bond of unity. The New Testament speaks about us being unified in Christ over and over again! Do you cry out in your prayers like David did, 'Create in me a clean heart, O God. Renew a right spirit within me'? Is that your prayer? Is it your deepest desire? Are you willing to allow it to happen? You will have to change direction from a self-focus to a God-focus. Exchange your desires for the things of this world to the things of God."

Soon the sermon was over and several people came up to E and thanked him for handling the legalism issue so well. Jack Burns was boiling red-hot with anger as he waited in the room where the deacons met after morning services. He had enough and now he was going to take action.

As John Givens entered the room, Jack, seething with disdain and discontent, exclaimed, "John, I'm so sick and tired of him using his pulpit to 'call out' people that he disagrees with! I knew what would happen today. And now it's time to do somethin' about it!"

John Givens, the chairman of the deacons, looked at Jack, dumbfounded, and asked, "What *are* you talkin' about, Jack? The pastor called on us not to judge anyone unless you know their heart, and only God knows a man's heart. If you and those cronies of yours would've stayed for the sermon, maybe you would've learned something."

Jack's face turned beet red. *Did I miss something?* he thought, as he quickly exited the room and wandered off down the hallway in a daze to find his friends.

The day's ugly climax had been diverted by E's message, but Azazel wasn't finished yet. There would be another opportunity soon. For thirteen years and six months, E had kicked against the goads of suffocating conformity and watered down spiritual power in his denomination and in Pearl Rose. The year before, Elise's father had died suddenly from a heart attack. He was E's confidant and biggest supporter. Now, E had no one to fill that void. The culture of Christianity was something he fought against most of all. Forcing a Christian agenda on the population, to him, would backfire and turn the population against the church, having an upside-down effect on all Christian values at some point in the future. Christianity was not "things you have to do," but "the person you want to be because of a loving relationship with God." If you go through life thinking you can be a Christian without the walk with God, you will never get to the point of "to live is Christ and to die is gain." He was sick and tired of the pretentious separation of church and state, of which the

Constitution never speaks. The separation of Sunday from the rest of the week is adhered to by many. And, the separation of secular from spiritual. Satan had been very successful pitting race against race and denomination against denomination. The body of Christ was detached, tangled, and mangled, rendering it dangerously close to a point of uselessness.

He was tired of fighting the fight—not the fight against the world or even Satan, but the fight with other Christians. Soon the three J's, along with others they had successfully dominated, went to the state director to protest the activities of Pearl Rose and its pastor. The very idea of personal freedom, which, of course, implied freedom from them and their controlling legalism, was unacceptable.

"Now, men, let's see if I get this right. You're saying that Brother Ethan is a rebel that doesn't adhere to our explicit denominational guidelines and regulations?" the state director asked.

The group nodded their heads affirmatively.

Then, the director asked, "Well, do you have substantial proof for this claim?"

Jack looked at the director calmly and said, "Yes, sir. I have this petition of over sixty names from people who think like we do."

The director continued, "Well, that's all very interesting, but what's your proof? What has he done that's opposing to the gospel of Christ?"

John looked over at Jack and waved his hand, wanting to interject a few words, stating, "Sir, Brother Ethan is a false teacher. He distorts the truth of God's word and makes it say what he wants it to say. He gives people false hope in healing that never happens and deliverances that are farces. He preaches love, love, love, but in reality, he's just watering down God's judgments."

The men hadn't made a good case for any investigation, but when the director got a call from Jack's uncle, "the senator," things changed very quickly.

Jack's teenaged daughter, Katherine, was dying of cancer and there was very little the doctors could do for her. Jack wanted to bring the deacons in and lay hands on her and anoint her with oil, but E refused.

He said, "Jack, at this difficult time. God's calling you and your family to think unselfishly. He's calling you to think of others."

E's statement enraged Jack and caused him to spin out of control like an autumn leaf, bound to hit bottom eventually. Instead of hearing E out, he got a handful of deacons to pray for Katherine and lay hands on her anyway.

"Now, Katherine, this is the list I told you about. All these people have cancer. What I want you to do is start working your way down that list and pray for all these people by name. When you get to the bottom, start over," E told the girl.

Jack and his wife, Elizabeth, didn't listen to the rest of what E had to say, but Katherine did and she was obedient to God. After three weeks of her praying for others, the doctors finally saw positive changes in her. She seemed to have more energy and her appetite returned.

Jack gave the credit to the impromptu laying on of hands, but Katherine knew why she was feeling better.

Soon, the denomination's state office instigated an investigation. "Brother Ethan, my name is Tony Daio, and I've …" the man said.

E cut him off with, "I know who you are, Mr. Daio, and I know why you're here."

Daio looked surprised, because his arrival was supposed to be very hush hush. He asked E, "Oh, did someone tip you off?"

E looked into the empty eyes of the pretentious man and answered, "You could say that."

Soon he had thoroughly perused the files and interviewed several members in the church including the staff and deacons.

"Brother E, I'm paid to find things, and that's what I intend to do. Now, can you tell me what the Celeste Missions in Mexico is? I see that the church gives quite a bit of money to it? I can't seem to find it on my list of approved denominational ministries," he asked, knowing that Jasper's mission was not accountable to any denominational oversight.

E looked at him with a half smile and walked off, not saying a word. He was not interested in Daio's traps or his game-play. He had bigger fish to fry.

Soon he was at the hospital checking on Katherine. He would pray with her while her mother was gone to pick up the other kids from school, unencumbered by the faithless eyes of her parents. They became good friends, and E found her to be a very strong Christian for someone so young.

He would tell her, "You have a lot of faith, my little Kat."

Within a month, the official certified letter from Mr. Daio was sent to the church office to the attention of the deacon body. Here's what the letter said:

> Gentlemen:
>
> We're all aware of the autonomous structure of our denomination's churches. However, we've shown ourselves capable of all manner of cooperative endeavors when we choose. The most obvious example is international and state mission work, but the denomination also provides financial services for clergy, maintains an archive of historical records, and sends out media to teach and learn by. Given that congregational autonomy doesn't preclude a cooperative denomination-wide effort for these other endeavors, it shouldn't preclude a denomination-wide effort at censuring clergy when necessary. Surely, we don't intend to say that the ecclesiological legalism of congregational autonomy renders our denomination's state and national organizations powerless to make correctional statements toward the ministerial ranks in our churches from time to time.
>
> It's been my finding that the leadership of Pearl Rose, specifically the pastor, has been grossly negligent in its duties to its members, its denomination, and to the community at large. The failures of Pearl Rose lie directly on the pastor's shoulders. The freewheel-

ing nature within Pearl Rose is confusing to the congregation as a whole. Specific examples of this are questionable faith healings, showy demon extractions, the excessive use of laying on hands, use of musical instruments other than the piano and organ, the inclusion of some music that's not denomination-approved, and incessantly stating that Jesus shed His blood for our sins. These sorts of things sound like they come from some other denomination or religion. Lastly, and most importantly, the substantial monetary support that Pearl Rose gives to one of the pastor's family members in mission work not even affiliated with our denomination has to be sending a mixed signal to new Christians and even seasoned ones. If integrity is not a standard in our clergy, how can we expect it of our church members?

In my assessment, Pearl Rose could grow and prosper under the right leadership. Reluctantly, I recommend that the church vote to remove Reverend Moses from his duties as pastor immediately and start the process of finding an interim pastor. If the church chooses not to remove Reverend Moses, my findings will be sent to national headquarters and the church could face expulsion from denominational affiliation indefinitely.

Thank you for your cooperation in this matter. My office will help you in your transition as much as possible.
Sincerely,
Anthony Daio
Vice President, Ethics and Religious Liberty Division

As the deacons made their way inside the packed room, they lacked the camaraderie that usually occurred at their meetings. E and the staff walked in the door, and all eyes fell to the floor as if they had been shamed. Nevertheless, E made his way around the room, shaking hands and asking questions about family and personal issues.

At exactly seven o'clock, John Givens called the meeting to order. "Now men, we've invited the staff here tonight because of a letter we received. Mr. Daio conducted an investigation and has sent us his troubling recommendation. Johnny, would you pass these out to everyone?" he asked. "Brother E, he's recommending your dismissal. We, as a deacon body, wanted to give you an opportunity to reply before we bring this matter before the church. You have the floor."

E, visibly shaken by the letter, slowly stood with tears streaming down his face and sadness in his eyes that hurt all the deacons deeply. As he sniffled, he stated, "Men, there's only one thing you can do to keep the unity of this church intact and that's to bring it to a vote. I would like to have a few minutes to respond to the charges beforehand, if you don't object."

Then he slowly sat back down, taking his handkerchief out of his back pocket to wipe his eyes. John was visibly shaken by E's emotional stance, but he tried to keep his composure while conducting church business.

With John and E both shaken by the indelibly caustic letter, David Whitmore stood and said, "I think this is a time for faith, men, not fear. I stand in solidarity with my pastor."

Immediately, the whole room was on their feet. John looked at the men and said, "Well, if you truly mean this, we'll announce it before the vote is taken."

Soon the Sunday E dreaded was upon him, but so was God's Spirit. On the day of his walk into the furnace, he'd never felt so invigorated and excited in his life. Elise was praying at home and Jasper had his entire family and staff praying in Mexico.

"You're everything that I live for, Jesus. You've given me an unbelievable life full of grace. Everything is filled with hope and not despair in my life, because you control every single beat of my heart. There's hope in this helpless situation. There's healing from hurtful words and attitudes, and you never let go of me through storms, pain, doubt, and rain. Amen," E prayed while in his study. Then, he got off his knees and walked out to make his way to his seat behind the podium. The deacons had determined that the situation was too tense to have the business meeting after morning preaching, so they decided to make the worship hour a prayer and singing time, followed by the reading of the letter and then E's response.

After the reading of the letter, you could hear sniffles and crying from the entire congregation. E slowly approached the pulpit and the whole church felt a reverence they had never felt so strongly before. The whole place seemed to glow brightly. It was as if God was saying, "This is my servant, with whom I am well pleased," as light shot through the stained glass windows of the church, illuminating him supernaturally behind the pulpit. Everyone felt the strong presence of God, even those who had signed the petition to bring about the investigation. E looked into the crowd as if he was seeing his family for the last time before leaving for some far away war.

Then he began, "John Locke once wrote, 'If the Gospel and the apostles may be credited, no man can be a Christian without charity and without that faith which works, not by force, but by love.' I kept hearing one scripture over and over while I was preparing for today, 'Make my joy complete by being of the same mind, maintaining the same love, united in spirit, intent on one purpose' (Phil. 2:2). Friends, if I'm causing any disunity in this church, it is my firm plea that you vote yes for my removal.

"It's all right to have differences of opinion on non-essential matters like worship music or pre-tribulation rapture or post-tribulation rapture, Arminianism or Calvinism. Whether you believe one or the other or you're not even sure what you believe doesn't affect your salvation. Yet far too many of us use these differences as justification for division and sometimes even anger and violence in our dogmatism. When that occurs, the love of God in our hearts is sacrificed to our own pitiful pride. Instead of saying to one another, 'I'm right and you're wrong,' we should be saying something like, 'It's certainly possible that you're correct. Now let's work together to expand His kingdom.' It's Satan who wants us to fall into the self-abuse of division and bickering. However, there's a time for division in the body of Christ. When an individual or church group denies clear Scripture and remains unrepentant after being admonished, then it's time to break fellowship with that person or group. If I have done any of those things, please vote yes for my removal from this fellowship.

"Primarily, it's the Holy Spirit that unites us through the saving work of Christ. Secondarily, it's the essential doctrines that define us. We have, as a common heritage, the blood of Christ that's been shed for the forgiveness of our sins. The central message of Christianity *is* atonement—it is the concept more than anything else that separates the Christian faith from the gamut of 'works religions,' where man earns his own salvation. If you disagree with me on what I consider apostasy, then vote yes for my removal.

"True Christians serve the true and living God and we know Jesus in a personal and intimate way…1 Corinthians 1:9. The blood of the Lamb has redeemed us. Furthermore, we have the body of God-inspired scriptures, which tell us the essentials of the faith, and deviating from these essentials means to be outside the camp of Christ. It's the essential doctrines that we must know and unite in. I'm no faith healer, but if you have a problem with me following the Holy Spirit's leading when He tells me to heal, cast out demons, or lay hands on someone, as Jesus and his disciples did many times in the New Testament, then vote yes for my removal.

"For the new Christians who might be confused by a mixed message I send to them. To you I say, my message is clear, concise, and to the point. Jesus is my Lord and personal Savior. I believe that Jesus died for my sins, that he rose from the dead in victory over sin and death, and that I was saved because of Jesus's death and resurrection. This is God's freely given gift called 'grace,' and I can't earn it. My faith is a byproduct of that wonderful grace. It's not a work of my own. If that message is confusing to you, please vote yes for my removal.

"For you who have a problem with this church funding the Mexican mission of my friend and his wife, who happens to be my biological sister, then I would ask that you not call me brother. If you're going to be pretentious in your spiritual relationships with me, which are far more important than biological ones, I would rather be someone who's not related. So vote yes for my removal." Then he turned and walked out the side door.

E went back to the parsonage to Elise's hugs and kisses. She said, "It'll be okay, honey. God's in control. If they vote to remove you, God has other plans for us—it's that simple."

He smiled knowing she was right, but what made him smile was the providence of God in putting Elise beside him. She'd been a constant friend and companion, but most of all, she kept him grounded in his purpose. He stopped right then and thanked God for her.

"Well, sweetheart, you better get the boxes out of the attic. There's no way this will end well," E said.

"When there seems to be no way, God can make a way. Besides, I haven't heard a fat lady sing yet!" she said while giggling at him.

"Well, ole' Miss Edwards was lookin' like she was goin' to start singin'!" E said, smiling.

Elise walked over and popped him on the arm.

As he said he would do, John Givens, who was visibly shaken by the delivery that E gave, reported to the congregation the deacon vote of solidarity. Then he motioned for the deacons to hand out the ballots for the vote. It was a solemn time with very little conversation. The significance of the event was on everyone's face as they checked their ballots and waited for the deacons to pick them up.

As soon as all the ballots were handed to the counting committee, John stood back up and walked over to the pulpit. As he started to speak, the front doors flew open with a loud thump and rushing wind as Katherine Burns walked through them, full of life and with a glow that radiated throughout the entire sanctuary. Meticulously and with resolve and poise, she made her way down the aisle and up the stairs to the pulpit.

She looked out into the daunting crowd unafraid and said, "I regret being a member of this church that my pastor and good friend envisioned and was faithful to see finished. He's my earthly hero, and you act as if you have some power over his God-given calling. If it weren't for him, most of you wouldn't even be here." She shook her head for a moment and started again. "I don't know what the vote will be today, but I've already heard that if there's one vote against him, he'll consider his mission done here at Pearl Rose. I see that my parents are sitting out there and I want you and this church to know that I've been healed. God told me last night that it was done. Daddy, you're mad at Brother E for the way he reacted to my cancer, but he was only being obedient to God. As I look through the Bible, Jesus healed everyone differently, according to their needs or their personalities or even their beliefs. It reminds me that He's a personal God and not a God who adheres to our ways or traditions. God will bless Brother E and his family, and I'm sure He'll move him to a place that *will* appreciate him for the wonderful person that he is."

John Givens just sat there with his mouth open as she walked back down the aisle past her parents who were trying desperately to get to her. Finally, Jim Winter came barreling through the side door, not knowing what had just happened. "John, I have the vote!" he said excitedly.

John got behind the pulpit to read the results, but he couldn't. It was like the Spirit had closed his mouth. He stood there for a moment while everyone waited, but all he could say was, "We've been deceived by Satan and led astray." Then he stepped down and handed Jim the folded sheet of paper.

Jim just stood there staring with big eyes, not understanding what was going on. The whole church seemed to evoke a weeping spirit and a deep sadness as Jack proudly made his way up to the pulpit to give the report on the vote. He slowly opened the sheet of paper that he grabbed in a hurry from the counting committee and stared at it for several seconds. He couldn't believe his eyes. Then he looked over at Jack, who was waving his hands to be recognized from the floor. Still flabbergasted, he stated, "I recognize Jack Burns from the floor."

Jack said, "I believe that the voting on this particular issue wasn't handled correctly and I move that we have an immediate oral revote from the floor to correct it."

John Givens immediately seconded the motion.

Jack finally made it behind the pulpit and whispered something in John Cooper's ear, and then John asked, "Everyone heard the motion and second. All in favor of the revote from the floor say 'aye.'"

The whole church exploded with a resounding "aye." Then, while holding his breath, he asked for any opposed. You could have heard a pin drop the silence was so deafening.

John then asked for the vote "yes" to keep Brother E as the pastor and again the whole church exploded in affirmation. Then John asked for any opposing and again silence. Jack looked over at his wife while trying to hold back the tears and nodded his head up and down with a gleaming smile.

"Jack, can I show you somethin'?" John Cooper asked with wide eyes while both men stood confused behind the pulpit.

"Sure. What?" Jack asked half-heartedly. John slowly opened the piece of paper that had the vote count written on it and showed it to Jack.

"Are you serious?" asked Jack, grabbing the paper from John's hand.

John proclaimed with a white face, "All it has is just a big zero written in red!"

Jack, with his mouth still open wide, gave a very large sigh and got his handkerchief out of his pocket to wipe his eyes. He couldn't say anything; he just went down to hug his wife and daughter as they went out the side door.

John Givens was walking over to the parsonage to tell E the good news when Jack quickly caught up with him. "John, I realize that you should be the one who tells the pastor, but I need to apologize to him and Miss Elise, so would you mind greatly?" John just smiled and motioned for him to go ahead.

"E, honey, someone's at the door!" Elise said as she cracked the door of his study where he was praying on his knees. As he opened the front door, three happy faces were looking at him.

"Hello, Brother E," Jack said. Katherine ran over with a big smile and hugged E and Elise.

There was an inquiry into Pearl Rose Church three months later from national headquarters, but they ended up chastising Mr. Daio and his staff instead. He was moved to a lower office that had no dealings with local churches. Although the state denominational office wrote a formal letter of apology to E and to Pearl Rose, there was still quite a lot of animosity between them through the years.

It was soon the end of the '50s and a new age of revolt and revolution was in the air across America. E and Elise stayed on their knees as they watched their beloved country tumble down a dangerous path of arrogance and selfishness. It was the "I" generation. Moral resolution was bent to individual preference and God was dead in the hearts and minds of many Americans. A progressive way of thinking was introduced and many bought into the "change is what we need" message.

On the Road to Emmaus

E had been at Pearl Rose for thirty years. Apollo 13 had safely splashed down in the Pacific and the Vietnam Conflict had officially been going on for eleven years. Many of the books published in the '70s revolved around the general theme of man's alienation from God. E felt that the seventies were much like the thirties. After a decade of free love, drugs, and decadent lifestyles of non-conformity, many found their way back to their spiritual roots.

While sitting outside watching the waning moon slowly cross a tranquil sky, E turned to Elise in a pensive mood and said, "I think we're in a forty-year cycle, honey, sorta like those hard-headed Israelites in the wilderness. Forty years to get their heads screwed on right and then another decline. We might not see this spiritual awakening again until 2010, so we better make hay while the sun's shinin'!"

Elise looked over and giggled at the prospect and announced, "Well, E-bee Jeebee, you might be gettin' a little old by then. I might have to do it without ya, hun!"

E scowled at her, not because of her joke, but for calling him "E-bee Jeebee." Their youngest daughter, Grace, and her friends would call him that behind his back. Elise thought it could be her new pet name for him, but he totally despised it, so she decided to use it to get under his skin, only to see if she could change his demeanor back again. It was a game, but she truly loved him and had fun teasing him.

Pearl Rose kept modest numbers in Sunday school and worship services throughout the fifties and sixties, but the numbers were escalating at a breakneck speed by 1970. New life was entering the church, but new problems developed as well.

E got in bed next to Elise, sighed for a moment as she rubbed cream on her face and hands, and then started, "Elise, I'm not sure I'm up for this. After all, I'm sixty-seven. I mean, we have the charismatics out there stirring things up in the church, but there needs to be balance to all this. If you get a close, personal relationship with God without learning and appreciating His Word, you end up stumbling, no matter what spiritual gifts you have. It's like a flower planted in rocky soil. It might bloom for a short period, but eventually it wilts and dies. These kids are right about the power of God not being tapped into though. Our generation dropped the ball."

She looked over at E and said with loving eyes, "Honey, you've been preaching for years the things they're just now figuring out. Who's to say that you didn't have some small part in the tide turning? We celebrate our fortieth wedding anniversary in less than three years and you're supposed to retire. Didn't God tell you to "hang up your hat" after thirty-three years? What I suggest is that you ask God to find your replacement, because I have some traveling to do before I leave this earth!"

He looked into Elise's beautiful eyes illuminated by the moonlight coming through the window. It was like the first time he saw her as the dim light softened the lines in her face. He lovingly said to her, "Honey, God has been dealing with me all day about that and you just confirmed it."

"So do you know who your replacement is?" she asked inquisitively.

"Oh, I have an idea it might be David Wolfe. And God didn't say for me to 'hang up my hat,' by the way, just to stop preaching at Pearl Rose," he proclaimed while giving her a kiss on the cheek and turning over.

"Oh. So what does that mean? I hope it doesn't mean that you're going to look for another church?" Elise asked sharply.

E turned back over and answered, "Oh, no, honey. But God and you have me for the duration of my time here, I'm afraid!"

She just giggled and turned over to go to sleep.

As he walked into his study the next morning with his cup of coffee, he couldn't sit down. For some reason, he was restless and soon found himself pacing around the sanctuary. He walked back into the office and told the secretary that he was going for a long walk.

She looked at him and said, "Pastor, you had a call from David Wolfe. He wanted me to tell you that he surrendered to the ministry."

E smiled and exclaimed loudly, "Yes!" as he jumped up in the air with great energy.

Then she continued, getting caught up in E's emotions, "He's going to be a missionary and he was on his way to Mexico to stay with Jasper for a while. Isn't that great!"

E was proud of David, but at the same time disappointed in the news. He thought for sure David was the one who would take over after he retired.

Soon, E was walking over the covered bridge across Clear Creek and toward town, feeling sorry for himself for losing David. A stranger seemed to come from nowhere and started walking next to him. He thought it was someone who had been fishing by the bridge and asked, "Catch anything?"

The man answered, "Oh, no, I was just resting."

E, not really looking too intently at the man, kept walking and said without a flinch, "Well, you will only find rest in Jesus. Let your old life crumble and fade. If you're looking for a place that you can truly rest, I can help."

The man grinned, shook his head, and said, "Well, I'm looking for a place... You're right."

E looked over at the man just as he put his head down to conceal his face under the brim of his hat while flicking a coin up in the air with his thumb.

"So where you from, son?" E asked, letting his curiosity take control.

"Oh, I lived in Dallas until I went to college and then on to seminary," the man answered.

E knitted his eyebrows together and exclaimed, "Well, I'm originally from Texas, too, and a seminary boy. How 'bout that! Were you raised in Dallas? What seminary did you go to?"

The mysterious man, noticeably fidgeting at the new line of questions, turned and said, "Well, tell me about yourself, sir."

E, trying to get a glimpse of the man's face again, answered, "Sure. I'm from a community called Artesia in northeastern Texas. Ever heard of it?"

The man just grunted and walked on.

"Well, tell me your name, son?" E begged, beginning to get frustrated with the answers he wasn't getting.

"Dr. Moses. And yours, sir?" the man said as he tipped his hat and looked off into the distance.

E stopped dead in his tracks as the man walked on for a few steps and turned on his heels, almost in military style and looked straight into E's eyes. E had seen that confident swagger before. It was his own. E's eyes began to well up with tears as he looked intently into the young man's face and asked, "You're twenty-seven, aren't you?"

The young man started to smile. Then, it grew into a large grin as he answered, "Yes sir, Uncle E."

E couldn't contain his great emotion at seeing James's son again and enveloped him in an unending embrace. The last time he had seen him, his mother was remarrying to a man from Dallas. He looked into his face and saw so many features of the family. Ole Grandpa Nick was in his eyebrows, his mother, Hannah, in his soft caring eyes, and that walk, that unmistakable walk of Oswald Moses made over ... He couldn't believe his eyes. For several seconds, E couldn't say a word as he kept shaking his head and putting his hand over his mouth.

He finally got his composure back and asked, "So what are you doin' here, son?"

James Jr. smiled, raising his shoulders, and said, "Well, I wish you could tell me that. I couldn't sleep last night. So I prayed and God told me to come to Pearl Rose. I got dressed, packed a suitcase, and here I am."

E, smiling as big as a Cheshire cat, asked, "So why didn't you come up to the church?"

"God told me to wait here by this bridge. I got the feeling that somehow it meant something. So can you tell me what this is all about?" James asked as he wrinkled up his eyebrows like Poppa Nick used to do.

E smiled for a moment, started shaking his head up and down, and answered, "Oh, yeah. I know why you're here. Could you tell me what time you couldn't sleep? No, don't tell me ... I'm going to tell you. It was straight up ten, right?"

James looked over at his uncle, nodded his head affirmatively and smiled. E put his hand around James's shoulders and started walking back toward the church. "I have lots to tell you, Dr. Moses, and I can tell you all about that gold coin in your hand, too. Come, let's see Aunt Elise and sit for a while."

Soon, E filled James in on God's plans, and for the next three years, E taught him everything he knew. After the third year at Pearl Rose as associate pastor, James was ready to grab the reigns. He had fallen in love with Katherine Burns and they were married in June of 1973. E had kept up Miss Margaret's big house in Artesia over the years and they were looking forward to moving back and settling into a peaceful retiree lifestyle. On July 8, 1973, E preached for the last time at Pearl Rose. It was a packed house as he got up to give his delivery. He looked over at the pew where his girls always sat; there they were with their husbands and kids.

He looked once more out the windows he had seen installed and then over to David Wolfe and said, "'Seek first the kingdom of God and His righteousness, and all these things shall be added to you.' Have you ever realized how revolutionary those words from Christ were? Even if you're a pastor of a wonderful church, those words sting in your ears. I mean, after all, God, I have to clothe and feed my family. I have to make a living. Jesus is not only saying that a right relationship with God is vital, but it should precede everything else in your life."

As he continued, the congregation smiled at him and thanked him for his many years of service that had always taken precedent over his own life.

Downwardly Mobile

Dr. James Moses had settled into the parsonage with his new wife, and everyone had cried as E and Elise drove away across the creek bridge.

"No looking back, Elise," E said, knowing how emotional she would get if she took a last look. "We'll be back visiting before you know it!" E said, trying to calm Elise as well as himself. "Besides, I have a surprise for ya, and I can't have you lookin' all sad."

Elise turned her head and looked out the side window saying, "E, I don't think I'm ready for any surprises right now, if you don't mind."

E looked over at Elise, smiled, and said, "Sure, honey, you just tell me when you want to hear about it." He knew her well enough to know that it wouldn't be very long.

They had been driving only thirty minutes when she looked over at him, giggling, and asked, "Okay, okay. I can't wait any longer! What is it?"

E put his hand into his inside coat pocket and pulled out an envelope.

"These are plane tickets to Italy!"

"Are you serious?" she asked with great surprise.

E, trying not to get emotional, just shook his head up and down.

"I have another surprise for you, too," E said a few seconds later.

Elise was still looking at the tickets and asked, "And what's that?"

E looked over at Elise, trying to prolong the anticipation and just smiled.

"Okay E-bee, what is it?" she asked more resolutely.

Well, Jasper and Janie are joining us!" he said as she howled with excitement and hit his arm.

"Jas and Janie, it's great to see y'all!" E exclaimed with enthusiasm.

"E, you old codger, you're lookin' pretty old and worn out, but my cuz over there looks younger every time I see her. Did you find the fountain of youth over in the Louisiana Purchase, Ellie?" Jasper asked with a laugh.

"Oh, shut up, Casper. Nobody wants to here your silly ramblings!" Elise said as she hugged him.

"It's so good to see y'all. It's been too long!" Janie added as she hugged everyone.

"So what's the agenda?" Jasper asked.

E pulled out all of his brochures and threw them on the table, then looked intently at all of their excitement and said, "I have yet another surprise." All eyes were on E as he held out for a brief second or two and then blurted out, "The Donaldsons will be joining us in Florence for our trip up to Venice!"

Elise excitedly looked over at E and asked loudly, "Jack Donaldson?"

E added with a nod, "And his wife, Matilda!"

E had told Janie and Jasper about their experiences in Venice and they were looking forward to meeting part of the Moses family folklore. E and Elise had kept up with Jack as he traversed the outback of Australia for many years. When he left them in Venice, he went over to the asylum where his wife was being held, and told them to "let her have a go." He wrote E and said that he told her that she was going to have to "buck it up," that he had mission work to do and she was part of it. They ended up with three kids and were blissfully happy.

Dallas was noisy and clamorous as they stepped out into the big city. "So where ya takin' us, E?" Jasper asked.

"Sonny Bryan's, of course!" E said as if everyone should know.

Elise looked over and said, "Do you ever get tired of that place?"

E just smiled and shook his head from side to side.

The night flew as they all caught up on each other's lives. Before they knew it, morning had arrived and it was time to go to the airport. The DC-10 had a new smell and was adorned with the seventies fashion colors of burnt orange, brown, and lime green. They flew from Dallas to Florence with stops in Chicago, London, and Milan. Bleary-eyed, out of sorts, and looking less than their best after so many hours of flying, layovers, and transfers, the foursome made their way out of the airport as if they were getting off a very tumultuous roller-coaster ride.

"I'm gettin' too old for this!" E said, as he sighed heavily, dragging his luggage behind him. Elise was more chipper than everyone else as she floated through the air, defying gravity. She could feel the intrigue of Florence and exploration was in her veins. The renaissance city was beautiful and full of color; she couldn't wait to see it all.

"Elise, your eyes are gonna get sore from lookin' so much!" E told her as she rushed ahead of the group.

Jasper caught up with E and asked, "So where are we meetin' the Donaldsons?"

E, looking at his watch, said, "We have to get the luggage to our rooms and then we'll go down to the train station."

Jasper asked, "Is that where we're meeting 'em?"

"Um hum," E said with a nod.

"So you're not gonna tell me much about this are you?" Jasper asked, raising one side of his mouth. He knew E pretty well and knew how much he liked to surprise people with good things. "Okay, I'll play along, but do any of your plans include sleep?" Jasper asked with a chuckle.

"Jas, you'll have plenty time to catch up on your rest when you're dead," E stated with a chuckle, as if it were his motto.

Jasper looked at E, rolled his eyes, and said, "Coffee is a wonderful thing in Italy—strong and smooth. For some reason, I don't think I'm gonna get nearly enough of it!"

Soon they were at the Santa Maria Novella train station. The Donaldsons were waiting there and quickly spied E and Elise.

"*Glorias oame*, it's great to see ya, mate!" Jack said as he grabbed E around the neck and gave him a sideways hug and a rub on the head. Elise hugged him too as he brought his wife over to introduce her. "This be Matilda, my missus!"

E asked with a grin, "I thought you called her *Galah*?" Matilda popped Jack on the arm with her palm and said, "*Galah,* you say! So I'm a silly person, you ole bloke?"

Jack laughed and said, "Oh, what do I know? I'm just an ole' Taswegian from beyond the black stump!"

Shelia looked at him and said, "Just an ole crow eater, you are!"

"Hey, Tiny, what do you call a boomerang that won't come back?" Jack asked.

E just looked dazed and shook his head.

"A stick!" Jack answered with a boisterous laugh.

E grinned at them and said, "I think both of you are playin' to the crowd! And, by the way, the crowd is my good friend, Jasper, and his wife and my sister, Janie."

Jack shook Jasper's hand and tipped his wallaby to Janie. He looked back at E and said, "Oh, Tiny, you spread the good oil, you do, lad! So what's with drownin' worms? Let's hit the frog!"

Elise looked over at E and shrugged her shoulders. He just rolled his eyes at Jack and said, "So what ya say we speak the King's English?"

Jack smiled and answered, "Ya got'er mate, so let's stop dilly dallyin' and go find some tucker."

Matilda looked over at Janie and said, "He's always hungry!"

Elise exclaimed, "Which king exactly are you quotin', Jack? I think you've been upside down too long in Oz! Besides, we have an hour on the Trenitalia to Pisa before we eat!" Everyone laughed as they walked over to the terminal.

"So where *are* we dining, may I ask?" Jack said with a proper English accent.

Elise just pushed him and said, "We're not lettin' you off the train. You can eat your tucker here!"

Matilda said, "There ya go, Elise. He's got kangaroos loose in the top paddock."

E looked over at Jack, laughing, and said, "We have reservations in Pisa."

Elise added, "Anticca Focacceria San Francesco!"

Jack laughed again and asked, "Well, we've made it all the way 'round to California, have we, Tiny?"

Matilda hit him again on the arm and Elise said, "Isn't that arm sore, Jack?"

"Beat to a bloody pulp, it is," Jack answered as he laughed hardily.

After seeing the leaning tower, they made their way to the restaurant. Elise ordered the *spaghetti alla Norma* and started a trend for the table except for Jasper, who ordered the *involtini di pescespada*. After a sumptuous dessert and a walk around the leaning tower, they were ready to get back to Florence and to bed.

On the train, Elise asked Jack in her best Australian accent, "How's it goin', mate? You were eatin' like you had a holla leg!"

He laughed and said, "Elise, you're a candy. I'm full as a fairy's phone book. After I go and have a cuppa, I'll be better than fine."

Elise turned her head and said, "I'm gonna take a guess that's coffee?"

Jack, fully surprised at Elise's abilities to understand him, said, "Crikey, I believe she's got me pegged! E, your cheese and kisses is somethin,' she is. We had a flamin' good time tonight and we appreciate you including us in this expedition of yours, mate. It's been just great to see you and Elise again and to finally meet your sister and brother-in-law, just blimey great!"

Anyone who has ever studied art dreams of visiting Florence, and Elise was no exception. It's home to many of the great Renaissance masterpieces including Michelangelo's *David* and Botticelli's *Primavera*. The other things on Elise's list were the Duomo, the Palazzo Vecchio, and the Uffizi Gallery, and she had the impossible task of seeing it all in one day.

E was interested in one thing in Florence. Michelangelo's *Florence Pietà* had intrigued him for years. The unfinished sculpture is so unique that many believe that Michelangelo placed himself into the work. If you look closely at the face of Nicodemus standing behind Mary, he looks remarkably like Michelangelo. This makes perfect sense because Michelangelo originally planned it to be his own funeral monument.

After seeing the Duomo, E stopped dead in his tracks. Right next to the Duomo was the east door of the Baptistery, which was created by Lorenzo Ghiberti. The bronze door, which took him twenty-eight years to complete, is made up of ten panels, each depicting scenes from the Bible. They include:

1. Adam and Eve being expelled from Eden

2. Cain murdering his brother, Abel

3. The drunkenness of Noah and his sacrifice

4. Abraham and the sacrifice of Isaac

5. Esau and Jacob

6. Joseph sold into slavery

7. Moses receiving the Ten Commandments

8. The fall of Jericho

9. The battle with the Philistines

10. Solomon and the Queen of Sheba

They were all mesmerized by the incredible detail of each scene. E was impressed by everything he saw in Florence, but he was far from satisfied. As they made their way to the second floor, there it was to the right at the top of the stairs. *Florence Pietà*. E was not disappointed in its presentation as he approached the masterpiece. With each work Michelangelo completed, he became more intensely spiritual. E saw a yearning to merge his soul with God's in the sculpture, as he stared at it for almost an hour. The rough and dramatic angular lines were much more feeling than any of Michelangelo's earlier polished works and captured the emotion of the dramatic moment when Christ's limp body was being carried to the tomb for burial. Satisfaction overcame E as he walked back down the stairs with a perpetual grin.

Soon it was time to leave Florence and travel to Venice. As the train approached the water city, there was a silent reverence E and Elise shared as they looked out the window of the train. It had been forty years, but the city still looked the same. Venice is one of the most surreal places to arrive by train. They pulled into a pretty common station and left the front doors to be presented with the Grand Canal with its water trams and grand buildings rising up from the water. Immediately, E and Elise slipped back through time to a place where they had started their lives together. They walked slowly down the streets lined by canals and laced with bridges. Time had truly stood still for them until they glimpsed down at their inter-laced aged hands and suddenly realized the truth. The other couples were shaken by the experience as well and didn't say much as they followed close behind. Jack was reliving the moments of their first encounter together and his encounter with God on the Aegean. Jasper and Janie were just soaking in the ambiance of a rare gem—enticingly gorgeous. They were completely oblivious to anyone or anything else as their eyes ran across the expanse of canals and intri-cate architecture illuminated by a golden sun. Everyone was on an unending field trip of wonder, excitement, and mystery.

Once they had taken the Vaporetto down the Grand Canal, they ended up at St. Mark's Square and went inside the Basilica, which was even more beautiful and ornate than they had remembered. They climbed to the top, overlooking the Square, and saw a wed-ding couple posing for pictures below.

As they turned to go back down, an old man came over and stared at E for several seconds. Then he asked, "Ethan Moses?" E looked at the man for a moment, then it hit him. It was the priest they had met forty years earlier. E quickly started thinking back in his mind for a name.

Finally, he blurted out, "Father Caravello!"

Father Caravello said enthusiastically, "God told me that I would see you again!"

E looked surprised at his command of the English language and said, "Father Caravello, I'm impressed. Your English has improved immeasurably!"

"You might remember that man over there, too!" Elise said excit-edly, as she motioned toward Jack.

"Mamma mia! How wonderful, how very wonderful to see you! You have no idea how I've wondered about all of you. So tell me, what are we all doing in Venice? I know it wasn't to see me, or was it?" Father Caravello said with a belly laugh, as he kissed them all on the cheek.

E smiled, looking deep in his eyes, and asked, "Father, I believe you've had a revelation?"

Father Caravello smiled with a gleam in his eye and said, "I don't know if that's Mark the Apostle's bones in this church, but I do know they have no power, no special magic. Even if they are Mark's bones, he's not here. What I do know is that I should act on what revelation God does give me, when He gives it to me. If I don't obey the light, it will turn into darkness and overcome me."

E, impressed with the priest's command of scripture, said, "John 12:35."

The priest smiled and added, "And Matthew 6:23."

With great anticipation, E asked, "So what's the revelation?"

Father Caravello put his index finger up to the side of his mouth and pushed up slightly. Then, fanning his hand out expressively, he said, "Malachi."

E raised both eyebrows and asked, "Malachi?"

Father Caravello smiled with raised eyebrows and nodded his head up and down raising his shoulders. Just then, a wonderful idea popped in his head, and he said, "How would you like to experience Venice through my eyes? I'll be your guide and tonight is my treat. What do you say?" Everyone was excited about the possibilities and immediately said yes.

As the sun set over the lagoon, the group made a left on the corner of Salizada San Lio and Calle Paradiso. Next to Hotel Bruno was La Boutique del Gelato where they ate a wonderful meal. Later they went to Pasticceria Ponte delle Paste for some homemade pastries. The lights from the old lanterns on the gondola piers were reflecting in the sloshing water of the Grand Canal. It was a great escape from the tyranny of automobiles, scooters, and bicycles—there were none. Everything was a picture postcard as they walked to peaceful chatter and the clanging of boats in the water. The women were exhausted, so the men walked them back to their hotel and left them to rest.

E wanted to get to the bottom of the Malachi question, so he pushed the men back onto the street and started with, "So tell me about Malachi, Father Caravello."

He looked over at E with a glinting smile and answered, "First, call me Francisco, and then I tell you about Malachi."

E laughed and said, "Okay, Frank."

Father Caravello's whole body laughed as he blurted out, "'Frank.' Well, okay. Good enough." Jack came up to the other side so he could hear, and Jasper stayed close to E's right shoulder.

Francisco humbly looked at the men and softly started, "First, let me say, I realize our differences. I'm Catholic and you're all Protestant. I know that we have regrettably waged war with each other in the past, but God has revealed to me that you, E, are the one I must come to with this. I was reading the first chapter of Malachi one day where God admonished the priests of Israel. He said, 'A son honors his father and a servant, his master. And if I'm your Father, where is the honor due me?' They were making things easy on the worshipers. As we would say, 'anything goes,' just so long as they came. They were bringing lame and diseased animals to be sacrificed. The way the priests responded to God was peculiar. They were surprised that God would complain. After all, they were getting the numbers up. God was furious and said they needed to shut the temple doors and not light useless fires. I can't tell you how much God has played this story over and over again in my head. Can you help me make sense of it?"

God had already enlightened E on Malachi before their trip. He looked intently into the man's gray-blue eyes with great love and respect and said, "First, I'm impressed with your humility. We've been calling you Father or 'Frank,' but I heard one of the waiters call you, 'Your Excellency.' I can see why God has chosen you to reveal His truth. I, too, was in Malachi and God revealed the same verses to me."

E continued. "As Christians, we think that the sacrificial system doesn't exist anymore, but we are to be the sacrifice. What God is telling you is He is tired of the church lowering its standards and allowing anything just to get people in the door. If you have no standards and you stand for nothing, then how is the world going to see any differences? He's not just talking to the church in general. He's talking to the church of this age, and I believe this age is the Laodicean Age. What God is telling you and me both is we've dropped the ball."

Francisco wiped his eyes, looked off over the lagoon, and said, "I was afraid you were going to tell me something like that."

Jack interjected, "Boy, you two are givin' us a good ear-bashin,' but to me, the priests were serving themselves and their egos and not God, as we do so many times ourselves."

Francisco looked at the men and said, "I'm glad to know you men, but if we are the Church of Laodicea, heaven help us."

Jasper looked over at both men, smiled with a gleam in his eye, and said, "The great news is God hasn't given up on us yet. After all, He gave you two men revelations for some reason."

Francisco smiled and asked, "So tell me this, why couldn't God just tell me what He meant? Why did He need E to tell me?"

Jack interjected, "Beg yours, but I think God loves our unity and our relying on each other. The unity of the body of believers makes God chuffed."

Francisco added, "And, I think He's also saying, 'Don't think you, your church, or even your country has all the answers.' God brought an American Protestant here to open my eyes! So where do we go from here, men?"

E looked intently into his face and said, "Your Excellency, we do nothing but make ourselves totally available to God and His leading."

All the men agreed and continued to walk across the Rialto Bridge, through the market, and back toward the hotel. As Francisco dropped off the men, he said "*Ciao!* Oh, E, could I speak with you privately for a minute?"

E stayed as the other men went inside the hotel. As they walked to the water's edge and found a seat, Francisco said, "I didn't want to say anything in front of them, but I had pretty much figured out that scripture. Everyone just confirmed what God was telling me."

E looked at him and knew there was more to the story. He studied him for a few moments and then asked, "So there's more, Your Excellency?"

Francisco smiled at E's perceptiveness and began in a whisper, "Well, I have a Jewish Rabbi friend I've been working on for years. He's extremely close to believing that Jesus *is* the Messiah, but he decided to put me to one more test. He's the reason I was studying Malachi. I believe that God is not going to blind the Jews forever."

E looked at him and agreed, "Me too. But what's so important about Malachi?"

Francisco looked over at E with a grin, but his eyes were somewhat sad. He answered, "I'd been telling Fishel for years that I could find Jesus anywhere in the Old Testament. I was successful in helping him discover many prophecies that Jesus fulfilled. I revealed to him that the two angels in Jesus's tomb at the head and foot were like the angels on the top of the ark and that Jesus was the fulfillment of the law that was inside the ark. However, recently he told me that if I could show him Jesus in the very last book of the Old Testament and the very last prophet to the Jews, he would no longer doubt my words and he would believe."

E looked at him with a stoic face as if he had been removed from his body for a few brief moments. Then he began to smile and his smile grew into a glowing expression of joy. Francisco looked as E and asked, "So I knew you would have something. What is it, my friend?"

E stated, "In Malachi chapter four, it says, 'But for you who revere my name, the Son of righteousness will rise with healing in His wings.' It's the last chapter of both of our Old Testaments and yet it talks about Jesus."

Francisco was thrilled, but with a sincere face, he asked, "That's so wonderful, but how do I convince my friend that the scripture is talking about Jesus?"

E smiled and answered, "In Luke chapter eight, Jesus is almost crushed by a large crowd of people wanting to get to Him. A woman who had been hemorrhaging for twelve years came up behind him and touched the hem of his cloak. If you know your Greek and know anything about Jewish traditions, you realize that he was wearing a *tallit*, or a prayer shawl. It was a garment that all Jewish men wore— a rectangular-shaped piece of linen. In each corner was a tassel that hung down to almost the ground. These are called *tzitzit*. The woman had grabbed one of the *tzitzit* in the corner of the prayer shawl."

Francisco interjected, "Although this is very interesting, E, I don't see the connection."

E smiled and continued, "Oh, you will. We know that Jesus was wearing a *tallit* because the Pharisees and the Sadducees would have had a fit if he weren't. So here's the important part. The Jews call each corner where the *tzitzit* is located 'wings.' So do you see now?"

Francisco shook his head with a big smile as tears started to stream down his round cheeks. He looked at E and said, "Healing in His wings," as he shook his head up and down. E smiled and patted him on the back. Francisco reached around E, gave him a big bear hug, and said, "Thank you, my friend. God truly uses you, and I can see why. You have no agenda of your own. You have no preconceived notions of any kind. You have no contempt for anyone and you have perfect humility. Tomorrow I'll take you all on a personal tour of my city by boat. As soon as everyone has had something to eat, meet me here by the water. Oh, and call me Frank." E smiled, gave him a nod, and walked inside to greet Elise and the others.

The next day was magnificent with blue skies, bright sunshine, and seventy-three degrees. The men with their Gondolier hats and blue striped sweaters were already serenading the tourists as they stepped aboard for a relaxing ride around the city. The traders were out and the shops were all open. Everyone met Francisco at the dock at ten and got on board. During their unforgettable tour, they floated along parts of the Grand Canal and other smaller canals then made their way across the lagoon to the island of Murano. They took a short stroll through the fairy-tale streets and perused the world-famous glass-blowing shops, buying souvenirs and watching demonstrations.

Elise was in heaven as she danced her way to each destination. "Frank, I'm so glad you have a big boat or we would've tipped by now!" E told Francisco, looking at Elise running along the bow. "Tomorrow all the couples are going their own way for our last day here. A little personal time, you understand?" E asked Francisco.

"I understand, but tell me that you will stay in touch," Francisco asked with resolve while walking into *Trattoria da Giorgio ai Greci*. "And let me treat everyone tonight, please," he said, while speaking to one of the waiters. E smiled and nodded. It was a wonderful restaurant and their table was canal-side with a beautiful view.

E looked over at Francisco and said, "I'll stay in touch and you do the same. I want to know what happens with your friend." They both smiled and enjoyed the rest of the night.

The next morning, everyone took advantage of the breakfast that was included with the rooms and left to go their own way for the day. E and Elise took a walk along the canals and decided to go up into the bell tower opposite the Basilica. Once at the top, they took in the whole of Venice, plus the two islands next to it. It was lovely to look at from such a high view.

They found a coffee shop close to the one they had visited on their first trip to Venice and sat there looking over the water, reminiscing about days gone by. Elise slowly approached the water's edge and proclaimed, "Once again with great sorrow, I must say good-bye to you, my sweet Venice."

"Don't get too emotional, Elise. I plan to come back and go to Rome next year!" E stated, trying to liven up the tense moment.

As everyone met for supper that night, it was with the greatest reluctance and empty wallets that they left, only to hope that they might return someday.

The Isle of Patmos

Artesia had changed vastly, but E and Elise soon adapted and made it their own again. E would supply for churches in the area and even took some interim positions while churches found new pastors. Elise, however, decided to start a Christian ministry that provided meals and the gospel for the homeless, helpless, and downtrodden. Elise's mother had died in 1980, so she decided to call the ministry Miriam's Hope. Over the next several years, they ministered together, traveling several times a year on mission trips to Mexico, Honduras, Argentina, and even Australia.

"Jas, it never ceases to amaze me. Every time I come down here to Mexico, it's as if I went back in time. This morning, I got up to a rooster crowing and a donkey braying! No interstate noises. In fact, I heard no cars! Where can you find that in the States?" E asked Jasper with a laugh.

E and Elise were on their annual pilgrimage to Jasper and Janie's mission in Mexico. It was early May, but the weather was already hot and muggy. "Jas, I gotta call from Pearl Rose before we left," E said with his head raised.

Jas looked at his old friend with a smile and asked, "Don't tell me they want ya back?"

E laughed vigorously and answered, "As a matter of fact, yes—for a one-night-only engagement! They're dedicating the new sanctuary next month. Can you believe it's been twelve years?"

Jas smiled as he looked off in the distance and answered, "I can't believe it. James is doin' a great job with the church and we continue to get contributions. In fact, the contributions have more than tripled since you were there, old man!"

E had a long, self-deprecating laugh and asked, "Why do you think God took me out when everything was just startin' to build?"

Jas looked into his old friend's eyes and realized that he missed being a pastor. Then he said, "Paul said, 'I planted, Apollos watered.' You were the seed sower, my friend, but your nephew, he's the reaper of the harvest. We all have our parts, don't we?" There was a slight pause, then Jasper started again. "You know, my son's doin' more than I'll ever do here. He's been raised with these people. He knows Spanish as well as they do. In fact, he speaks their dialect. He'll really be the reaper in this ministry, not us."

E looked over at his tired old friend and announced with fervor, "Well, I'm not down for the count yet, old codger!"

Jasper chuckled, patted E on the back, and said, "Have I ever told you how much I appreciate you? I really do. You've helped me through some hard times, my friend. You've listened when I needed an ear. You've chided me when I needed a good, stiff kick in the pants. And you've loved me and supported me when I was unlovable and not worth a dime. I really do appreciate it."

E looked at Jasper with an appreciative smile and said, "I could say the exact same thing about you. I do appreciate the good words, though."

They all went to a restaurant for a nice meal before E and Elise left for the States the next day. As they were getting up to go, Jasper collapsed on the floor. E ran over to see what he could do, but Jasper was gone just that quick. Everything seemed to go into slow motion as he looked down at his friend and over at Janie. She had a face like she expected it, but E was taken by complete surprise.

"E, he's been gettin' his affairs in order for some time now," Janie said with a sad smile.

E found himself thinking back through the conversations he'd had with Jasper that night. He had given E some riddle that Stout had stuffed into a journal in that safe deposit box. Jasper knew that it had something to do with the Pearl Rose land, because the man who had sold Stout the land had given it to him.

"E, I want you to have it. Before I gave you the land, I went to see if I could figure the riddle out, but I couldn't. I don't know if it will be any help to you, but it's yours as well as the pot of gold you find," Jasper said with a laugh.

Then E remembered something even more ominous about that night. Jasper had said, "This is my last time to see you for a while, my friend."

E had relied on Jasper so much through the years, and now his good friend was gone. After preaching Jasper's funeral back in Texas, it was time for E to prepare for the homecoming event at Pearl Rose. His heart wasn't in it, but he felt a profound duty toward God, the church, and his nephew, so he marched on even without his friend to bounce ideas off of.

"Well, Dr. Moses, you've done very well. The people seem to be growing spiritually," E stated with pride as he hugged his nephew.

James looked over at E and said, "Uncle, please don't call me 'Dr. Moses.'"

E laughed heartily and said, "But I'm proud of ya, son. It's not derogatory!"

James smiled and replied, "I know, Uncle, but it's absurd that you persist in addressing me with that prestigious title when you have the experience and the wisdom. If you insist on calling me 'Doctor,' I shall call you 'Master E' or somethin.'"

E laughed hysterically, hitting his leg hard with his right hand, and exclaimed, "No, ye shall not! You call me 'Uncle.' That has a much nicer ring to it."

Changing the subject, E looked around the new building and said, "This is unbelievable. This place could hold several thousand people!"

James, not taking his uncle's bait, said, "Uncle, I need to talk to you about the other building. They wanna tear it down to make room for more parking. Is there anything I need to know or any wishes you might have before that's done?"

E was touched that James would ask and he just stood there soaking up his nephew's humility for a moment. As his eyes widened, he abruptly asked, "Son, what're you planning to do with the bell?"

James answered, "The bell? Well, we have no plans for it. Maybe we could give it to another church?"

E smiled at his benevolence and commanded, "Let's take a walk. I have some things to tell you and they have to do with your father."

After their walk, James was noticeably shaken. His head was down and his eyes were red as he tried to regain his composure. "Uncle, I know that our new sanctuary doesn't have a bell tower, but what do you think about building a separate bell tower on that hill behind the church overlooking the water?" James asked.

E smiled and asked, "The hill where your aunt and I used to sit and watch the sunset?"

James nodded his head up and down. E answered with a bright smile, "I believe that's an inspired idea, and your father would love it."

James's eyes began welling up with tears as he tried to halt his emotions. E, trying to change the subject, quickly said, "Son, I have something else I want you to help me with before the services tonight. Aunt Elise is taking a nap, and if I don't do this now, I may never get the chance."

James quickly cured his melancholy state and asked, "Sure, Uncle. What is it?" As they changed clothes, E filled James in on the riddle and the circumstances surrounding it. James was excited and ready within minutes. It took E a little longer to get ready.

"Now, here's the riddle that was written on a yellow piece of tattered paper from Jasper:

Forty paces
From steel to steel branch
Walk toward the crossed arrows
Until darkness flees
Then lift up your eyes unto the hills
For He is the cornerstone
And no man is an island
At seven hands

E continued, "The only thing I've figured out is the steel part. We found the remains of a forge when we built the covered bridge years ago. 'From steel' would be our starting point, and I think maybe the 'steel branch' would be Steele Fork at forty paces east. That was the name of that fork in the road many years ago."

James interjected, "To Indians, an arrow wards off evil spirits, but crossed arrows mean friendship."

E looked intently at James for a moment and then blurted out, "*Amicitia!* That's the name of that old settlement to the north! It means friendship in Latin, I think. Let's get some gear and get over there!"

As they drove, James kept reciting the next line: "Until darkness flees."

Suddenly, E almost screamed out, "Light's Bluff! It's now a dumpsite, but many years ago, it was a beautiful place, from what I hear."

Soon, they stopped at Light's Bluff and got out of the car. The stench was so terrible they had to get back in the car, but they sat there looking out the windows for several minutes.

"'So lift up your eyes unto the hills'? That's a Biblical reference! 'Your help comes from the Lord'!" E said.

James pointed up to the adjacent hill where there was an old, over-grown, abandoned cemetery with a cross over the entryway. E leered over at James and said, "It would have to be that old spooky bone orchard! I always tried to stay away from that place. It gave me the creeps."

They finally made their way through the briers, vines, and under-growth covering the dilapidated limestone archway of the cemetery. As E and James stood there, they were almost ready to abandon the idea of buried treasure, especially if it had something to do with dead corpses.

Then suddenly James pointed to the right front corner of the cemetery and recited, "For He is the cornerstone." A very old, dark gray headstone with a cross on top was sitting undisturbed with the faint inscription, "John Donne—He lived to bless others."

E looked at James, shook his head, and exclaimed, "I don't think this is going to amount to anything. Besides, I'm not diggin' up some corpse. I don't care what he has in his hands!"

James excitedly announced, "Uncle, look closely. That's the only monument that has no date on it, and John Donne wrote, 'No man is an island'!"

E smiled with bright eyes and said, "Son, I'm glad I brought you along! I would've never gotten that!"

E and James began to dig, and at a little over twenty-eight inches (seven hands), they hit a large, square stone vault that measured forty inches by forty inches. They finally got the top stone off only to find another liner box made of cedar that was pitched with a tar-like substance. In the large, tarred box were these seven items:

1. A Colonial Bible in a carved box

2. A British heavy cavalry saber

3. A British cutlass with sheath

4. A large arrowhead pipe with some beads

5. A large lead box containing a British Angel Coin with a depiction of an angel on one side, seven gold bars, eight gold chains, including two that were over three feet long, thirty Spanish silver pieces, over a hundred guineas, seventy-five crowns, thirty-three half-crowns, forty shillings, and thirty sixpence.

6. A very old, handwritten copy of the English Magna Carta on papyrus.

7. A note written with incredible penmanship on a dried skin that said, "My name is James Elias Clear. I am an émigré from England who settled here in 1677. I came under fire from the Georgia Colony elders when I began expounding my theology. I believe in a covenant of grace,' in which faith alone is enough to achieve salvation. The men that dominated my colony disagreed, and I was banished and excommunicated from all the Colonies, so I came to settle here with the help of my Indian friends. I have secured this bounty to later retrieve when it becomes necessary for my use. If you have found it, that means I never made it back to claim it. Let it be known that if you have ill will for my treasure, I hereby curse your venture. But for you who have a pure heart, may God bless you through this finding."

E and James were enchanted as they made several trips to the car to load their treasure. James asked, "What are ya gonna do with all this, Uncle?"

E smiled and answered, "Well, you heard the man; we have to make sure our intentions are pure." Right then, E got a scripture in his head: "Go your way, sell whatever you have and give to the poor, and you will have treasure in heaven; and come, take up the cross, and follow Me." E stated, "I propose that we sell it to a collector as a complete set and give the money to Miriam's Hope."

James smiled and said, "I should've known you wouldn't keep anything for yourself."

E knitted his eyebrows at his nephew and said, "But I did! I had the adventure of a lifetime with my favorite nephew. I couldn't ask for more. After all, I have an unfailing treasure in heaven."

James looked over at his uncle, smiled, and asked, "Do you think it would be honorable to take some of the money and build that bell tower we talked about?"

E smiled and answered, "A great idea! You take your half and build the bell tower, and I'll take my half and give to Miriam's Hope."

James smiled at his uncle with a renewed respect and asked, "Uncle, do you think Clear Creek got its name from that man?"

E answered, "I think so. I always thought it was because the water was clear!" James looked over at E with big eyes and started to say something, but E said, "I know what you're thinkin', and you're probably right. This land was ordained to be church land long before we were ever thought of. I have an idea that God made a promise to that man and we benefited from it."

The dedication program started on time as Elise sat with James and Katherine.

E preached, "In Matthew 28:18–20, Jesus said, 'All authority has been given to me in heaven and on earth. Go, therefore, and make disciples of all the nations, baptizing them in the name of the Father and the Son and the Holy Spirit, teaching them to observe all that I commanded you; and lo, I am with you always, even to the end of the age.'

"We look at this passage as the so-called 'great commission' to the church, but do we understand all that it's saying? Not only to go, not only to baptize, but also to teach and make disciples. We get all caught up in saving, when it's not even mentioned there. We want to save the world, but we can't. We can invite, we can inform, we can seek, help, heal, feed, and baptize, but we don't save anyone—not even ourselves. The Spirit pricks the heart, but Jesus alone saves. Do you see what Jesus wants here? He wants quality Christians—Christians who know wrong from right, darkness from light. Christians who are unique because of their relationship with Him, not because of some religion they follow."

E continued, "We can get a good idea of the church's mission through some other scriptures too. For instance, John 3:17, 'For God did not send the Son into the world to judge the world, but that the world should be saved through Him.' There are some among us who tend to believe that we are the 'sin police,' the moral judges of the world already knowing who's going to hell and what type judgment they will receive. They put people down, talk about them, and try to ruin them because they know who is evil and they're trying to help God out. Friends, if Jesus didn't come into this world to judge, I feel very confident that He wants us to follow that example. A lot of you might 'amen' that, but I'm fixin' to step on some more toes. In Mark 10:45 it says, 'For even the Son of Man did not come to be served, but to serve, and to give his life a ransom for many.' Christ didn't come to be served, but to serve. Did you hear me right? Are you serving your church? Well, that's commendable. Are you serving your community? Well, that's great. Are you serving your neighbors? Well, that's just wonderful. But are you serving the undesirable, the down-and-out, and the unclean? If you are, you're getting close to what Jesus is calling you to do, but no cigar. Are you serving your enemy? The people who are unkind to you? The type of service that Christ is calling you to is not service with strings attached. It's acting as if the least of these were Christ himself. Are you serving like that? The good news is God supplies you with what you need to serve fellow man. So if God saves, if the Spirit pricks, and if God gives you the tools you need for His purposes, what is He calling you to do? One thing, my friends, and one thing alone—*availability*." As he finished his sermon, over a dozen people came up to rededicate themselves to Christ's plan for their lives and three came up to be baptized. James and Katherine hugged E and Elise, telling them they wished they lived closer.

By late summer, Janie had moved back to the States and was helping Elise and Mary with Miriam's Hope. Janie and Mary made it possible for Elise to go to Australia with E in the fall. E had gotten a distressing letter from Jack and wanted to get over there to make sure he was okay.

In his letter, he said, "Tiny, I've seen the wonders of God on earth, but I'm truly ready to give the wonders of His heaven a burl and rest for a while with my wonderful wife who died at Christmas."

By the time E and Elise got there, Jack was gone. His son, Ethan, was so excited to see his namesake again, but he was sorry that they had made such a long journey. E still used the opportunity to pay respects to Jack and Matilda and to instruct Ethan in his future ministry. They did what they could for three weeks, helping him get things in order and giving him a hand. While they were there, Elise had some dizzy spells and E wanted to get her back home soon, so they said their good-byes and headed back to the States.

The next Monday morning, Elise walked into Miriam's Hope and collapsed to the floor. She looked over at E in the hospital and said, "Somefing's wong wif me, honey."

E smiled and said, "Nothing that we can't get through together. You don't worry, sweetheart, I'm here. You just get some rest."

She smiled at him with a tear running down her cheek and gripped his hand tightly. He suddenly had a flashback to the place where he had proposed to her, holding her hand so tightly, never to let it go.

As he sat there by Elise that night, he began conversing with God. "God, I feel so helpless and this darkness makes it hard to see, but that's when I must trust you more. I trust that you make all things good for those who love you and there's a reason for everything. God, you keep bringing me back to the Isle of Patmos in my dreams and in my studies. Why? Is it because John was alone, too?

He was exiled to the solitude of a small island without friends or family. Would John have been so available to you otherwise? Maybe he would have been running around to all the churches, putting out fires, but you wanted him still, focused, and alone. What a vicious tyrant meant for evil, you turned to ultimate good. I can look and see your hand in his life, but I doubt he realized the impact his revelation would have on the world. Help me to have that kind of trust in you, God, trust that knows you are in total control, even when it looks so chaotic and out of control. I have tried to pray for Elise's healing, but you stop me each time. I can't pray that prayer, but God, help me to know what to pray. She's my wife and we are of one flesh and I do ask that you have your will in her life as well as mine." There was a long silent period, then he prayed, "God, please don't take Elise. Please. I beg you, God." After his prayer, he collapsed from exhaustion in the chair next to her bed.

As he went into a deep sleep, he dreamed. It was a very dark place, but the moon was out and the stars were bright. You could hear the surf from all sides as the wind blew softly, rustling the Tamarisk trees. It was a quiet place, a very lonely, dark, and solemn place. Almost immediately, he saw an old man with a gray beard. He was sitting on a large rock with a cane in one hand, praying, just praying. Then it was over. The dream ended very abruptly with the image of John praying on Patmos seared into his head. He jerked his head up and then he was awake.

Elise was looking at him with the most loving eyes. She reached out her hand and put it on his cheek and said, "My E-bee Jeebee." Suddenly he realized how much he loved her and how much he would miss her laughter, her singing, and her love if she were gone.

"I know why, God," he said in a small whisper. "I know why it had to be Patmos. 'Tribulation' comes from the word, *'thlipsis,'* which means 'pressure.' You had to put him in a place of great pressure where he would pray that you would bring him deeper into yourself, and then the very straits that he was in had served their purpose. He was praying because he was continually praying—not for himself but for the churches, for the saints, for your will to be done. You want me to continually pray, too. You want me to be a prayer warrior. But God, why do you have to take away everyone I love to make that happen?" He laid his head down on Elise's bed and cried himself back to sleep.

The doctor ordered blood tests, which showed that she only had a vitamin deficiency. Monthly injections seemed to combat the problem for a while, but her memory was slipping. Although she had periods of appearing to be normal, there were other times she seemed to be very confused.

Elise was in the first stages of Alzheimer's and her body and mind were wasting away slowly, but God's love for her and E was still as strong as it had ever been. They would continue to pray together each morning. One morning, she got up, got dressed, and said she had to make breakfast for the girls before they went to school. It made E very sad, but right after that, he got a scripture from Genesis in his head. "Enoch walked with God…" He continued to drive himself with even more resolution to make Elise's life as comfortable as possible and to do that which God had called him to do—walk with Him. A true test of spiritual maturity is not measured by what a person does in the extraordinary times, but in the ordinary times when there's nothing noteworthy happening and no one watching. Those are the times that bring you to your second wind, spiritually. To walk with God, you have to get into His stride and into His viewpoint on every level.

"Honey, I've been thinking that I need to write some memories and thoughts down so I can remind myself when I forget. Would you get me a journal?" Elise asked.

E just looked at her with a peaceful smile and said, "Of course, honey. I will get it today."

He didn't tell her that she already had three journals. The following is an excerpt from one of them:

"It's a Wednesday and it seems like Saturday to me for some reason. At some future point in my disease, my dear E, you will probably have to consider placing me in a nursing home. You will be forced to make a decision you would rather not make, and I realize that hurts. I know you love me, E-bee Jeebee, and I love you more than life itself. I know that our love surpasses anything this life doles out and it can't be defeated by some disease. Even if I don't know you one day when I wake up, please know that it's only temporary. As much as I would like to be by you to the end, my dear, I know that things happen and I want you to continue with your life. If you place me in a nursing home, there are some real advantages, including a well-trained medical staff and programs that are designed specifically for my problems. I know you, E, and I know that you will put everything into caring for me, even at the detriment of your own health. That's not something I want you to do."

Within three years, E had to be checked into the hospital for exhaustion and malnutrition. Joy had found him on the floor, and Elise was curled up next to him with her head against his. She had poured pills on top of his body, knowing something was wrong with him and trying to help.

"Hope, I know that we have ta do something, but you know Poppa," Joy told her sister.

Hope said, "Well, I'm gonna insist that he hire a nurse to stay with them during the night and for a few hours in the morning. Grace has already moved a hospital bed into the house."

"Well, I've talked to a friend of theirs who wants to help out. I think we should see if we can pay them to cook at least one meal a day and maybe clean twice a week," Joy insisted.

Hope exclaimed, "I think that's a wonderful idea!"

Soon, a nurse and a housekeeper were hired part-time to look after them. For the next several years, E stayed on his knees and in the Bible studying, as Elise gradually slipped further and further away from him. The housekeeper was a strong Christian lady and loved serving E and Elise. The nurse was not a Christian, so E made it his calling to lead her to the Lord and gave her a Bible. He wrote in the front of it:

God says He loves each of us (John 4:10)
and He thinks of each one of us continually (Psalm 139:17, 18).
How amazing is that?
He is willing to daily bear our burdens (Psalm 68:19)
and Jesus will give us abundant life (John 10:10).
He has given us the Bible,
full of wonderful promises and hope.
If you will read it and
ask God what He is trying to tell you through it,
your mind will be opened in a new and marvelous way.

The Test of Time

> "Distance tests a horse's strength. Time reveals a person's character."
>
> —Chinese Proverb

I, Levi, was sent by God to three churches in and around Port Arthur, Texas, to test them. The results of the test will not only ensure blessing on those who pass, but will curse those who fail.

"Hi. My name is Levi, sir, and I was wondering if you could help me. I'm having some hard times, but I'm willing to work," I said to Dr. Polk as he was coming out of his elaborate church office at 3:30 p.m.

He proceeded to direct me to Christian Services Mission downtown, which helped "people like me."

I insisted, "Sir, I've been there, but I was really hoping for some work to get me back on my feet. Anything would do, and I'm a very hard worker."

Dr. Polk was tired and he had a large party at his house to attend. He looked at me with disdain as he grunted and announced, "Mister, there's nothing I can do for ya. Now, you just go down there to that mission and look for Mr. Matt Huggins, and he'll fix ya up. Tell'm I sent you." Then he hurried off toward his big, fancy car with his big, fancy suit and jumped in like he was escaping from an armed robber, leaving a plume of gray-blue smoke behind him.

The second church was on the outskirts of town and was not as large as the first church. "Yes, ma'am. My name is Levi and I …" was all I got out before the church secretary motioned for a man who was standing across the room to "deal" with me.

She said nothing at all to me as she went back to scratching paper with her pen and sipping her Earl Grey, like I was sub-human rot that had oozed off the street and into her prim and proper world. The man came over and forcefully pushed me back out the front door.

I continued to speak to him. "Sir, could I ask for your help? You see, I'm a little down on my luck, but I'm willing to work. I'm a hard worker and …"

Before I could finish his sentence, the man had shuffled me out the door into the street and left me there. He looked back over his shoulder and almost screamed, "And don't come back!" shaking his finger at me. Three years later, God dismantled that church, brick by brick.

The third church was larger than the second, but smaller than the big church downtown that I first visited. As I walked into the office, two deacons were walking out of the conference room.

I appeared in front of the secretary and said, "Ma'am, I hate to bother you, but I'm a little down on my luck and would appreciate some help. I'm willing to work, if you know of anything …"

George Raymond, the chairman of the deacons, overheard the conversation and before the secretary could say anything, looked over at me and asked, "What's your name, sir?"

I answered, "My name is Levi."

"Come on in here, Levi. I want you to meet our pastor, Reverend Hudson Taylor," George said enthusiastically.

Hudson was just finishing up with a deacon's lunch meeting and the topic they had focused on was "How can we be better ministers to the downtrodden?"

"Hudson, I would like you to meet Levi. He's a little down on his luck and needs a job," George stated as he smiled at Hudson.

"Well, George, here's your opportunity to minister; why don't you give'm a job?" Hudson said.

George's grin turned into shock as he saw the tables turned. "Well, I—" George started.

Hudson cut him off with, "Oh, come on, George. Give the man a chance. If you will, I'll get him some clothes and a place to stay."

"Okay, pastor. Have him at my office at seven in the morning sharp and I'll find somethin' for him to do," George said.

Hudson looked over at me smiling and asked, "Are you hungry, Levi?"

"Well, it's been some time since I ate," I answered softly.

Hudson pushed a button on the phone to talk to Margery, his secretary in the front office, and said, "Marge, would you bring that extra lunch box in here, please? Here you go, Levi. Eat up and then we'll get you some clothes to work in. I'll be in the front office when you're finished," Hudson said as he gave the box of food to me.

Soon, I came out and Hudson motioned for me to have a seat while he finished his conversation on the phone. "Okay, Marge, I'll be back in about an hour," Hudson said, while he motioned for me to follow. As we got into Hudson's truck, the clouds seemed to be pushed away and the sun finally broke through. After Hudson went over to get some clothes for me, he talked to another deacon who had a furnished one-bedroom apartment above his horse stables. It wasn't fancy, but it was available and comfortable. Hudson left me at the apartment and drove back to the church.

"Marge, I'm back. Any messages?" he asked as he zipped through his office door.

"No, pastor, but didn't you give that lunch box to that man?"

Hudson came back out of his office and answered, "Yes, why?"

She said with a confounded look, "Well, Lily was cleaning the conference room and noticed that it hadn't been touched. It still had the seal on it and everything."

Hudson looked puzzled and said, "Huh," and then went back into his office.

The next day came early for Hudson. He had gotten a call from a member who had a relative involved in a car accident, so he didn't get back home until 3:00 a.m. He rushed over to the apartment that he had left me in and knocked on the door. I was ready to go as we made our way to George's shop where they made custom cabinets.

After I filled out all the paperwork, they sent me over to the nurse for a urine sample. "It's a drug test, Levi, and everyone has to take it," George said, in case I might get the idea that George was discriminating against me. "Levi, Ernie will show you the ropes today and maybe tomorrow we can get you started on some real work," George said as he retired upstairs to his office.

By ten, Ernie had shown me everything. "Well, Levi, you have any questions?" Ernie asked.

"Only one, sir," I said.

"Well, what is it?" asked Ernie, thinking he was going to have to go back over everything.

"Well, sir, when can I get to work?" I asked.

"Well, I hardly think you're ready to do much work yet, Levi," Ernie answered as he laughed.

"Well, I'm very familiar with cabinet work. I can do anything you ask," I said.

Ernie's curiosity got the best of him. Besides, he had to break the "new guy" in right, so he blurted out a whole set of dimensions on some kitchen cabinets he was working on and told me to figure out how it needed to be built and take a shot at it. He had been working on the job before I showed up, but there were so many crooks and turns in the dimensions, he had almost given up. Soon I was finished and the cabinets were a work of art.

"Levi, I've never seen that kind of quality work, especially that quickly," George stated.

For two solid weeks, I worked for them. I was there at seven a.m. and left at seven p.m. The shop was very far behind on orders before I came, but I helped them to catch up on so many levels. It was payday, Friday the seventh. I had worked hard and George wanted to hand deliver my check.

"Levi, it gives me great pleasure to present this check to you. Thank you for your hard work," George stated with pride, reaching for my hand to shake. I bowed humbly and took the check.

All weekend, George excitedly thought up more things for me to do. He wanted to pick me up himself Monday morning. As he knocked on the door of the small apartment with a bag full of sausage biscuits, the door swung open.

"Levi?" George said forcefully. He went inside and walked around. It was if no one had been there in months. It was very clean—almost too clean. He looked in the pantry and saw that all the food that was given me was unopened. He went into the bedroom, and on the end of the single bed was a neatly folded stack of clean clothes. On top was the un-cashed check for two weeks work. George quickly called down to the church ... but I was not there. As they all thought back, they realized they never once saw me after work.

As both George and Hudson sat in the conference room discussing the matter, Marge bolted in unannounced and said, "Guys, y'all are not gonna believe this. They ran his social security number and that number hasn't even been issued yet."

Hudson squinted at George and Marge, saying, "Look, you're not goin' to get me that easy! Okay, he's gone and he was a great worker, but that's it. So I wish him well and good luck."

Marge said, "There's more, pastor. The last name that he gave, 'Sarim,' means angel prince in Hebrew! And he left a note…well, if you call it that."

"What note?" Hudson asked with surprise.

"Well, it has your name on it, but it was just a red circle drawn on a white sheet of paper with the Bible verse, Luke 2:14, written on it," Marge said with large eyes, waiting for a comeback.

Hudson just looked at the two of them, rolled his eyes, threw his hands up in the air, and exited the room. I had issued part of the blessing for passing the test, but you can't out-give God. The biggest "blessing" was yet to come.

The Full Circle

As E emerged from his excursion through time, he found himself sitting by the lake with his feet in the water. Soon it was time to go home. He sat down in his appointed seat in the back of the big car and readied himself for the long trip back to Artesia. As he straightened his fancy kerchief in his suit, he looked over the water of Cross Lake and smiled at his life and all the experiences that God had given him.

"What do you mean, 'he's out of money'? They had three hundred thousand just over two years ago! Do you mean to say that medical expenses have been that extensive?" Joy Lyons said to her sister, Faith.

"Sis, that was over three years ago, and look, this isn't going to be easy for anyone, but what do we do? Poppa won't let us put Momma in a 'home'—he wants to be with her. You have the only place that can accommodate both of 'em right now. We're getting ready to move. Besides, we'll help you monetarily as much as we can. John has already said he would pay for the full-time nurse," pleaded Faith, the oldest of three girls.

"Look, we're selling the old place. Daddy wants us to divide up the furniture, the dishes, and Mother's crystal. The money we get for the house, I'll give to you for expenses. He wants to keep the photo albums and his truck and boat, though. What do ya think?" Faith asked.

"Well, does Grace want this too?" Joy asked.

"Yes, Grace has already been over to straighten, clean, and box up things. We need you to come up as soon as possible," Faith said.

"Okay, I'll talk with Frank tonight and see what he says," Joy said cautiously while her hands shook with anticipation.

Soon, E and Elise were on their way to Port Arthur to live with their daughter, Joy. Things were cramped in the bedroom with a small bath, but E made the best of the situation. He placed the large hospital bed in the middle of the room and set his cot up in the corner near his wife's head. Most of their earthly possessions were either sold or passed out to the family. Joy was the second oldest and the closest to her mother. However, Frank Lyons, her husband, was not a good host, to say the least. E couldn't help but wonder if he was in the lion's den like Daniel.

"Poppa, I'm sorry about this. I wish I could offer you somethin' better, but it's the best we can do," Joy said as they moved into her humble suburban home. "As you know, Frank's been disabled since the accident and we're struggling ourselves to make ends meet."

E looked intently into his daughter's eyes with a peaceful smile and said, "Joy, we have all we need. I appreciate you taking care of us and letting us stay here."

Joy and Frank had a troubled marriage. They stayed together without satisfaction and learned to live lonely lives without intimacy or harmony. Maybe it was because they wanted a stable lifestyle modeled for their kids, or possibly it was because they couldn't afford lives apart, but they stayed together. E was very aware of the situation, even though they tried to hide it.

He would say a few well-placed words to Frank and Joy from time to time to get them thinking, like, "Life's a journey to our God and relationships are the roads we take to get there."

Joy was grieved that her father knew of her "failure," as she considered it, but he never judged either of them. He would whisper to Elise, "Our very purpose in life is to love. It strengthens us, brings us to greatness, and encourages joy and peace in our lives. I'm afraid that our little Joy has had very little joy in her life, and that saddens me. It's time for us to pray very diligently for both of them."

From the start, Frank was threatened by what he considered an "intrusion into his personal life." He might not have been abusive physically, but he was very abusive emotionally.

"Joy, you need to tell your father to keep quiet about his views. This is my house and I don't wanna hear anything from a failed, old preacher. If he would've saved his money and planned better, he wouldn't have to beg from us!" Frank exclaimed.

"Frank, that's my father you're talkin' about, and they didn't have retirement plans back then. Besides, he had savings, but mother's been sick for a very long time."

Frank asked a little louder and with a snap in his neck, "Well, where's God then? Did God forsake them? They gave their lives to God and God's work, and look where it got'm—broke without a pot to pee in and living in a borrowed room in south Texas. Pathetic!" Then he left to find something to do in his shop.

"Joy, some marriages are like the man who wrote the IRS a letter stating, 'I can't sleep: my conscience is bothering me.' He encloses a check for $50 in the envelope and continued, 'If I still can't sleep, I'll send you the balance."

She looked at her father apologetically and said, "Look, this whole thing will work out, Poppa. Just give him some time."

E continued, "Put everything into your marriage, and believe that marriage can make you something more, not something less that you are, and learn to enjoy your differences."

Joy said, "Daddy, why don't you just say it. I have a problem with my husband because I've done something to deserve it. I get it."

E said, "I never said any of that. What I'm tryin' to say is you have to get past your own picky criticisms of yourself before you can truly let anyone in. Your purpose in life is to love, but you first have to love yourself. Open your heart, Joy, and then everything will usually follow suit. If they don't, have the fortitude to move past it and choose not to suffer, thinking it's somehow your fault."

Joy said, "Okay, Poppa, but if you know what's best, you'll stay out of our lives, especially Frank's."

E looked at Joy and smiled. She had seen that smile before. It said, "Don't ask me to promise anything."

The weather was beginning to look like spring on that cool, blue March Sunday morning. There was a little church within walking distance of the house, so E decided that he was going to explore its treasures. He went down to meet the pastor the week before, but he was threatened by E's presence and acted like he was much too busy for any conversation. When he first arrived, E had felt tension in the air. Something was definitely very wrong there and the Spirit let him know it quickly. E immediately tried to intercede, but no one was talking. He decided to kneel and pray right in the hallway of the church.

Just then, the Spirit started speaking. *He hasn't added My virtues to his life. His goodness is limited to intermittent occasions with his family and friends. His knowledge is limited to only what he can study and read, but it only leads to vanity and self-glory. It's only doctrine without intimacy with Me. He has no self-control, exhibited in his sexual relationship with the church secretary. Self-control is necessary to understand the greatness of his salvation. He's abandoned his "point" in a very serious war. The whole church has suffered because he has not persevered. My character and precepts are opposing views to him. You were his last test, brotherly kindness and love, and he failed miserably. He's been condemned to lose everything he holds dear, even his family.*

Suddenly, E had a sadness deep inside his soul and a lament for the man. "God, please don't be hasty in your judgments of this man. A man should be entitled to be judged by his best moments, not his worst. Please let me try to get through to him. After all, you did call him to your purposes and he *is* your child. Please, God?" E waited for several minutes without an answer from God. He stood his ground and continued to insist. God finally said, *E, you have forty days and then my judgment is final.*

Pastor Bob Small looked at the old man on his knees in the hallway and thought, *How pathetic—the old preacher has to stoop to such measures to get noticed by me.* He walked over and asked, "Are you all right, Brother E?"

E answered, "Brother Small, I was just prayin.' Hope you don't mind."

Bob said, "Well, of course not, but we do have a room for that." E had already seen a problem in that one statement. He had compartmentalized his life—one side for Church and God, and the other side for him and whatever he wanted.

"Oh, I think we need to stay in constant contact with God all the time, don't you think, Brother Small?" E asked, as he cut his eyes toward Bob.

Frank and Joy had been attending the little church, but had never joined and were not even regular attendees. "Poppa, I don't think you're gonna like it there," Joy had already told him. E knew the little church was not where God wanted him to end up, but he had to try and save the pastor from inevitable ruin.

"Brother Small, you ever studied 2 Chronicles 33? That story says to me, 'It's one thing to overlook God from time to time, but to have utter disregard for Him is another.' When we ignore God long-term, it leads to serious consequences. David was an adulterer and a murderer. However, it was Saul who paid the biggest price, and he did none of those things. Saul never turned back to God. He never repented and he never learned from his mistakes," E said with authority.

Bob Small felt it very hard to breathe. His ears turned blood red and his face was on fire. He knew it was only an old preacher who had spoken to him, but he felt as if God himself had spoken to his soul.

"Brother E, I'm sorry, but I have to get ready for my sermon," Bob announced as he hurried off down the hall.

"I think you just got your sermon," E whispered under his breath.

After the pastor left, E went down the hall to the office. There sat Polly Mead, church secretary and Frank's mother's younger sister. "Good morning, Mrs. Mead. And how are you?" E asked as his eyes darted in a piercing stare.

Looking much too busy to respond, she gave him a quick nod and continued with her duties.

"You know what I've found out?" E asked her, trying to get a response.

She looked up from her computer with wide eyes, trying to hide any nervousness his question might have raised, and asked, "What's that?"

He immediately responded to her with, "I've learned how to avoid the snares of the enemy and walk without fear or worry."

Her curiosity got the best of her as she started wondering what the old man knew about her indiscretions. She looked at him with insincere boldness and asked, "So how'd you learn that?"

He looked deep into her eyes and answered, "By learning where all the traps are."

If she wasn't sure before, she was sure now. The old man knew. But how? She'd been very careful to cover her tracks. "Well, I'll take care of that old man," she said to herself as she shuffled off to the sanctuary.

"You either leave this alone, or I'll make sure your life is a living hell. Do you understand me, old man?" Frank commanded to E as if he were in charge of those sorts of things.

E just looked into Frank's eyes. He was not about to go against God. Frank could tear him limb from limb, but he had already resolved to continue his quest.

"You know, Frank, when we ignore God, we forget the very source of all blessings. It will not turn out good to live as if we are the origin of everything good in our lives," E stated to Frank after several seconds of silence.

"Look, old man, save all the religious mumbo-jumbo for Joy or somebody else. I don't wanna hear it. You just make sure you do what I say. You stay away from my aunt. She's a good person and she don't deserve your remarks!" Frank yelled as he bounced a fist off the doorsill and exited.

E looked over at Elise and said, "Making decisions according to our own pursuits and desires is a recipe for disaster. We have a lot of praying to do." Elise looked at E as a small tear ran down her cheek and he realized that she understood. "You know, Elise, I could be doin' a lot of self-pitying, but self pity is from Satan. If I wallow in these things that seem to be swallowing me whole, I can't be used for God's purposes. We have to trust God, no matter how things look or what happens to us. Trust is the opposite of fear," E continued as he bowed by Elise's bed.

The next day was calm and beautiful. E had gotten only three hours of sleep, but somehow he felt rested. He kissed Elise on the cheek and walked out the door of the house to the stillness of the morning. A mockingbird swished by his shoulder and chattered something that sounded like, "Today's the day!" The leaves were a glimmering light green, signifying new life from the dead. E knew the Spirit was giving him a picture of what seeds had to be sown— repentance, forgiveness and restoration, then the wonderful liberty of new life. He felt as if he had wings to fly, but his old legs were not about to bring him to take-off speed.

The church was cool from the night and silent, similar to the silence before a storm, but E had his full armor on and his sword was drawn. As he turned the corner and approached the church office, he felt a shift in the wind. It was as if it were going before him, clearing the way.

"Good morning, Mrs. Mead," E strongly stated as he entered the front office. Mrs. Mead and the front office were barricades that Azazel had placed there to block what needed to be done.

E looked into her eyes and continued, "'To those who believe in His name, He gives the right to become children of God,' John wrote in his gospel. Sadly, some people don't have a father who shows them love. But God's the perfect parent. It would be totally against His character to mistreat any of His children."

She was stunned. Her eyes became fixated on her Bible that was sitting on the edge of her desk, open to John. She thought, *How did he know about my relationship with my father?*

She never even saw E go past her desk and straight into Bob's office. He walked right up to Bob while he was on the phone and motioned for him to hang up. "Bob, let's take a walk," E commanded.

Bob slowly pushed his chair back and walked around his desk as if he had no recourse but to obey. As they walked by Polly's desk, without eye contact, Bob said, "We'll be back soon."

While they sat behind the church on a picnic table, Bob said emphatically, "Look, Brother E, what's it gonna take for you to leave this alone? I don't wanna cause you problems, ole man, but you need to stop putting your nose in this, you understand?"

E looked at Bob with love and said, "The Lord's sending you a message through me and if you don't receive it and turn from your sins, there are serious repercussions. Do *you* understand?"

Bob was not going to be thrown that easily. He stood puffed up, his eyes flaring with anger. "Look, old man—," was all he got out before a large wind almost tipped him over while he was speaking. He got his composure back and continued, a little more respectfully, "Look, Brother E, I know that you think you have the best of intentions, but you have no idea what you're messin' with. I'm asking you to let this alone. Please?"

E started to look larger than life to Bob. A supernatural glow seemed to envelop him as he stood and proclaimed with his index finger, "Bob, be on your guard so that you won't be carried away by the error of lawless men and fall from your secure position. But grow in the grace and knowledge of your Lord and Savior. To him be glory, both now and forever."

After E finished quoting scripture found in 2 Peter, he walked back down the road to where Elise was waiting. "Elise, he didn't listen. This is going to be a lot harder than I thought," he whispered to his wife as he got her ready for the nurse.

Polly had been busy on the phone all day, trying to find out where E got his information. She made sure to spread the rumor that he was making trouble, especially for the pastor. Frank had been working at the stockyard, helping to herd cattle into the corral for the auctioneers. But when he took his break, Melanie Barge, a church busybody, was waiting for him. "Frank, you gotta stop your father-in-law. He's gonna end up splittin' the church!" she exclaimed in a frantic gobble.

"What's he done now, Melanie?" Frank asked with a red face and tight jaw.

"Well, Polly says he's meddling in personal things. He even knew about her problems with her father!"

Frank was fuming as he kicked open the gate with his boot. "That's it! I told him to leave this alone. Now, he's really gonna pay!"

Melanie let her curiosity get the best of her and asked, "What're you gonna do?"

With nostrils flared, he answered, "Not sure, but it won't be good."

"So, Shorty, how much will you give me?" Frank asked his friend who owned a used car business in town.

"Well, the boat's in great shape and the truck looks like someone kept it in a museum. I'll give you top dollar for 'em. I even think I have a buyer," he answered.

"Great, I'll bring you the title tomorrow," Frank stated with resolve.

The next day was hard for E. He had been up with Elise most of the night. She seemed to be restless about something. As he walked out the door, E immediately noticed his truck and boat were missing. He went back in to ask Joy about it, but she knew nothing. As she looked over at Frank, he nonchalantly replied, "I sold them. We needed the money." At that very moment, the lights flickered in the old house. God was not pleased with Frank. He had come against God's anointed, but God would reserve judgment, giving him time to repent.

E walked outside, staring at the place where his truck and boat had been. He was looking forward to fishing, but now he had nothing to look forward to. Then, at that moment, he snapped out of his pity party and proclaimed, "God, I'm sorry. For a moment there, I took my corrective glasses off. I forgot that my point of view should always be from eternity. I'm content to know that you care for me and give me everything I need." He suddenly got a huge smile on his face and a peace in his eyes as he walked back inside.

Frank and Joy had been feuding and she was very quiet while cleaning the kitchen. Frank was sitting in the den with a smirky grin, reading his paper and thinking that he had finally put the old man in his place.

"It's a beautiful day, isn't it?" E said, as he seemed to float through the house back toward the bedroom where Elise was waiting.

Frank was in shock. He thought, *What did I do wrong? If anything was going to bring the old man down, it had to be selling his fishing boat and truck. Was he off his rocker?* Frank was completely perplexed as he sat there, staring into space with his mouth open.

Joy smiled and said to herself, "That's my Poppa."

E couldn't let himself be taken off task; he only had seven more days before the forty days were up. He had to try again. He got on the phone and called the church. Polly was out for the morning, so Bob answered the phone. With great authority, E said, "Bob, we have to talk. Meet me downtown at Eleanor's Diner for lunch."

There was a big pause while the Holy Spirit was clutching Bob's heart, then he conceded, "I'll be there. Twelve o'clock."

Now, E had to figure out how he was going to get there. Joy and Frank were leaving to see their kids in Houston and they had the only car. "Joy, what's the name of that place where Frank sold my truck?" E asked.

"Poppa, it's Cowboy Auto Sales, but I think it's already sold. Why?" she asked.

"Oh, just wanted to know," E answered as he walked back to his room.

"Shorty Charms, please?" he said, as he waited on hold.

"Yes, Shorty? This is Frank Lyon's father-in-law. I was wonderin' if you could give me the name of the person who bought my truck? You see, I need to tell them some things about it," E said.

"There's nothin' wrong, is there?" Shorty asked.

"Oh, no. It's all good things," E answered quickly.

Shorty, thinking that it would only make him look better to the buyer, said, "Well, it was a pastor. His name's Hudson Taylor."

As he got his phone number, E thanked him and immediately dialed the number.

"Pastor Taylor, this is Ethan Moses, I understand that you bought my truck and boat from Cowboy Auto Sales?"

"Well, if your truck was red with a boat behind it, I guess I probably did," Hudson answered with apprehension.

"Congratulations, but I need to share some things with you. Nothin' bad, it's just that Bessie is particular about some things."

"Well, Mr. Moses, was it?" Hudson asked.

"Reverend Moses and I'll be waiting at eleven. Just pick me up at thirty-three Morning Star Road," E answered and then hung up.

Hudson was left scratching his head. He said to Marge, "I just had one of those *Twilight Zone* moments. That was the guy that owned my truck and boat and he wants me to pick him up so he can tell me all about 'Bessie'!"

Marge laughed and said, "Well, you have to go. I mean, it's interesting. Anything that can shock *you* is very interesting. I almost wanna go myself," she said while laughing.

"Go ahead and laugh, but the best part is he's a preacher," he said, shaking his head.

"Well, that does make it interesting. So when is this chance meeting?" she asked.

"Well, in a few minutes. I'm not even sure I have enough time to get there," Hudson said.

Marge grabbed his coat off the rack, tossed it to him, and said, "What 'ya waitin' for?"

As he pulled up to the old house, he started to wonder what kind of preacher E was. Soon, E bolted out of the door with his coat in hand and said, "Hudson was it? Glad to meet you. We can talk while you drive me to the diner downtown."

Hudson was beginning to get the picture. An old retired pastor, no transportation, and a sucker driving him to his favorite place to eat…he didn't lose his truck, he'd gained a chauffeur.

They were soon at the diner, so E thanked Hudson for driving him there and said, "I'll see ya Sunday, preacher," as he flew out of the door and into the restaurant. Hudson shook his head and drove back to the parsonage to eat a bite before going to the hospital to visit the sick.

"Look, Bob, the way I see it is, Christians are dieting on God and gorging themselves on the pitiful, spoiled meat of this world. I was very concerned about your sermon on Philippians four. It's not a 'name it and claim it' verse. It's not to be used as some magical potion for personal victory. All it means is that he could handle any situation God gave him, for better or for worse, because the Lord gave him the ability to be content in everything. And John 14:13–14 is not a way to worldly prosperity; it's a call for spiritual obedience. Don't twist your scriptures because it fits your appetite at the time. God will really come down on you for perverting His Word like that." E looked over his shoulder at the old diner and noticed a sleazy man who had been very attentive to every word he said.

E said, "Bob, let's move outside to the patio tables and talk some more." E was on a roll and he was making strides, but he had just begun. As they sat outside, E continued, "Look, Bob, I'm not here to condemn you but to help you get back on track. I know you're doin' some things that you shouldn't be doing."

Bob was really beginning to come around. He was broken and willing to receive what E was saying. Suddenly, E looked around and saw that same man from the diner, trying to hear what was going on. E quickly got up and went over to the man and said, "What's your name?"

The man just mumbled "Azazel" under his breath. E looked into his eyes and saw something very unsavory about him and exclaimed, "You have no power here. In the name of Jesus, I command you to leave immediately and not come back!"

The man spun around and jumped up like he was standing on hot coals and then ran as fast as he could down the alley away from the diner. Bob was visibly thrown from the occurrence, but E tried to stay on task by continuing, "Bob, you have to set this right in the church. I can't tell you how the church will react, but I know that God will react positively with your repentance and I know that He's not done with you yet—He did send me."

Bob was broken and crying in his hands. He asked E through his tears to go with him to see his wife. "Be glad to," E said with a caring smile.

"Hello again, Mrs. Mead. Good to see ya," E stated with great sincerity, as he walked into the church office. Polly was already aware that E had been talking to Bob. She suspected that he knew everything.

"Brother E, how are you?" she said with curtness.

"Oh, good. Just wanted to check on ya and see how you were doin'. Have you ever read John chapter eight, Mrs. Mead?" E asked.

She looked at him like she was being cornered and said, "Can't say that I have."

E continued, "John recounts the Lord's forgiveness to a woman caught in adultery. Though Jesus rescued her from a stoning, she didn't get away with the sin. However, anyone could see her genuine regret and repentance after Jesus's love had covered her. God's willing to give you another chance too, Mrs. Mead. Our God forgives and cleanses so we have the privilege of starting anew. Receive His great love today."

By the time E was finished, she was crying into his handkerchief. She looked up at E and said, "What about Bob?" E knew she was concerned about him.

"Bob is going to be fine. He's resigning Sunday and going back to seminary. He's been wanting to do that for some time anyway," E said, trying to relieve her of any other worries. He prayed with her and told her that even though she was a widow, she needed to ask forgiveness from her family.

Frank was hanging his head low around the house. He'd really acted childishly and on bad information from Melanie. "Daddy E, I wanna apologize for my behavior. I really am sorry," he said to the old man with sincerity as his head lowered.

E looked at him with tender, caring eyes. "I don't condemn you, Frank. I know this is a precarious situation we're all in here. Let's just forget it," E said as he gave the big man a firm handshake.

You Can't Out-give God

"Hud, you think you could pick me up? The sheriff called and wants me at the jailhouse now," E quickly asked. Before Hudson had a chance to say a word or ask questions, E continued. "I'll be waitin' out by the road. Just hurry, okay?"

"Well, I—," was all Hudson was able to say.

E started again, "Alrighty, just hurry!" Then he hung up.

After Hudson's initial introduction to the old preacher, he had an occasion to take him to lunch as his "good deed for the day" but Hudson learned quickly that you can't "out-give" God. E had his eye on one waitress in particular. Her name was Betty and she seemed to be happy enough; at least Hudson thought so.

"Well, tell me about yourself, Brother E?" Hudson began, but very soon, it was Hudson who was blabbering on about his life and ministry. He thought, *How did that old man get me to talk about myself?*

E kept in the conversation, but you could tell his mind was elsewhere. As Betty passed their table, E touched her on the arm and said, "There's no name sweeter than Betty, because God loves her and He's ready."

At first, Hudson thought he had a dirty old man making rhymes to young waitresses, but then he saw Betty's face and realized there was something much deeper going on. She gave the old preacher a smile but quickly excused herself to wait on other tables. Before long, Betty was giving E preferential treatment. Hudson thought, *Well, the old man has really charmed her.*

They ate their meal and were casually talking when Betty came by to check on E. "Oh, we're fine, Betty. You've waited on us so well, but you know, God is still waiting on you," E stated with somberness. Her face looked like she had seen a ghost. Tears started welling up in her eyes as she swallowed hard. She smiled and thanked the men for coming and excused herself hastily.

As they walked toward the old truck, E looked over at Hud and said, "You go ahead. I'll just be a minute."

As E stood outside the restaurant by the curb, Hudson felt bad for the old preacher waiting for someone who wasn't going to come. Then, at that very moment, Betty came bolting out of the restaurant crying her eyes out. After several minutes, Betty was smiling and hugging E and they were exchanging pieces of paper.

"Well, Hudson, what were you sayin' about your new buildin' project?" E asked as he hopped into Hudson's truck.

All of a sudden, Hudson saw a pathetic picture of himself in the rearview mirror as he backed out. Suddenly, he realized that his priorities and his values were way off from God's. He asked, "Brother E, what just happened?"

E just said, "Oh, a mini-revival, I guess. She'd been runnin' from God. You know, there's only one letter difference from 'grave' to 'grace,' but they take you two different directions."

Hudson just kept wondering to himself, as he went to pick up E, what blessing he was in store for today.

The old jail looked like something out of a Western, with a bulletin board full of black and white mug shots, cold iron bars, and a locked gun rack on drab, green walls. Hudson didn't frequent jails and as he walked in, he withdrew back from the scene, hugging close to the front door. He watched as Brother E walked right up to the sheriff, shook hands, and made small talk. "Okay, give me the key, Sam," E commanded.

Hudson wanted to shake some sense into him, but he was too far away.

"Now, are you sure, Reverend?" the sheriff asked as he raised his brow and looked sideways at the old man. E just shook his head in a fashion that made you think the sheriff was wasting his time.

In the middle cell stood a very large black man taunting the officers. He yelled with contempt, "You just try to touch me and I'll kill you!" He had grabbed an oak chair that was sitting too close to his cell and ripped it apart like it was a twig. He had the back spine of the chair in his hand, shaking it at anyone who came close. E quietly went up to the cell and started to unlock the door. Hudson was so scared he was frozen in his tracks as his mouth dried to dust. His eyes were burning from not blinking. The man started yelling at E in a rage, daring him to come closer.

The sheriff looked over at E and said, "You can't go against that man. He'll kill ya. Leon, give him your club."

Brother E gestured for the men to keep quiet and just shook his head no. Hudson, standing there in shock, had an epiphany. He was watching David and Goliath played out in front of him—the taunting giant and the man of God, one smaller and frailer and the other looking like he could tear anything apart. Then a scripture came to him, "David said to the Philistine, 'You come against me with sword, spear and javelin, but I come against you in the name of the LORD Almighty…'"

With Bible in hand, E opened the door and walked right up to the man. Brother E was tall, but he was looking up at least three inches into the big man's red eyes. The big man started to speak but was quickly cut off by E's words, "You have no authority here and you can't speak unless I ask you to."

The rest were whispers, but Hudson watched with amazement as the club in the man's hand slowly came down. Then he started to lose his prideful composure and humility replaced it. Soon he was lying on his cot in a fetal position, crying as E sat there by him. The old preacher finally stood up, took the big stick from the floor, and laid a Bible by the man's head. He patted him on the back, gave him a slip of paper, and told him that he would be back to see him. And just like that, it was over. The old preacher came out of the cell, gave the keys to the sheriff, and talked for a moment before going over to Hudson.

E looked at Hudson, who was pretending not to be shocked and said, "Well, Hud, are ya ready to go? I'm real sorry for taking you away from what you had planned."

Hudson almost cried as God gave him yet another lesson in priorities. He replied, "Brother E, nothing's more important that what you just did. And, by the way, what did you just do?"

E looked over at Hudson over his spectacles, smiled, and said in a nonchalant manner, "That man was just full of demons, you know? Hey, could you take me by the sporting goods store to get some new fishing line? It won't take me but a second, I promise."

"Oh, no problem. Could you tell me something, though?" Hudson asked with a puzzled face.

"Sure," E replied.

"Well, I couldn't hear much, but I did hear you ask him to tell you who you were? Why did you ask that and why did he say, 'the Holy One'?"

E smiled and raised his brows at Hudson, "Ya know, Hud, you have a lot of learnin' to do. Hang around me and I might be able to teach ya somethin.' I didn't ask the man who I was, I asked the demons who I was, to be sure I was talkin' to them."

Hudson stared at him, grimaced, then asked, "So when the demons said, 'the Holy One,' they were seeing Christ?"

"No, they were seeing the Holy Spirit in me," E answered. "Hud, we've all been given authority over this earth through Him, you know?"

Hudson sat there stunned, with his mouth open, in the parking lot of the small sporting goods store just staring into space. Hud said to himself, "How could he be so relaxed about what just happened?" Then it came to him. "It's just so commonplace for him. The unusual is the usual for that old man." He got a warm feeling in his heart as an excited E crawled back onto the seat of his truck with his little bag.

"Is there anywhere else I can take you, Brother E?" Hudson asked, almost hoping for another adventure with the old man.

"No, I guess I better get back to check on Momma. Thank you for being available, Hud," E said as he looked in his bag. Hudson almost felt like God himself had just spoken to him.

"Hud, I've been prayin' for that man that's singin' at that church across town tonight and God really started revealing some things to me about him. Would it be too much trouble to take me? I really need to talk to 'em if you don't mind," E asked as he studied his spool of fishing line.

Hud just looked over at him, smiled, and said, "Be glad to."

Bus-ted

The crowd was massive and the big church was starting to bubble over with louder and louder chatter. As Hud's truck came to a stop outside, he barely got it in park before E had bailed and was in a fast dash to the entrance. Again, Hudson saw the sea of people as an impossible journey; after all, they were late getting there. He was sure the performance had already begun.

Hudson started making his way slowly toward the door when E bolted out and headed for the large impressive bus that sat next to the church. By now, Hudson wasn't surprised at anything. He just shook his head and without being cued, continued walking toward the entrance. John Bryant was performing that night and it was "standing room only." He was a popular contemporary Christian singer and songwriter who had just won several awards and the crowd was beginning to get annoyed that he was late starting his concert.

Rap! Rap! Rap! was the noise as E thrust his fist into the bus door for the second time. Finally, a tall, handsome man reluctantly opened the door.

"I'm comin,' just gotta get my shoes on!" John exclaimed, thinking he was speaking to someone from the production crew.

"John, God knows what you're up to and I know that the guilt is about to kill you," E said while John stared at the old man with an open mouth. "I'm not here to condemn you, son. I'm here to restore you. Are you ready to be restored?" E asked.

John just looked down at the floor and squirmed. The old man had really taken him off guard. He was having an affair with a girl on tour with him. He had that look of, *It's too late to do anything. I've botched up my entire ministry and there's no hope for me.* E had seen the look before.

He looked at John and said, "Look, God sent me to you tonight to restore, not to ruin … to redeem, not to charge … to free, not to imprison. You've done all those things to yourself. Don't get me wrong. It'll be hard. But you can do it. I've prayed that God not only restore your ministry, but also make it better than ever before. Most of the greatest figures of the Bible were spiritual failures at one time or another. And though they failed, often very significantly, they learned from their failure, confessed it to God, and were, more than often, able to be used in even mightier ways. The first step is confession. Let me pray with you?"

John just nodded up and down shamefully as his eyes welled up.

"God, we acknowledge you're in charge of everything. This man has been condemned to die as we all have; however, your Son has paid that price and we come to you tonight, wishing to be restored into your presence and forgiven for our trespasses in sin. God, touch this anointed man of yours tonight in this concert so that You may touch others. Thank you, God, for using broken vessels, broken bread, and poured-out wine. Amen," E prayed.

As John opened his eyes, the bus looked much brighter and his spirit was invigorated. He reached out his hand, but E just grabbed him around the back and gave him a giant hug.

As he let go, E could see that the big man was tearing up and said, "Look, now's the hard part. You'll need to confess to your wife first, then to your church, and then to your fans. But tonight, just sing your heart out. Here's my address and phone number—stay in touch."

John just smiled and nodded as they went out of the bus. While E and John were talking, Hudson grew anxious watching the deafening crowd of young people around him. He started to pull back toward the entrance. As if it had been planned, E walked into the entrance with John and stood by Hudson.

John sang that night like never before, feeling God's great presence and His grace, and many came to a saving knowledge of Christ.

Turning Dallas Upside Down

"Hud, don't you think you've paid your debt? Done your 'good deed'? I mean, it's impossible to be around Brother E and dislike him, don't get me wrong, but—" Hud's wife pleadingly asked.

He forcefully interjected, "Honey, that man's incredible! He's so genuine and sincere, and he's taught me more about ministry in a few days than I ever learned at seminary or anywhere else, for that matter. Brother E doesn't seek God's presence; he lives in it all the time! To him, it's like breathing air. At first, I really felt like he wasn't even aware of his impact and God was micromanaging him without him even knowing it. But that wasn't it. He just makes himself totally available to God's leading. It's truly a sight to behold!"

As he told her some of the things that he had experienced with E, she realized a deep change in Hudson. "Well, Hud, you know that pastor's conference is next week. Maybe you need to invite him to go with you?" she asked, testing his resolve.

"That sounds great! I'll talk to the organizers and see if he could open with prayer or something," Hud said excitedly.

"Miss Dorothy, I need to speak to Dr. Polk, if I may. This is Hudson Taylor," he said as she put him on hold. Dr. Polk's church was in charge of the pastor's conference.

"Hello," answered Milford Polk.

"Yes, Milford, this is Hud. Say, I have a question for ya," Hud said.

"Yes?" Polk asked.

"Well, I was wonderin' if I could bring an old pastor friend with me to the conference and maybe he could do a prayer?" Hud asked.

"Sure, Hud! Sounds great. Who's your friend?" asked Polk.

"Well, his name is Ethan Moses," answered Hud, and then there was a very long pause.

"Well, Hud … I've just been handed the program for the conference and I really don't think we can fit him in," Polk said, slyly trying to backpedal.

"Well, maybe I could just bring him along then?" Hud asked, getting another very long pause.

"Hud, I don't think that would be wise. Well, I have to go—lots of work to do. God bless," Polk said, not waiting for a response before hanging up.

Hud was puzzled, and he wasn't one to let sleeping dogs lie.

"Bobby, this is Hud," he said to his minister friend in a nondenominational church.

"Hey, Hud. What's goin' on?" he asked.

Hud proceeded to ask Bobby what he knew about Brother E and why he was getting a cool response about the pastor's conference. Bobby knew everything about everybody and Hud thought he could help shed some light on the mystery.

"Well, Hud, he was quite the rebel in his day. He really went up against the 'men in power' on racial issues, preaching love instead of judgment. Also, he believed in 'spiritual gifts,' and you know how well that went over," Bobby replied with a deep sigh.

"Wow, I knew he was different! Is that all you have?" Hud asked swiftly.

"Is that all I have? You know me better than that. What do ya wanta know?"

"Well, tell me 'bout the racial thing," Hud asked.

"Let's see. He was totally against the separatist movement. It's been told that he even got death threats," Bobby said.

"What's wrong with his view?" Hud challenged.

"Well, nothing nowadays but back then... not a popular opinion!" Bobby answered with a high pitch to his voice.

"What about the love thing? He doesn't believe in God's judgment?" Hud asked, thinking that had to be the big deal.

"Oh, yes, he believes in judgment from God. He just doesn't think that judgment is something that Christians were called to do. They were called to show God's grace to others as we have been shown God's grace ourselves," Bobby answered.

"Again, what's so wrong about that?" Hud asked, getting increasingly annoyed.

"Well, nothing. But even now, Hud, some use judgment and guilt as leverage against their members," Bobby answered.

"And what about the 'spiritual gifts' thing?" Hud asked, trying to hurry things up a bit.

"Well, Hud, you understand that you really need to get this information firsthand. I only know what others have said," Bobby said.

"Yes, yes... so tell me," Hud said.

"It's been told more than once that he healed people at some of his revivals and even at regular church services!" Bobby answered, followed by a long pause.

A scripture out of Matthew came to Hudson: "Then he said to the man, 'Stretch out your hand.' So he stretched it out and it was completely restored, just as sound as the other. But the Pharisees went out and plotted how they might kill Jesus."

"Is that it?" Hud asked.

Bobby answered, "No, no, there's more. It's also been told that he has actually performed exorcisms!"

After another long pause, Hud asked, "Well, is that it?"

"No, in a couple of his tent revivals back in the '40s, some say he waved his hands across the crowd and several fell out cold in the front pews!" Bobby answered, with a great exhale of relief as he finally finished his list. "Of course, all these things may be exaggerated in great degree, you understand?" Bobby said, finishing his synopsis of E's ministry.

"Well, Bobby, I have to say, I have no problem with any of that. I can see why God uses him for all those things, though. I've never seen a minister more humble. Others might get a big head if God allowed them to do half of those things, but you would never see it in him," Hud said to Bobby, thanking him for the information.

He had found out what made Milford Polk squirm. Then at that moment, Hud got another scripture in his head: "But the Pharisees said, 'It is by the prince of demons that he drives out demons.'" Then he thought, *the religious leaders didn't seem to like Jesus very much either.*

Protocol for Meeting Royalty

"Hud, I want you to meet Elise. She had a good night and she's dressed to receive guests," E said, as he motioned for Hudson to come in.

From what E had said about her, Hudson was expecting to meet the Queen herself. As he entered the small room, he noticed that she was in a large bed, unresponsive to anything or anyone. As Hudson looked at her, he noticed that someone had tried to dress her, but her contorted body made it hard for anything to fit the way it was designed.

"Elise, this is Hudson Taylor, who I told you about. And Hud, this is Elise," the old man said, gesturing with his hands as if he were introducing royalty.

Hudson just stood there for a moment in silence as he looked upon the old lady, thinking to himself how outward appearances seem to make us all judge prematurely. Then he said, "Miss Elise, it's my great pleasure," tilting his head in a bow of respect.

As E was getting his jacket and hat on, Hudson noticed a picture sitting behind some others on his little desk. It was a very old sepia photo of a small, white, clapboard church and in front seventy people were standing.

"Wow, Brother E, all those people were members of that little church?" Hud asked.

"Oh, no. That's not the members," E answered, as he dropped the conversation and combed his hair.

"Who are they?" Hud asked, wanting to know more and more about E.

"Don't get the wrong idea, Hud," E answered as his old eyes looked over at Hudson.

"What do ya mean?" asked Hud.

"Well, I don't wanta boast; it was all God, every bit God," answered E.

"What are you talkin' about?" Hud asked, letting his curiosity get the best of him.

"Those were the people who accepted Christ at a revival I preached there," E said almost apologetically. Hudson was stunned as he exhaled quickly. He wasn't expecting that answer.

As he looked around the room, he saw a plaque that was small and discolored on the corner of the dresser. Hud could tell it was a cheaply-made plastic relic from some passé trophy shop.

"What's this, Brother E?" Hud asked, as he examined the relic in his hands.

E smiled with a big grin. You would have thought he had been given a million dollars.

"That's for seventy-five years of service," he said, as his eyes glistened with emotion.

Hud looked intently at the plaque and thought, *How cheap can they be?* He was embarrassed that anyone would give such a "Cracker Jack prize" to a man of his stature and worth.

"Brother E, is this all they gave you?"

E just looked at him with a puzzled look.

"I mean, did they give you a luncheon or something...I hope?" Hud continued.

"Oh, no. I wouldn't let 'em go to that trouble. It's great to have the accolades of man, but that's not why I did it, Hud," E answered as if he had been transported to a faraway place.

"Now, honey, we're goin' to a pastor's luncheon, but I'll be back soon," E said as he leaned over Elise and gave her a kiss, whispering to her that he loved her. As E went out the door, he motioned for the nurse to take over.

"Hud, I know you see an old, unresponsive, contorted woman in that bed, but I see her the way she looked that first night I met her," E said, as he climbed into Hudson's truck with a wide smile. Hud was still shaken by the whole affair and was feeling guilty for judging so many on looks alone. Then he started thinking about how he had done the same to E. He just looked in the rearview mirror and shook his head at himself as he pulled out onto the main road.

The pastor's conference was booked solid and to Hud's chagrin, he was unable to get Brother E on the list. Dr. Merewether was a well-known author who had been a pastor of a very large church in Dallas for several years. Now he was speaking all over the world on what he had learned in his ministry. He was pushing his new book called *The Price of Wisdom*. The conference went well, and on the last day, Dr. Merewether let everyone out at noon to attend a large luncheon at a restaurant downtown. The large private room was adorned with all the things that make a gala fancy. Hud had signed up for the luncheon but was not about to leave E out of that equation. He had slipped his name onto the roster as well. As he drove down the road with the old man, he thought about how it might go down. *They will ignore us for sure. Like being in grade school again with all the cliques,* he thought. They arrived early and the waitresses seated them at the end of a very long rectangular table. Soon Dr. Merewether came through the door of the restaurant and was stopped by someone eating at one of the tables. The large entourage of pastors who were hanging on to him went ahead into the private function room where E and Hud were sitting. As Hud had predicted, the men went to the opposite side of the long table without speaking and started arguing amongst themselves about where Dr. M would sit.

It was only a few minutes, but Dr. M finally walked through the door of the room and you would have thought a famous warship had pulled into harbor. As the men motioned for Dr. M to come over and sit by them, E just sat there and took a sip of iced tea from his glass. Hud was watching everything like it was on the silver screen. Dr. M went over to the guys at the end of the table, shook their hands, and then proceeded to walk right over to E.

He started asking him questions like, "Brother E, what would you tell a young pastor who had so much strife in his life he couldn't concentrate on his ministry?"

Without hesitation, E answered, "I would tell him he's being self-centered."

Dr. M let out a boisterous laugh and made himself at home there by E. "Tell me, Brother E, what would you tell a young Christian couple who had been married only a few months and were already having problems? What books should they read? Should they concentrate on communication skills?" he asked.

E looked intently into Dr. M's eyes and said, "Communication's good, and a book is good too, as long as it's the Bible. But they need to work on their communication with God. They need to read His word every day and pray together. Tell them to get their lives right with Him and I'll guarantee that their marriage will be a great success. Can any book guarantee that?" E asked with his brow raised.

Dr. M was taken by E's frankness and his speed to answer questions that seemed complex. "Brother E, would you mind if I sat here by you? This is good stuff," he said, while getting his notebook out of his briefcase. "Tell me, Brother E, what do you think about subjects like devotion, piety, and high ethical standards?" Dr. M asked.

"All good things, but a faith that's built on devotion, piety, including your 'high ethical standards,' but omits love and kindness is like the house built on sand—it's a beautiful house, but it's lacking the essential foundation. Jesus lived out that example of universal kindness to all persons, and it should be the central theme to the faith of all who say they follow Jesus," E answered as Dr. M quickly wrote down what he said.

Dr. M, taking full advantage of the old man's wisdom, then asked, "So Brother E, what is the shortest gospel in the Bible? I mean, if you're trying to explain it to someone and you don't have much time."

E looked at the man over his glasses and stated, "Ephesians 2:4."

Dr. M stopped writing, looked up at the old man, and asked, "Just that one verse?"

E took a sip of tea and replied, "Oh, heavens no! Just the first two words of the verse." Dr. M was baffled as he sat there with his pen, waiting for an explanation. E continued, "The first two words say it all in a nutshell—'But God...' We were once foolish ourselves, as it says in Titus 3:3. We were disobedient, deceived, enslaved to lusts and pleasures, spending our lives in malice, *but God*, being rich in mercy, because of His great love for us even when we were dead in our sins, made us alive together with Christ through His marvelous grace by which we were saved."

Still writing fervently and without looking up, Dr. M asked, "What about the Ten Commandments? I mean, are they out of date? Do they convey a church not willing to bend, a church with too much legalism and not enough grace?"

E looked at the man and shook his head. "The Ten Commandments are God's virtues, his very nature and character. You ever idolized a major league baseball player? Didn't you want to know everything about him? Didn't you want to mimic his very life, be like him in every way? So God has given you His baseball card with all His stats. Do you want to discard it or try your best to be like Him?"

At that very moment, Hud looked down at the end of the table where the other pastors were. Every one of them had their mouths wide open in disbelief as their "star" lowered himself to ask questions of an old man who didn't even have a doctorate and hadn't even written a single book. Hud vowed to remember that picture in his head as long as he lived. He thought for a moment and realized that he was looking at a picture of the Last Supper with Christ … all the men gathered around, asking who will have the prestigious appointments in His kingdom? Who will sit by Him? And Hud could just hear the scripture in his head: "God opposes the proud, but gives grace to the humble." E continued to give page after page of notes on every topic as Dr. M wrote, trying to keep up with the old man. On a couple of occasions, the men at the table's end would try to pry Dr. M away with no success. The foot-washer was speaking.

An Open Invitation

As everyone left, Dr. M pushed a piece of paper into E's hand and thanked him for his time. Hudson was truly impressed with the old man. He had really shined and the dapper Dr. Milford Polk just looked foolish and small at the other end of the table. E had told

Hudson once that he was well on his way to having a doctorate himself many years ago.

"Brother E, why didn't you go ahead and get your doctorate? You were so close," Hudson asked while they got into his truck.

"Hud, having a doctorate is great, don't get me wrong. Just don't buy into the lie that a doctorate is where you get your knowledge. And it's definitely not where you get your wisdom. Do you understand?" E asked.

"Not exactly," replied Hudson.

"Well, if you look at Paul's life in the Bible, he really knew his Bible. He was a Pharisee of Pharisees, but his 'revelation' came from Jesus. His book learning served him well, but only as a basis to start with, not a basis to end with. In First Corinthians chapter eight, verse one, he says that knowledge makes you arrogant, but love edifies," E answered.

Hudson just looked more puzzled, so E continued. "Look, Hud, the most important person in our world is the Holy Spirit. Without Him, there is *no* knowledge. You can study the Holy Scriptures for years, but without the Holy Spirit enlightening and illuminating, you have nothing. In Luke chapter twenty-four, verse forty-five, it says, 'Then He opened their minds to understanding of the scripture.' And in First John two, twenty-seven it says, 'As for you, the anointing which you received from Him abides in you, and you have no need for anyone to teach you…' A doctorate is not the key to the Bible. The Holy Spirit is the key that unlocks the Bible," E said as he pulled the piece of paper that Dr. M had given him out of his coat pocket. He got his thick glasses out of his shirt pocket and tried to make out the small print that was on the napkin, but couldn't.

Then he said, "Look, Hud, book learnin' can lead to a dangerous and precarious arrogance. It's fine to get that doctorate, but focus on the skills of doing—selfless God-led doing."

Hudson reached over, and E placed the note in his open hand and continued, "Hud, Bible study is only part of ministry. Seminary taught me a lot about the Bible, but nothing about people or living the Word of God, and they taught me very little about God's spiritual gifts," E said.

Hudson shook his head in agreement and, looking at the note, exclaimed, "Well, Brother E, it seems that you have an invitation to speak at Dr. M's former church in Dallas!"

After a few weeks of planning, Hudson and E were on their way to Dr. M's former church. While Hudson entranced himself into the ebb and flow of Dallas freeway life, E took a short nap with his old, tattered Bible resting in his lap. As he slumped there with his thick, black glasses riding low on his nose and his page magnifier holding his place, Hudson couldn't help but wonder how he would perform on the big stage. He recollected only one time that he had actually heard him in front of a large crowd. Could he "cut the mustard" in a large church setting with hundreds, if not thousands, watching him? Would the television cameras help tell his story or would they be unkind to the old man?

The alarm clock was an unwelcome reminder of the beginning of a hectic day. Both men got up and sat on the edge of their beds, trying to get their bearings.

"Hud, I need to call and talk to Momma's nurse. Could you make us a pot of coffee?" E asked while he reached for the small bedside table to brace himself for his ascent.

"Sure, Brother E," Hud answered as he jettisoned himself from the covers onto his feet and leapt like a grasshopper over to the small coffeepot on the other side of the room.

E was still trying to balance and straighten himself. As Hudson made a cup of coffee for E, he was thinking, *I'll probably have to help the old man around this large city.*

"Brother E, what's your topic for the sermon today?" Hudson asked without eye contact, in case E didn't want to reveal any secret.

"Brokenness," E said without hesitation. "And if I don't get this sermon out, I think I'm gonna pop! Say, Hud, afterward, let me show you the town. I'm gonna take you to this great barbeque place on the west end—Sonny Bryan's."

Hudson just shook his head in amazement. *Old Brother E might look a hundred on the outside, but he's a teenager on the inside.*

As they got closer and closer to the church, E got more and more anxious.

"Are you nervous, Brother E?" Hudson asked, noticing him fidgeting.

"Nervous! Ha! Not a bit. Just excited. God's Spirit is all over me; I can hardly sit still or breathe! If I can manage to get all this out that He's pouring into me, I'll be doin' wonderful," E answered with great exuberance.

To no less than five thousand people and countless thousands over the airwaves, E slowly made his way on stage. He looked intently at them, using the leverage of a silent microphone to create reverence in the room. For several seconds he stood there on the verge of starting, waiting for the Spirit's cue. Then he broke the silence.

"Are you a broken vessel?" Then he paused and waited for the exact moment to punctuate his question before beginning again. "Broken vessels are the only vessels God uses. Broken vessels not only know the love of Jesus, but they show the love of Jesus through their cracks. Broken vessels are the only vessels that allow the grace of God to flow through. Broken vessels are not prideful vessels, not beautiful on their own merit, but beyond beautiful through God's grace. Broken vessels are available vessels, vessels desiring to be filled continually to overflowing with the Holy Spirit, never holding in God's grace, but continually releasing it. Are you a broken vessel? That's the question God is asking you today."

He took his Bible, flipped it under his right arm, and scooted to the edge of the stage. Hudson's eyes welled up with pride. He felt a big lump in his throat as he gazed at his earthly hero.

After the special music, Dr. Merewether formally introduced E. Again, E stared into the crowd and slowly started. "Now, what is brokenness? The Hebrew word found in Psalms is *abad*—to lose oneself, and by implication, 'to perish!' Jesus said, '… whosoever will lose his life, the same shall save it,' in Luke 9:24. Almost everyone tries to save himself. Even many of the most notable, seemingly successful religious leaders try to save their own lives and their own ministries. Jesus says it must *all* be surrendered. Would you continue in a life with prideful and pitiful fruits, or would you choose brokenness, as David and Jesus and Paul did, so that the perfume of the Spirit in you will spread beyond your church, beyond your life, beyond your tombstone, and into the decades, generations, and ages to come?"

E continued by giving scripture references on David's life, Jesus's life, and Paul's life. He was all over the Bible, turning the pages like the most accomplished surgeon performing a procedure that he alone had devised and perfected. By the end of his delivery, three hundred people had come to the front to rededicate their lives, and over a hundred had accepted Christ as their Savior. Endless others had made professions over the phone line from the television broadcast.

Afterward, the deacons, pastors, and elders of the church barraged E, so Hudson made his way to the podium to get E's Bible. As he reached for it, he looked intently at it and got a tenaciously serious look on his face. He was frozen as he stood there, totally flabbergasted at what he saw.

One of the deacons came up to Hudson and, shaking him, asked, "Are you all right, Hud?"

Suddenly, he snapped out of it and looked the man square in his eyes and stated, "It's upside-down."

The man squinted, pooched out his lips, and gave Hudson a puzzled look. Then Hudson pointed his index finger toward the pulpit and continued, "The Bible. It's upside-down."

The man just smiled and shook his head. Hudson picked the Bible up and realized that E was relying totally on his memory and the Spirit to get him through the scriptures so decisively. He didn't know how that church would be changed by E's message, but he knew that his life and ministry would never be the same.

My Brother's Keeper

"Brother E, I'm ready to go home," Hud said with a sigh as they finished their meal.

"Please stop calling me Brother E," E said with a smile on his face as they drove home from Dallas.

"But, what do I call you?" Hudson quizzed.

"How 'bout E?" he said, crimping up his eyebrows.

"But that sounds so disrespectful!" Hud exclaimed with frustration.

"Look, Hud, all that 'brother' 'sister' stuff was started to break down boundaries between us all, wasn't it? I mean, by calling someone 'brother,' you're saying they're family. However, these days, it's a formal title that someone that's a minister wears. There's even a racial division it's used for. It defeats the purpose for which it was designed," E stated.

"Wow. I never thought of that," Hud said as he stared out the car window.

"What's the first and greatest commandment?" E asked.

Hud stared into E's eyes and then announced smartly, "To love God."

E pointedly said, "Jesus said in Matthew 22:37 it is to love God with all your heart, soul, and mind. The word for love there is *agapao*, which means to totally give yourself over to it. It means to stay in a continual pattern of His will and not yours. But Hud, what's the second greatest commandment?"

Hud was stumped. As he sat there thinking, E's eyes widened as he glared at Hud over his spectacles and said, "Jesus continued with a second greatest commandment after telling the Pharisees and Sadducees the greatest. 'Love your neighbor as yourself. There's no commandment greater than these.' Both had love in them. One was to love God completely and the other was to love others wholly. Basically, we're called to love God and love man," he said, as he rested his head back on the seat. Hud just shook his head in amazement.

After a long interval of reflection and silence, Hud asked, "E, why did you pack that old gas can? I have plenty of gas and I never run out."

E looked over at Hud, smiled, and answered, "I have a sentimental attachment to the old can, and it reminds me to keep myself emptied out so that God can fill me."

Hud had a pensive smile as he studied the road ahead.

"Slow down, Hud," E blurted out abruptly.

"What is it?" Hud asked with urgency.

"You see that van that's stopped there by the road? There's a little boy waving a sign in the back window. Looks like it says, 'Help, out of gas,'" E said as he pointed with his index finger.

"Yep, that's what it says," Hud answered with an anxious nod.

The two men stopped in front of the van and E got out, went to the bed of Hudson's truck, and waited for Hudson to pick up the can. E looked at the scared woman in the driver's seat and pointed his finger toward the gas can.

She slowly lowered the window and asked, "How did you know I was out of gas?"

E answered softly, "We saw the little boy in the back window, ma'am."

She just looked at E with a shocked, pale face. "There's no little boy here. It's just my two daughters and me. We were just praying that God would send someone to help us," she said with great emotion as tears welled up in her eyes.

E looked over at Hudson with a smile and motioned for him to put the gas in the van. While Hudson was pouring the gas, E took the opportunity to talk with the woman and gave her a slip of paper and some money. She said her thank yous to the men and they walked slowly back to the truck.

"E, every time I'm with you, stuff like this happens! And then you give them a piece of paper. Would you mind telling me what's written on there?" Hudson asked with a big smile.

"Oh, that's simple, Hud," E answered coolly and continued, "It's just my address and phone number. A long time ago, God showed me that we're not usually called to come into someone's life once, but we are called to be disciples. Do you really know what that word means? We're God's representative to that person, and you can't do that in passing. I think God puts certain people in your life for reasons that are beyond what you can see or understand. I also think it's like rings that loosely hold us all together as one. No man is an island, you know. I think that God keeps building these rings into infinity."

"Infinity?" Hudson asked with a heightened sense of curiosity.

"Yes, meaning that He had no beginning and has no ending," E said with a chuckle. "Did you know that the infinite circle is a symbol for God?" E asked, shifting and rearranging himself in his seat.

Hud was getting chill bumps and started squirming with discomfort while E was talking about circles. He suddenly remembered that big "O" on the sheet of paper that I had left for him with a Bible verse written on it. He sat there trying to remember the verse and then it suddenly came to him from nowhere, "Glory to God in the highest, and on earth, peace to men on whom His favor rests."

While Hudson was in deep thought, E continued. "In numerical systems, the 'O' is the first symbol to be considered, as it is the first from which all others proceed. I was talkin' to a Jewish Rabbi friend of mine and—"

Before E could finish his statement, Hudson stopped him abruptly and asked, "You have a Rabbi friend?"

E continued, "Yes, Fishel Menk." As E pulled a letter out of his coat pocket, he continued, "Anyway, we were talking one day and he made the statement that the God that Christians worship is much smaller than the God the Jews worship. I asked him to explain and he went to the very first chapter in the Bible and asked, 'What does that say to you, E?' as he pointed to the verse, 'In the beginning God created the heavens and the earth.' I looked at it intently and tried to think like a Jewish rabbi, but I missed the mark. I answered, 'That God created all things.'

"Fishel just looked at me, shook his head, and said, 'See, that's what I mean. If you believe that God is everywhere and He never has an end or beginning, then you would look at that differently. To me, it says that God removed himself from an area first. It means to me that He sacrificed for us at the very beginning of time, drawing a compass circle from Jerusalem to the edge of a great void to show us His tremendous power. We both look at the circle as a symbol for God. However, I look at the outside of that circle as where God never ends, but you look at the inside of that circle and say, "That's God. That's where He lives." Christians compartmentalize and belittle God.'"

E unfolded the letter that he had in his coat pocket and handed it to Hudson. The top of the letter had an illustration of the ark of the covenant on it with the words "Third Temple Foundation" underneath. It gave Hudson chills as he looked upon the ark that was mentioned so many times in Holy Scripture. Here is what the letter said:

Dear Ethan,

It's been so very long since I have sat to pen you a letter, and I apologize. You're a very dear friend, to whom I owe so much gratitude. It was you, my friend, who convinced me to move here and it was you whom G-d used to open my eyes to so many things. Since your visit, we have made lots of progress. As you know, the great entryway into the vault that encases the ark was found with the seal from the Levite family that was in charge of it. However, until recently, we were not totally convinced the ark was still there. Through new X-ray equipment, we're not only sure that the ark is there and intact, but also that there are other relics as well. It's still encased in forty inches of stone, but for now, that's a good thing.

Everything else has been prepared and we will be ready to start building the Third Temple soon.

On other news, certain German officials came to us and asked if we wanted to make the bunker where Hitler killed himself into a Jewish historical library. Berliners are very sensitive about their past errors and nothing marks the fact that the bunker even exists. However, we're very excited about the prospect, and three of our colleagues have already met with them and laid out a rough set of plans.

I'm so sorry to hear about your wife, Elise. She was so full of life; her enthusiasm and energy are still felt here with us and will always be a part of our lives and those who come after us. Take care, Adi.

Barukh ata Adonai Eloheinu melekh ha-olam,
Rabbi Fishel Menk

"What does that salutation mean, E?" Hudson asked with a wrinkled brow.

"Blessed are you Lord, our God, King of the universe," E answered as he smiled.

"I was taught that the ark was taken up to heaven. This letter sounds like some Indiana Jones movie. Are you kidding me? They can't really have the ark, right?" Hudson asked naively.

E looked over at Hudson, emitted an amusing cackle, and said, "I thought the same way once."

With a pensive stare into space, E continued, "I had a dream not long after a meeting with my friend, Fishel. He was claiming to know the whereabouts of the ark and I thought he was crazy. As you, I'd always decided that God took his ark home many hundreds of years ago. My dream was more of a premonition with smells, sounds, color, and everything. I saw the crucifixion of Christ as it was happening. I saw the clouds, the darkness, and I felt the earth shake beneath my feet. There was a very pronounced sense of awe as I stood there. Suddenly, I was inside a vault deep within the earth, looking square at the ark in front of me. It was so daunting that I tried to move back from it, but the walls were close in and I had nowhere to go. As I looked up, I saw a crack appear above the ark and begin to grow. It went four different directions. Then I realized that it was forming a cross on the ceiling over the ark. Soon the earth stopped shaking and my eyes were directed to the mercy seat beneath the angel's wings on top of the ark. I noticed a bright red substance dripping from the crack above, hitting the seat, and with each hit the earth shook. Soon the whole seat was covered in red. Then I realized that it was blood and that I was under the crucifixion site of Jesus. As I looked at the seat for a while, it turned from a deep red to a snow white. After it changed color, the whole ark seemed to radiate with a marvelous golden glow. I felt my knees give way and found myself on the ground with my face in the floor.

"Then I heard God's voice say, 'My ark is for ministry and to pronounce blessings; it was then and it still is now.' Soon everything was dark as pitch. I couldn't see a thing. I started to panic, and then His voice came again: 'I will not stay in darkness forever from my people.' Then it was all over."

"Wow, do you ever seek confirmation on these things?" Hudson asked with his head cocked to one side.

"Of course. I found what God said to me in the Bible in Deuteronomy 10:8. And about the darkness, there are several verses, but the one that God gave me was Exodus 20:20–23," E answered with a grin, realizing that he was really asking Hudson to bite off a lot at one time.

"E, you're one interesting man! It's never boring around you, that's for sure," Hudson said as he chuckled and watched the road before him.

"Experiences with God are never boring, Hud," E said as he looked over at Hudson with a calm, cool stare.

"Say, what kind of name is Fishel?" Hudson asked as his brain went into overload.

"It means 'little fish,'" E said as his eyes sparkled, looking over at Hudson with a smile.

"And what does *Adi* mean?" Hudson asked.

"Well, Hud, that's Fishel's pet name for me," E answered.

"But what does it mean?" Hudson asked.

"It means 'jewel,'" E stated nonchalantly, with a mysterious twinkle.

Hudson just shook his head in amazement and exclaimed, "Hitler's bunker, the ark of the covenant...What in the world's next? The Jewel of the Nile? One day, you're going to tell me about some hidden treasure you found!"

E just smiled with great reflection as he looked out the window into the distance.

Hudson had put the old gas can back in the bed of the truck before they left the van miles back. This time, he was more careful how he handled it, treating it like it was a great trophy. He couldn't help but think about me and the note. Did his encounter with E have anything to do with me? Was it one of those circles that E was talking about? His mind grew tired of speculating as he drove back toward Port Arthur.

The Best Fishing Hole

Three days later, Hudson pulled up under the outstretched limbs of the huge oak tree in front of E's daughter's house. It was after nine in the morning, but it was still warm from the preceding hot day under the searing Texas sun. Hudson got out, dropped the tailgate, and sat down, waiting for E to surface from the humble, suburban, pre-war home on the outskirts of Port Arthur. It was not an ostentatious place, but when Hudson looked at that stately oak with its overreaching branches, he wondered if God was trying to tell him something about the man who lived inside.

He had gotten a frantic call from E that morning about a man who was going to be at a sporting goods store in town. Hudson had told E that he had several things to do, but E wouldn't hear any of it. He had almost begged Hudson to take him over to the store, saying, "Hud, I can't tell you how crucial this is. God placed this man's name on my heart early this morning while I was praying and I have to talk to him immediately."

Hudson was E's new prayer partner since he couldn't pray with his old one anymore. Hudson figured that he was talking about his wife, but he didn't ask out of respect for his feelings. The first time Hudson came over to pray with E, he had encountered God so strongly that he began to spin in his spirit. He could feel himself not only spinning, but growing bigger and bigger. He had mentioned something to E about it, but E just looked and him, smiled, and said, "Hud, that should happen to you every time you pray. In scripture it says, 'God inhabits praise.' What it really means is that He spins around in it. What you were experiencing was God inhabiting your praises."

"Okay, E. Give me fifteen minutes and I'll be there to pick you up," Hudson said on the phone before he left. Now he was waiting for the old man. "Boy, I really need to get going. I hope he surfaces soon," Hudson said to himself, putting his head in his hands, trying to be patient.

That same moment, E came barreling out the door, moving faster than Hudson had ever seen him go. Before he made it halfway to the truck, he motioned for Hudson to get it cranked and before Hudson had turned the starter a second time, E was already seated with the door closed.

"Let's move," E said as he braced himself in his seat.

"So what's this about?" Hudson asked as his demeanor softened.

"I was prayin' around three o'clock this morning and God said very clearly, 'Go and get the newspaper,' so I did. As I was lookin' through it, I ran across this picture of a guy beside a fish in an enclosed case. The caption read, 'Andrew Walker from Poplar Bluff, Missouri broke the record for the largest bass ever caught. The official weigh-in was twenty-two pounds and seven ounces.' God just stopped my eyes on his face and said to me, 'One day as Jesus was walking along the shore of the Sea of Galilee, he saw two brothers—Simon, also called Peter, and Andrew—throwing a net into the water, for they fished for a living.' It's Matthew 4:18," E answered.

"Still, I'm not understanding. What does any of this have to do with you?" Hudson impatiently asked.

"God's calling him into the ministry. He's been running for a long time. Now, since this has happened, it's going to be a lot more difficult to make the right decision. I'm sure that all the brands will be after him for endorsements."

Hudson had a hard time finding a parking place in front of the big store. People were everywhere. As they entered, Hudson saw all the cameras, reporters, and vendors and he realized this was an impossible task, even for E. Hudson, once again, hugged the front door and watched as E barreled toward the frantic crowd at breakneck speed. He tried to get the old man's attention, but his focus was not on Hudson. Then the most amazing thing happened. As E walked through the crowd, it seemed to part like water. As he walked up to Andrew, there were lights and cameras everywhere, but suddenly they all turned from Andrew. E walked right up to his face, talked to him for several minutes, and handed him a piece of paper. They hugged with tears, and then E walked back toward Hudson. As he left Andrew, the cameras swung back around, the microphones moved back into place, and the reporters again turned their attention toward the man with the fish.

As Hudson watched E move toward him, it was like the water was going back into place behind him. Then Hudson heard a voice say, "Then Moses stretched out his hand over the sea, and all that night I drove the sea back with a strong east wind and turned it into dry land." Hudson was paralyzed and his knees were shaking. He couldn't believe what he had just witnessed or heard, yet none of the people who were involved saw God's great hand at all. He wondered why he was privy to it and became very humble, almost to the point of tears as his eyes welled up. He felt like getting on his knees right there.

E, seeing that the scene visibly shook Hudson, went up to him and whispered, "You know what's so amazing to me, Hud?"

All Hudson could do was shake his head and blink a lot, trying to keep the tears from rolling down his cheeks.

"That God gives us so much privilege. You see, I caught the biggest fish," E said with dignity, as he opened the front door and went outside into the sweltering heat. Hudson humbly followed behind, seeing E in a whole new light that day—not as just some old washed up preacher, but as a chosen man of God. A true jewel and a marvelous blessing to those his life touched. He was just as important to God as all those men in the Bible. Nothing separated them— nothing. But one thing bound them all together, God's tremendous unmerited love, favor, and power.

The Promised Land

He was lower than he'd ever been. Elise had passed away in the night and tears streamed down his cheeks as they carried her lifeless body away on the cold stretcher. Years ago, he was struck with the piercing pain of losing so much of her—the hugs and special moments of celebration together. So long ago, he'd lost the conversations with her while reading the newspaper and sipping coffee. Now he'd lost even her presence. He'd given so much of himself to her, getting very little sleep every night to make sure she was comfortable. He would turn her, bathe her, feed her, talk to her, read to her, and pray with her.

As he lay there on her bed, he had a vision of drowning in dark swirling water. He'd always been an excellent swimmer, but for some reason, it was pulling him down into a never-ending abyss of darkness. Then he saw Jesus with His outstretched hands standing there.

"E, stop swimming and reach up for my hands," Christ instructed lovingly.

E resisted. If he stopped swimming, he thought he would surely go under. He tried using one hand, but it didn't work.

"E, you have to surrender all or you will go under," Christ continued with patience.

Finally, E stopped fighting the water and raised both hands and put them in Christ's hands. Jesus didn't just pull him to the surface of the water, but kept pulling him closer and closer to His face. E noticed that Jesus had blue eyes as he got closer and closer.

Then he noticed that both his eyes were Earth swirling around. As he looked into the pupil of His eyes, he heard, "Let me show you the wonder of my great love. Take my right hand and let me give you refuge from your foes. I will keep you as the apple of my eye and hide you in the shadow of my wings."

E was mesmerized, but he couldn't help but ask, "What do you want of me, Lord?"

Jesus continued, "E, I just want to show you my love and I want you to know my peace. You can let go now." Right then he heard a scripture: "The LORD bless you and keep you; the LORD make His face shine upon you and be gracious to you; the LORD turn His face toward you and give you peace …" (Numbers 6:24–26).

Elise was standing to the side of Jesus. He thought, *She must've been there the whole time.* As he looked at her, she said, "You can let go now, E." As quickly as it started, it had ended. He just stared at the ceiling for what seemed like hours.

That same night as he slept, he had a dream. He was standing in a beautiful meadow. Colorful butterflies were fluttering and birds were singing beautiful songs. It was the most beautiful place he'd ever seen. While he was wondering where he was, a graceful one-horse carriage appeared in the distance, trotted slowly, and stopped right in front of him. The horse was not bridled and seemed to know where it was going. A woman dressed in red was already in the carriage when E got in. She rode with him a long distance until the horse stopped, and E helped the lady out and onto the ground. As he sat back down, the woman took her hat off and locked eyes with his as she swept the hair out of her face. He suddenly realized that it was Elise and the horse was Goosebumps, his horse from his youth that had died when she ran through a fence in a terrible storm. Then, suddenly from nowhere, Micah came running over the hill and rubbed against his leg as E got out of the carriage.

Elise was more beautiful that he had ever remembered. Her golden hair was flowing in the soft breeze and her beautiful blue eyes sparkled as she looked resolutely into E's soul. It was that same look that she had given him in the tent revival so many years ago. She just stood there for a moment and then she put her arms out for him, saying, "E, it's time to come home." He felt like a great magnet was drawing him closer and closer to her and then, suddenly, she took his arm and patted it, speaking softly with a giggle, "My E-bee Jeebee."

They both were buried on a hill under the shadow of a large cherry tree overlooking Steeple Creek. Autumn's color had long since faded and fallen, and the air had taken on a wintry chill. The birds were silent, and clouds seemed to appear from nowhere, forbidding the sun to shine and dropping moisture to the earth that looked very much like tears. The man who slayed giants had died and the world would go on as if nothing had changed. But for Hudson Taylor, everything did.

He remembered Brother E saying, "To those who much is given, much is expected, and I've been given so much." It was hard for Hudson to see the "much" as he looked at the slim crowd inside the church that morning for the double funeral. He thought, *Here's a couple who gave their lives for people, serving them, feeding them, being there for them, but where were the people now? Had the weather kept them away? Had the couple outlived all those they had loved and served? And, even so, how many people are affected even today because of them? How far did their reach really go and could anyone ever fathom its depth?*

E had given Hudson his favorite black sports coat while they were in Dallas, and Hudson wanted to wear it to the funeral as a tribute. Of course, he knew he didn't fill the coat out as well as E. As he sat there, he ran his fingers into the inside coin pocket and pulled out an old, tattered, yellow piece of paper. There was a Bible verse handwritten on it: "So be content with who you are, and don't put on airs. God's strong hand is on you; he'll promote you at the right time. Live carefree before God; he is most careful with you. 1 Peter 5:6" He thought, *The old man is still speaking to me from the grave.* His heart pounded and his eyes blinked feverishly to keep the tears from running down his cheeks.

"As we excuse the family, the pianist will play and sing a song that E and Aunt Elise requested for this day," the associate pastor said as he motioned for the pianist to start.

She played and sang:

> *I was sinking deep in sin, far from the peaceful shore,*
> *Very deeply stained within, sinking to rise no more,*
> *But the Master of the sea, heard my despairing cry,*
> *From the waters lifted me, now safe am I.*

Hudson felt his chest tighten as he listened to the words of the old hymn, realizing Brother Moses was gone.

As Hudson parked his truck after the funeral, he picked up the fishing rod that E had given to him and noticed that some words were meticulously scratched into it. They read, "*Here's the patience and the faith of the saints. Rev.* 13:10." The other side read, "*Patient for God's timing and faithful to know that there are fish.*" Hudson knew he was not talking about fish.

It was at an auspicious ceremony when E gave him the rod. Hudson had just given a speech about "our purpose" to a group of young teenagers. "I've got somethin' for ya, Hud," E stated with pride and continued, "Take care of it. It's given me a lifetime of satisfaction."

Hudson looked at the rod that couldn't be more than a year or two old and said, "This rod and reel?" E just looked at him with his gleaming blue eyes and smiled. Hudson thought, *He had a way of making his eyebrows talk too.* He knew that he was speaking much deeper than a rod and reel, but at the time, he didn't put much thought into it. As he looked back, he suddenly realized that the etchings on the rod had a much deeper meaning too. He began thinking of the words E said as he walked away from him. It was as if God had shielded Hud from hearing them until that very moment. Then, he paused, realizing that it was not haphazard at all. It was all part of God's plan!

He remembered E saying, "And, my little Timothy, take care of that mantle, would you?" as if he were rewinding a tape in his mind. Those were the last words he said to him before he died, the very last words, and Hud was baffled. He suddenly became flushed and weak at the knees as all of his blood rushed to his vital organs. "Elijah's mantle?" he began his soliloquy. "In a fishing rod? That couldn't be. A mantle is an Old Testament thing—not meant for today. But the fishing rod could be the physical manifestation of a spiritual truth? Moses did have a rod, didn't he? I'm to be a fisher of men; I think I'm getting it! And he called me Timothy...like Paul's Timothy?"

The Big, Red "O"

Hudson continued to study the emotionally charged day, resting his chin on his right hand. While he was sitting there, a big, white car pushed its way into his driveway as the wheels moaned from the change in direction they were commanded to make. The tinted windows didn't allow for scrutiny of the inhabitants as the monstrosity came to a stop only a few feet from Hudson. Soon the back door swung open wide and a tall, lanky man that looked unbelievably like Brother E slowly emerged and stood beside the car.

"Reverend Hudson Taylor?" the man asked, squinting toward Hudson with one hand above his brow to keep the sun from his eyes.

Hudson slowly stood. His hands started to tremble as his eyes widened. "Yes," he said nervously, allowing only one step toward the familiar-looking man who had to be part of a premonition.

"Reverend Taylor, my name's James Moses. My uncle told me all about you. I tried to catch you before you left the funeral, but I'm havin' some trouble gettin' 'round these days," James said, as he slowly limped his way toward Hudson with help from me, his olive-skinned chauffeur.

Hudson was relieved that Brother E's ghost wasn't paying him a visit, but he still felt strange around someone who looked so much like the old man. "Well, I don't think I saw you at the funeral," Hudson stated nervously as he continued to get his bearings.

"Oh, I was there, but I just got out of the hospital for knee surgery, so they wouldn't let me climb those steps to the podium. It was better that I didn't get up there, anyway. I would have blabbered all over the place. You see, those two were more like my parents," James said as he pulled a piece of paper out of his coat pocket and wrote on it. "Reverend Taylor, what does this mean to you?" James asked, as he held up the piece of paper.

Hudson looked intently at the white sheet of paper with a big, red "O" on it and felt his face ignite as blood rushed to it. He swallowed hard and answered languidly, "Well, it's a symbol of our infinite God."

"Reverend Taylor, are you familiar with Matthew 5:10?" James asked, as if he were moderating a quiz show.

Hudson looked up in James's aging blue eyes with a growing smile and answered, "Yes, the often wrongly interpreted, 'Good things will happen to people who are hungry and thirsty for righteousness, for they will inherit Heaven.'"

James released a thin smile as his voice suddenly sharpened, "Well, Reverend Taylor, what does that mean to you?"

Hudson paused, met James's eyes again, and answered, "Well, it's not promising you eternal life. Only faith in Christ can do that. It's saying, 'When you crave the things of God, you experience God and His blessings here and now.'"

"I have to tell you, I was very skeptical, but you've convinced me that you're the man for the job," James added vigorously with a chuckle as he reached into his coat pocket and pulled out a crinkled letter written by Ethan Moses. "It seems that my uncle was convinced that *you* were to be my replacement at Pearl Rose and not my son," James continued, clearly taken by him as he handed Hudson the letter.

Hudson was fascinated at this turn of events and a tremendous peace fell upon him like he had never felt before. The old man had left an indelible mark on him and goose bumps were all over his skin as he broke into a satisfying smile. The remnant of God's great awakening continued—the mantle had been passed.

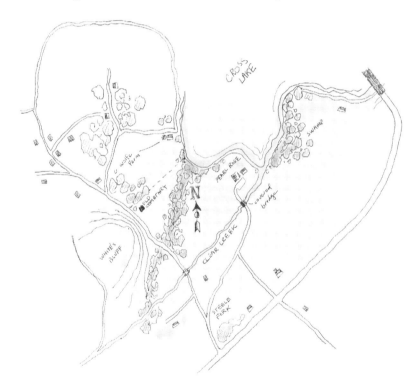